CALDIVUM
PUBLISHING

Ross Robertson was born in Scotland and although he adores spending time surrounded by the jaw-dropping landscape of his beloved Highlands, he has always wanted to see and learn more. In other words, he had a desire to travel the world. He has almost achieved that. In doing so, he has experienced a myriad of beautiful places and many wonderful people of humility who have given of themselves immeasurable love, kindness and generosity. However, throughout this great journey he has also laughed and cried at the countless imbeciles he has encountered who, in contributing immensely to the folly that is our world today, masquerade as citizens of integrity, good standing and moral fortitude. For it is not only their unadulterated and shameless gall that provokes hilarity and tragedy, but also the extraordinary influence they wield. With this in mind he has often found himself asking the same question over and over again-

'Who stole the compass?'

He has lived in Scotland, Ireland, England and the US and has worked as a business consultant for a variety of organisations: some respectable and some not so... He has also been a columnist and contributor to a number of publications: some respectable and some not so...

He is in love with the girl he hopes to spend the rest of his life with. Before that happens however, he thinks it might be a good idea if she first made a few appointments with her therapist!

Praise for 'A Yearning for Jacob's Son'

"...gripping, enlightening and bloody good fun"

"We've always known the Queen loves Scotland. Now we know why."

"Fast, caustic, shocking and controversial ...the research is astonishing."

"This novel is ambitious ...A Yearning for Jacob's Son could be one of the most controversial British books in decades!"

"Robertson has brought the history of Scottish achievement to the street in a novel which is just as entertaining as it is unpretentious."

A YEARNING FOR
JACOB'S SON

ROSS ROBERTSON

CALDIPUM
PUBLISHING

First published in Scotland, the UK, Ireland, and Worldwide in 2009

Copyright © Ross Robertson 2009

www.rossrobertson.co.uk

A CIP catalogue record for this book will be available
from the National Library of Scotland and the British Library.

Paperback ISBN 978-0-9559930-0-8

Set in Times

Cover Design by Creative Direction and Design, New Jersey, USA
visiondesign@optonline.net

Original Front Cover Image - 'Oil Drilling Platforms in Storm'
© Mick Roessler/Corbis

Website and PR by Roundsquare, Dublin
www.roundsquare.ie

Caldivum Publishing
An Imprint

<u>Thanks</u>

Robert Burns   For everything he ever thought, wrote and sang. Born
                          250 years ago this year, he is still alive in my heart.

Elizabeth Ross Robertson   A loving mother always knows what her child needs!
                          A few years ago, she presented me with a fascinating
                          book. Reading it changed everything.

Diane, David.........and Smudge

Gordon

Johnny (or Iain!) Robertson

Niall

Eoin MacHale and Roundsquare.ie

Paul S. Carroll

The Watson Family of Huntershill, Bishopbriggs

Graham, Stephen, Myles and Dalippe

Peter, Groover, Clunk, Podge, Scotty, Copie and Topper

Glamis Castle, Kirriemuir, Scotland

And

The People and Landscape of Scotland

Special Mentions and Inspired Reading

Neal Ascherson:	*'Stone Voices: The Search for Scotland'* ©2002 Granta Books
Tom Nairn; RMIT:	*'Globalisation and Nationalism: The New Deal.'* The Edinburgh Lecture - 7/3/2008
European Journal of International Law:	www.ejil.org ©*1998-2007*
www.OpenDemocracy.net	
Arthur Herman:	*'The Scottish Enlightenment: The Scots' Invention of the Modern World'* ©2003 Fourth Estate
Tom Devine:	*'Scotland's Empire 1600-1815'* ©2004 Penguin
Tom Devine:	*'The Scottish Nation 1700-2000'* ©1999 Penguin
Tom Devine and Paddy Logue:	*'Being Scottish'* ©2002 Polygon
Alexander Leslie Klieforth and Robert John Munro:	*'Scottish Invention of America, Democracy and Human Rights'* ©2004 University Press of America
Elspeth Wills:	*'Scottish Firsts'* ©2002 Mainstream
George Scott Wilkie:	*'Understanding Robert Burns'* ©2002 Neil Wilson Publishing
Mark Calney:	*'Robert Burns and the Ideas of the American Revolution'* ©1996 Mark Calney
Christopher Knight and Robert Lomas:	*'The Second Messiah'* ©1998 Arrow
Michael Baigent and Richard Leigh:	*'The Temple and the Lodge'* ©1992 Arcade
RealmofScotland.com:	*'The Great Deception – GERS – 2004/2005'* ©2007 Niall Aslen
Philip Roth:	*'American Pastoral'* ©1997 Vantage
Hunter S. Thompson:	*'Hell's Angels'* ©1966 Random House (This book has nothing to do with this novel; it is just a brilliant read!)

In no way would the author presume that the above authors and websites share his opinions and interpretations expressed herein. If there are similarities, it is neither intended or implied and is purely coincidental. Furthermore, because there may be some overlapping of certain historical and philosophical interpretation and facts, the author would like to acknowledge the above authors and websites for their contribution to the various subject matters contained herein, and the inspiration they have given the author in the writing of this novel.

Wee Ditty

Although I didn't know it at the time, I started to write this novel fourteen years ago. At my mother's request, I had returned from the States the previous year to finish my degree in Edinburgh. What's more, I made some new friends that final year, one of whom was kind enough to send me an invitation to her wedding. It was to be in the summer. The ceremony was to be held in Rosslyn Chapel while the Reception would be at the Balmoral. I was excited.

The Balmoral! Wow! *The* five star hotel in the centre of Edinburgh with its grand ballroom and rosette dining. Bloody hell, I'll need to hire a kilt. Will I have enough money to buy more than one round? I hope the bride's father has forked out the spondoolies on shit loads of complimentary vino. Like my country, I knew of the world I would be entering. I was just not familiar with its nuances.

I also realised I was not that familiar with the beauty of Rosslyn Chapel, either. By now, most of you who are reading this will have heard of Rosslyn and its new found fame. Some of you might actually have paid it a visit. If you have then you'll know I'm not talking nonsense when I say it is a special place ...a very special place! I also wonder whether you can get married there nowadays.

The wedding ceremony was wonderful, a very Scottish affair: the pipes, the crunching of leather shoes on the gravel, the whispers of appreciation and the smell of whisky on the breath. The chapel walls echoed the deep tones of the minister and the timid mumbles of the bride and groom. Smiling faces were aplenty. The gargoyles up above nodded in agreement as the snake danced in ecstasy around the Apprentice Pillar. It was a heart-warming afternoon.

Afterwards, as I stood waiting for the bus to take me and the other guests back into town and to the Balmoral, I took it upon myself to have a wee wander. I marvelled at the architecture and the thousands of sculptures. I wanted to find out more. How old is this place? How come I had never heard of it before? I also wondered as to why there were a few pictures, of some low-key visits made by the Queen, hanging from the walls of the tiny café and bookstore. I never knew the Queen had been to Rosslyn.

I browsed the three small wooden bookshelves. There could only have been about forty books: mostly Scottish History, the odd one on the Sinclairs of Rosslyn, four or five telling the story of the Chapel and two or three on some ancient group called the Templar Knights. I picked one up and leafed through. Interesting, I thought.

But Scotland was overloaded with history. There was just too damned much. And I was content with my Scottishness. I didn't need to prove it to anyone.

Later at the Balmoral, I danced, I spun to the Dashing White Sergeant, I drank and I gibbered. The next day I awoke with some good memories and a banging sare heid!

A few months after the wedding, I was sitting in my cold and empty Edinburgh flat, contemplating what to do on a dreary Saturday in October. In a few minutes, I was in the car and heading south. The trees were shedding leaves and grey clouds hung over the city with intent. As my mother would say, it was a dank day.

Rosslyn Chapel was quiet. The Sinclairs, and no one else for that matter, probably had no idea what the future was to hold. I think they savoured in the notion the world knew little of their home. Parking the car outside the local pub, I bought a small guidebook and wandered alone in the chapel grounds while gawping at the ancient engineering. The place had my utmost attention. I began to think. When I left, I bought a couple of books.

My initial interest focussed on the Templars Knights and Rosslyn Chapel but I have always been more intrigued by the here and now. Of course, it was interesting to read of feudal politics and the historical relationships with Freemasons and other secret societies but was there any significance to the present day? The following year I realised there was and I found myself asking the hows and the whys. What followed has been years of research and theorising. My friends used to laugh. They had other things to worry about!

Not long after, in the Fall of 1996, the Stone of Destiny was returned to Scotland after seven hundred years of captivity in Westminster Abbey. A couple of years after that, the political landscape changed forever. The people had voted *Yes-Yes*; Scotland was to have its own Parliament again. The politics of Scotland and England were now my prime concern. My research had become the here and now! Significantly, however, and as much as I read and studied, and read some more, I was also presented with an opportunity to travel, live and work in many other parts of the world. It was a journey of enlightenment. For not only was I struck and influenced by the unflinching loyalty, good and bad, which ordinary people maintain in their nations, I also came to reconsider patriotism and national aspiration, and what it means to belong. Furthermore, and regardless of my growing irritation with Scotland's rancid clan of apathetic apologists and political entrepreneurs of poverty, I also realised how providential (yes, and sometimes frustrating) it is to be Scottish and to belong to a country where most of its people possess an inherent and ancient belief that great personal and collective value can be drawn from justice, equality, humanity, learning and enterprise.

It has been fourteen years since I attended that wedding and it has been fourteen years since I decided to learn more about my country. I have learned much and much more than certain people have probably wanted me to know. However, you may be surprised to learn that this novel has little to do with Rosslyn; in fact, it is mentioned only three times. Nevertheless, it was where I began this quest; and that, to me, is very important. Because as well as having discovered a place, I think, to be of even greater significance than Rosslyn, I have also experienced the joy of being touched, warmed and inspired by the landscape and people of my country to a level I could barely have imagined possible. Consequently, I have attempted, maybe foolishly, to write *A Yearning for Jacob's Son* for a broad spectrum of readers: the well read and not so well read, the young and the old, nationalists and unionists and those undecided, Scots and non-Scots, and those with an interest in how the western world, and its major organisations which have such enormous influence, came into being; and how nations, and our lives and rights within, are affected and manipulated without concurrence. Moreover, I want to make history and politics accessible to those with neither the time nor the access to the great libraries of the world, and to those who want to be entertained while learning something new. However, in being a Scot myself and from a re-energised movement within, I have no doubt that commentators from certain political and cultural persuasions will do all they can to dismiss this novel because it is in their, and their superiors', insidious interest to do so. Regardless, I have to defer it is also their right. On the other hand, I know there will be many others who will welcome and appreciate this novel's premise. That is most definitely their right.

At the beginning of 2008, I finally put fingertip to key and although much has changed since then, and will continue to change, there are specific constants that will always remain.

I hope you will find some meaning in what I have discovered. If you don't, you can always kick back, put your feet up, have some fun and enjoy the story!

RR - February 2009

"If I'm designed yon lordling's slave,
By Nature's law designed,
Why was an independent wish
E'er planted in my mind?
If not, why am I subject to
His cruelty and his scorn?
Or why has Man the will and pow'r
To make his fellow mourn?"
-Robert Burns

"Breathes there the man
With soul so dead
Who never to himself hath said,
'This is my own, my native land!"
-Sir Walter Scott

"Being Scottish is more than a nationality... it is a state of mind."
-Arthur J. Herman

"Whenever I hear a politician talking about financial considerations in
relation to Scottish self determination I know they're talking complete shit.
It's not about that at all, it's about democracy."
-James Kelman
(Booker Prize 1994)

"No man has a right to fix the boundary of the march of a nation. No man has
a right to say to his Country; thus far shalt thou go and no further."
-Charles Stewart Parnell

1

don't fuck with the veracity of instinct

Friday 6th June 2008

4.38 pm – The West End - Glasgow

Dixie paused for breath, just for a moment. Looking around, she decided she didn't care who might be listening in. And she wasn't going to lower her voice, either. After all, it was Friday, she was in the pub with friends and this was Glasgow.

'There's no fucking way she was an angel. Absolutely no way. The media, including me, only portrayed her in that light because we all feared a backlash from our so-called loyal readers whose creepy and sanctimonious veneration made me vomit. Christ, you couldn't say one bad thing about her without being hounded by the committee of the Bi-Polar Fan Club who had donned the Union Jack waistcoats, spent a fiver on the insta-matic cameras and torn open the umpteen boxes of man-sized tissues. But we all knew the truth, didn't we? As I said, we were just too scared to print it in case we upset Reggie the piano man, Georgios the public toilet stalker, and Nigel the fucking weirdo from Borehamwood.

'Look at the public's reaction. For fuck's sake, it was as if their soulmate had just died. The best friend all those sad tarts and gushing queens never had. Someone they could confide in when they first gave some guy a blow-job and someone to comb their hair while they were watching Corrie. What's worse, they all really believed they knew her; like really knew her. They

1

even talked about her as if she was one of the family, sitting beside them at the kitchen table while a discussion was held on which bedside lamp to buy from the Swedish Meatball and Furniture Factory and how many Cheese and Onion and Ready Salted pounds they were going to shed before next week's FatWatchers. WWDD? Fuck me, it was a national display of how pathetic we had become.

'Mind you, I can't say I wasn't pissing myself laughing as I sat there watching the fat-fingered loners weeping their eyes out in St. James's Park while cuddling a wee framed picture of the woman and telling Bear News it wasnae fair. Or the group of hairdressers from Birmingham who bunked off work so they could go down to London, light a few sparklers and hold an all-night wailing vigil. It was brilliant; the hysterical mass hysteria of howling good-bye to the big-nosed Norma-Jean. And all because *we* hounded her to her death. Aye, right. It was all the fault of the Press so it was.

'Yet they still ignored the ironic tragedy between their undying loyalty for her and the job we do. If it hadn't been for the Press, they would have never acquired that god-awful, self-righteous love for their beloved English rose in the first place. We were only playing along, giving them what they craved. And laughably, if it weren't for us as well, they would have found out a long time before she took a joyride through the streets of gay Paris that she was just as ruthless, unhinged and scheming as we were. Were they really that stupid? You bet your life they were. What's more, she was just as fucking bad.

'I mean, all that bowing of the head and peeking up towards the camera with those sad eyes and moaning about there being three people in the relationship. Jesus, who in their right mind goes on national television and discusses that sort of nonsense? I'll tell you; poor sods from council estates in Burnley looking for a couple of hundred quid and narcissistic celebrities seeking sympathy and pleading for forgiveness for annoying the shit out of us for the duration of their pathetic careers. Yes indeedy, she had taken the Springer philosophy to a higher level.

'Come on, you just don't take on the Establishment. It

2

was like watching West Brom play Man U. The no-hoper putting up a brave fight for sixty minutes before Fergie says enough is enough and sends on the first team to teach the upstarts a lesson.

'But oh no, she wanted to go into extra time so she made sure she got that picture taken. You know the one, where she's sitting at the end of the luxury yacht looking pathetic and heartbroken and lonely when in all probability she'd just been down below in the gold plated captain's cabin enjoying some wave crashing coitus.

'Nope, she didn't grasp any of it. Not one bit. It was all about an heir and a spare, and they got that with Mr. Ed and the wee ginger Nazi. Sorry but time's up, the game is over. Yep, the poor girl just never understood what she was getting into. And whom she was taking on. But you had to give her credit, by god, she was a trier: the legs akimbo picture in the gym, the book, the see-through dress, the rugby player, a fiasco with an Iberian, that numpty of an Army captain, and a multi-millionaire whose daddy owns a shop who, coincidentally, was the unluckiest of the enchanted fuckers in that all he probably wanted was to shag someone famous. But nope, he ends up dying in the car crash as well; a mangled wreck where everybody copped it apart from the bodyguard who, as we were to find out later, went on to conveniently lose all recollection of both the incident and his fucked-up life aside from his name, rank, serial number, where he lived, where he went on holiday and where his local pub was.

'And still the great British public didn't get it. They even turned on Lizzie herself; calling her an unsympathetic bitch and demanding she come down from Scotland to publicly support the national cause. Christ, what national cause was there for her to support? If my daughter-in-law had decided that her way of seeking revenge on my wayward son was to take the more than occasional visit down to the officers' quarters for some blue-blooded pleasure, then I can't say I would be too forthcoming in popping on my black hat and sniffing away the tears. I mean, the girl was so popular in the Mess they'd given her a nickname, strapped a saddle on her back, tied her to the stable door and left her there with a bucket of water and a pile of straw!

'And therein lay one of the many idiotic examples of the great British public's sickening hypocrisies. Now those very same worthless mourners who were holding wakes in Wycombe and funeral parties in Falmouth have forgotten all about her. Fuck me, it's only been ten years since they were suffering from what the shrinks then were describing as a vicarious mass pilgrimage of delusional, self-serving, self-perpetuating and grief-stricken fucking lunacy; where throwing a huge bunch of flowers on a moving vehicle was considered a show of loyal devotion and not as it should have been; Aye, causing another fucking car crash! And now, instead of venting their anger and organising some bitter reprisal at the despicable Establishment, they are singing its praises from the roof tops. Wretched souls so they are. However, we all know they aren't the only ones who should be implicated. Oh no! Cos we, the Press, the good wee message girl, has decided to print what they want to read ...again. We are the ones who are just as culpable and only too willing to provide them with the new opinions of the nation.'

"Isn't it great that Lizzie came through it all much the stronger?" "Ah, bless him; the wee, fat, baldy piano player really deserves his Knighthood." "Actually, I think Horsey-Face looks good in that dress." "I'm going to vote for Butler Boy in 'Arseholes in the Jungle'."

'Nope, she and everybody else for that matter should have known you just don't take the power-brokers on. They are the almighty. As long as we play all along, everything will be hunky-dory. In fact, never are they happier than when we all sing and celebrate our togetherness, our wonderfully prosaic, fucking togetherness!'

Dixie's bloodshot eyes glistened for a moment beneath her short and shaggy auburn hair. Though her jacket from her pin-stripe trouser suit had already been thrown over the back of the bar stool, her white linen shirt still had a need to cling to her perspiring curves. Nearby, a group of coked-up stockbrokers were letching after her, their evening dose of machismo having kicked in early.

Exhausted, she was gulping down rather than sipping on a large glass of cold Sancerre. Oh yes, it felt good inside her mouth. It was also providing an instant rebirth to the senses only a glass of fine wine, or maybe a double orgasm for that matter, could do to release the built-up anxiety of another fractious week. Nevertheless, she was enjoying herself for the first time in a while. And why the fuck not, she thought. Why shouldn't she let go and give it laldy, especially after a long day of worry, anger and strife?

She had first woken up on the sofa in the early hours before staggering off to bed in a dry-mouthed daze, only to be up again at six to discover that Catriona had fallen ill. Rather than take the day off, she had driven her daughter and son across town to her parents. Unfortunately, things didn't improve on the way into work either, as she had to slip a tenner to a couple of station guards to help her out when her car picked up a puncture just behind Central Station. It had been a bloody awful day and to further enrage the wee man stomping on her temples, it had ended with a stand-up row with her editor who was still trying to persuade her to shelve the story she was working on.

Now she was free, at least for a few hours.

She was standing in an old bar just off St. Vincent Street with her two best friends, Johnnie and Paul, and her recently employed assistant, the eager Rory Hamilton. At this moment, she adored her world. She was turning down the gas. For the rest of the evening she was not going to be judged by what she said or what she wrote.

The Ploughman Poet was her after-work local and a favourite of the city's wealthy professionals keen to stay in touch with tradition. It was a pub of brass fonts and dark oaks and huge mirrors advertising old whiskies. It also a damn good wine list. Aquascutums mingled with Hugo Boss and balding heads bobbed amongst hair gel while the bar staff, wearing black ties, white shirts and long black aprons, served without fuss. They were all men. Small jugs of water lay idle on the bar while the tiled floor below -laid by immigrant Italian hands- withstood the weight of sixty or so Glaswegians preparing to touch down at

Steamin' International. Up above, the ceiling was another reminder there had once been a need for specialised tradesmen. It was also a reminder that once upon a time the law would have permitted her to light up and drag on a well-earned fag. She cocked her head back and smiled. The plastering may have been a musty yellow and full of cracks but the cornicing still maintained, remarkably, a refined elegance.

She wondered if it was her own sweat she could now smell, the muggy summer's day having rendered the pub an alcoholics' sauna. She laughed. The pub wasn't quite minging yet but it was pretty fucking close to stinking. Malt whiskies blended with Mexican beer while pints of lager and thick stout sharpened the pungent breath of smokers returning from the beer-garden. She gagged. At the far end of the bar, the open space contracted into a narrow corridor of small enclosed snugs guarded by wooden frames and crinkled glass. She imagined the days when the only sounds coming from them were the grunts and moans of sex starved punters and hookers from the docks. How times change. She sighed and she smiled. This evening they were packed full of young office workers laughing and joking and shrieking with drink induced joy. Behind her, the magnificent stained glass windows kept the outside world at bay. And thank goodness, she thought, for that.

She took another drink of wine as Rory spoke.

'Aye, but it's no use us standing here and mouthing off about how pathetic everyone is and how we're all being led a jolly jig,' he said. 'At least the public back then had the balls to stand up for what they thought was right, even though they were so evidently misguided and wrong. You had to give them that.'

'Of course you did,' she snapped. 'But that was the damn problem. The Establishment, in being ill-prepared for the back-lash, allowed the Press to paint her as some poor soul who had been given a raw deal in a difficult marriage when in reality we all knew it was different. She may have been a loving mother but she was a liability. What's more, while certain others were hoping and praying she would just go away, it wouldn't have been good business for the public to know what she was really like. But when the Press subverted the real truth, the country went into Mental Vigilante mode, and that created a scenario where the event of her death was far, far worse than the calamity we would have suffered if the public had discovered what really had been going on.'

'But then,' reasoned Rory, 'all hell could have broken loose. The Media needs to be controlled in some way.'

'Of course it does,' she stated as if to end the discussion on her terms. 'But at the expense of the truth and free speech, I beg to differ.'

There was an uncomfortable silence. Johnnie and Paul knew it best to let her give-off when she was in a mood like this. Stand back and let the pistols pop. But Rory was trying to impress. He was just getting to know the real Dixie.

'Ah, the young philosopher speaks a good game,' smiled Johnnie. 'But you've a lot to learn before you can take this girl on and win. She's from the generation of protest and anger, ideals and ethics. Something, I presume Rory, you've not been exposed to in your world of Lad's Mags and Wee-Wees.'

Rory bowed his head while Dixie's mouth almost broke into a sympathetic smile. Paul, also feeling sorry for Rory, was quick to jump to his defence by using his well-honed flyting skills on Johnnie. 'Listen Wop-Head,' he grinned, 'it is Nintendo Wii, not some kid's urinary deposit. So please, spare us the grandiose clichéd shite. Or better still, tell it to that arsehole from Saturday night television for I'm sure, just like you, he thinks the world is just one big fucking stage. It's all right for Dixie and me, we've had twenty years to get used to your philo-sophical and thespian pish but Rory here is just a sprat and I for one wouldn't wish him to be subjected to your nonsense for any longer than needs be. In fact, it would be better for all concerned if you fucked-off sooner rather than later to wherever the hell you're going for your next shoot.'

'Argentina, by the way. Good wine so there is. And even better women,' laughed Johnnie.

The four of them were just warming up.

This was what she had promised herself. Take a break

from work. Enjoy your friends. It was also the third evening on the trot she had decided to get well and truly off-her-legs drunk. Tonight, however, was slightly different. She was in the company of friends, and that was a much better proposition than feeding the kids, playing with bone-grating toys and nodding off to James Waterman as he attacked yet another arrogant and thoroughly unprepared politician on News Line.

The previous night's drinking had begun as soon as the kids had been shunted off to bed. Before collapsing on the sofa, there had been a nifty dash to the fridge and out with a bottle of wine, uncorking it faster than a seasoned jaikie on Argyle Street. The agony still fresh, she hadn't noticed the drinking becoming a routine. Her excuse was that it eased the tension but in reality it was about loneliness and fatigue and being a single mother. Fucking separated. Often there were tears and moping around, and sulking and self-loathing. Nevertheless, it couldn't all be her fault, could it? Surely, he was the one to blame for the mess she was in. He was the one who didn't understand the long hours and the public pressures of what she did. Yes, it was definitely his fault that for the last six years she had preferred to work late than subject herself to night after night of his monotonous tales of his company's P&L and his enthusiastic endeavours in playing squash, talking squash and masturbating over squash!

In more sober times however, she knew he was a good man and a good father but why get married in the first place? They had been so different. Her mind was full of things that affected the world while his was full of things that affected the family. But opposites were meant to attract were they not, or so she convinced herself when the knot was tied. Unfortunately, that fairytale had long since ended and mercifully, he had had the gumption to end the misery. It wasn't doing either of them any good. It wasn't violent and there was no one else involved: just the end of the road. Neither could she say, sadly, that it had been all fun and games. The sex had lost its zeal and the laughter had long since ended. Nevertheless, throughout all of their woes, it had been comfortable and easy, and he had pushed her to grow as a person. What's more, when they did part, he didn't even bother to contest the custody of the kids. Now, he would visit often and take them away on holidays. And he would still love her. It's just a shame the feeling wasn't reciprocated.

Oh, fuck. What a selfish bitch!

Before the first bottle was finished, she had been on her feet and sliding across her open plan lounge and dull walnut floor to ambush the fridge once again. But the drinking didn't mean she was an alcoholic. Alchies didn't have the time nor the inclination to savour a thirty quid bottle of Chablis. No! This was only a short-term predicament and time would see her grab her life by the clitoris again. There were people to interview, leads to investigate and stories to write. For the moment though, she would sit back, drink, and reflect. She would snigger at those she had exposed, fume at those who denied her information and become irritated by those who were thwarting her ambition. And the bottle would tilt; again.

Lying back on her large white sofa with her cognitive process in overdrive was always her moment to escape, with the drunken lucidity of what she should do always ending with a yelp and a dogmatic slap of her hand on the table. First, there would be frustration, followed by her self-insistence on righting a few wrongs and, with the glass in her left hand, ending with the scribbling of unintelligible notes on discarded envelopes and the corners of newspapers. And all would be fine; the morning would bring a better day. Yes, it would. What's more, it was time to switch on the tele. It was time for News Line.

Waterman had always been the best entertainment of a lazy evening. Lately, though, the political assassins' favourite assassin was becoming too good, his researchers too sharp and his prey far too weak. No one, nowadays, wanted to go on News Line if "he of the short legs and huge head" was sitting there with a hand on his cock and an eye on the cross hairs. Political careers were far too fragile. Furthermore, why spend ten minutes twitching uncontrollably beneath the glare of the studio lights as the sweat trickled down the crack of your arse when it was by far the more sensible option for a politician to take the Fifth, switch off the mobile, lock the bedroom door and have a wank.

Waterman was brilliant but at this moment on a Thursday evening, he couldn't even buckle her wee brown shoes. He was a grandstander who courted attention and who took great pleasure from invoking a rise in his detractors. He had even dissed her beloved Burns. *Arsehole!* No. She was the only one who got to the nub of any political nonsense that really mattered. She was the one with her own people on the inside and she was the one who could disarm and destroy anyone brave enough to defend a political decision she disagreed with. She always got to the truth. Or so she thought.

She had become a media enigma. In other words, her readers thought her to be credible and unbiased. What's more, they trusted her. Okay, so she had an experienced editor who knew that a year rather than a week was a long time in politics and a newspaper owner unmoved by political persuasion, but she always ensured she never pushed her personal agenda when it came to reporting the facts. It didn't matter whether her targets were the First Minister or a Toon Coonciloor from Irvine; stories were always about how politics affected the people.

She had always felt that way, even back in Uni when she was an antagonistic left-wing pain in the arse. But then again, she reminded herself, everyone in the eighties was. And then there were the years writing articles in every publication deemed important enough for such an acclaimed student as she. After that, it was straight into employment as a junior reporter for the Tribune. No more manky flats, no more tinned spaghetti and no more bottles of Thunderbird. The stone washed jeans had been discarded, the left-wing extremism abandoned and the hair shaped into a clean cut bob. She was now a professional.

The Tribune was the paper she had always seen as taking her to the top. Unlike the other broadsheets in Glasgow and Edinburgh, the Tribune's hacks had a sense of freedom about what they did. No pressure to create half-truths, just good old-fashioned journalism. It had also been reassuring to know that the paper wanted her, even allowing her time to speak to a few of its journalists before she signed a contract. And she just loved the office. "Yer tellin' Toni" journos with greying hair, droopy balls and Bi-focals hanging from an old piece of chord hunched over modern workstations while sucking in expensive beer guts and persisting to type with the fore-finger of each hand. Gallows humour and piss-taking echoed round the wood panelled office. The guys at the Trib identified with the city. They lived it. It was their life. It was her life.

This was the reason that writing for a tabloid was most definitely out of the question. Back-stabbingly competitive with little time for sentiment it was all smash and grab. These papers didn't have opinions, only twisted statements of "fact" scrawled by young attack dogs out to make a name for themselves and a weekly slot on a regional radio show. Shite piled upon shite; a murder one day, a double murder the next. And far too many column inches given over to football. No, the Tribune was the only paper she had ever wanted to work for.

The following years saw her endure the endless tedium of covering council elections and the Constitutional Convention, excitement at Labour winning the General Election in '97 and immense pride at the re-opening of the Scottish Parliament. She quickly became top dog, or top bitch, to those in the concrete and wooden caves of Holyrood. Moreover, it hadn't prevented her from making in-roads at Westminster as well. Holyrood might have been growing in prominence, but at the turn of the century Westminster still made all the big decisions. However, exposing corruption, social negligence and political mis-management were not what made her a pest. What annoyed politicians was her ability to see both sides of an argument and write stories accordingly and, as much as she found it frustrating that her words in the Trib' could never really reflect her true anger at some of the Government's policies, emotional reporting was a big no-no. Iraq, Cheney, Crime, Blair, Health, Education; they were all sensitive subjects but as long as she remained detached, she was doing a good job.

Nevertheless, she had wanted more of the limelight. She wanted to be considered as the best and though her editor had carpeted her on more than a few occasions, she had made sufficient impact with some of her controversial articles to be marked out as a future political editor. There was the one on a certain political party's clandestine association with a Christian fundamentalist group, another on the financial neglect of public housing projects in Glasgow and, in a wee bit too close to home as it transpired, there had been the exclusive she had penned on a corruption scandal involving the police and a gang of Russian mobsters. All three stories sparked media-wide interest but unfortunately, as well as becoming an instant celebrity in the world of journalism, she had pissed a lot of people off. But what the hell, she was doing a good job, wasn't she?

And that's exactly what her boss told her after she received international recognition for the first time. Her story was all over the news channels. Even Alain DeWitt's BEAR TV had decided to cover it.

The Trib', against its lawyers' advice, had published her piece on a tri-lateral strategy involving the British, American and Dutch Governments who, by applying pressure on the trade agreements of four small oil producing countries, had engineered huge tax concessions for the world's largest oil companies. It was the big bad West up to its old tricks again: supporting the multi-nationals and appeasing investors while small countries in Africa and South East Asia suffered. What did the world care that a tribal village wouldn't acquire a clean water supply for another year? What did it matter if the infant death toll went up a percentile or two? At least the shareholders were happy.

As Dixie reminisced, she raised the glass, toasted herself and took another drink.

She had even been asked to appear on the dreaded News Line and BEAR Live to discuss her investigation but had declined the offers. As it turned out it hadn't been the smartest of moves as she and the Tribune had been pilloried in the right-wing press. And worse was to come as her line of enemies in London grew increasingly longer. At the top of the seething queue stood both the Government's Director of Communication and the CEO of a major broadcaster. What's more, as she sought a hiding place on a Caribbean beach, those men of influence had been joined by the Minister for Enterprise and the chairman of

UKES plc who, along with his counterparts at Shell and BP, happened to be one of the most powerful men in the world. Unfortunately, it was widely known that the boss man at UKES wasn't the most endearing or magnanimous of souls, especially when pens and Dictaphones were stuck into his flabby face by determined hacks like her.

Such were the hindrances of what she did and how she went about it. But fuck them, she wasn't going to change. She had already lost her husband and much, much more so she was damned if she was going to lose her professional respect!

It had been two o'clock in the morning when she opened her eyes to the sight of the second bottle lying empty on the coffee table beside the grimy and finger printed wine glass. Her head had nipped, strands of hair had stuck to her greasy face and drool had encrusted in the corner of her dehydrated mouth. She had struggled dizzily to her feet, grabbing the remote control and switching off the television chattering quietly in the corner. She hadn't the energy to think about the morning when the hair would need washing, the kids dropped off at the crèche and a meeting held to discuss the story on the Hutchinson Group.

Now, however, it was early on Friday evening, just after five. As the pub filled up, she comforted and protected another wine glass while smiling into the eyes of her two best friends. She had just about managed to forget about last night and to see out the day without losing it. And that was more than enough cause for a minor celebration.

*

5.05 pm - A3 - London

Sitting in the out of town traffic on a Friday night was not Elliot Walker's idea of post-work relaxation. After all, he had a loving wife waiting for him at home.

London traffic was a grind at the best of times but come the weekend, the trek out to Surrey was everything he despised; mile after mile of Porches, Bentleys and SUV monsters all competing for the minimal space the A3 could afford. Elliot scoffed. Inside these double-axled tins of wealth, pseudo Greek gods preened themselves in the rear-view mirror while taking leering glances at any female with a pair of tits and a decent looking arse. It was their dream time, the chance to peacock themselves in front of the poor minions standing at a bus stop and to hallucinate of fucking a twenty-three year old secretary who so obviously wanted someone like them. Further-more, as long as the traffic jam continued to jolt and trundle towards Sunningdale, the bastards at the wheel didn't have to think about sleeping with their botoxed wife of ten years who as well being past her prime, was more content to sit in an Ascot brasserie discussing the sex lives of professional golfers than her poor kids who had been packed off annually to boarding school.

Hating himself for being bitter and green like this, Elliot sometimes felt he was just as bad as those he was privately mocking but as arrogant and aggressive as they could be, at least they had gumption. They had balls. They were courageous risk-takers with a vastly different approach to what Elliot thought appropriate when dealing with power and control. They got into people's faces whereas he took cover behind the Law and his expert knowledge of it. Sure, he could be a ruthless bastard if he wanted to but his aggression came in the form of paper and ink and the backing of UKES plc. Nevertheless, in the big, bad real world, in day to day transactions with stroppy train conductors, dodgy shop owners and traffic wardens, he daren't piss anyone off. Deference was his ally, his friend. He would suppress his petulance and his retributive thoughts. And he would cringe at his inadequacy in not being a little more hot-headed.

Elliot dreamed of the day when he would make a stand. Just complaining about being overcharged in a pub would be a start, or telling some young chav to quit smoking on the train. Anything. It would at least allow him to walk a little taller. But he was weak, petrified that any altercation would compromise his position within the company. And he knew it. His entire life had been about making the best of scant resources. No, he dare not impose himself. He had worked too damn hard to throw it all away and though his self-persecution would frustrate and disturb, his disinclination for controversy was a small price to pay for sleeping easy or rather this is what he assured himself when analysing his now waning justification. After all, he had a loyal and beautiful wife, a well-paid job as a top corporate litigator and a whopping big pension coming his way. What's more, his longing for home had never left him and as much as he would miss his London friends and the corporate membership to the St. George's club, he would retire early and return home to the big sky of Lochaber.

Elliot loved going home and like most exiles, his image of Scotland was of the more romantic nature. He adored the wild magnificence of his land. He had no doubts; the Highlands were a truly remarkable landscape. It didn't matter what time of year he was there, the colours of the changing seasons, the selfish Atlantic winds and the astonishing remoteness of being, made each visit seem like a trip to somewhere undiscovered. It could be warm, it could be freezing, the rain could pour sideways and the sun could shine at eleven at night. It was a heavenly place, a spiritual place. It was home.

Kirsten and he would often bag a Munro in late summer. From high up above their world, they would sit on a lonesome rock surveying their own mystical and infinite paradise. Holding hands, they would dream and look down on pockets of singing sands, sacred mountains and saintly lochs. At the end of a clear day, as the sun was setting, they would inhale the pine trees and wild flowers while gazing over to the Cuillins, the table tops of the Small Isles and a hundred different peaks of blues, purples, greens, browns and golds. They would sip on a malt whisky and count the small boats drifting at peace in the waters thousands of feet below, and they would cuddle up to each other and shelter from the evening breeze. They might have felt wee and exposed and fragile in this cathedral of nature but they felt alive.

When he was home, Elliot always hoped that he'd be able to spend time with one of his oldest friends who would also be taking a break in the Highlands. Johnnie Di Marco and Elliot had been at university together and had shared many great times, but whereas Elliot had grown up and settled down, he couldn't help but smile ruefully, and with pride, at Johnnie's incredible good fortune. After college, Johnnie had dedicated himself to his craft, first playing bit parts in the odd television series before being spotted by a Hollywood actress who as well as obsessively ingratiating herself with Johnnie's bedtime prowess, had pointed out his acting talent to her agent. The rest they say; but Johnnie had remained grounded and in touch with his roots. Of course, being an A-list actor meant Johnnie could now travel the world first class and shag beautiful girls without trying, but he was loyal and he adored his friends.

Talking late into the beguiling nights as the Northern Lights sparkled and danced in the sky above Johnnie's cottage, they would hoot and joke, take the piss, sing old folk songs and drink just a little too much. Elliot loved Johnnie's company. An entertainer, he was enlightening and good fun to be around. Nevertheless, as much as Elliot knew his life to be fantastically uninteresting in comparison to Johnnie's, he was never made to feel anything other than special. Johnnie had that knack, the ability to make him feel as if he were the most important person in the world, often asking Elliot how he was getting on while gently mocking his life in London. *"Why don't the two of you move back to Glasgow? You could still have the city life and be only a couple of hours from this place."* Elliot also respected that Johnnie never much discussed himself and his "dreadfully intrusive" lifestyle, preferring instead to ask about the peaks Elliot had climbed and pleading to see the pictures he had taken. Johnnie was a good man. He was a good friend.

Elliot's day at the office had been routinely unexciting. There had been much posturing by his latest legal opponents and much berating from his chairman, Sir Alexander Lamont, about not giving the bastards anything. This, of course, was not what the workers at the Forth Oil Refinery would have wanted to hear, so broken were they by seeing their benefits and rights reduced to almost nothing over the last few years.

'Listen Walker,' shouted the chairman, 'if they didn't already know that oil is the most precious commodity on the planet, they do now. And that means they're going to demand more cash, higher pensions and shorter working hours, and I'm damn sure I'm not going to give them back as much as a sniff of what I've taken. In fact, I've had enough of those sponging Scots, yourself excluded of course, so if it's a battle they're after then they had better come well-armed, for it will be more than polite negotiation around the table, it will be a full-out industrial war. And I, of course, will not be on the losing side!'

Sir Alexander hated losing. It was part of what they call nowadays as his genetic make-up, or as Elliot observed after four years of working alongside him, a belief that life, and everybody else for that matter, had bestowed on him the right to be a big obnoxious bastard. Unlike Elliot's last boss at Shell, Sir Alexander didn't care whether it was his wine collection, his art collection, his club memberships or his holiday homes; they just had to be the best, the biggest, the most expensive and the most exclusive. Being just another son of just another old-moneyed family wasn't enough for Sir Alexander. He had to be someone who was respected. He had to be revered. And God help anyone who stood in his oily path.

Elliot began to realise this three years ago when he had mentioned to Sir Alexander in the passing about Kirsten's love of horses. Sir Alexander loved to ride himself and while Elliot ignored the innuendo, the old man apparently knew what he was talking about: *"Hunting. Rathcombe. Down near Swickington."* Having never heard of Rathcombe or not knowing where the fuck Swickington was, Elliot wasn't in the mood for pursuing the subject. Nevertheless, he was more than a little taken aback when only a few weeks later he and Kirsten had been invited to join Sir Alexander's hunt for a day. Kirsten was delighted. She had heard about the Duke of Rathcombe and his ancestral home on the Fairmont Estate. "It is *the* hunt in all of England, for goodness sake." Yes, Kirsten was more than delighted, she was ecstatic.

Having grown up with two of her own, Kirsten adored horses, galloping for hours across the beaches and hills north of Inverness. This, on the other hand, would be an entirely new experience. But she wasn't going to let that spoil her fun. Within hours of Elliot telling her of the invite, she had bought all the gear. Expensive? Yes. But, hey, it would be a weekend of shiny new boots, tight fitting jodhpurs, shorter hair and a brand new riding hat. The saddle would be buffed and the whip feathered. She was going to have a blast.

Elliot, however, was a self-proclaimed novice horseman; more inclined was he to ride just to keep Kirsten happy. Horses made him nervous and the thought of being bucked through the air like a drunk from a Bronco machine petrified him. But he couldn't refuse Sir Alexander Lamont. It would have been bad for his career prospects and even worse for his marriage.

Sir Alexander's PA had checked them into the Melford Manor Park Hotel, a few miles up the road from the Fairmont Estate. The hotel was in a place of American fantasy; a snoozy little Cotswolds village of old stone, tiled roofs, winding lanes, small windows and a village pub sitting on the corner of the main street awash with regalia and antiques of the ancient Hunt, which for four hundred years had hunted deer and then, after some old Duke realised that venison was becoming much less frequent on his banqueting menu, some two hundred odd years of chasing Basil Brush over fence and hedge and stream.

Elliot, though, wasn't anti-hunting. Having grown up in the country, he recognised that life could be very different from the city. Hunting was a heritage, an ancient culture and a source of employment for many. What's more, as Elliot and most of the real world were aware, the fox was a wee pain in the arse, most notably to many a mangled chicken and many a dead sheep. The four-legged killer was also the essential component in the lives of the huntsmen, farmers, blacksmiths, furriers, saddlers, and all the other businesses in the countryside who relied on hunting to provide them with a living. However, times were changing. Now that the Ban had been brought in, those who hunted were doing their best to keep tradition alive. There were club shows, dog shows, horse shows, legal challenges, the Countryside Alliance, the storming of Parliament and the odd maverick Hunt that when not trampling on Cathy the Crusty Campaigner's head, still enjoyed chasing the real thing and the murdering savagery it conferred.

The Rathcombe, however, obeyed the law; as much to avoid the PR nightmare it would incur because of its aristocratic connections, as it was for the fact that people like Sir Alexander couldn't be seen, publicly at least, to be taking the law into their own hands. Nevertheless, the Rathcombe Hunt and many others like it continued to thrive, and good for them, thought Elliot. It seemed like rare fun. In fact, if he was going to jump on an enormous horse, stand on the occasional foxhound, get pissed before eight in the morning and hang on for dear life as Trigger flew across a six-foot hedge while chasing a pack of slavering mutts who in turn were chasing an old rag dowsed in Vulpinic odours, then it only seemed appropriate he embrace the local customs and get dressed up for the day. Elliot smiled. Misguided might have been an understatement for the bizarre outcome to the controversial anti-Hunting affair but the irony wasn't lost on Elliot. No more could one hunt a fox with hounds, not in Britain anyway, but if Old MacDonald happened upon one darting across his fields then the farmer was more than welcome to load a couple of shells into a shotgun, take direct aim and blow the poor thing's arse to Kingdom Come!

As they waited to be picked up, they could feel the sun burning through the early morning mist as it drifted peacefully through the trees and up towards the sky. It was a fine but chilly autumnal morning and it would be a fine, if not excruciatingly painful, day. Kirsten, belonging inside her well-fitting riding clothes, was chapping at the bit to make a start while Elliot, struggling with an ill-fitting riding hat and endeavouring with little success to find some kind of genital comfort zone within his nippy and extremely tight-fitting jodhpurs, wasn't so keen

Right on seven, a large and dirty blue Landrover came skidding to a halt on the gravel outside the hotel and out jumped a healthy-looking young man with wild fair hair and an enormous set of white teeth. Christ, thought Elliot, if he was any more hyper, I'd be jumping on him right now, cracking the whip and shouting, 'Come on Biscuit, one more furlong!'

Biscuit's real name was David and he was wearing an open-neck, navy cotton shirt rolled up to his elbows and tucked inside a pair of white jeans held up by an ornate buckle and belt. He walked with purpose, which was not surprising considering he had on a pair of black leather boots that seemed to travel up his legs forever before stopping just above his thick knees. He was smiling and polite, and full of energy. 'Good morning. Kirsten and Elliot is it?' he asked as he opened the front door for Kirsten while leaving Elliot to clamber in to the back unaided. As the engine roared before driving off, David turned to Kirsten. 'First time down at the Rathcombe?' Elliot was still shuffling with his gonads when Kirsten replied from the front seat. 'Oh yes, but I've heard so much about it. I can't wait.'

'You'll have a great day and our country is wonderful. Everything you need for a good day's riding.'

A few minutes later, after listening to Kirsten and David talk enthusiastically about riding in the Cotswolds versus riding in the Highlands, Elliot was relieved to feel the Landrover slowing down and drawing to a stop behind a another pub in another small village. His baw-bag was fucking killing him.

They hopped out and as David led them to the gathering, Elliot saw Sir Alexander holding court with two other riders. He was drinking whisky from a small silver tankard and barking his opinions as usual. If Elliot's tadger hadn't been gasping for air, he would have laughed out loud at the sight of his boss. Elliot noticed the tiny riding hat first, clipped tightly underneath moustache, three chins and fat ruddy face of the older man. Taking an eyeful, Elliot studied the unique uniform of the Rathcombe Hunt -navy blue riding coat with gold buttons and cream coloured buff facings- while also struggling to disguise his ridicule as the riding coat made no apology for exposing Sir Alexander's huge and lumpy arse, which, like Elliot's crumpled cock, seemed to be suffering from asphyxiation. However, that was just the warm up. When Elliot caught sight of the short, little brown boots on Sir Alexander's long, fat legs, he couldn't resist letting out a whispered snort. 'Bloody Hell, it's the English Yosemite Sam!'

'Morning, Walker. Where's that gorgeous little wife of yours?'

'Hello, Sir Alexander,' replied a sheepish Elliot. 'I think she's gone off with David to have a look at her horse.'

'That's the spirit. Straight into things. She must like a good ride,' roared Lamont, much to his own amusement.

What an arsehole!

As he joined the small gathering, Elliot could feel his social ineptitude. To his relief, the tension quickly eased when one of the many non-riding members here to follow the hunt shoved a hot toddy into his hand.

'So, Walker' demanded Sir Alexander, 'rode out before have we?'

'Eh. No. Not really. Only with Kirsten. A few gallops across the heath at Windsor. In fact, I'm a bit nervous.'

'Ach, don't be lad. We'll make sure you're all right. Just follow the pack and don't jump anything you don't think you can clear. I mean, we don't want a broken neck do we? You can't be dealing with my affairs if you're winched up in some bloody hospital can you?'

Elliot smiled but underneath he was fuming. Was this Sir Alexander's idea of fun? To make an employee look foolish and subservient? You bet it was.

He stood obediently as Sir Alexander introduced him to an Alain DeWitt and a Sir Peter Milligan; two men Elliot didn't know, and reckoned he would probably never see again. Not because he wouldn't be back here any time in the future but rather the two men had a presence of immense power and influence. They were at ease, the consequence of a quiet and unassuming power. As they turned to Elliot, he could feel their eyes giving his character a good going over. Elliot presumed they didn't normally mix with serfs like him but ultimately didn't care if he wasn't their type of man because they were most definitely not his. They were complicated and intense, and far from Elliot's ideal choice to have a beer with. But what the fuck, he was here to enjoy himself.

Standing slightly back, Elliot relaxed a little while he

was subjected to Sir Alexander's gossip concerning a couple of fellow members at the old man's private club in London. Sir Alexander guffawed at his own importance while the two men grinned politely. Their intense gaze shifted back and forth between Sir Alexander and Elliot who was standing in silence wondering if they were thinking what he was thinking; how in the hell can you work for this guy? Elliot attempted to fake an enthusiastic interest in his boss's monologue by nodding occasionally and chuckling at Sir Alexander's childish jokes. It was as if Sir Alexander couldn't wait to tell his audience of his latest house purchase in the Caymans, his newly acquired winery in France and his rather large contribution to The Rathcombe so it could continue the brave fight against the new Countryside legislation. Oh yes, he was most definitely the man.

'Anyway, chaps, what are we going to do about this Scottish mob?' prodded Sir Alexander. 'They're becoming a wee bit big for their boots, wouldn't you say?'

Just like yourself, big man.

Elliot had always presumed that Sir Alexander kept his opinions confined to his office. Obviously not. 'I mean, they could win the bloody Holyrood election,' continued the old man. 'Can you believe that? It's enough to scare the hell out of any self-deserving Brit, is it not?'

Elliot bowed his head in discomfiture. Not that he agreed or disagreed with his boss, rather it was early on a cold October morning in the middle of fucking nowhere and here he stood, with his nut sack knocking frantically on the door of his colon, listening once again to Sir Alexander's bluster.

The two men were uneasy. Waiting for Elliot's reaction, they quickly turned to Sir Alexander with a look that informed him that this was neither the time nor the place. However, Sir Alexander read their guardedness. 'Don't you worry about Elliot here, chaps. He's my best boy and one of us. Oh no! Nothing to worry about at all.'

But the two men weren't forthcoming in widening the discussion. After a couple of mumbles, and a few ums and ahs Elliot could feel they just wanted him to bugger off.

He did.

Making his apologies a few minutes later, Elliot left to join Kirsten in choosing a horse. The village square was busy with horse boxes, 4x4 jeeps, wax jackets, green wellies, a couple of dozen non-riding members, fifty or so riders and about thirty yelping hounds. The air was sharp and the early morning breath steamed out from a hundred yapping mouths. The excitement was most definitely intensifying. It was a different way of life, but then again, they were a very different people.

Kirsten was trotting her horse up and down a narrow laneway when Elliot arrived at the row of horseboxes. David was standing waiting and although he had changed into his hunting attire, his smile was gone. 'Sorry Elliot, but the Master of the Hunt has changed the course for today. It's awfully difficult so I think it better you didn't ride out.'

Elliot didn't know whether that was a good decision or not. He wasn't in the mood for hanging around all morning doing nothing but then again he didn't fancy breaking his neck, either.

'But Sir Alexander reckons you can follow on with some other members. That'll be good fun,' said David, trying to ease Elliot's apparent disappointment.

'Ach, not to worry, David. I'll be fine. I'll just go and tell Kirsten.'

Kirsten could understand where David was coming from. Riding could be dangerous and as much as she wanted Elliot to have fun, she was more than a little secretly pleased that she wouldn't have to keep looking over her shoulder to see if Elliot's horse had dislodged him into a dung-infested field. She could go hell for leather and enjoy it even more.

At eight o'clock, the Master of the Hunt blew his little copper horn. The thermos flasks and silver cups were packed away, the Landrover engines purred, the huntsman, whippers-in and riders moved towards their mounts, and the foxhounds went mental.

Elliot had read that the hounds had been part of the Hunt since the seventeenth century and in being mental, it was no surprise they were treated like royalty. The paperwork on their breeding was detailed and historic and apart from a controversial introduction of Welsh hounds into the bloodline in the thirties, they were pretty close to being complete blue bloods. However, now that the Ban had called a halt to their genetic instincts, preventing them from ravishing and ripping the odd fox to pieces, they were being used more and more as entertainment; the most ridiculous of which, as Elliot observed with much hilarity later in the day, was being made to race and jump two-foot high fences in a nearby field with what looked uncannily like a brightly coloured, fluffy clown collar wrapped around their necks. It didn't help, either, that they had names such as Bovina, Prizzy, Porky and Flapjack!

Just like a Saturday night in Sloane Square!

The riders trotted out of the village as the hounds barked and weaved amongst the horses' hooves. The Huntsman, in his green jacket, led the way. Once inside the nearby field, he fought to control the hounds who had begun to sniff the ground and pound the grass. Kirsten was in the main pack of horses and a few lengths behind Sir Alexander whose poor horse must have thought that a quick and painless transformation into a bucket of glue would have been a much less painful proposition that lumping Sir Alexander's fat arse around the countryside for another four hours. But Sir Alexander didn't care about whom or what was hurting. He was off on the gallop across the field, was first to reach the hedgerow and didn't flinch as he glided over. He was at the front and intended to stay there. Elliot laughed. It wasn't even a bloody race! Kirsten, meanwhile, took things easy for the first few miles. Listening carefully to David's advice, she began to relax, soon feeling comfortable enough to start jumping like the seasoned point to pointer she was.

Elliot, however, could not have felt, or looked, more ridiculous. Yes, he had giggled at Sir Alexander's pomposity but his now public and pathetic predicament had inflicted upon him his own humiliating strain of portentousness. There he was, with whip in hand, blinded by an oversized hat bobbing up and down and scraping his nose. Jesus, this wasn't the kind of carry-on he

24

had expected this early in the day, especially as his plum-sack now resembled his granny's left elbow. Maybe it was a blessing he could hardly see or feel a thing because he now felt like an eejit of pantomimic proportions.

Okay, so he was dressed up in appropriate hunting gear: *Not a bother!* He was following the horses: *Nae problemo!* He was also admiring the landscape and listening for the horn: *Nothing wrong with that, big boy!* Unfortunately, there were no reins to grab hold off and, courtesy of fucking Davy-boy's desire to invoke the Hunt's new and improved Health and Safety initiative, no finely polished leather saddle on which to park his skinny white arse. Too late, Porcelain-Pus, the nutbag is already in intensive care. Predictably, of course, there was no require-ment now for Elliot fucking Walker, he of the Useless Pathetic and Insignificant Wanker Association, to go anywhere near any form of equine transportation. Oh, fucking no! He had to settle for this. Arse and screaming testies on the back of a quad bike, holding on to the waist of Arabella; a chubby and malodorously fetid elderly woman relishing and revelling in the task of driving through the horse shit like a recently sectioned rally driver.

What a numpty!

Elliot knew he was different from those he had met that day on the Hunt. It was most definitely a case of them and us. He didn't feel subservient at first but after a night of heavy drinking and silly songs, he could sense the change in his hosts. As much as he thought most of them good fun to be around, he knew deep inside there was an incestuous subtlety to their relationships. They were a family who knew each other well and knew each other's histories even better, a club who didn't mind the odd visitor but a club all the same, and a club who enjoyed the position it held in society. He could sense their superiority and how no mortal was to be worshipped. And as much as they strived for it not to happen, all their talk went in a downward direction. Like the interest they showed in Elliot. Oh yes, it was a "wonderful achievement" to have worked hard and defeated the tough life of Lochaber to become a top lawyer but it was nothing special to them. Certainly nothing like the joy his mother and father had shown at his graduation. Furthermore, what Elliot had achieved was insignificant and in a deprecating way, beneath them. Lawyers were like tradesmen who existed for the sole purpose of making the privileged lives of the well-connected even better. What's more, Elliot noticed the distinct difference in how they spoke to each other as compared to those outside their circle of privilege. Elliot didn't have the bloodline, the connections or the power, and as much as they had been hospitable and kind and friendly, he was most definitely an outsider.

But couldn't everyone be an outsider, he asked himself. If one of those he met that day happened to stumble into a party in a South London flat and witness Chantelle-baby gyrating her crimson tide on top of Dewayne's bulbous Calvin Kleins, then Elliot was sure the chauffeur would be receiving a call sharpish. Moreover, if a family sat down for lunch next to a group of wealthy farmers at the Harrogate Show, he was damn sure there wouldn't be a fawning scramble to nominate and second the unfortunate Mr and Mrs Patel for membership to the local agricultural society!

That day reminded Elliot of the difference between the culture he grew up within and the culture in which he now lived. Of course, there was snobbery and elitism on either side of the border but Scotland didn't have the same class inflicted baggage as England. No, Scotland had an inverted class system where the entrenched and bewildering ethos of small town Scotland ensured anyone on any given day could be spitefully and wilfully excluded. Small artisan golf clubs, council estate communities and old mining villages all had their "who the fuck do you think you are" exclusion zones. It was about protection. Protect a way of life, protect the cultural history and make sure you come out on top, regardless if one was living on incapacity benefits or sipping cocktails in a Miami bar courtesy of daddy's inheritance. However, that time with the Hunt a few years ago had been a one day experience of the lifetimes of others, and it was, as they say, enlightening. Furthermore, as he sat thinking in his office earlier, and now in his car as it trundled slowly down the A3, he began to realise how drained he was of Sir Alexander's never ending struggle for dominance. It had been wearing, as had Sir Alexander's increasingly Unionist rants of them and us. He was worn-out with Sir Alexander's quest for power and of the rising tension between London and Edinburgh. Britain, he had once thought, was surely stronger as a collective entity and it had been proven time and time again but now he wondered if the situation was changing. Was London really losing its grip?

Elliot had never been a Scottish nationalist. Sure, he liked the idea of being Scottish but it wasn't the end game for him. That result belonged to his wife and hopefully his kids. Nevertheless, there was a time he did believe in the strength of the United Kingdom and what Scotland gave to London was a respectable trade-off against future investment. If Scotland could shore up the UK treasure chest every once in a while then the least Westminster could do was ensure Scotland was taken care of. Now, however, having been at the table to witness Sir Alexander Lamont rip the soul from those in the Forth Oil Refinery, Elliot was beginning to question his motivation; not from a nationalist point of view but from an opinion that not everybody could be dismissed as a mere inconsequence. Furthermore, devolution politics had been developing a bit of an edge lately.

Having been in London for about ten years, he had first seen the country being led by a Scot before being replaced by another. Now he could feel antagonism in the air. Moreover, these two haughty leaders had been well aware of the growing resentment as well. The former was a Prime Minister who never talked about his Scottishness; more intent was he in lying to the world about weapons of mass destruction in Iraq, socialising with brain-dead entertainers and defending his peculiar looking wife from her mouth and everything that spewed out of it. His successor, meanwhile, avoided his more conspicuous Scottish-ness as much as a Z-Lister eschewed the concept of personal dignity. Embarrassed he held no genuine, everyday power over his constituency, he was now completely absorbed in the defence of his position. And by wittering on constantly about the strength of Britain and Britishness, and thinking it was a sensible public relations move to sit down for afternoon tea and a chat with Margaret Thatcher, the poor bastard had not only forsaken his roots, he had also forgotten how to run the bloody country. He was in a "lose-lose" situation and unless the political gods could deliver unto him an FDR or a Churchill epiphanic moment in international crisis aversion, then the Press was never going to let him forget where he came from.

Elliot shook his head. He couldn't even raise a smile.

Beginning with the occasional anti-Scottish joke in the opinion columns of the London evening papers, the sniping had developed into full-blown articles in the national media. The ordinary English man and woman were apparently pissed-off with the Scottish Raj. Unfortunately, the erroneous frustration of this minority was becoming more vocal: on radio, in letters, in comments on elongated online threads and more importantly, in Parliament. Elliot's unease was growing. Things were definitely changing for the worse. But should he be that concerned, he asked himself. He never felt like a foreigner in London: just someone from a different part of the world. Leave the politics to the politicians was his mantra. Fighting over what, he wondered. The world would still go on. Starbucks would still sell a decent coffee, a Big Mac would still taste brilliant after a night on the beer, Bono would still be sporting his four-inch platform boots while harping on about the poor defenceless Africans, and he would still have Kirsten to go home to after a long day at the office.

2

forever the pig in shit

Saturday 7th June

6.00 pm - West End - Glasgow

'Hey Boss,' started a nonchalant Charlie on the other end of the line, 'that razor blade any closer to your wrists yet?'

Dixie wasn't in the mood for casual conversation, nor Charlie's quips of gentle mockery. 'Just about. Nappies full of shit, Walt at his brainwashing best and a four year old son who's quite content for me to be a major shareholder in Toys'4'U. Fortunately, his sense of perception has not yet reached the point where he understands my potential to be a wicked mother who has no qualms in dispensing the sleepy solutions!'

'That good, eh? Well, let's hope I can cheer you up.'

According to his tax returns, Charlie Norton was a freelance photographer. However, as Dixie's profile had risen, he had quickly become her un-registered private investigator; a chameleon able to retrieve information Dixie could only acquire by lying on her back for fifteen minutes. People trusted him; for no other reason than he didn't appear threatening. He could crack jokes with the lads, discuss art and philosophy with academics and was a genius at persuading women to love him. What's more, he knew it. Nevertheless, Dixie made sure she kept him close. As much as he was a joker with an inclination to fuck around, he was a decent man and he was bloody good at his job.

'Okay Charlie, what do you have for me? And please tell me it's been worthwhile. I'm in the middle of getting ready for dinner with Hastie and if some inside scoop is on the menu from the big man in blue, the last thing I need to be worrying about is you having been caught with your camera up somebody's arse.'

'A bit touchy are we, Dixie?'

'Damn it, Charlie. What have you got?'

Charlie knew Dixie was on the edge. She had been for a few weeks now. A divorce in process, a big story in the works and two kids to love and take care of was more than enough for him to understand that his teasing would only be tolerated for so long. 'Not only did our men have a round of golf at Gleneagles but also a long lunch in Fairlie's.'

'And?'

'Yep, we got the pictures. But you owe me. The security was so tight it took all bloody day.'

'And you're sure nobody saw you?'

'As sure as I can be,' laughed Charlie. 'Not only did I become a golfer for the day, I also called in a favour from my little mate Dave and his wife. They're members at Gleneagles and regulars in the restaurant so if I was made they would have the back up.'

Dixie breathed out, a smile passing her lips for the first time since she held Catriona that morning. 'Brilliant, Charlie. I'm sure you'll be suitably rewarded.'

Charlie's work was over for the day. Beer and sex were now at the top of his agenda. 'Thanks. I'll be sure to spend it with prudence on some worthwhile extra-curricular activity in town tonight!'

'You just do that, Norton,' grinned Dixie. 'And when you drop into the STD clinic on Monday make sure you show them your loyalty card.'

Driving through the West End on a summer's evening was a joyful release for Dixie. With the roof down and Stuart Murdoch's melodies uplifting her spirits, she breathed in the city air. It was fresh and damp, and smelled of summer rain and cherry blossom. As her tyres squeaked gently on the tarmac of the quiet streets, she had time to smile as party invitees squeezed their cars into non-existent parking bays beside small fenced-off gardens in the centre of residential squares. Moments later, they would be disappearing through the old stonework and polished black door of a five-story townhouse to enjoy expensive wine, Indy music and a barbeque on the back patio.

As she drove further down the road and away from the exclusivity of the moneyed avenues, the streets widened and the re-furbished tenements grew in number. Corner pubs stood alone, protecting the silent thoughts of their patrons from behind large, stained glass windows while next door the addictive smell of newly fried fish and chips, and salt and vinegar, wafted out from an Italian chippy. As she stopped at a traffic light, a cyclist flew by on her inside, its pilot rushing home after a busy day working in a fashion store on the Byres Road. In an hour, the girl would be changed into her best togs and anticipating a good night out. Every so often, the ancient spire of the university would peek its head above the skyline while down below, in the bars tucked peacefully down old mews, waiters cleaned and polished tables, set out ash-trays and turned on the side-walk gas heaters. Nearby, in dead-end alleyways, bands tuned up and sipped on cold bottles of beer.

There was a hyperactive contradiction to the West End: the accessible and the discreet unobtainable, the peculiar and the habitual, the classical and the downright diabolical. Not always to everyone's taste but it nevertheless ensured that even its most nonsensical of residents could avoid the humiliation of being exposed as extremely fucking stupid. The West End was most definitely Scotland's intellectual and cultural powerhouse. Not only did it have the feel of an environment in constant change, it also had the smell of practical purpose. Its foundations had been constructed on the concept of innovation. Things were always happening, always changing. It was always on the move.

This journey would occasionally take her mind back to her student days when the neighbourhoods surrounding the old university were awash with combat jackets, peace signs, purple hair and the sounds of Hue and Cry, Scheme, Neal Young and god forbid, Depeche Mode. She remembered how she fooled around with Paul and Johnnie, and how poor Elliot always bore the brunt of their humour. She loved her friends and the freedom she had as a student. She smiled. It was still evident in today's new creed heading to the Oran Mor for a night of music and debate, and hopefully, sex.

Dixie enjoyed the emancipation back then because she wasn't a threat to anyone, just another outspoken student with no idea of how the world worked and oblivious to the effects of real power. Now, things were different. In the last twenty years, the world had become a much smaller place and instead of fighting for justice for their fellow countrymen, students now protested against the power of multi-nationals, the decaying state of the environment and the labour conditions in Asian sweat shops. Unidentifiable people in unidentifiable places. It was easier that way, thought Dixie; much easier than facing up to the ugly world of inner city estates only a few miles to the east where it was now generally accepted that the paupers in the tower blocks only had themselves to blame. It was their problem the world couldn't care less. Because didn't everyone have an opportunity to break out from the ghetto? What's more, if the junk disciples couldn't bother their arses to grasp it, then why should anyone else shed a philanthropic tear if the contemptible fuckers ended up reaping benefits which saw crime arrive on their door-steps with a daily delivery of extortion and violence, only to be followed by a couple of pissed-off policemen gearing up to serve ASBO number three. Mournfully, these spurned and pathetic communities within the concrete slums had become much more than a laughing stock: political correctness declaring that you couldn't mock anyone nowadays; anyone, that is, apart from the rotten and stinking underclass of society. They had become fair game on the battlefield of guilt appeasement. Disillusioned, helpless and eternally fucked.

Tonight, however, Dixie didn't have time for protest marches and charity runs. She was on to a story she had been preparing for all her life. It was as if destiny had incurred upon her the opportunity to speak for a helluva lot of people. It also scared the shit out of her that the ramifications of her story could transpire into a threat to her own personal safety. Nevertheless, they were nowhere near as frightening as the possible outcome if she ended up saying and doing nothing.

She pulled up a few doors down from the restaurant, giving her hair and make-up a final going over before stepping out and locking up. She stood for a second, checking herself out in the window of the car door and eyeing her choice of dress with perked-up satisfaction: a little green and black linen number from Iona Crawford. 'Not bad!' And, considering she had two young kids, she was also grateful that God had bestowed on her torso some damn fine healthy genes.

'Dixie, good to see you and thanks for indulging an old man,' said Deputy Chief Constable Michael Hastie as he reached over the table and planted a light kiss on Dixie's cheek.

'Mike, you're only fifty-two for goodness sake. There's sure to be some life in your old ticker yet.'

'Ah, flattery will get you everywhere. Please, sit down.'

Dixie squeezed between the tables and carefully took a seat on the cream leather bench-seat facing out towards the main body of the restaurant. She didn't like being fenced in like this. Breathing deeply, she glanced at the bottle of wine sitting at the edge of the table. It was red: Malbec 2005. A good wine but not her choice for such a humid evening. The policeman fiddled with his cutlery as he waited for the waiter to pour Dixie her first glass and his third. A quick toast and large sip later, he spoke. 'Hope the wine is to your liking and since you'll no doubt want to go Dutch, it's a damn good price as well.'

Dixie smiled impishly. 'What's this, a man of substantial means not treating a lady like myself?'

'Dixie, I'm so sorry, I just supposed you'd...'

'It's okay Michael. I'm only winding you up but I must say it's very gracious that you see me as one your peers.'

She lifted the glass slowly and as much as she wanted to knock it back in a one-er, her good manners and self-awareness permitted her only a sip. She breathed deeply before continuing.

'Anyway, I don't suppose it would look good for the DCC to be seen buying dinner and drinks for the political editor of the Tribune, especially after the corruption investigation we forced on you chaps a couple of years ago?'

'No, I guess not, but you know as well as I do that that bullshit was instigated from down south in order to take the heat off them after the subway shootings!'

'I know, I know. I'm only pulling your leg. Still in work mode, you see. And still protecting my corner.'

'Fair cop, to excuse the busman's parlance. Anyway, you look good tonight.'

Dixie was taken aback by the softness of his words, she not being used to the big, powerful policeman showing another side to his usual tough persona. She blushed. Hastie picked up on her blood-shot cheeks and glanced down, changing the conversation immediately. 'So, hungry I hope? The main man is in the house tonight so we had better indulge ourselves.'

She had warned herself earlier to avoid any displays of her inbred cynicism but regardless of any attempt she would make to offer up some humour, she knew she couldn't help but fall into that uncomfortable mind-set between the two. 'Is he, now? My goodness, that's rare; considering he's on television these days just as often as the Six O'clock News.' It was a feeble retort. Not that she was embarrassed at what she said; just that she could never extinguish her irreverence. If he finds it funny then so be it. If not, then fuck it. She had long since passed the point of embarking on a character make-over. 'Ah ...the world's favourite chef, cooking for little old deary moi? How delightful!'

As they finished off dinner with an agreeable but pricey Burnt Cambridge Cream and double espresso, Dixie offered a timid smile as the candlelight flickered in her eyes. 'Tell me Mike; is your presence this evening a sign that the Strathclyde Force is willing to re-open communications with the Trib?'

Hastie leaned forward in his chair, disguising his usual self-aggrandising nature. 'First of all, Dixie, it really is good of you to have dinner with me and although we both know relations between the Force and the Tribune have been bordering on the, how shall I say, fractious, don't you think its time we moved on? Life's far too short to be worrying about personal vendettas and one-upmanship.' He looked down at the table and swept away the crumbs left by an exhausted waiter. 'Of course I want to open up communications again. I wouldn't be very good at my job if I didn't. However, I do believe I'm a man who cares for the greater good and if we, the police, screw up then we deserve a hammering in the media. On the other hand, when you guys start sticking your snouts into things that could be deemed to be of no concern of yours, then I think we have every right to make your life difficult. There are a lot of dangerous bastards out there and it's our job to ensure they don't threaten the status quo.'

Dixie didn't want to broach the corruption scandal again, thinking it better to move things on. 'You're sounding very political, Mike. Thinking of bigger things?'

'I don't know,' offered Hastie with more than a hint of caution. 'I'm fairly happy with my lot here but I do feel I have much more to offer the country. Maybe London is the place for me. And now the kids have grown up and I'm single again, there's nothing really to hold me back.'

'What's this? Not by any chance thinking of a role with the Intelligence Community are you? The National Security Department maybe?' asked Dixie mischievously.

Hastie smiled at Dixie's perceptiveness. Nothing passed her by. 'I'm not too sure but I'm pretty well up the pecking order with the NSD. When a top job comes along down there, I might just consider it. As I said, I've a lot to offer.'

'So why are you telling me?'

'I don't know. Probably because there are very few people I can discuss it with. And from a political point of view, maybe the Tribune will understand my position if I do move on.'

As they both took a sip of their coffee, Dixie hoped the policeman wouldn't see her mind going into overdrive. *Why is he telling me? I know we've had our difficulties before but this is a bit out of left field. Mike Hastie is one of the best cops Scotland has had in the last thirty years, and highly respected in the corridors of power as well. What the fuck is he up to?*

'Well, I don't think it has anything to do with us, Mike.' continued Dixie. 'It's your decision but if you moving on creates a vacuum then we will have something to say.'

'I understand, Dixie. But if I do, I hope I can leave the place in a more stable and secure position.'

Dixie could almost touch the unyielding hardness in Hastie's voice. This was a threat. 'Mike, I hoped this would be a cordial evening. I was also hoping it wouldn't all be office talk. And as much as I'm well aware of my workaholic tendencies, I do occasionally need some time off, you know.'

'Does that mean your covert working practices differ from that bloody photographer of yours? I hear he's working weekends and taking up golf now.'

Dixie was stunned. *How did he find out so quickly?* The look of shock on her face was evidence enough for Hastie. He definitely knew something about the story she was working on. But as to how much, she didn't have a scooby.

She gave nothing away. 'Look Mike, if the head fixer of the Hutchinson Group just so happens to be on a golfing trip to Scotland and we're not on the case, then it renders us as pathetic professionals who have no clue whatsoever as to how to do our jobs properly. It's our duty to find these things out just as it's your duty to protect. I mean, he was only playing golf …wasn't he?'

He knew she was a crafty bitch but he was tired now. He opted to finish and move on. 'Yep, he's only here to play golf and that, I hope, is how you'll report it.'

'That's what I thought. I take it then that there should be nothing much to worry about?'

'Nothing at all.'

'Good. Then shall we retire to the bar for a nightcap?'

'Now there's an idea.'

3

playgrounds for bulldogs

Monday 9th June

6.55am - Grosvenor Square - London

Four floors below, the traffic was already backing up towards Oxford Street and Park Lane, yet for Peter Buchanan the madness of a London Monday morning seemed much further away than eighty feet as he sipped quietly on a coffee in the office of Sir Alexander Lamont. He loved the early hours, he could think. Wondering how the city had changed in the past twenty years and how much it would change further still. How the rise in the financial industry had given birth to a happiness of sorts and how it had taken away the city's soul. But wasn't that the exact nature of England's capital city. Evolving, tempting, abusing, ejaculating, manipulating?

As relaxed as he was though, he smiled in sympathy as buses, cars, motor bikes and delivery vans honked their horns while taxi drivers shouted obscenities and homeless people grovelled inside industrial wheelie bins. These days, it had become a war of attrition just getting to the office. Patience was a distant virtue and every second seemed like a time to strike, especially for those not propelled by oil and gas who weaved unthinkingly through the chaos with newspapers under arms and briefcases held tight within white knuckle fists. He had been one of them once but had learned to shield himself from the daily abuse. He had a good defence.

London was made for prize fighters, a lonely city where loyalty was only as strong as your bank balance and integrity a slight on your character. And it created monsters. It nurtured them, fed them and ultimately destroyed them before casting them into the River Thames to drift out to sea alongside all the other shit the city no longer had the need for. However, as he stood over this demesne at the centre of an historic kingdom, Peter could only smile as he contemplated the future. It would soon be his, this city. He would be its king and he would set out to change the Britain that had so tragically lost the faith of its people.

'Ah, Buchanan,' heralded Sir Alexander Lamont as he marched into the office. 'Glad you could make it at this ungodly hour but in my world, as you no doubt know, there are no mornings, noons and nights. The oil keeps pumping and we keep selling.'

'No, this is fine, Sir Alex. In case you have forgotten, I have two young kids.'

'Ah yes, of course you have. How are the little buggers? Well, I hope?'

'Oh yes, well enough to wake me from my slumber two or three times a night.'

Sir Alexander placed his old leather briefcase by the side of his enormous chestnut desk before hanging his jacket inside the built-in closet. He strutted over to the window, stopping to pour himself a coffee. 'What, doesn't your wife tend to all that business?' he joked. 'Wasn't like that in my day. Anyway, how is she? I haven't seen her, or you for that matter, since …when was it …ah yes, the wedding of the Duke's daughter. Damn fine occasion wouldn't you say? However, you would have thought the miserable bastard would have splashed out on some decent Bordeaux for his daughter's big day!'

Sir Alexander returned to his desk while slurping on a coffee and coughing up his early morning phlegm. Peter resisted a reaction, and throwing up, at the man's lack of good health and general manner. Having heard his bullshit much too often, he knew that Sir Alexander could change in a second. He hoped this morning wouldn't be one of those times.

Peter had known Sir Alexander Lamont since he was a young boy, his father and Lamont having been old acquaintances. Lamont would often visit the Buchanan's estate in the Highlands where there had been many a long day on the moor ending with Peter humping Lamont's pellet ridden birds back to the castle. He loved being around Sir Alexander back then. He was a man who cut a good figure in his tweed and as the results from the shotgun had proved, had an eye as sharp as his mind. He told the rudest jokes, shouted the loudest profanities and obliterated the most pheasants. Nevertheless, he had always been bloody good fun. Peter even remembered when Sir Alexander had first taught him how to fire a shotgun and how it felt like the easiest thing in the world to do. Advising him to watch the tips of the heather, he was to check the wind and wait for the beaters' sudden stop. 'Always be ready, young Buchanan,' Sir Alexander would bark. 'There's no use doing anything in life unless you are thoroughly prepared. Check out all the possibilities, weigh up your options and take good aim. And always have your finger twitching on the trigger otherwise your petrified prey will be gone forever and you, young man, will end up, sadly, with nothing on your table.'

Those days on the moors had taught Peter a valuable lesson; men like Sir Alexander always had an advantage. They made it their business to make it so, by whatever means.

His father, though endowed with a healthy generational legacy, had preferred honesty and perseverance to ensure the family's continued success. However, this work ethic had not been easy for Peter to understand, his father spending weeks and sometimes months away from the family home. He could be down in London or in the Far East making deals so Peter could be sent to the best of schools and provided with the best of opportunities. Peter was thankful for the leg-up but resentful at the absence of a father figure. That was why, as a boy, he came to mistakenly admire the man now sitting opposite. Peter craved inspiration. He needed someone to follow. It was also why, at the end of a long wet day, he would often sit by his father's feet and listen wide-eyed and enthused as Sir Alexander discussed everything from hunting bears in Alaska to banking and politics in London. Sir Alexander, with strategies mapped out for all eventualities, had all the answers. Who would support him with this, who would oppose him in that? Single-minded, he had one aim: to increase both his already considerable personal wealth and his far-reaching power base. Furthermore, most of the time he was to be proven correct. Inspired by these late night conversations, Peter discovered his own appetite for banking, and for politics.

There were also a few times when Peter would be sent to bed early, only to find he couldn't sleep as he listened to his father and Sir Alexander shouting wildly at each other. From his bedroom high up in the castle, he would hear the echoes of Sir Alexander's over-zealous demands in between the slamming of old wooden doors. In the morning, as his father sat quietly at the break-fast table while Sir Alexander continued to rant, Peter would feel ashamed. Why had his father not stood up to Sir Alexander? What had been wrong with him? Was he just weak? No. He had misread his father, and on the odd day they did spend time alone together, Peter began to understand his father's way of getting things done. He learned of humility and respect and of understanding how even the smallest of decisions could affect someone or something. His father would tell him stories of people in Indonesia who would fall at his feet and beg for food while his company ransacked the country for the benefit of a few people back home. He would also tell Peter of his pain as he stared into a starving child's eyes while he wore the best of linen suits and the finest of watches. He knew what he did wasn't right and nor was it fair. Nevertheless, as much as Peter could sense his father's guilt with the family's accumulated wealth, he could also feel his father's pride. There were stories of charity and investment and of giving something back. Maybe that was his father's greatest gift to Peter before he passed away: to provide people with hope. Sure, it was politics and corruption and theft on a grand scale but he had to be prepared to give something in return. His father was teaching him of responsibility. Not just to oneself but to others. He wanted Peter to appreciate the goodness in men and to understand that even the most under-privileged deserved respect. Knowing he had been born lucky, his father was trying to tell Peter the same thing. Being privileged meant just that.

His father never much discussed Sir Alexander Lamont except to warn Peter to watch out for his kind. However, with the power Lamont held, and the influence he exerted in the City, his father advised to keep the likes of Lamont close. Choose the wrong team and Peter would suffer. Be seen to offer support, whatever he thought personally. And he had to be smart, street smart. He was to think of what was best for the majority while providing assistance to the minority. If he didn't then Peter's life would be riddled with bad decisions and remorse. And remorse, determined his father, was the worst feeling of all.

Peter hated feeling guilty and despised making mistakes. And he had made a few. He had been pompous, self righteous and arrogant but then so had most people he had grown up with. The difference, he felt, was that he could change. He didn't like making a fool of anyone either, even feeling sorry for the Prime Minister when facing him across the floor. However, as much as Peter attempted to display humility and integrity, he had learned something from his father about Lamont. What's more, he had been prepared to betray his morals to do something about it.

A few years before, when Peter first came to London to take up his position with Parker Milroy Private Banking, he set about developing as many well-connected contacts as possible. It was the only way to the top. He also used these contacts to build his own private dossier on Lamont, quickly discovering that his father had been excessively generous with his character assassination. In fact, Lamont was much worse. He practically ran the bloody country!

There was the much-publicised scandal of the small oil producers in Africa and Asia, as well as the ruthlessness in how Lamont dealt with the Unions. But there was much more. A couple of old school friends had laughed in perverse admiration as they told Peter of when Lamont, in demanding tax cuts for

UKES, had reduced the last Tory Prime Minister to tears. If the tax cuts weren't forthcoming then the whole world would get to know about the ex-Prime Minister's bit on the side. What's more, if that wasn't bad enough, UKES received the tax breaks and Lamont still leaked the story to the Press. Peter had winced as he listened to his friends flaunt their wicked approbation.

There had also been the bribery of the Minister for Trade and Enterprise who in rushing through new legislation, proffered huge financial gains for the City's hedge funds. Then there had been the covert surveillance carried out by NSD -the National Security Department- of the CEO of a Big 4 bank picking up a rent boy on Clapham Common, resulting in improved banking conditions for UKES and larger dividends for its investors However, above all these was the Cornwall Summit; a secret meeting in a country house down on the coast where Lamont had been instrumental in completing a deal between British arms producers and Libya, the outcome of which saw the UK selling weapons at a discount price in return for cheaper oil. Peter had gasped when he heard who was in attendance: the chairman of a major UK weapons manufacturer (who had boasted about drinking goat's milk in a Bedouin tent), the chairmen of three US airlines, two Swiss bankers, a Government minister, two Libyan officials and, of course, Lamont. Yes, Peter had done his homework. Lamont was a ruthless bastard.

Peter reckoned this power had everything to do with privilege or, in Lamont's case, the lack of it. Unfortunately, his heritage was far from aristocratic; no matter how often Lamont would lead people to believe it was. Peter's contacts, as well as his father's, alluded to as much by stating that Lamont's family had forced itself upon the Establishment from as far back as the early nineteenth century. They had been tobacco traders in the economic explosion that struck Glasgow and the River Clyde, transforming it from a small trading port into the European gateway for the lung searing commodity. The Lamont's wealth expanded with grand houses having been built in and around Glasgow and positions of power taken on the Shipping and Revenue Boards. With such influence, it wasn't long before the inevitable happened: their diversification into high finance and private banking. However, as hard as they had fought, and succeeded, to develop their reputation in Scotland, the Lamonts had found it difficult to establish a foothold in Victorian London. They had given much to the Arts and Education but still found it nigh-on-impossible to be accepted. At first, the Lamonts thought it was because of their Scottishness but after some quiet words from a Society insider, they discovered their rejection, to their horror, was down to the plain old simple fact that they just weren't a likeable family.

Therein lay the inexorable flaw inherited by the seventh generation Sir Alexander. Being polite or diplomatic wasn't in the Lamont make-up. Moreover, being educated in finance and business and economics wasn't enough, either. They still knew nothing of the ways of London Society. In other words, they lacked the necessary breeding. Nevertheless, their lack of grace and good manners hadn't prevented them from making inroads, especially when others discovered the size of the family bank account. And when a young aristocrat or two thought it a good idea to start up a business franchise in the Far East, in stepped the Lamonts with an offer of finance. If they weren't going to be invited through the front door, they may as well sneak in through the back. Beginning by having the aristocratic entrepreneurs in hoc, it wasn't long before the ambitious young men of London became addicted to the Lamont cash. Moreover, as long as that was the case, the politics of the day ensured there would always be the odd invite to a Duke's estate and a few reluctant honours from the Palace.

The Lamonts quickly built up a colony of influence in London and, over time, been grudgingly accepted. However, though their children, and then children's children, had been sent to the finest of schools, accepted to the best of universities and awarded high-ranking commissions in the armed services, they still remained universally unpopular. This long-held rejection, reasoned Peter, was most probably the catalyst for Sir Alexander becoming the man he now was -omnipotent, all-threatening and all-controlling- and undoubtedly why he had been offered the chairmanship of UKES plc. Both the Government and the City required someone who would neither flinch nor yield when defending Westminster's corner and a tough negotiator prepared to break any rule necessary to ensure investments were secure; someone exactly like Sir Alexander Lamont.

"Supremely Influential" was how Lamont once described his family. However, as much as the Lamonts had become a powerful British institution, they had yet to break through the bricks and mortar, and rivers of blue blood, surrounding the El Dorado of society. In other words, they had never received as much as a smile from the grand house on the Mall, regardless of how manipulative or indiscreet they might have been. There had even been tales of Lamont's grandfather and his courting of a young cousin of Victoria, as well as his desperately unsuccessful attempt to marry-off Lamont's father to a cousin of a former King. It had been humiliating. Furthermore, for once in their history, the unthinkable had happened; a Lamont patriarch had been unable to purchase the future. Consequently, a long-standing bitterness towards the First Family ensued, a bitterness enthusiastically inherited by Sir Alexander. However, this acidic animosity had little do with any objections he might have had to the idea of there being a hereditary head of state but rather to a twisted belief that certain souls in the Household had their own personal aversions. As Sir Alexander reasoned, the Palace just didn't like people who were wealthier, more successful and more powerful than it was.

Bollocks, thought Peter. It had much more to do with Sir Alexander's perfidious attitude towards Scotland. Unwilling to accept and acknowledge that the Queen and Queen Mother's heritage lay deep within their Scottish roots, Sir Alexander was always a little too quick in putting Scotland down, inclined to think he would be more popular with the London political establishment if he were more English centric. What's more, his personal motivations and ambitions had led to a tempestuous discord where Sir Alexander hadn't just stopped with mocking Scotland; he had come to privately mock the Queen and her love for the country. *'Who in hell does she think she is? Buggering off up there for weeks at a time when she should be down here. In fact, it's a bloody liberty. Here we are in London, working our arses off to provide for her and her off-springs, and there she is, off singing songs of wild mountain thyme and opening old folks' homes in Aberdeen. By God, someone should have a word!'*

In contrast, Peter was sympathetically discerning of the how the relationship worked between the Palace and Scotland. It definitely ran much deeper than was apparent to Sir Alexander: much deeper.

Peter had always considered himself an acquaintance of sorts; not well enough to declare them as firm family friends but enough to have earned their respect and trust. He had been at school with a couple of cousins, had partied with a son down on the Med, hunted with another in the Highlands and dined alongside the family at a few private dinners. He liked them. They were good fun with a wicked sense of humour drowned with dry wit and devoid of deprecation. They cared deeply about their role in Society and just as much about their family history.

Although he could have been widely mistaken, Peter felt most of them kept a keen eye on the political situation, as he had discovered on more than one occasion after being interrogated, intriguingly, about his plans. The drink would flow, their Staff would disappear and questions would come faster than Magnus. He learned early not to give much away but since official protocol was non-partisan, he felt he could discuss his strategies in confidence. He would offer his thoughts and listen to their opinions. He would lead late night debates and be a catalyst for broader discussion. He sensed they enjoyed his company, and he most definitely enjoyed theirs. Up to speed on most current issues, some of them were, undeniably, politically astute: despairing for the people troubled by the Credit Crunch and hitting out at the rising energy prices. However, when the conversation switched to Scotland their eyes would shift quickly back and forth, glancing to each other for support. Peter reckoned the short, ensuing silence was a prelude to a heightened intensity. As they turned to him, Peter would feel their eyes hold his stare for an extra second as their points of view became much more considered. It was raw. Two of them, specifically, would be uneasy, Peter perceiving a quiet anger. Of course, they could never, ever, say anything publicly but he felt Scotland, and its political situation, was discussed as much as any other topic, even sensing tones of endearment as they talked about Andrew Drummond -their First Minister, and sympathised with the disadvantaged in and around Glasgow. Moreover, they would affectionately comment on the positive things happening in Scotland: the new sense of pride and confidence, the success of its old and renowned universities and the ground-breaking environmental initiatives. Peter felt as if they knew more about what was happening up there than he did. In fact, he was almost embarrassed at their insight. Most of all, they talked of the peace of mind they had when walking their estates and how much they cherished the solitude and the freedom. It was as if they were talking about home.

This morning, though, Peter would disregard Lamont's obsessions and protestations until the time was right. As Lamont had once told him, Peter would make sure he was fully prepared before pulling any trigger. First, though, he still had a couple of things to do and one of them was to become Prime Minister.

'So Buchanan, you know why I brought you in here this morning?'

'I've an idea Sir Alex, but no doubt you'll want to be more specific than you were on the phone.'

'Oh yes, the time has come to be a helluva lot more than specific. It's time to sort out this bloody mess once and for all.'

'Well, hopefully I can change it all in a couple of years.'

'I'm afraid we haven't got a couple of years. We have to do something about it now. Two bloody years and it could all be too late.

Lamont sat back in his chair and threw his feet on the desk. Peter fought with his anger, trying not to think of how the old fiend was going to manipulate him.

'So Buchanan, my boy, what do you think of all this nonsense up in Scotland? It's not exactly what we would call beneficial to the grand scheme of things, is it?'

46

'No, it's far from ideal, but it does open the door for the Tories down here.'

'Maybe so, but I'm sure we'll see just as many being slammed in our face in return.'

'Why do you say that?' enquired Peter, closing his eyes and taking a deep breath.

'Things could become complicated down here,' growled Lamont. 'We've a helluva lot more tied up in Scotland than the people realise. First, and always first, there's the oil and the gas. Second, there is the impending financial crisis and though we don't yet know as to how bad it will be, you can be sure, if the government has to borrow its way out of the bloody mess, which it looks like it will, then we'll need to use my North Sea reserves as collateral to underwriting our borrowings. Finally, and much more important in the immediate short-term to both the country, and myself, we have Faslane and the Nuclear Defence Prog-ramme to concern ourselves with. Along with the North Sea, Faslane is more than just critical to the economic success and defence of our nation, it is an absolute necessity.'

Here we go again. Good old Blighty's interests at heart.

'So Buchanan, your priority will rest with Faslane. Don't you worry about the other concerns; I can take care of them.'

Oh really?

'The subs up there not only protect us, Buchanan; they also provide the country with thousands of jobs, with standing in the international community, with a damn good relationship with our friends across the Atlantic, as well, of course, as the rather large contribution they make to our accumulated wealth.'

And a few million for yourself, of course!

'However, there is more than just a couple of dollars at stake here, especially when you consider the country is contr-acted to spend a further seventy-five billion of them on the Nuclear Defence Regeneration Programme, which, without the bloody oil and gas revenues, it most definitely won't have. So have no doubts, Buchanan; this is an extremely big business.

'As you know, research is conducted at Aldermaston and Burghfield, the nuclear reactors are manufactured in Derby, refits and decommissions are carried out at Rosyth, Devonport and Portsmouth, and Vickers builds the new subs in Barrow. Then we dock them at Faslane, which, as you also know, was overhauled a few years ago at a cost of even more billions. However, as much as this business contributes enormously to the economy, it may all become redundant if the big players with significant interest and investment in the programme, most notably the Hutchinson Group and its clients, decide to run off with their cash elsewhere. In other words, it is the likes of Hutchinson who we really need to look after. If we do, they will ensure their investment into companies such as Dobbie and McGregor, who we've already contracted to run the bloody Aldermaston operation, continues. Furthermore, in return for Hutchinson's commitment, we have also sanctioned a significant US shareholding in the overall programme, thirty-eight percent to be precise, which not only entices the Yanks to place some rather substantial Defence orders with our suppliers but also creates an environment for them to generously invest in some of our other industries such as energy, finance and research.'

Oh yes, it's all for the country. All for the flag

'However, it's not just a one way transaction,' continued Lamont. 'We invest in their defence and energy industries as well, including the lease agreement we have on their missiles and the covert permission we provide for Faslane to be used as a base for their North Atlantic activities. Unsurprisingly, all this contributes to our noble and very special relationship, and the development of our ...how do you say ...shared capabilities, which has benefited both our countries for years.'

'Yes, Sir Alexander,' sighed Peter, 'but if all of this is being taken care of, why so much concern?'

'The concern does not lie with us or the Americans, but with Scotland and its political situation. You know how fragile it is at the moment. Any negative news about our role down here means more votes for the SNP up there. They already have the power in Holyrood albeit with a minority government, but the more the Westminster Government continues to screw things up down here, the greater the chance of that Scottish minority turning into a majority. And if that happens, we could be looking at the entire nuclear operation shutting down in the next fifteen years. No more Faslane, no more investment; and no more investment equates to an economic disaster!'

Peter could see where the conversation was going and it did not make for pleasant listening. For years he had listened to Lamont's rhetoric about the troublesome Scots and how they should be kept in their place.

'So the bad news,' announced Lamont, 'is that that bitch Armstrong, in her disloyal persistency, has been sniffing around our negotiations with the Hutchinson Group.'

'But there's nothing new in that, Sir Alexander. She is forever thinking Westminster has dirty hands. Thankfully, she and the Tribune never quite arrive at the truth.'

'Yes, I know, but my sources reckon she is on the verge of breaking a story about my, and therefore the Government's, various business dealings. And we can't be having that, can we. Nevertheless, above all my conceited protectionism, what really concerns me is that this could only be the beginning. Negative revelations denotes more SNP votes, and more SNP votes will transpire into a threat to my North Sea oil revenues. And if we get to that stage, then we could be talking about meltdown.'

His revenues?

Peter took a moment before his riposte. As much as this was about money and power, it was more about saving face for Lamont. It was also about Lamont being in control, and for once in his life, the old man could see it being taken away. *Oh no, that just wouldn't do, now would it?* 'Well, thanks for informing me, Sir Alexander, but don't you think it's up to the people of Scotland to decide? In fact, it's all this surreptitiousness that irritates them in the first place. And in any case, what do you want me to do about it?'

Peter's deficiency in revealing any kind of impassioned support was fuelling Lamont's agitation. 'What I want from you, dear boy, is to prepare for the future. So, I've arranged for you to meet with my chap from Hutchinson to iron out some details and then to meet his boss. I've already informed them that the future of Faslane and the Nuclear Programme is not something with which they should be overly concerned, and that there will be no issue whatsoever, politically speaking, with the SNP and its promise for a nuclear-free Scotland. In other words, I've been brave enough to ensure there will be no change to the current state of affairs in British politics, and that Faslane will remain open and under Westminster control.'

Peter's head jerked up sharply as he listened to Lamont's premature promises. How could Lamont be so sure that the political situation in Scotland wasn't going to change in the next few years? It was a rash prediction. Unless, of course, he knew something no one else did.

Lamont saw the perplexity in Peter's eyes. 'Don't you worry about the mechanics in all of this, Buchanan; I always deliver. If you stick to what you're good at, everything will be fine. What Hutchinson needs is reassurance. They need to hear from a future PM who is on their side and prepared to sign-off on future developments. Like you and me, they are also planning for the years ahead.'

Lamont stared into Peter's eyes, making sure he understood. The rebounding look may have been one of bewilderment but it confirmed to Lamont that the politician knew what was expected of him.

'Yes,' continued Lamont, 'it is always an encouraging and pleasant experience meeting your benefactors, Buchanan. It's a kind of ...reassuring feeling to know that what plans we make in life eventually bear fruit. However, being confident and self-assured may not be enough in securing our future demands with our allies. Moreover, as much as my continued affirmation, and your commitment, will go a long way in appeasing their concerns, you have to realise their world is all about rewarding investors with reliably high dividends. And if that means playing dirty then that is what Hutchinson will do. Similarly, my mission is to ensure the country continues to prosper, but if that just happens to include playing dirty as well, then my men will be in the sewer of contempt tomorrow. In other words, there may be some tough negotiating to do first. You see, when the UK and

US governments sit down to draw up agreements, there has always been this mistaken belief that we are both on the same side. Unfortunately, I have realised that this has not always been the case. And it would be wise for you to remember that.'

'But Sir Alexander,' pleaded Peter, unable to halt his contradictory opinions. 'I'm not so sure it's such a sensible idea for us to be making injudicious predictions at the moment.'

Lamont fell silent for a couple of seconds while Peter closed his eyes. He sensed the old man was about to blow.

Elliot Walker was also on the fourth floor of the United Kingdom Energy Sources' HQ in Grosvenor Square. He was in his office, perusing the newspaper reports of the weekend meetings with the Unions. He liked his place of work. There was an ambiance of distinguished history about the furnishings, the interior designers having avoided the clichéd, clinical and modern design trends. It wasn't dark either, which coming from a childhood of protracted winters in the north of Scotland, turned out to be a welcome blessing.

He had just arrived at work and was feeling the need for his third cup of coffee of the morning, having already had a quick one at home and another at the train station. It had been a tiring weekend made worse that he and Kirsten had to cancel their anniversary trip to Devon because of the trouble at the refinery. She was furious when Sir Alexander called late on Friday, and even more insulted when Elliot had been ordered to spend the weekend at the Office of Arbitration, preparing legal information for the company's spokesman being given the full treatment by the television news cameras. Kirsten hadn't been happy and he had borne the brunt. In fact, he had been glad to get back to the office because his guilt had been getting the better of him. It could be bad enough being a senior litigator for a huge multi-national like UKES but there was nothing more frightening than a disgruntled woman from the Black Isle.

It was just after seven-thirty when he went to collect his coffee. As he passed the Chairman's office, he noticed the door ajar. Glancing inwards, he saw the two pairs of legs, as well as hearing a voice he recognised but couldn't place. For no other reason than to be a nosey bastard, Elliot stopped at the desk of Sir Alexander's PA. 'Hey Marie, who's that in there with the big man? I know the voice.'

'Elliot, I thought a man of your intellect would recognise the Leader of the Opposition. It's Peter Buchanan, for goodness sake. Isn't that voice sexy?'

'Eh? Yes, yes, it is, isn't it? Not in that way, Marie but I think I know what you mean.' Glancing over at the door, he leaned over the desk and whispered. 'So, what's he doing in here at this time of day?'

'No idea. You know the boss, tells me everything and nothing all at the same time. Anyway, did you have a good weekend with that gorgeous wife of yours?'

He only heard the first two words. He was now staring at the back wall, not listening.

'Elliot, did you hear me?'

'Sorry Marie, what were you saying?'

'Nothing Elliot, it doesn't matter.'

'Er …Okay …thanks. See you in a bit.'

Elliot walked back to his office. It was a few yards along the corridor from Sir Alexander's. Just before Elliot reached his own door, Sir Alexander let out an almighty roar.

'Listen boy, you'll bloody well do what you're told.'

'I hear you, Sir Alexander,' winced Peter Buchanan, 'but there's not a lot I can do at this moment in time. I'm not the PM yet.'

'But you fucking well will be soon, and there's no way we're going to give up Faslane, and absolutely no chance I'll be giving my fucking oil back to those objectionable bastards in Edinburgh. There'll be chaos down here, do you here? Bloody hell, I wish Labour was going to win the next election and not your group of arse bashing little boys. Unfortunately, they are £25 million in the red and being led by a man who doesn't know how to talk properly, let alone run the country, so there's no fucking chance of that, is there? The idiot even wants to hold a State Funeral for Thatcher. Can you believe that? Christ, we used to rely on Labour keeping the Scots on a leash, which is more than can be said for your mob, but with Labour on the way out, it leaves us with one big fucking problem, especially if Scotland goes ahead with the Referendum. And trust me, that's the last thing you or I fucking well need!'

'But Sir, aren't you Scottish yourself?'

Lamont scoffed at the suggestion. 'Of course not! Maybe my ancestors were but certainly not me. I'm British, first and foremost. Anyway, that has nothing to do with it. Who and what we have to concern ourselves with is that arsehole Drummond and the SNP. If we're not careful, he'll have us over some very expensive barrels of oil after the next election: and that includes you, son. And don't you bloody well forget it. Now fuck off and get some strategy sorted out, and be back here as soon as you and your old school chummies have had a little chat.'

Elliot Walker was stunned. He had never heard such a vitriolic tirade coming from his boss. Sure, he'd seen him angry before but this was a new line in persuasion. Something big was definitely up and he was going to find out what it was. Maybe, he thought, it was time he had a chat with an old friend.

*

11.16 am – Gleneagles, Scotland

'Brad! How's the old country treating you? Enjoying the tropical climate?'

'Yeh, sure. Rained twice already. And suffering a little bit today. Had a few too many last night.'

'The water of life not living up to its name? No sympathy my end, I'm afraid. So, you've met our men?'

'Yeh, played golf Saturday with our big man from the military. Then met with our Government man last night.'

'First things, first; how did it go Saturday?'

'Pretty good. He's confident he can deliver for us on the continuation but believes the Scottish Administration will be no push over. Says the country has just about had enough of outside interference so he's advising us to bring more than our usual to the table. Meeting him again today to finalise his inventory.'

There was a short silence on the end of the line. His boss could be easily distracted. 'And last night?'

'Even better. Says he has to run things by his boss before making a commitment.

'Good work, Brad, but be careful, the Scots are a crafty bunch; and I should know, my grandfather was one. What's more, if our deal isn't strong enough, we could be out of the picture pretty darn quick and if that happens we both know I'm gonna be fending off an irate mob of investors reminding me of the goddamn fact. Anyway, there's no need to tell you again Brad but there's a helluva lot riding on this, and now that our asshole of a vice-president and his Pinocchio are no longer in the loop, that's the message coming out of Langley as well. So keep pushing and keep me up to speed.'

'Sure, Drew. I'll be on to you later today.'

'And everything hush-hush?'

'Come on, Drew. Who's gonna follow me to Scotland? Hell, no one lives here.'

'Just be careful, got it?'

'Drew, how many times do I have to tell you? I'm the...'

'Yes, Brad, We all know you're the best in the business. Anyway, St. Andrews next on the magical mystery tour, is it?'

'Sure is. Can't wait. Heading there as we speak.'

'Brad, know what?

'What?'

'You're a goddamn lucky bastard!'

Brad Zimmerman was 'The Fixer' for the Hutchinson Group, a private equity firm named after a famous Scottish banker from the nineteenth century. Its office was located in the heart of the U.S. capitol, on Pennsylvania Avenue, close to the FBI Headquarters and the Department of Justice, and only a few hundred yards from both the White House and the Senate.

One of five firms known collectively as the world's shadow banking system, Hutchinson had experienced some rough times recently, PR wise, with several journalists having exposed its sinister political connections to former Presidents and Prime Ministers, as well as its investment deals with several Defence firms. Nevertheless, behind closed doors, the company's worth and combined assets had grown to well over $269 billion, in most part down to some brilliant lobbyists it had on its books, as well as several ruthless and opportunistic politicians. However, as Brad had often struggled to highlight to his boss, it wasn't the journos that Hutchinson should be worried about; it was the investors. Hell, countries would always be at war so better to be inside the shop and buying the goods than looking in from outside with nothing in your pockets.

In developing his own brand of ruthlessness, Brad never allowed his conscience to affect negotiations. It was work and it was money. Sure, Langley and the CIA were always sticking their noses in when it came to strategies of "National Defence", a phrase Brad was keen to re-phrase as "International Attack", but it was a small price to pay when the annual bonus landed on his desk and his portfolio increased with another piece of Manhattan real estate.

Brad had been keeping investors happy since he joined Hutchinson in the late nineties. He loved his job: as much for the excitement as for the money. He was the great illusionist. He had also learned much, especially from his boss. However, there was always an historical perspective to negotiations when it came to Drew Wilson and boy, could his boss talk some real shit. What's more, Brad didn't care about History, which annoyed the hell out of him personally, as he struggled with a wilful inability to listen to his boss's lectures. Nevertheless, Brad had been smart, discovering over time that as much as he could gleam from the old man, he could learn much more about insider politicking from the lobbyists on Capitol Hill and the agents in Langley.

Within these circles, the secrecy of decision-making enthralled him. Drew Wilson might have given him the leads and the contacts but it was Brad who did the deals. He was the man who investors spoke to when they wanted something done and he was the man to whom they turned when it came to increasing the pressure on corruptible politicians. The people he dealt with didn't know whether to run from him or fall at his feet and worship him. And that's what he craved; the silent power of influence. Others were welcome to the fame. When he was at college, though, he never envisaged he would eventually land a job whose title would be as it was. Officially, he was Director of Investor Relations but in the real world, he was The Fixer. Welcomed with lavish gifts and afforded five-star status wherever he went, he was the man with the finger on the "send" option of international money transfers. And only he knew the access code.

As much as Brad disliked the thought of being a loner, his job demanded it; his success depending on never becoming too close to those with whom he did business. He could play one against the other without feeling. He had goals to achieve and money to make. It could also be tiring but it never stopped him from having fun. Hookers in South East Asia, drug dealers in Mexico and penthouses in the Middle East, he could enjoy them all without the guilt of going home to a suspicious wife. However, he never enjoyed his sojourns to Europe. The people he dealt with here didn't seem as desperate as others across the world. Moreover, they were far too conceited for their own good. Sure, they wanted and needed investment but not if it made them look bad. They were to be regarded as the initiators, the old world instigators. Brad, wisely, didn't give a shit what they thought. They spoke with funny accents, talked down to him and had a particular distaste for the US, especially those in London. Americans were brash and outspoken with no need for decorum, they thought. Americans were stupid, they thought. In some cases, they had a point but at least Americans weren't afraid to parade their true colours. As for being dense, Brad didn't agree. His country had some fine intellectuals and some outstanding universities but nevertheless, if he had to play the typical Yank to get his way then more fool them. Hell, they had a nerve calling him a dumbfuck when their own government was involved in just as much bullshit as his. Oddly enough, their mockery quickly disappeared when billions of investment dollars were on the table. Especially that asshole in charge of

UKES!

Brad had met with Sir Alexander Lamont on a number of occasions, taking an instant dislike to him at the first meeting, and not seeing it improve on any subsequent visit. He soon discovered it was reciprocal. Nevertheless, he had to remain cordial. There was much at stake.

He first met Lamont in London to discuss the possibility of obtaining cheap oil from Libya. The US airline industry, haemorrhaging cash, had its representatives come to Brad asking for help. Therefore, with a veiled threat to withdraw investment form the UK's Nuclear Missile Defence Programme, he set out his proposals. The next thing he knew he was sitting in a private club in London, hammering out a strategy with Lamont. He may have been old, but he was one helluva confident dude and there didn't appear to be a goddamn problem on the planet he couldn't solve. The second time he met Lamont hadn't been so pleasant. Hutchinson's investments in the Far East and Africa had been taking a battering, with Brad's last resort being once again to meet Lamont. However, this time Brad's requirements didn't offer Lamont anything in return. Acquire what he could from the small oil producing countries, Drew Wilson told him. Anything! Drew didn't care how much. Lamont huffed and puffed, calling Brad a cocky little shit, and whom did he think he was asking for more help. At one point, he thought Lamont was going to have him thrown him out. Furthermore, when Brad threatened to withdraw investment from the major banks in the City, he could see Lamont's fist clench. The old man was furious. His face reddened, his eyes exploded and his veins popped. 'Just who the fuck do you think you are, Zimmerman?' he screamed. 'How many times have I had to bail your country out? And you wander in here, demanding this and threatening that. Bloody Hell, we should never have given you lot your damned Independence. Fucking little upstart!'

The raging fury had no effect. Brad allowed Lamont to blow, knowing UKES had a shit load to lose if they didn't play along. Brad received the tax concessions for his Asian investors while Lamont also reaped in some action. In fact, Brad couldn't understand why the Lamont had lost the plot in the first place.

And they say Americans are loud and obnoxious.

Today, however, was not about Lamont and his antics. It was about Hutchinson and its investments. In understanding how the political landscape was changing in the UK, Brad could sense the mounting stress in his investors. Scotland and England were at breaking point, leading to those investors and some big-hitting politicians getting on the phone to his boss and demanding Hutchinson sort things out. There was concern for the huge investment in North Sea Oil, shredding nerves from the potential fall-out from the tumbling stocks in the world's financial markets and the declaration by the Scottish Government to withdraw from the Nuclear Defence programme. All these combined had more than a few chairman shitting themselves over the loss of even more orders, money and jobs. Brad knew it wouldn't be easy but he had to get things fixed. As well as looking after loyal investors, he had to ensure he kept the politicians on-side. He had to be shrewd in how he played the game. Furthermore, as Brad's boss had been at pains to tell him, Scotland was a good friend to the States. He had to make damn sure he didn't screw things up.

Brad, though, now had time to switch off his mind for an hour or two. He was being chauffer driven on a minor road beneath the Ochil Hills. It was his first visit to Scotland and as well as being impressed by the country's blend of the historic and modern, he was also surprised by the quality of the roads, which in most cases seemed to be of a much better standard than those at home. Furthermore, the houses he saw from the road were well constructed and not at all 'twee' as he had envisaged. There were precious few signs of the kilts, the pipes and the shortbread but just enough to know he was in Scotland. Overall, the place seemed to be clean and in good repair. The car also passed the famous Strathallan School, boyhood institution of many a politician. 'Impressive!' As were the small villages they drove through such as Dunning and Newburgh.

'Can you believe it, Willie?' said Brad to his driver, 'I'm going to be in St. Andrews. In all my life, I never thought I'd have the chance to play the Old Course but to have dinner in the Royal and Ancient clubhouse as well? Fucking hell!'

'Aye, St. Andrews is a very special place. There's just something about it that ye cannae put yer finger on. Maybe it's because it was our ancient capital or maybe it's the mystique of the seven hundred year old university, or maybe it's just the Old Course itself. In fact, it's probably all three. Just make sure you soak it up because once you've been you'll never want to leave.'

'I'll try, Willie. I will.'

Brad's heart missed a beat as the car drove into the auld grey toon. His security guard, sitting in the front seat, picked up on his nerves. 'Sir? You alright?'

'I'm fine, Tony. Just fine.'

A minute later, Brad was jumping up and down in his seat and thumping the window with his fist. 'There it is, Willie. There it is!'

'Aye, Sir. There it is, the Royal and Ancient. You're like a child coming home so you are. I hope you enjoy your day.'

'Fuck me, Willie. Enjoy it? I'm gonna fucking love it! In fact, I've not been this excited since the blessed Carla Martinez dropped to her knees at summer camp and permitted my cock its first encounter with the female orifice.'

The car drove by the odd looking Old Course Hotel on the left before passing the famous Russacks Hotel and some of the old member clubs of St. Andrews farther on. Brad couldn't quite get his head round the idea that they looked more like town houses than they did country clubs. Turning left at Auchterlonies Golf Shop, the car drove quietly down Golf Place towards the Old Course.

Having dropped Brad and his bodyguard off at the R&A, Willie drove his unassuming Ford Mondeo a little further down the street, parking it just behind the Scottish Museum of Golf. It was time for his afternoon nap while "Nancy Boy" was off having a wank on the first tee. 'What an arsehole,' he mumbled. 'Just a fuckin' arsehole.'

Taking stock, Brad walked around the clubhouse, first staring inside the huge windows at the panelled oaks and leather chairs before glancing up at the ancient clock. He then turned his gaze to the land God made for golf. This wide expanse of brown and yellow grass couldn't be a golf course. There were tourists and golfers and cars all over the place. Hell, there was even an old man walking his dog! Was it not private, he asked himself. In the distance, he could see a group of golfers having their picture taken on the Swilken Bridge while over to his right he recognised the beach where Chariots of Fire had been filmed. *What the fuck?* He felt like an extra in Brigadoon!

Pulling himself together, Brad approached the clubhouse door with Tony behind, struggling with golf bag and suitcase. As Brad rang the bell and waited, he noticed the Claret Jug in a glass presentation case, just inside the lobby. 'My God! I'm about to enter the most hallowed halls in all of golf. Jesus H!' However, before his childish nerves could attack his defenceless bladder, a dour but smartly dressed receptionist-come-security guard came to the door.

'Yes Sir. How can I help you?'

'Hi. Zimmerman. Hutchinson Group. I'm here to see...'

'Of course you are, Sir. Your playing partner is already waiting inside. Can I help you with your clubs?'

'Oh no, Tony here will help.'

'Oh no, he won't, Sir. He's staying right there. Members and guests only, I'm afraid.'

'Listen, Boy; Tony has to be with me at all times.'

'Well then, I suppose that means you won't be playing golf today, Sir. As I said, it is members and guests only.'

'But... but...'

'No buts. Big Tony stays outside or you don't play. What will it be?'

'Okay Tony,' sighed Brad, 'give the boy my bags and wait for me over there by the eighteenth green. I should be back in about five or six hours.'

'Very good, Mr. Zimmerman, that's the spirit. And one more thing before you come in?'

'Yes, yes, what is it?'

'My name's Jim, Sir. And I'm forty-seven years old.'

4

yes, we can … well, maybe!

Tuesday 10th June

2.20 pm – The Mound - Edinburgh

Having strolled halfway down the steep hill from Edinburgh Castle, Jamie stopped for a rest, taking a seat on a bench just outside the gothic and haunting National Kirk of Scotland. Needing a few minutes to digest the fine lunch he had just shared with his uncle, he breathed in the warm summer air and looked north across the city while daring not to turn around and remind himself of where Margaret Thatcher had given her notorious "Sermon on the Mound" speech. It was too good a day to let the old tyrant spoil his everlasting sense of homecoming. Unfortunately, it wasn't just the Iron Witch who could bug his head; his phone was at it again. Having no desire to answer it, he screened the caller ID. 'Bloody hell! Persistence must be this guy's middle name.' It was Oliver Graham, one of Jamie's London counterparts in the world of political advising. 'Oliver! What's up?'

'Jamie, me old mucker,' offered the denigrating chief advisor to Peter Buchanan. 'Need to confirm a time for next week. Eleven good for you, old boy?'

Jamie didn't have an option. 'Eleven's perfect. How long will your man have?

'An hour or so. We've an interview scheduled with the Tribune at one. Location?'

61

'Not sure yet. Will let you know nearer the time.'

'Excellent. Looking forward to seeing you both. Ciao.'

Jamie snapped his phone shut. 'Asshole.' It wasn't that he didn't have time for Oliver Graham; it was just that Graham, ever since his boss had taken a huge lead in the Westminster polls, had been nigh-on unbearable. Closing his eyes for a moment, Jamie recomposed himself. He just wanted ten minutes alone time. He could do with enjoying his city.

Edinburgh was busy today and its majesty a far cry from the monotony of suburban America. Sure, San Francisco, the Pacific Ocean and the drive up Highway 1 to wee towns like Mendocino were examples of the good life but just south of San Fran was no place for someone like Jamie. He was much happier now. Glad to be gone from the smell and the heat of the dying embers left by the explosion of population that was Silicon Valley, glad to find an exit from the sprawling edifices creeping out the back of California's beyond, glad to escape from the dust bowls of concrete and soul-stripping polarisation of community, and most definitely glad to be liberated at last from the mental fuckers wandering the streets alone with needle in arm and gun in hand. Only a few years ago, he had been both fascinated and impressed by the Idea of America. Like many, however, he feared the grand plan was unravelling and unless a new direction and a renewed hope arrived soon, there would be no halting the monumental and cataclysmic shift of power to the Far East

As a young IT specialist in the Bay Area, Jamie had been a man in demand. Having both the skill of a developer and the intuition of knowing what the public wanted, he could mark trends, gauge public feeling and sense frustration. He was also customer centric, a priceless commodity in the IT industry that translated into only one thing for employers; keep him, whatever the cost. Though Jamie's heart and his head, and his soul, had never left Scotland, he was still a little embarrassed that back then he had been the dreadful, stereotypical bore: watching the SPL and Six Nations live on satellite, having his grandma send over his favourite foods and spending hours trawling the internet sites of the newspapers back home. He had however, made a concerted effort to avoid the awful parodies that were the Scottish and Irish bars. He much preferred the real thing. But in preferring the authenticity, and as much as he respected what Scotland stood for, he had found himself in the awful paradox of contemplating what being Scottish meant to him. In other words, he could never quite come to terms with what others in a foreign land thought of his country. Immensely proud to be a Scot, he couldn't help but feel that heart-ripping sensation when discussing where he came from and what the place was all about. Not because it was Scotland but rather with what he perceived others thought about Scotland. It was frustrating, almost paranoiac. They would smile politely: always. And then he would observe that instantly recognisable, non-verbalised response across their faces; most people just didn't think it was real nation. There were those who thought it was all castles and kilts, there were those who thought Trainspotting was a modern day depiction and there were those who thought it a poor outpost of the Empire. There were even those who still thought it a part of England. That really pissed him off, especially when he watched TV and read the newspapers. She was the Queen of England. He was the English Prime Minister. It was the English Olympic Team. It made him unbearably nauseating to be around and as much as his friends loved him, they could only take so much of his monotonous and migraine-inducing spouting on about the old country. Jamie reckoned it was an in-built self-defence mechanism most Scots had when it came to self-identity in the world. Being both important and pointless at the same time, his petulance would always surface when discussing British politics and culture. His friends, however, just didn't understand. They had their country. He would even attempt to bring the Queen into the conversation and describe her as the Queen of Scotland, and he would ridicule the decisions made by the Prime Minister of Scotland and the pathetic but courageous, limb-severing exploits of the Scottish Army in the Middle East. He was looking not for appeasement but for reaction. At a loss, his friends would laugh and shake their heads but he would feel much better about himself. Much better. He had given his little bit to redress the cause. Moreover, this made him wonder why he had become an IT specialist in the first place and, considering his other interests, how he had ended up on the other side of the world. Yes, it paid well but it wasn't exactly fulfilling a life's dream. For a man with ambitions like Jamie, there was only one place to be. He had wanted more and he had more to want.

Jamie adored Edinburgh. Imperious and historic, he was in love with his city. Tourists sat with picnics in Princes Street Gardens beneath the imposing, ancient castle while shoppers scurried between department stores on Princes Street and George Street. Investment bankers strolled with purpose around Lothian Road and St. Andrews Square while street entertainers up on the Royal Mile performed in vain to make David Hume smile. It was a magnificent city, an international city, and now that it had slowly morphed into being more Scottish than it was British, it had become much more than a token capital. With Holyrood firmly established, it was thriving. The Old Town was now a World Heritage Site, the old docklands had been transformed into a buzzing, cultural quarter and it was now recognised as a world financial centre. And the New Town, well, that was much the same as ever: stunning architecture, wide open boulevards and shit loads of wealth. The people were finding their feet again. The people of Scotland were now beginning to believe in the benefits of a Government and Parliament on the doorstep.

The Parliament building, however, was still a source for debate amongst the lay architects of the world. To the untrained eye, it had the look of a particularly hideous lump of concrete, denying its workers and visitors the impression of Scotland its designer envisioned. Jamie thought that to be an heroic pity because the building complemented both the physical and psychological attributes of Scotland. The inspired craftsmanship of its rooms and offices and chambers represented the landscape of Scotland: the land, the sea, the ships, the trees and the mountains, whereas the astonishing movement and light and space prompted and encouraged enlightened thought, reflecting the architect's profound reading into the Scottish psyche and Scotland's reputation as a country of both inventive, practical idealism and tempestuous, dualistic disposition. Above all this, however, Enric Moralles's greatest legacy to the people of Scotland was the Parliament's contradiction. It was to be a building of unity and equality, a building from which every true believer of democracy could take pride. It was a mirror image of everything good about Scotland. Well, just about everything, considered Jamie, apart from the odd bout of stupidity that is!

To Jamie, it was more than gratifying to have, at last, the government and parliament returned to Edinburgh. Though Jamie struggled to disguise his conceit that the workings of the Office were now being admired throughout the world, it was also right for the people to embrace it. With members of the public able to log onto Holyrood Television and giggle at the honourable members being humiliated during FM's Questions, as well as digitally participating in non-chamber debates and contributing to parliamentary committees, it had become the most interactive parliament on the planet. Dynamic and ground-breaking, it also had one of the highest proportions of female representatives of any national legislature and its fortunate MSPs only worked from nine through five. What's more, for the most anal amongst the IT literate electorate, one could also read, if one so wished, the mind-numbing Health and Safety directives for Scotland's Public Convenience Facilities. Jeez, thought Jamie, Jim the Joiner could probably send in a few bob and play the weekly sweepie as well. It was the most un-English of political establishments. And it was working ...most of the time!

Jamie, however, reckoned the interactive openness had stretched beyond reason, especially Visitor Information. Okay, so he thought it quite legitimate that the website could be read in both English and the Gaelic, and if you were an international student or recent immigrant, in Catalan, Spanish, French, British Sign Language, German, Dutch, Italian, Polish, Russian, Urdu, Chinese, Swedish, Arabic, Japanese and Bengali. However, if you were really up for a good laugh you could also view it in the old Scots language. Not that Jamie thought that was wrong, just very fucking funny. Nevertheless, it was the language that felt completely natural for most Scots to speak, most of whom still used its colloquialisms in day-to-day conversation. It was also a language Jamie adored, taking the example of Burns to prove that Scots could sound romantic and exciting and passionate, unlike the parliamentary administrators who he had presumed to be taking the piss when, in encouraging the public to drop in for a coffee, they had announced to the world that, "Ye'er walcome tae visit the Pairlament tae hae a keek roon or fin oot aboot whit wey the Pairlament warks."

Jamie smiled. Everything may have been changing in the world of Scottish politics but Edinburgh would always have a reassuring constant; the monuments and museums, the wide open spaces, trains chugging into Waverly and the amplified ramblings of tour guides on open top buses. There seemed to be a dignified progression to the city, a sense of control, which, unlike his bloody mobile phone, provided him the opportunity to relax once in while. Turning it in his hand, he looked at the screen. No caller ID.

'Jamie Houston.'

'Auld Reekie smelling of roses today?'

'As always. Secure line, I presume.'

'Got it in one. You know, I don't care what anyone says about you, Houston; I think you're rather intelligent. So, how do things stand with our man?'

Jamie chuckled. 'I'll tell you something, he's a smooth son-of-a-bitch, if a bit predictable. And he's sharp and efficient, that's for sure. What's more, I think he's ready to do a deal.'

'Really? This early in proceedings?'

'Yeh, seems like it. Meeting him next week to verify his offer.'

'Mmm ...interesting. We'll wait and see shall we. And our covert emissary? Still holding up?'

'Oh yeh. He's solid.'

'And he's still comfortable with the risk he is taking?'

'No reason for him not to be. He's a no-lose situation. No, he's fine, whichever way the referendum pans out.'

'Okay Jamie. Things appear to moving forward. Keep up the good work and I'll be in touch.'

Jamie closed his phone, slowly this time. His patience restored, he blew out a long breath. Oh yes, this was much more fun than the States.

Born and educated in Scotland, Jamie had relocated to America's west coast in the early nineties. Opportunities in IT were many back then and having become a leading player in Silicon Valley, he had built up a network of business associates willing to invest in his future. But it had never been enough. With Jamie's homesickness taking priority over all else, he moved back home in 1999, the year the Scottish Parliament was reconvened. It had also been a sign for Jamie to try something new. The IT business had been destroying him from within, his soul suffocating. He craved for something else.

He remembered his first introduction to Scottish politics, a monthly meeting of Labour activists in Leith. It was a wet night in November when he walked into the public halls. The walls were yellow, the air damp and the light bulbs naked. Doors slammed and voices echoed around the ghostly rooms as cars outside splashed through the rain. Fortunately, he had made time to re-quaint himself with the political situation. He learned of the major players and their ambitions, and he reviewed policy. He also watched and listened as New Labour steamrolled their way through massive cultural change. There was optimism, a new hope. It was time for someone other than the Tories. It was time for the Party who pushed through Devolution. It was time for Jamie to see what Scotland's largest party had to offer.

Jamie's political stance was centric. Despising excessive government interference just as much as he did a laissez-faire approach to business, he believed in a healthy combination of the two. It was only logical then, on hearing the then PM declare his "support for the disadvantaged while making every attempt to curb the ambitious drive of the megalomaniacs", that Jamie should be drawn to New Labour. Jeez, how naïve he had been. That night had been more than a wake-up call, it had been a motorway travel lodge, middle of a pissing wet night, rampant fire alarm, and much, much different from what he envisaged when being an international laptop patriot some 8,000 miles away.

Walking into that room, he was the stranger walking into the Nowhere Bar. As they glanced over their shoulders at the well-dressed stranger standing alone, the talking stopped and the mumbling began. He could see them asking each other who he was. He could sense their arrogance and fear. Who was the interloper? Jamie introduced himself to a small group: two men, one woman. The older of the men had silver hair, a moustache and was smartly dressed in a shirt, tie and brown sweater. The other was unshaven with scraggy hair and sporting a Billy Bragg t-shirt. Ridiculously, he also wore a mid-length leather jacket more suited to a gangster than a political activist.

Fuck me. It's the Brothers Smug.

The woman's hair was tied back and indented with crinkled grey strands frizzing their way through her mousy mop. She wore a flowery skirt, combat jacket and specs. Over to the side, an older woman was busy making tea and keeping quiet.

'Hi. I had a chat with the local secretary last week and he told me I should come down here and meet you guys.'

'Well then, you must be our Yank, eh?' grunted Younger Brother Smug. 'What, the good ole U S of A not work out for you, eh? Only come home when things are good, eh?'

Jamie laughed, hoping they would see in his smile a sign of immediate embitterment. 'Yeh, I suppose you could say that. Nothing like jumping on the bandwagon is there.'

'Well, I hope you're prepared to put the work in, not like those other pseudo-intellectual wankers we had with us last year. Those bastards joined up thinking it would help with their fucking networking options but when we asked them to canvass up by the Fort, they were off back to Lib-Dems quicker than a Leith hooker dropping her kets!'

'Actually,' answered Jamie with no hint of humour, 'I'm just feeling my way.'

'Feeling your way?' muttered Older Brother Smug. 'You don't come to a Labour meeting to feel your way. We've a job to do and that's to stay in power.' He winked at his two associates. 'We've already seen off the Tories and now we need to build up our member base. Oh yes, pal, things can only get better.'

Jamie listened to the Brothers Smug mouthing off about their party's success. The MASH reject said nothing, her eyes conducting an examination of Jamie's face. She trusted no one. It was obnoxious. There wasn't even an introduction. No hand shakes, no names, no welcome. This was their castle.

He sipped on the tea the elderly lady had given him while another man, who was more akin to a Haight-Ashbury cast-off, tapped a tea cup with his spoon and asked everyone to take a seat. It was clichéd and remedial, a school classroom full of neandrathals being taught by a failed artist. All the meeting needed now was for Dead-Head to make a move on Combat Woman and Older Brother Smug to let rip a smelly.

The meeting lasted no more than an hour, the discussion covering only one topic: how to sign-up new members. There was also by a pitiful and mundane "Voter Demographics" presentation made by a stuttering statistician on an old overhead projector. Jamie smiled at the lack of credible scientific methods in the stats. It was a post-code breakdown of *No's, Maybes, Probables* and *Definites*: nothing else. Jamie shook his head gently as the Brothers Smug gloated with pride. They bumped each other's shoulders while smirking over at him. He could almost smell the self-satisfaction oozing from their arses. They were delighted, as were the twenty or so other activists in the room, and even more thrilled when Dead-Head read out a letter from the local MSP, offering thanks for all the hard work they had done at the Holyrood election. Nevertheless, Jamie understood that these people, and many millions like them, had suffered for eighteen years at the hands of the Tories, so to see Maggie's bastards wiped out in the '97 landslide could only result in this adulterated joy. It was their time.

After the meeting finished, Jamie expected there might have been an opportunity to discuss the bigger picture over a few pints, to contemplate new ideas and to think of new policies. But they wanted none of that "pretentious bullshit". It was all about power. Policies came second and new ideas weren't even on the agenda. Not for them would there be more fiscal autonomy for

Scotland and not for them the anti-nuclear campaign. Some of them were so full of hypocritical shit they even denounced the Holyrood Parliament as useless and incompetent. Short sighted was an understatement. Could they not see the benefits? The future? No. They didn't care. As long as places such as the 'Fort' remained riddled with poverty, it was more votes for the party and no more Tory rule.

Jamie's interest in joining the Labour Party hadn't lasted long after that depressing November night. He wanted to make a difference, not stay in power. He did begin, however, to take a wee bit more interest in what had been accomplished. It had not been the most uplifting of experiences. 'How dare you?' he once roared at the television. 'Is it any wonder the people have lost their confidence?' Jamie was humiliated. 'How could you?' he screamed. 'Especially the oil. It is certainly more than a fucking "bonus"; it is a legitimate resource: like the people, like the wind, like the land. How would you like it, pal, if we started describing London's financial sector as a fucking "bonus".'

He joined the SNP shortly afterwards. And not because he was an old nationalist with anti-English tendencies, either. Like the vast majority of Scots, he was anything but. What's more, Jamie understood nationalism to be an ideology whose premise had changed dramatically over the past hundred years. Nowadays, it was all about a liberal or civic nationalism based on what one could do to benefit the land in which one lived, and in Scotland's case, it was about the country being intelligent and brave enough to survive on her own without intervention from a distant administration. Sure, there would be negotiations and trade agreements but at least they would be decided by a Scottish Sovereign State, rather than an institution wanting to impose its big brother globalised economy on others. Jamie's Scotland would be free from old nationalism and engrained with a common purpose. He signed up with the SNP because the party offered the only alternative to the established political parties' loyalty to the inequality within the Union; an inequality that had been gut-wrenching to a country that had given so much and an inequality that saw Scotland being treated as a dominion state and its people transformed into what McIlvanney had described as a "bunch of fearties".

Fortunately, Jamie never had that fear. Sure, Scotland was small, but as for being petrified of becoming an economic pariah, no fucking way! What's more, Jamie was sure he could persuade the people that Scotland could survive on her own; that after Secession the companies of the world would still want to, and, more importantly, need to trade in Scotland. The world would still go on. He desperately wanted to shake the country out of its inherent pessimism and to school Scotland in the advantages of controlling one's own destiny. He wanted to assert then exploit the great Scottish personal contradiction -a country full of educated but dogmatic individuals who cared deeply in community. First, though, he would have to hope they would stop shitting themselves.

Jamie had also been inspired by a speech given a few years ago by a young female MSP called Jessica Scott. She was smart, she was sharp and she provided inspiration. Most of all, she cared. Moreover, it didn't bother Jamie one bit when three years later she became Deputy Leader and neither did it bother him that her agenda rarely included philosophical discussions and too much red wine. Like the Labour Party meeting in Leith, there were still voters to be converted and stats to be analysed. Unlike the Labour Party in Leith, the SNP was working towards a better Scotland. It saw its power as a means to change things, not to make sure the other side didn't win.

As Jamie's role within the party grew, so did his influence. He became the whiz-kid flying lieutenant out-flanking the opposition in every battle. He was ahead of the game and considering the opposition seemed to be on some other planet when it came to winning and then losing votes, it hadn't exactly been a Fischer-Spassky confrontation. Yes, the Labour Party had been good for him.

It had taken Jamie some time to realise that Labour had been holding Parliament back, not because they didn't have one or two positive initiatives but rather its Administration was still being controlled by its central office in London. It was a ludicrous situation where no decision could be taken unless the then First Minister called up Downing Street first. Was it any surprise that some people in Scotland scoffed at Holyrood? It was insulting but that wasn't the only thing pissing Jamie off. Westminster still controlled Scotland's defence strategy, its corporation tax powers, its media and its oil, the very things standing between an already prosperous Scotland and the Scotland of Jamie's dreams. He wanted self-determination and self-fulfilment, and that, of course, could never happen as long as subs were docking in the Gare Loch, the likes of the Royal Caledonia Bank still paying its billions of corporation tax into the UK Treasury, the national broadcaster still controlling the media from London and the huge revenues from North Sea Oil still propping up the London economy. Furthermore, there was no bloody way it was ever going to happen as long as his irritating and infuriating phone continued to ring. This time, however, there would be no bad mood. This was a call he dare not ignore.

'Okay Jamie, I'll be quick. I'll be in Edinburgh next Wednesday. Staying overnight at The Strathearn. How about we meet there around two?'

'Sounds good to me. Can you reserve a private room?'

'Won't have to. I have a suite on the top floor.'

Jamie laughed. A sycophant he wasn't but this was business. 'Very good. I won't even ask you how much the room is costing you.'

'Too much for you to ever afford, young man. But hey, you're the man who chose politics. Maybe, like those mongrels in Westminster, you should try fiddling your expenses more often. Live the high life once in a while.'

'Oh yeh, I'm sure that would go down well with the voters. Anyway, two o'clock it is. See you there.'

Jamie switched his phone to silent before hiding it inside his jacket. No more calls would be taken for another ten minutes. He closed his eyes and shook his head. 'Yeh, I'm the man who chose politics, alright. Well, let's see if you're still enjoying the fine hospitality after I've finished with you.'

It had been a long and difficult journey for Jamie but when he joined the SNP, he could sense things were about to change. Consistently portrayed as antagonistic no-hopers by the two main political parties, his party had seized upon the ridiculous and law breaking anti-Scottish antics of Thatcher and the self-mutilation of the Labour Party to push themselves towards a power in 2007 that both hurt and angered the opposition. The SNP was now running the country with a vision that the people of Scotland should matter first and not old school, short term, political gain. Things were still, and would be, complicated, especially with a minority government but that only served to heighten Jamie's glee in witnessing the Labour Party implode in its bitter and petty jealousies and the dissolution of its self-proclaimed belief in having a divine right to rule Scotland. In contrast, Jamie and his Party were just not intent on liberating Scotland; they wanted to rid large parts of Scotland of its self-defeatism and self-doubt. Jamie longed for Scotland to stop moaning and to reach out from its apathy and stop rewarding ignorance with a seat in government. He needed Scotland to see that it was Westminster to blame and not the normal guy in an English street. He craved for Scotland to stop accepting the Union was working when all one had to do was witness the cap-in-hand mentality of the cities' poverty-stricken neighbourhoods. He wanted to inspire Scotland to stand alone as the respected country he knew. He wanted to reignite what Scotland was renowned for: practical idealism.

Once the pipe dream of the embittered St. Andrews student, he could almost touch it, smell it, hold it. Secession. It was Scotland's turn now, thought Jamie, the people deserving better than to be kept in check by Westminster, a far off place where being British was a prerequisite for becoming a Member of Parliament and the ultimate aim being the defence of the old Parliament. It was the palace of glorious empire, of self-preservation, regardless how it dressed itself up as being open-minded and tolerant.

There was, however, a juxtapositional impasse within the Devolution process and as much as there had been a furtive growth in anti-Scottish sentiment down south, England, too, had been given a raw deal, especially those in the out-lying regions. Scottish Westminster MPs voting on English-only issues was at the heart of the problem. What's more, Jamie knew it was unfair. It was only to be expected, for goodness sake, if on hearing of an MP in central Scotland voting nay against a bill that might have improved the environment in Northampton or Basingstoke or Derby, that the citizens of England would be mightily pissed-off. Especially when said MP had very little influence in his own constituency. It was widely recognised as a distorted represent-tation of power, but nevertheless, until Westminster withdrew its power of veto on Reserved Matters and the administrative and political set-up changed for the better in Scotland, there was no way that Right was ever going to be relinquished. What's more, Jamie didn't feel one little bit of sympathy with this English predicament. As long as the power exerted by Westminster cont-inued to be covertly pro-London and typical of an unbalanced powerbase where the big controls the small, then Scotland was going to do the same. Fuck 'em!

Unfortunately, unless Secession became a reality, Jamie wondered if things would ever change. History had taught him that the relationship between Scotland and England was a political enigma, maybe more so than any two nations in the world. Scotland and England were step siblings, each with its own diverse culture and each with differing legal, educational and ecclesiastical systems, and each with its own vision of where it stood in the history and future of the world. Yet, they had been brought together for the convenience of a few, and still being kept together, Jamie suspected, for the convenience of a few. What's more, Jamie didn't like it one bit. Nevertheless, as much as Scotland had a very different cultural ethos and international outlook than its neighbours, there still remained the shame of the Great British Paradox. Brilliant legislative minds from both countries had been at the forefront of the wicked colonisation crusades; not something to admire, thought Jamie, but a reality all the same. Ironically, the present set-up hadn't changed much, with both Scottish and English politicians, as representatives of the United Kingdom, taking leading roles in NATO, at the IMF and World Bank, on the United Nations Security Council and in administrating G8 summits. Jamie scorned. 'Oh yes, the ever-lasting Great British Paradox!'

Regrettably, however, and herein lay the real issue, far too many of Scotland's subjects had been left in squalor as Britain first turned the world pink with ambition, then red with the blood of conquest. From the Highland Clearances, to the Piper in the plague-infested trenches, to the Glasgow Shipyards and Lanarkshire Steel Plants, Scotland's people always appeared to be a Westminster after-thought. Not any fucking more!

Jamie Houston was one of the new breed of nationalist politician. He knew that the large retail chains would still need to trade in Scotland, and Energy companies would still see Scotland as the world-leader in energy research and technology. International development companies would still be standing with their hands-out looking to borrow a few quid to fund a project in Asia and mutli-industrial powerhouses would still be knocking on the door of research companies asking for a wee bit of help in developing their products. They weren't going to disappear just because Scotland and England opted for a divorce. Their bank accounts and shareholders wouldn't let them. But that was what many voters in Scotland, who didn't understand economics, thought. It was the politics of fear.

Jamie liked to dream but in being a pragmatist it didn't happen very often. He was also trying hard to have more of a conciliatory mind-set. If England wanted to run its own affairs, it would be free to do so. What's more, as much as Scotland would work alongside its neighbour, Jamie felt it was for the people of Scotland to decide Scotland's fate and not a few hundred MPs based in another country.

Which meant there were still strategies to devise, PR campaigns to run and dirty political fights to be fought in the battlegrounds of Scotland's marginal seats. And in being the chief advisor to Scotland's First Minister, Andrew Drummond, Jamie felt the SNP stood alone in the battle for Scotland's future. The opposition parties were trying their best but with one hand tied behind their backs, it wasn't easy. Particularly Labour, who had a self-proclaimed culture of thinking the people of Scotland were daft enough to think that it was the party of the people. In engendering an employment culture where almost thirty percent of Scotland's west coast either worked for or relied on the State, Labour had thwarted ambition and created a culture of dependency and fear amongst the lower classes, which illogically had it boasting of economic and development success when, in reality, all it could deliver was the odd call-centre here and there. It had even led the Party to believe that they had done enough to secure their politicians' seats in both parliaments. For fifty years, it had worked but the people of Scotland were telling Jamie they wanted more than handouts, they wanted to build the country themselves. Now, with a new sense of hope, they were coming over to Jamie's party in droves. And with the increase in demand for its industrial and commercial expertise, it scientific research and its natural resources such as oil, wind and water, the future was looking decidedly good for Scotland. If she could only seize the opportunity. If only the "fearties" would not prevail.

The evidence pointing to a prosperous Scotland as an independent nation was mounting. Though Jamie knew that, he also knew that a large number of people in Scotland still had to be persuaded that that was the case. They needed to understand and see the new way in action. They needed proof. Three hundred years of having Westminster in control wasn't going to change in a few years. In becoming used to the security, many of the people considered having adopted parents as better than having none at all. The family might be dysfunctional but it still put food on the table. But Jamie had grown up; and thought Scotland should do the same. He wanted to find his real father, his true family history. He just wished his brothers and sisters would agree with him. Nevertheless, as much as there remained an underlying wish for Scotland to go on its own, the voters would still require a cast iron assurance it was the right thing to do; and in understanding that changing a voter's behaviour was dependent on their attitudes changing first, Jamie had found it an arduous task. The younger voters had been easier to persuade.

All they had ever known was the Holyrood Government and along with it, had grown into adulthood with a new sense of confidence. Jamie's main concern, however, was with a large number of the older generation. Being loyal to the Union, they would take some shifting. He had to pinpoint those voters who would sway towards his party. He had to convince. And with the power of the Internet, the message was sifting through.

Jamie, more than most political analysts, identified with the Web and its influential sites powering the rumour mill. He also knew that Scotland was a small country. Online newspapers were as widely read now as the hardcopy, making it possible to comment on stories. This medium was critical to his strategy. Other voters would see they were not alone, understanding there were thousands of others who believed that Jamie's party was making a difference. In organising teams of activists to trawl the Web to ensure the message was heard, he had created one big problem for the newspapers that supported the Union. Their message and scare-mongering was still blatant but whereas in the past the drip feeding of anti-Nationalist sentiment could be interpretated as the truth, there were now thousands of voters ready to contradict a story. It had become more difficult for editors to manipulate opinion and it had become nearly impossible for journalists to write a story without all the facts. And this is where his party had stolen a march on the opposition, who still relied on scandalous and prejudiced headlines, and barefaced lies in the broadsheets. Jamie even had young activists on the social networking websites come together online to encourage each other and plan activities. The world had changed and Jamie knew that. He only hoped the newspapers wouldn't shut down his beloved Comments threads. They were his oxygen.

However, it was in fund-raising and voter research where Jamie excelled. According to his boss, he was the best in the world. He had set up a donation system that danced its way throughout cyberspace. Facebook, My Space and Twitter; the movement was growing, as was the Party bank account. More importantly, he had developed consumer and voter identification software with which not only simple demographics could be analysed but also the lifestyles, behaviour and culture of the population. He could accurately predict who was a SNP voter, a Labour voter and where a bloody Nazi polished his jack-boots. He could analyse where floating voters were most likely to live, what they thought and what they bought in the shops. It was priceless and it was key to most of his strategic initiatives. And now that it was working, he felt so close to success. In fact, he was so confident, he was sure the Party would overturn a 13,000 Labour majority and win the upcoming bi-election in Glasgow.

5

submarines and racing machines

Friday 13th June

12.05 pm - Southern Highlands

As Dixie drove out of the small village, she pressed the button to wind up the roof on her convertible and switched on her Dictaphone. Yet again, the village had mirrored the divisive complexities of the country. She had much to report.

She admired the serenity of Garelochead, a small village about thirty miles west of Glasgow. Perched at the head of the dangerously beautiful Gare Loch, Victorian houses overlooked the bay while yachts rocked on the gentle current and retired men sat on the jetty with fishing rods and flasks of tea. At first glance, there were many villages in the Southern Highlands like this: each at the end of a deep chasm of water, each with its own hotel and each with an eye on the tourist dollar. And why not, thought Dixie, the lochs and mountains of Scotland were an ideal place to escape. However, whereas most other remote village hotels had progressed with the times, the second of the small and friendly white-washed hotels in Garelochead was a reminder of days gone by. The Lounge Bar, with its log fire, tartan upholstery and higher prices was to the front of the hotel and facing the loch. No doubt, it would be frequented by the hiking brigade. The locals, on the other hand, could be found in the Dirty Bar around the back. With its cold stone floor, pool table and twenty pence puggy, it was a tourist free zone. The hotel may have been a distant outpost but when the log fire was burning on the weekends, it was warm, welcoming, and full of patrons. In the cold weekdays of the off-season however, Dixie reckoned it would be empty and disturbingly lonely. Entrapped by seventies wallpaper, its bedrooms would, more than likely, be drowning in dampness while the echoes of its creaking staircases would drift through its haunting carcass. Outside, above half a dozen gas canisters lying next to the back door, a white plastic banner advertising football on satellite and discounted American beer hung limply from a side wall. Along the street, the local shop sold newspapers, paperback novels for under a fiver, stamps, cheap toys, bread, tins of beans, new world wine, packs of Player Blue, six packs of beer for £3.99 and, of course, the yellow-labelled, brain-shriveller otherwise known as Monkjuice. Like most village shops, it also doubled up as a Post Office where pensions could be collected and dole money dispensed.

Two hours earlier, Dixie had parked her car on the loch front. The village had been quite. Looking around, most of the houses she saw were traditionally built in old stone whereas the residences dotted around the odd back street could be much better described as modern traditional, which in Dixie's words meant the *"cooncil hoose"*. With rickety wire fences hanging over pavements, rusty swings creaking in the back garden and garbage bins (with the house number squiggled with industrial white paint down the side) standing at ease, they couldn't quite be described as aesthetically beautiful. What's more, if all that wasn't enough evidence to sit down and write a letter to the planners with, one just had to glance at the outside walls. They were greywashed and covered with harling: a dour, ugly and idiosyncratic pebble-dash insulation found only, for some inexplicable reason, on the sides of less architecturally creative Scottish households. Dixie, though, knew it was the people who really lightened up these wee towns like Garelochead, where it wouldn't be out of the ordinary to walk into the local bar and listen to its punters harp on about football and politics while describing a villager's recent encounter with the Monkjuice.

"He went nuclear but what do you expect when he drinks

the stuff. It's fucking rocket fuel. In fact, that arsehole needs to bugger off and find a village without an idiot!"

In most cases, this would be a gentle and humorous reminder of life outside the city but in this part of the world, it carried a dangerous irony because only a few miles down the road there happened to be a highly-guarded storage facility actually stocking the real stuff. Dixie snorted. The Monkjuice might blow your head off but rocket fuel, high explosives and two hundred nuclear warheads were a much different kettle when it came to forgetting about your shitty existence.

She had spent most of the morning wandering around Faslane, a few miles south of Garelochead and home to the Trident Nuclear Submarine base. It was a disconcerting place. Quiet roads by the water and surrounded by inspiring mountains it would, in normal circumstances, be an ideal setting for a day trip for Glaswegian families loaded up with picnics of pan bread, Tesco's ham, Tunnock's Carmel Wafers and cans of Tizer as well as games for the kids and swimming costumes at the ready for a cooling off in the loch. Unfortunately, Faslane was not a place anyone could readily describe as normal.

Dixie had been up this way a few times since her student days and it seemed to change on every visit. Not only were the subs bigger and the security tighter, there was, now, spacious accommodation for the sailors and sports facilities good enough to grace an Olympic village.

Thirty years ago, the submarines had been the guardians of Polaris, the nuclear missile pre-dating Trident, but they had long since been sent to the decommissioning yard down South, only to be replaced, much against the protestations of CND and Tommy Sheridan being carted away like Jesus after the Crucifixion, by new and improved submarines which sat docked in the eerie bay like enormous sleeping killer-whales. In fact, enormous was an understatement, these things were fucking huge and much bigger in real life than they appeared on her television at home.

On most days the greyness of the submarines blended in with the dark shaded waters of the loch but today the sun was shining and these fantastic killing machines sat basking in the calm waters, readying themselves for their next trans-ocean hunting party. Dixie shook her head as she thought of the nearby Holy Loch and its warehouse of nuclear warheads. What an unfortunate name for these schooling waters.

She had parked her car on the main street and taken an inquisitive wander down to the well-armed gates of the facility. Royal Navy Police stood to attention as the security cameras perched high on isolated poles followed her every movement. She thought of playing the childhood game of trying to dodge the cameras but Faslane intimidated her. Hang around too long and an elite squad of American and British security teams would be out sharpish to quietly and firmly warn her off. Everything behind the miles of twenty-foot high fences and electric barbed wire was disarmingly quiet; no doubt the strategy required in masking the clandestine activity of checking on the validity of nuclear warheads and the daily configuration of missile launch codes! This place was built for death but also to make money. Billions had been invested in Trident, both from Britain and from the US, and it was in the best interests of those investors to protect their product. Unfortunately, for any unenlightened soul who dare breach the security fences, it wouldn't be unreasonable to conclude that they wouldn't be receiving a skelped arse and told to bugger off home to mummy; more like a few days in a grey concrete cell being battered and abused by grey men in grey uniforms. As well as inventing the colour grey to present the public with the opportunity of describing the sad bastard who bought his suits from a famous department store, someone also decided that grey should be the colour of naval camouflage. And such was the dullness and evil intent to the colouring that when these atomic serpents of the sea drifted into North Korean waters, Dixie reckoned there wouldn't be much chance of the commodore donning a multi-coloured morning suit and inviting Kim Jong-il to share a Pimms and Lemonade on the brig.

However, a few hundred yards down from the entrance, colour was in abundance as the long time residents of the Peace Camp did what they could to illuminate the drab and sinister surroundings. The Peace Camp had been at Faslane since the eighties, when CND was at is height. Nowadays, the dedicated souls who lived in canvas tents and rusting caravans had become as much a part of the local fabric as the church, the school and the local shop.

She had taken time out to sit and talk to the protesters and, as always, been inspired by their dedication but saddened by their ineffectiveness. Security had been upgraded since the days of cutting a hole in the fence, tying oneself to a submarine and unfurling a banner of protest. But still they persevered. The dreadlocks, pierced noses and green linen pants continued to be the choice of dress while strumming guitars and babies crying the soundtrack to their life-long mission. Nowadays, the Peaceniks were lucky if their protestations received a bi-annual five minute slot on the nightly news, so apathetic to the wrongs of the world had the masses become. Global capitalism and the environment were now the cause-celebre, as well, of course, as the occasional anti-Iraq march. There was, however, a saving grace in this cultural shift, in that the extremists had long since deserted Faslane, morphing into hooded warriors dressed up as clowns whose ill-thought out plans for world-wide anarchy included trashing the odd McDonalds and destroying a city centre supermarket while the nearby G8 conference held talks on the food shortage in Africa. Meanwhile, the determined soldiers of the Peace Camp struggled on and regardless that they were on speaking terms with the authorities, did succeed on occasion to block the road as the warheads arrived in trundling silence from Aldermaston in the middle of the night. Sadly, though, with arrests resulting in a just a fifty pound fine, very little of their glorious victories was reported. The MoD required, ironically, peace and quiet, and as that silence once again dawned on the Peace Camp, the occasional Crusty could only shrug his shoulders before wandering up to Garelochead for his morning supplies. They had become the great ignored.

It had been a sad and predictable morning and as she listened to lost causes and wasted dreams, she considered the determination of the few to see out their mission. She thought of their hopes and wondered if they had been defeated. If life was an unhygienic tent on beautiful but damp lochside, surrounded by screaming children, rotten vegetables and the remnants of a dole check lying inside an empty can of American beer then the answer was easy. It wasn't that they had been defeated; they just never had a chance of winning. When black and white combust it is always grey that emerges.

Dixie and Elliot had known each other since their University of Glasgow days. At that time they had been on opposite sides of the political spectrum; Dixie fighting for the rights of the shipyard and mine workers while Elliot didn't give a shit. She was the typical hot head firebrand to be found in any third level institution in Britain. There were marches to organise, banners to be printed, lectures to host and Margaret Thatcher to hate. She had been at the epicentre of university political life, which at Glasgow meant there were some pretty big shoes to fill, all of them great political and philosophical minds who had changed the world. However, as much as she had gained in knowledge, she was still a tad embarrassed at how she dressed back then. And Elliot wasn't going to let her forget it.

'I'll tell you something Dixie, your dress sense is a helluva lot better than when we lived on the Byres Road. You look terrific. In fact, it's amazing what a separation can do for someone? Who are you trying to impress then?'

'None of your business, shinty heid. At least I've stayed close to my roots, which is more than can be said for you, your multi-national lifestyle of manipulation and your mock Tudor house in the stockbroker belt.'

They were watching Elliot's wife, Kirsten, skimming stones on the loch. Dixie smiled with compassion. Despite his brave justification, she knew Elliot wanted home.

'Ah maybe so,' said Elliot defensively, but there's some damn good golf courses around Surrey and in my business they're a good place to be. I mean, if I have to listen to some tax accountant for four hours then why not do so with a six iron in my hand.'

Dixie laughed. 'Golf? A poor excuse for a sad bastard.'

'Anyway,' joked Elliot, 'your current stylistic attire is much sexier than striped stockings, Converse boots, a Dennis the Menace t-shirt and bright red hair.'

'Fuck off, sheep-molester. At least I had imagination whereas you thought you were the dogs: Welly boots, a woolly jumper and a fucking beard with less hair than on your skinny wee arse! Fuck me!'

'No thanks. I'm married.'

Elliot was still quick but had never been a match for her. He knew her mouth was still sharp, always ready for a rebuke and always eager to draw someone poor bastard into intellectual humiliation. It reminded him of her successful days on the debating team where in the space of four years the Uni had defeated all-comers in the World Championships. St. Andrews, Edinburgh, Oxford, Princeton and Cornell; all beaten into submission by the evil tongued All Stars of Glasgow.

They were sitting in the famous oyster bar enjoying both the lunch and the view of Loch Fyne. The restaurant was well known for its fresh sea food but just as well known for a wee hide away meeting between a fat guy from Hull who drove two Jags and a dour looking intellectual from Kirkcaldy.

'So, Mr. Walker, what do I owe this dis-pleasure?'

'Well, since I had a long weekend planned I thought it would be good to have a wee chat with you before we drive up the road to see the folks. We flew in this morning to Glasgow, hired that wee car outside and here we are. Mind you, I wish I wasn't so miserable with those hire car companies because I would have hired a huge mother of a driving machine to take me up to Lochaber. Imagine that, eh? Me driving through the sun-kissed mountains pretending I was in some sexy car commercial. Yep, eat your precious wee heart out, Hamster!'

'Okay, enough of your fuel-injected ejaculation. You've got me up here for a reason and something tells me it's not all about your perverted driving pleasure.'

Dixie could barely keep her lunch down on the drive

back to Glasgow. What Elliot had told her about the meeting between Sir Alexander Lamont and Peter Buchanan not only added to her theory but would vindicate her stance with her editor in pursuing a story he thought would come to nothing. Of course, continuing with the story increased the risk because, as Dixie had found out to her cost when she had exposed the trilateral oil scandal a few years back, Sir Alexander Lamont was not someone to be messed with, especially if she was prepared to go the whole way.

Lamont was well-known as a manipulative bastard but when the Tribune, again ignoring its lawyers' advice, published the story on UKES's and the Government's involvement, Dixie had felt the full force of his anger. There had been official letters from Whitehall putting pressure on the Tribune to retract the story, there had been disparaging remarks about Dixie in the London media and there had even been the harassment of late night phone calls to her house. Fortunately, the threats only served to deepen the resolve of both Dixie and her boss. The Tribune responded with further evidence to back up the story before launching an all out attack on the Government and its determination to hinder the rights of the free Press. "An Affront to Democracy" ran the headline, along with a published letter from the Tribune promising legal action. They knew it wouldn't have much effect but hoped it would send a warning signal that the Tribune wasn't going to back down. Dixie even took things one step further at a UKES press conference in Aberdeen when she questioned an unsuspecting Sir Alexander Lamont on UKES's role in the affair. Standing defiantly in the middle of the room as Sir Alexander and his aides resisted the temptation to answer her question with the truth, she persisted in her demands for an explanation. Sir Alexander laughed off any involvement before a company spokesman intervened, attacking the Tribune and its supposedly anti-business position. Unfortunately, when Dixie pointed out that the Tribune was, in fact, a good friend to the business world, the personal barrage began. The spokesman said she was being naïve and anti-British, and a journalist with socialist tendencies. He even sought to humiliate her as being a woman in a man's world and that she had no idea what she was talking about. But Dixie stood firm, demanding Sir Alexander reply. He had no come back, unless, of course, he had a wish to become embroiled in a full scale public debate in front of the news cameras. He continued to smile, dismissing any suggestion of impropriety on behalf of UKES and the Government, but Dixie could see the hatred in his eyes. Sir Alexander did not like to be humiliated and rather than go at it one-to-one with Dixie, made his apologies before being bundled away by his team. Dixie let out a childish grin as he retreated but persisted with her line of questioning. She shouted the question again and again but the throng of people surrounding Sir Alexander made an answer impossible. She had made her point that she was prepared to go all the way and if London didn't back off then that was what she was going to do.

As she drove on, Dixie heaved a smiling breath at her own foolhardiness and stubborn streak. As she enjoyed the play-back, the mountains reminded her of some other good yet difficult times. Deciding she needed a cigarette as well as a few minutes to think, she pulled off the road at the Rest and Be Thankful, a beauty spot atop of one of the steepest and longest roads in Europe.

She used to stop here with her then husband-to-be, and soon-to-be ex-husband, on the way back from their weekend breaks in Crinan. It would be their last stop before Glasgow. Parking the car, they would walk a few yards and gaze down at the magnificent glen below. They would walk a little further and stumble on the rocky ground before racing up the mountainside. Dixie would shriek with laughter as she struggled to pull him back down the slope as they fought over the last few yards. And then they would sit quietly in the biting wind, both thinking of marriage and both wondering if it was the right thing to do.

Now Dixie sat in her car wondering if taking on this story had been the right thing to do. 'Jesus,' she thought, 'is there anything Lamont won't resort to in achieving his aims?'

As she sat admiring the mountains, she lit a cigarette then shook her head. Was she in too deep for her wee wellies? She had already royally pissed him off once before and that had ended up in a right bloody mess. Was she prepared to get involved with the man again? And if she did, who could she turn to for help? Rory was just a kid, her boss would think it wouldn't be worth the hassle and DCC Mike Hastie had already warned her off. Was she all alone?

As Dixie opened the door to throw her cigarette out, she caught a glimpse in her wing-mirror of a lone man standing beside a black Range Rover. He was filming the landscape. She didn't want to make it obvious but she took an inquisitive look. Sharply dressed in a tailored grey suit with sunglasses protecting his eyes, this guy was no tourist. As she pulled the door closed, the angle of the mirror gave her a complete view of the Range Rover. Its door was open and another man sat talking on the phone, glancing occasionally over to Dixie's car. She then flicked her eyes back to the man with the camera. He was panning around the mountains but when Dixie's car came into view, he took just a little too much time filming Dixie for it to be indiscriminate. Pulling the door closed, she raised the roof on the convertible, breathed in deeply, started the engine and fixed her rear-view mirror on the slick black SUV. The two men were now talking to each other and both looking over to Dixie's car. She switched her mobile phone to Hands-Free, hit quick dial and slammed her foot hard on the accelerator. She felt a squeezy bum moment coming on.

'Time to hit the road!'

She bit her tongue, flicked her hair back and laughed in nervous fear as she waited for the number she had rung to answer.

DCI Paul Riley was at his desk when his mobile phone rang to the tune of The Killers – "Read my mind". He smiled when he saw it was Dixie's number on the screen. 'Well, hey-hey, if it isn't the troublemaker extraordinaire.' Pressing the green button, he lifted the I-Phone to his ear. 'Dixie, it's great to hear from you. How are things? I was just thinking that we had such a good time in the pub last Friday that we should maybe make plans to do it more often. How ab...'

'Paul, listen to me. No small talk,' stated Dixie in a calm tone betraying her fear. 'I've just stopped for a break by the side of the road and I noticed two men filming me.'

'Filming you? Do you think they're a couple of pervs?'

'No, definitely not. I think it may be worse that that.'

'What the hell do you mean, "worse than that"? Are you in danger?'

'I don't know yet but it's too long a story to tell you over the phone. Listen, I'm just short of shitting myself and I want to get back to Glasgow in one piece, that's all.'

'If you're not in Glasgow then where in hell are you?'

'Arrocher and heading back to the city. I've just had lunch with Elliot. I can't talk at the moment but I really do think I need your help. I actually think these guys are up to no good.'

'Is Elliot in trouble as well? In fact, what the fuck were you doing meeting Elliot up there in the first place?'

'Paul, enough with the fucking questions; I'll tell you all about it when I see you but first things first, how about doing your real job and saving my fat arse from these guys.'

'Ah, Dixie. I wouldn't say it was fat, just a little rotund.'

'For fuck's sake, Paul. Not now!'

'Okay, remain calm and keep driving. The nearest police station is in Balloch. I'll trace your phone and get your position. What's your car reg. again?'

Dixie told Paul her registration number. As the phone went silent for a moment, Dixie listened to Paul barking instructions in the background.

'Tommy, get some guys onto the A82 pronto. Just up from the Loch Lomond Club. Look out for a silver convertible BMW M3. Reg. number: Delta-Oscar-Alpha...One-Three-Two-Zero. One woman at the wheel. Driving fast and being pursued by a Black Range Rover. No ID on that just yet. Once you've picked her up, let me know and escort back to Balloch Station... Now!'

Paul came back on the line. 'Listen, Dixie. Don't drive like a maniac but don't drive like a typical Sunday afternoon driver, either. I've a squad car on the way and they'll bring you in. But stay calm; we'll get you home safely and I'll see you in Balloch. Have you got all that, Dixie?'

'Okay, but hurry, will you. I don't think these guys are of the "let's have a drink together" sort!'

Dixie hit the red button.

She had driven only a few miles when she saw the black Range Rover coming up fast from behind. It was in the middle of the road and flashing its headlights. Dixie didn't think they wanted to stop for a chat. She put her foot down but the Range Rover didn't seem to be retreating. Tears were beginning to trickle down her cheeks and her hands were sweating. 'Fuckin' hell!' she screamed.

She thought about Willie Macrae.

Dixie's car was flying down the side of Loch Lomond pursued by the men in black only fifty metres behind. Holding the wheel tightly, she glared ahead to the next bend. The cars swerved between the traffic, overtaking a small RV and an elderly couple out for a walk in the car. They peeked over in delayed shock as Dixie went flying by, quickly followed by the Range Rover. The first road sign Dixie saw read *Luss 5 Miles* and there was still no sign of a police car. Dixie drove harder and thanked the Lord she was at the wheel of a German flying machine rather than an American brickyard lump of steel. She took a wide turn at the next bend, narrowly missing a bus coming the other way. The water of Loch Lomond to her left was a sliver blur as the cliffs to her right edged ever closer. Dixie was beginning to feel hemmed in. Cars ahead pulled up as Dixie raced towards them. She could see the faces of the drivers gaping open mouthed as the BMW hit ninety. The Range Rover, transformed into a silent killer, commandeered the entire road. It seemed to be floating, and as Dixie slowed down for a series of tight bends, she first saw a hand, then a gun, appear from the passenger side of the Range Rover. Moments later, there was a sharp thud as a bullet ripped through her back window and into the dashboard. Dixie screamed as flashes of gun fire continued to explode from the side of the slick, black behemoth.

Her fear was turning into aggression. 'If it's a race you

want shitheads then bring it on! Bring it on!'

Dixie hadn't noticed her transformation from thoughtful journalist and loving mother into raving lunatic but she was damned if these guys were going to end her life like this. The BMW was trying its best to out run its pursuer and although she was a good driver, Dixie was obviously no where near as good as whoever the fuck was driving the Range Rover. Thankfully, their aim wasn't as good as their driving.

However, when her car hit the 100 mph mark just outside Loch Lomond Golf Club, her eyes strained as she focussed in on the blue flashing lights. Confirming that it was a police car coming in the opposite direction, she breathed for the first time in an age. Frantically, she flashed the lights of the BM but kept on going, eventually passing the police car that had come to a screeching halt after performing a hand brake turn on the other side of the road. Meanwhile, the Range Rover slowed before turning right on to a minor road towards Helensburgh. Dixie kept her foot down as the police car struggled to stay on her bumper. She was relieved that the Range Rover was gone but didn't feel the need to relax until she was in Balloch and the safety of the police station.

*

9.48 am – Piedmont Park - Atlanta, GA

Fourteen years had passed since Charlie Norton had been in Atlanta. From what he could remember about his days as an art student living off an overseas grant from the Arts Council, it had been a growing and confident city back in 1994 with Atlantans desperate to tell the world that not only was their city the capital of the South, home to Coca-Cola and the famous Atlanta Braves, it was also an Olympic city.

Its beautiful neighbourhoods like Buckhead and Virginia Highlands had been the places to be seen whereas strip bars like Hot Mama Gs were not. Of them all, he had preferred Virginia Highlands because it offered a greater variety of women from which to choose and where affluent sorority girls from Emory and Agnes Scott, with their plump and precious tits, and tight leggings, afforded him a splendid view of the odd camel toe. Always eager and willing to listen to his art critiques, in which he took great pleasure presenting in an affected English South Counties accent, they didn't take much persuading to enjoy a night of passion at his apartment. Chuckling to himself, he remembered his bullshit. For heaven's sake, he was a working class lad from Leeds and if they had known the truth about his background, he was sure his shagging success rate would have been well below the fifty percent mark.

Charlie loved Atlanta, a city renowned for the word *Civil*. The people, with a vestige of the old southern customs and manners in their genes, were civil almost beyond reason. It was also the town where Sherman finally broke the back of the Confederate Army during the American Civil War. Furthermore, it was the birthplace of the great Civil Rights leader, Martin Luther King. How ironic then that this great city, with so much heritage in civility and progress, had been burdened by having one of the world's largest producers of weapons in its own backyard.

Charlie had rented a Yamaha YZF for the few days he was in town, permitting him the freedom he craved from the constant traffic jams on I-75 and I-85. At anytime he could disappear from the mayhem and pop into the world of old southern charm to be found in Druid Hills and Peachtree and adore the grandeur of the ancient pine trees standing guard over the winding and twisting avenues of the old-moneyed citizens. He also found the small neighbourhood shopping districts irresistible. Parking his bike, he had taken a side-walk chair to watch the world drift by as he sipped on a coffee and inhaled the freshness of the warm air and pine needles emanating from every nook and cranny in the city.

Regrettably, Charlie wasn't here to reminisce, he was here to do a job. A job, he thought, that could be veering on the wrong side of risky, especially considering the new Homeland Security strategy implemented by these fucking nutters in Washington.

Charlie was proud of his surveillance skills just as much as he was of his photography now hanging in both the Glasgow School of Art and the MODA here in Atlanta, and so perfected was he in the skills of journalistic snooping he also considered taking covert pictures of arseholes of the suited variety an art form. Some had called him a paparazzi and some a sneaky fucking bastard but only Charlie and his boss knew him to be one of the best in the business. Leaning lightly against his bike parked on the other side of Fourteenth Street from the Four Seasons Hotel, the great silver monolith boasting the city's best view of the famous Piedmont Park, Charlie was dressed in jeans and black leather jacket; the standard uniform of the hundred or so couriers to be found around Midtown. Though he had a pretty good idea to where Brad Zimmerman would be heading this morning, Charlie thought it more beneficial to his general health and well-being if he remained incognito rather than hang around the gates of the international armaments company, and creator of the Trident missile, Dobbie and McGregor.

An hour had passed before a blacked out people-carrier arrived at the door of the hotel. Zimmerman and his security guard came rushing out and were in the car in seconds. If Charlie hadn't been as good as he was he could have easily have missed his first opportunity. Guys like Zimmerman never drew attention to themselves, hence the people-carrier and not a big fuck-off, pride of place in the brochure, Cadillac. Like Charlie, it was Zimmerman's job to stay in the background and everything he did took on this façade.

As the people-carrier drove off, Charlie took a couple of snaps but only after watching Zimmerman's car travel about a hundred yards did Charlie start the engine. Tracking him would be easy to begin with but what Dixie really wanted was an image of Zimmerman and whoever he was meeting. What's more, this assignment wouldn't be the piece of piss like Gleneagles was because snapping a target while he was playing a four hour round of golf on one of the most famous golf courses in the world could have been performed by anyone, including a wheelchair-bound, fingerless blind man. However, such was the secrecy within the Defence industry, this mission would an entirely different challenge. Arms manufacturers and private equity firms were not in the business of self-promotion. One badly planned meeting could destroy a deal worth billions of dollars.

He followed Zimmerman as far as the road leading off to the plant but ultimately knew his prospects for success would be useless unless Zimmerman, and whoever he was meeting, would be brazen enough to head out for lunch somewhere. Luckily for Charlie, their need for fine dining took precedence over secrecy.

The people-carrier came back along the road about two hours later, heading south into town. Charlie kept a safe distance until the people-carrier disappeared into an underground parking lot at Buckhead's Lenox Square. Continuing on, Charlie parked nearby, just outside a Reggae bar he used to know. 'Damn it,' he groaned, 'trawling a fucking mall looking for the little Bar Mitzvah Boy.'

He found his two targets in a fine dining restaurant just off Peachtree. 'Fuck it!' whispered Charlie. The location had been well thought out; no side views, tinted windows and a strong midday sun. Analysing the situation, he reckoned he was going to have to risk it. 'Ah well, lad. In for a penny.'

On his bike in a couple of minutes, Charlie was circling around Lenox Square before hitting Peachtree once again. He drove slowly up to the restaurant and in one movement was jumping off his bike and taking a package from his backpack. In the next, he was heading for the door and taking out a receipt book from inside his jacket. Couriers were known to keep their helmets on so there would be no suspicion. Well, not until he took out his Nikon and pointed it at the two unsuspecting guests! In he went, walking with a strut and a carefree attitude.

The restaurant was busy and quiet. In between small mouthfuls of food, small groups of businessmen and a few brace of wealthy MILFs sat whispering in eager but cautious tones. The décor was a striking blend of different shades of blacks and greys and silvers. Spotless mirrors hung on the wall while sharply dressed waiters and waitresses slothed gently between the tables. The tablecloths were bright white and the wine glasses lay empty, glistening in the reflection of the midday sun striking the mirrors. This was definitely a place for rumours, gossip and big decisions.

'Hey dude, got a package. You gonna sign for it?' asked Charlie of the Maitre D.

'Sanglante enfer!' muttered the Frenchman. 'How many times do we have to tell you? Drop-off is at the rear.' He tutted and shook his head. 'Quick, where do I sign?'

Seconds after handing over the sweet smelling package and receipt book to Froggie, Charlie was quickly reaching for his camera and taking aim at the table in the far corner of the restaurant. Zimmerman and his business associate, and more importantly, Zimmerman's bodyguard, were unaware of their role in the photo-shoot. Winding the focus, Charlie hit the quick-shutter button and listened as the Nikon took at least twelve pictures. Two seconds later, the hand of the Maitre D knocked his arm down.

'What the hell do you think you are doing?'

'Hey, what's the problem? I'm just taking a few snaps of your interior, dude. It's cool!'

'Give me that camera, now. It is forbidden to take pictures inside here. Our patrons require privacy.'

Charlie quickly swept the Maitre D's arm away. 'Sorry Jacques. Gotta go. See ya!'

He swivelled and ran, and was on his bike before the Maitre D had even reached the door. As he drove off, Charlie turned and laughed out loud at the sight of Froggie waving the receipt book in the air. 'God help me. Forever the righteous nation.' Knowing the Frenchman would not report the intrusion, Charlie smiled. 'Is it any wonder they could never win a war. C'est la vie, Monsieur Jacques. Apprécier les chocolats!'

6

ony wan seen the wean an' 'at

Sunday 15th June

12.10 pm – Glasgow

Dixie had already read the papers and taken the kids over to her parents. She was alone at last, driving across her Glasgow en route to look after a wee bit of business at the airport.

She loved that she was a part of this city, which as well as being mocked for the aggressive nature of its citizens and its vast swathes of public housing, also had an international and well-deserved reputation for producing great minds who had pushed the bounds of their chosen fields to the very limit of Reason. Philosophers, inventors, writers, artists and musicians; they were plenty and Glasgow drew privilege from them. Edinburgh may have taken then plaudits but Glasgow was the unsung hero.

Dixie also considered the self-deprecating nature of Glaswegians, smiling at the notion that Glasgow would be a beautiful city when it was finished. However, it was simply not in the nature of the vast majority of its citizens to *finish*. Imagine, she thought, where the world would be now if Adam Smith had put his feet up on his desk and announced to the world that, 'I'm done. I'm now the Chair of Philosophy at the University of Glasgow and therefore the brightest man in the entire world, so you two; aye, that's right, both you, Mr. James Hutton and you, Mr. Joseph Black, can fuck right off cos I'm off to the pub to get pished!'

Dixie sniggered at the conflicting nature of Scotland's education and its relationship with alcohol. Here was a country full of very clever people who thought nothing of the dangers of the demon drink. Hume, Smith, Kames and Ferguson would often fall in love with the claret while discussing world changing academic theories in the drinking howffs of Glasgow and Edinburgh. Was it any wonder no one could understand them? In fact, alcohol had become so entrenched in the country's psyche that she thought it hilarious that no other country in the entire world has so many colloquialisms for getting drunk. Aff yer legs, steamin, paralytic, smeekit, bladdered, huckled, stocious, trollied, jaiked, guttered, stoatin, rubbered, puggled, buckled, morocced, and banjaxed. And they were just the ones of which she knew! What's more, it didn't surprise Dixie to think that within this great culture of endless creativity, there was also this eccentric and obscure Sunday morning tradition she was now witnessing from her car. Unique to Scotland, it seemed that everybody and their granny would head down to the local paper shop, pop in to discuss topics such as world geography and astrophysics, as well as hangovers and the occasional bowel movement, before walking out with the worst Sunday paper in the world while gobbling on a two litre bottle of Ginger Fizz, Scotland's gum rotting, enamel stripping, stomach burning, but extremely refreshing national soft drink.

"Awe right there, Raju. How's it goin' big man?"

"Ach, nae bother, Billy. The other half is away up tae the Burrell Collection wi' the weans so I've got some peace for the day. How aboot yersel?"

"Aye, cool like. Me and the missus went oot for a curry last night tae yer mate Vivek's place. Braw meal so it was. But a'll tell ye something, not only did we get blootered, ma fuckin mooth's as dry as the Bolivian Salt Flats and ma erse feels like it's re-enterin' the earth's atmosphere at mach 9!"

"So Billy, a Sunday News and a bottle of Ginger Fizz?"

"Aye, yer a godsend, Raju. See you later, big man."

After leaving the West End, Dixie decided she would take the Clyde Tunnel and then the M8. It was the quickest route but she would have to drive past one of the city's two stadiums of hate. Though tentative efforts were being made to lessen the problem, it was both a coliseum and a weekend cathedral of worship for one of Scotland's biggest football clubs and more than the occasional ninety-minute bigot. Dixie shook her head and smiled at her own naivety. Like its counterpart across the city, the stadium didn't so much provide a stage for a collection of vocal bigots but rather a tribal homeland for a peculiar and absurd blend of rights defenders whose cultural objectives (of protecting their precious demesne from the abuse directed at them by a similarly dis-affected sub-group from within the very same religion) produced a nasty and sometimes extremely violent bi-product. Like many of the millions of forward-thinking people in the country, she had grown weary of the two great football teams in the city. She was tired of their hatred and their entrenched view-points. For over one hundred years, the two teams and their supporters had corrupted the image of Glasgow and neither was the situation helped by the tabloids whose pages were saturated with "exclusives" of the Old Firm. Consequently, if a visitor to Scotland was ever to enquire about sport in Scotland, they could be instantly forgiven for thinking it only played one: football. And it only had two teams: Celtic and Rangers. It infuriated her. The bigots had their tabloids to inform and their Orange Marches and Irish Republican bars to enlighten and entertain. Religion and tribal war was their life's rationale: playing flutes, calling for the Black and Tans to come out and play, banging the big lambeg, selling propaganda magazines, dancing the Hokey-Cokey, collecting money for the glorious cause. Indeed, these were two institutions who fed off the extremely fucking stupid.

Indeed, who the fuck are Chris Hoy and Andy Murray?

Dixie's M3 shot across town towards the tunnel. Leaving the West End, she drove alongside the re-generated River Clyde where once the great ships of the world had been designed, built, and launched with the Veuve before being replaced by post-modern apartments, strange looking bridges and science centres in the guise of exotic and distant animals. She hit the M8 near Govan with its surrounding social deficits and burnt-out and boarded-up apartments representing the myopic mistake of Sixties social planning. Although the football season was over, she could still imagine the hoards of red, white and blue heading to the stadium while the poverty stricken locals in their baseball caps, baggy white tracksuits and greased down hair swaggered with dangerous intent outside the gates. It was tragic. The second and third generations of the underclass Thatcher had left to rot. The Disenfranchised. 'Will they ever learn?' she thought. 'Do they ever want to learn?'

Yes, this great city will be quite nice when it's finished.

Glasgow Airport was busy this Sunday lunchtime and jammed full of tourists heading off on annual vacation. Dixie loved airports, especially at the weekend. It was a businessman free zone, which in turn created an anthropologist's dream landscape. There were eight check-in lines for Toronto, busy with families setting off to see Uncle Archie and Aunty Alice while alongside, the New York line chattered with fat-walleted suburban women prepping for the bi-annual shopping trip to the Big Apple. However, it was down at the far-end of the concourse where sociological research reigned supreme: the check-in desks for package trips to the Med! One could listen and watch for a couple of hours and an Eddie Izzard stand-up show wouldn't be any funnier. In fact, Dixie reckoned that if she could sell t-shirts outside with "I'm a stupid fucking bastard" emblazoned on the front, she was sure she could make a wee fortune.

Among the throng were those completely unaccustomed to airports. Pink jumpsuits, high heels, fake Louis Vuitton suitcases and six weans. No patience, no common sense and no fucking idea. And so worried were they about missing their flight they thought nothing of allowing the world to observe their illiteracy.

It would begin with a ridiculously early arrival to the airport, wearing clothes that were brand-spanking. They would saunter to the back of the check-in line. They would whisper and raise their eyebrows and complain that the line wisnae moving. There would still be four hours before take-off. *Plenny o time for a beer or two.* Yet still they would move no closer to the check-in desk. There would be an impending feeling of panic. The queue should be moving quicker. Irrational thought would take over. *Are we in the right line?* With the kids becoming restless, they would double-check with the family in front. Doubt would set in. *We cannae miss the flight.* They had been looking forward to the holiday for a whole year. She had even boasted to Collette in the hairdressers only last night. The beamer she would have in Asda on Monday morning. Aw naw, this just wouldnae do. *I'm gonnae check with the lassie at the desk.*

And then, with no sense of self-embarrassment, she would be off. *Look efter the weans.* The heels would click on the floor as the handbag brushed against the other passengers. With her stare trained on the check-in desk, her expression was one of indignation. The arse of her jumpsuit would be hinging as if she was wearing a nappy full of kak. She would offer no apology to those at the front of the line. She would slam her handbag on top of the desk. Her elbows would arch in readiness for attack. She would check one more time with the screen up above. In bright, yellow, luminous type-face, it still read *"WFUA 243: Malaga – 1610"*. She wouldn't even stop for breath. And then.

'Hey darlin', is this the check-in for the Whoosh Airlines Flight 243 to Malaga at ten past four?'

'Yes madam, it is. Now if you'd be so kind as to go back and wait in line, we'll get you checked in as soon as possible.'

'Are you sure this is the line, hen?'

Dixie could just imagine what the poor check-in girl was thinking. "Of course I'm fucking sure. Can you not fucking read the screen you stupid fucking half-wit. Or was that not part of your education when you were busy planting daffodils in the school garden!"

Fortunately, the fun didn't stop there. On a weekday, as Dixie headed for Heathrow or Brussels, the idiots at the final security check drove her insane with their heid-the-ba psyche. However, on the weekend these morons were brilliantly stupid.

There would be the uncomfortable looking middle-aged guy wearing a dumb grin while passing through the metal detector, there would be the group of lads on a stag whose drunken demeanour would insist that the female official perform the body sweep, and there would be the complete imbecile who had no fucking idea as to what was permitted through Security and what was not.

"Six leetars o' voddie, three cases o' Sooper, an' four oonses o' blaw. Whit je mean a cannae take it oan?"

Dixie walked up the stairs to where the holiday's day-one budget disappeared in minutes. Six pounds for a sandwich, three-fifty for coffee, nine ninety-nine for chips and rubbered haddock and …*"For fuck's sake …Five fifty? …For a fuckin' pint?"*

Thankfully, most of the customers today didn't give a damn. It was time for John Denver and there was plenty of cash and credit. The place was awash with trackie bottoms and white trainers and hair shaved to the bone. It was all part of the experience, even if it meant turning up four hours early to get gee-eyed at the bar!

God help me!

She saw him sitting in the corner with Kirsten, nursing a Sunday afternoon pint and unsurprisingly, looking none too happy. Another weekend had been ruined, although this time Elliot had been the instigator. When she saw Dixie, Kirsten's expression turned from fear into irritation. Thankfully, her body language appeared to offer protection for her husband rather than aggression towards Dixie.

'Hi folks, how was your weekend?' asked Dixie. 'Or is that a stupid question?'

A slightly piqued Kirsten pinched her lips. 'We were having a great time until you called on Friday evening.'

'I can only imagine and please believe me when I tell you that I'm really, really sorry. I had no idea but after what happened, I thought you'd better know.'

Kirsten sighed, the tension in her body easing. 'Och, I'm sorry, too, Dixie. It's just that last weekend was ruined by that boss of Elliot's and now this. As you can guess, it's not exactly a pleasant feeling to know you might be being followed. Not pleasant at all. And it's not made any easier by knowing that one of your friends was nearly murdered.'

Dixie didn't need a reminder. Things could have turned out much worse. 'Anyway, we're all still alive so we should be thankful for that. Has Elliot told you anything, Kirsten?'

'No, nothing apart from your wee Starsky and Hutch moment and quite frankly, I'd rather not know.'

'Good. Let's keep it that way, shall we?'

'That's all I needed to hear. I'll leave you two alone to talk shop while I pop off to buy some make-up. See you in a bit.'

Elliot waited until Kirsten was out of earshot before he spoke, 'Jesus Christ, Dixie! What the hell is going on?'

'I wish I knew, Elliot. It's not everyday someone takes a pot shot. Not unless you live in South London that is. All I know is that Rory and I have been working on this story concerning the Hutchinson Group. You know, taking the odd photograph, doing the occasional interview but this; this is completely out-with the norm. So I can assure you, having bullets smashing through my rear windscreen is all new to me. I mean, it's not as if I'm protecting some secret terrorist cell preparing to blow up another airport. However, after what you told me about your boss and Peter Buchanan, I'm beginning to think there's a lot more to this story than merely some government Arms deal.'

'What do you think it is?'

'I'm not quite sure. I spoke with Paul Riley on Friday night and gave him the summary picture of what I know but let's just say I have an old journalist's hunch, if you know what I mean?'

'No I don't, Dixie. I'm a litigator remember. Exciting stuff like tax, employee agreements, mergers and acquisitions. I'm a real James Bond so I am!'

'Funny you should say that.'

7

benny and george

10.01 am – Pennsylvania Avenue - Washington DC.

Brad Zimmerman was not your typical American private equity firm employee. For a start, he wasn't the best looking of guys. Well under six foot, he had an anaemic complexion not improved by a severe bout of teenage acne, red to fairish hair and a slight ponch, courtesy of a penchant for coke and pizza. His inherited genes had played a cruel joke. There were no "six foot tall and eyes of blue" moments in Brad's life and he had missed them all his life.

At school, he was always an outsider. Bullied by the jocks, despised by the geeks, sneered at by the girls and hated by the teachers, Brad had kept his head down. It was hard enough just getting on with his life. In the quieter moments of his depression he often thanked his then unlucky stars he hadn't grown into the regular, white-male, middle-class psychotic, aged between twenty-five and thirty-five, who made it his hobby to rape and murder innocent women while occasionally sitting down with a bottle of Pinot Noir and munching into Steak a la Little Sarah Jones with a side order of baby new potatoes, and all before heading off to Florida for a short holiday and a state sponsored injection of heart stopping chemicals!

Brad, though, had turned his many weaknesses into a significant advantage. As well as living in a beautiful apartment in Georgetown, he also ate at the finest restaurants alongside some of the most powerful people in the world. He had homes in Shanghai and Vancouver, a beach house in the Caymans and a property portfolio worth over twenty million dollars. And all because he could live life unnoticed. Not bad, he thought, for a little Jewish boy from Chicago.

Sitting in his plush office on Pennsylvania Avenue, he was thinking about his round of golf at St. Andrews. It had been a sunny and windy day on the Old Course, the perfect conditions for a round on the historic links. Having shot an 89, he was delighted with himself. Furthermore, for the first time in his life on a golf course, he hadn't taken a mulligan, he hadn't taken a preferred lie and he had counted all his strokes.

There was a knock on the door and Brad glanced at his video monitor. It was his boss, Drew Wilson. 'What now?' Brad muttered as he dropped his head in mock despair before pressing a button under his desk to open the door.

Drew Wilson bounced into the room. For an old man he was still agile and his tailor-made navy suit sat well on his frame, striking a gentle but handsome contrast with his silver hair. 'Brad, my boy, how was your weekend?'

Brad smiled but inside he wasn't laughing. He wondered what the lesson of today would be. 'Not bad, Boss. Took it easy, I'm afraid. Very tired after Scotland and Atlanta.'

Drew Wilson loved to play little mind games with Brad. As a history buff, he saw this as an opportunity to throw his fish some bate. 'Ah, Scotland and Atlanta, eh? And now you're on Pennsylvania Avenue. Connections, connections.'

'"Connections?" sighed Brad. 'I've absolutely no idea what you're talking about but please, Old Grey Hair, continue.'

'Oh, I am disappointed in your lack of enthusiasm, my young Mr. Zimmerman. In fact, before I depart this world to a better place, I may have to look for a new protégé for whom to pass on my learnings.'

'Drew?' pleaded Brad.

The older man poured himself a coffee before taking a seat overlooking the great city of power. 'Brad, do you see the

Washington Monument over there?'

Brad got comfortable.

'It's an Egyptian Obelisk, built not only to commemorate the first leader of our country but also as a tribute to our ancient Masonic fraternities. You know, with the pyramid at the top representing the phallic fallibility of men and our acknowledgement that the female, the Sun-Gods and the Superior Being in the heavens have much greater power than us.'

'Jesus! Really?' said Brad, making no attempt to disguise his sarcasm.

'"Jesus?" Ah, I'm afraid it isn't Jesus who you should be cursing, Brad. More like James.'

Brad looked up, his face contracting and eyes wide open both in his bemusement and in the apparent ridiculousness of the impending conversation.

What the hell?

Glancing back, Drew saw the uncertainty. 'Not to worry, that's another story for another day, young Z.' Taking a sip of his coffee, he smiled. 'Anyway, back to the "Connections". Fifty bucks says that when you were indulging your golfing nirvana at St. Andrews the other day, you failed to notice the monument just across the street from the eighteenth green.'

'Put it on my tab.'

'Well, it's an exact copy of that great monument out there, albeit a little smaller. Built in the 1800s by the people of Scotland to remember the Protestant Martyrs of the sixteenth century who lost their lives in the aftermath of a little spat with an oppressive Cardinal.'

'So?' asked Brad.

'So? So, the descendents of the very people who died for that monument were the very same people who created the ideals, and therefore the foundations and system of government, for this great United States in which we now live.'

'Gimmie a break.'

'No break required, Brad. Just sit back, listen and learn.'

Brad turned away, preventing Drew Wilson from seeing his eyes disappear into his skull. Taking a deep breath, he waited for his boss to continue.

'You see, Brad, beginning just after the execution of Mary, Queen of Scots, Scotland had set out to rid the country of the influence of Rome. It was a violent era, extremely violent, but also instrumental in a massive cultural and religious shift towards a strict Calvinistic doctrine. Somewhat appropriately, and due in no small part to the witch-hunts and gratuitous executions carried out by an army of mad fundamentalists, this era was known as the Killing Times. However, we mustn't forget that the violence was a means to an end, an end that resulted in a covenant being signed and an allegiance pledged to the new faith. Known as the Covenanters, the signatories sought and delivered a greater sense of religious equality, as well as playing a key role in the ultimate demise of the Stuart dynasty. More importantly, it set a precedent for a new form of religious democracy, which, as a consequence, guaranteed that local clergymen were voted into office by their parishioners and not, as was the case, appointed by a Cardinal or Archbishop. What's more, to ensure the movement grew and established itself within the national psyche, the new religious authorities built public schools all across Scotland so that all children between the ages of seven and fourteen could learn to read or to be more specific, read the Bible. Sadly, and regardless that the movement was a fortunate turn of events for my ancestors, the Covenanters didn't get everything quite right. For within their screwed-up idea of wisdom, they thought it wise idea to develop a new national characteristic: Miserableness. Nevertheless, Brad, Scotland was the first place in the world to give all its children a free education and that was almost four hundred years ago. Hell, the United States of America wasn't even an after-thought at the time!'

Drew took another sip of coffee. 'Want to hear more?'

Brad feigned interest. He was bored already. 'I'm in the Presidential box, Drew. The stage is yours.'

'Well, a few decades later, there just so happened to be the not too insignificant matter of the Act of Union between Scotland and England. Scotland, with no thanks to the spoiling

108

tactics of the English Navy, had lost a shit load of its GDP in some screwed-up colonisation scheme in Central America and was in dire need of some serious financial help. England, meanwhile, was still at war with France and was beginning to shit itself that the increasingly pissed-off Scots would take up arms and support the French. Soon after, amid corrupt payments, secret deals, and mass riots and protestations, the parliament in Edinburgh was dissolved and all its powers transferred to Westminster. Nevertheless, after the Act of Union, England was secure and Scotland, whose trade routes had been re-opened after the withdrawal of the English Navy, had free trade once more. All in all, I suppose it was kinda like a corporate merger of such, voted through by the boards of two companies but without the shareholders knowing what the hell was going on.'

Bar-keep. A drink, if you please!

'Fortunately, and as much as the Scots were pissed that their government had been sold off in the Union with England, it opened the door for Scotland to thrive. With Government and its petty bureaucracy having left for London, the thinkers, writers, merchants and universities pretty much had a free reign and what followed was a monumental period of philosophical enlightenment in which the brilliant minds of Hutchinson, Hume and Smith pioneered a new freedom of thought, eventually leading to the creation of the great economic behemoth we now call Capitalism. What's more, and just as important may I add, this phenomenal intellectual revolution paved the way for Scotland to make some serious money ...some really serious money.'

Drew Wilson wandered around the room as he spoke, picking up framed pictures and small plastic trophies and dusting them off with his shirt cuffs. He was lost in his own world. Brad's eyes didn't follow him. He had witnessed the show many times. Before continuing, Drew pulled at one of Newton's Balls and watched as gravity pushed the clanking silver spheres back and forth. 'But the real catalyst was the opening up of the North Atlantic trade routes. As soon as the English Navy stopped intercepting Scottish merchant ships in the Atlantic, it was boom time. Why? Because it took two days less to ship the cotton and tobacco to Glasgow than it did to Bristol. Glasgow became the busiest trading port in the world, and the richest. Wealth poured in and merchants built fine homes in Glasgow, Edinburgh and the Americas, and as one would expect in the natural course of events, the first great financial institutions were founded such as the all-powerful Royal Caledonian Bank and Principal Life. And if that wasn't enough, the country still continued to thrive as many of the great thinkers of Europe headed for Scotland to further expand their minds. Even Voltaire, in all his pomp, said that, "it is to Scotland that we should look to find inspiration in this new world."'

A quart of JD ...Please!

'Scotland's universities became the epicentre of the intellectual world, inspiring genius and invention, and educating great men such as our very own Benjamin Rush. Even to this day, if we think of Dolly the Sheep, the scientists in Scotland still lead from the front in many disciplines. You see, Brad, Scotland was, and still is, an intellectual gold mine. In fact, think of any major invention of the last three hundred years and you will receive no better odds than evens it was invented by a Scot; Natural Scepticism, Capitalism, Modern Surgery, Anaesthetics, Steam Power, Nuclear and Electromagnetic Physics, Aspirin, Quinine, Insulin, Penicillin, Telephone, Television, Geosciences, Radar, Radiography, Environmental Conservation, MRI and CT scans and the components of DNA. Hell, Brad, the list goes on and on and on, and it's not just in science and medicine and philosophy in which they excel, either. They also founded the Bank of England, played leading roles in composing and signing both the Declaration of Independence and US Constitution, created the US Navy, built Princeton, settled the South and the Pacific North West, discovered the North-West Passage, and put the phrase "In God we trust" on our money. Drew Wilson chuckled. 'In fact, since old George with the wooden teeth took Office, more than half of our Commanders-in-Chief have had Scottish ancestry!'

Oh, please. Go tell someone who gives a fuck!

Drew Wilson was enjoying himself. 'Which, Brad, brings us to the connection with Pennsylvania Avenue.' Pausing for effect, he turned to his disgruntled student. 'Who, may I ask, Brad, is Philadelphia's most famous son?'

'Who is; Benjamin Franklin?' offered Brad, sensing his present state of waking consciousness was now in Jeopardy.

'Of course he is. Old Benny boy was not only one of America's greatest ever citizens, he was also the bringer of light to these shores and, as you will have no doubt deduced, a Freemason as well. He was also the main man when it came to seeking support for an independent and republican United States and smart enough to realise he needed recognition and financial assistance from Europe to achieve his aims. With his persistence, and genius in political persuasion, Franklin's idea for the new democratic world gathered force in Europe. Unfortunately, with the Hanovers in control of Westminster and its government in desperate need of the colonies' resources, as well as a threat of sedition hanging over his wig, Franklin didn't have a hope in hell of receiving any help from England. Nevertheless, he didn't have to travel far for his ideas to receive a much warmer welcome. With John Adams as his rottweiller, Franklin's skills in intoxicating and slightly misleading the French led to an offer of support that had as much to do with undermining the influence and military might of Britain than it did with any new form of government.' Drew tutted. 'If only the French Court had known what was to become of them? Anyway, Franklyn still had to persuade many of his own people that his idea of a republic was a much better proposition than Westminster rule. However, he required the majority of his countrymen to back him, and they weren't going to do that without good reason; after all, they still had to do business with Britain, for goodness sake. He therefore had to motivate, inform and instruct the new intellectual class in America; to let them know that they had international backing, to let them see that others beyond their shores were thinking as he was. In other words, he had to let his own people understand that there were others of their ilk who were on their side. And there was only one place he was going to find that: the place where Franklin had turned to as a younger man to develop his political philosophies, the place where he knew great minds like his were working on a new framework for society, the place which had strong links with the colonies and the place which had an historic and perennial mistrust of England.'

Help me please!

'So Franklin set off on his many triangular trips hoping to garner support that would add sustainability to his ideas. And by that, I mean, is that he journeyed from Philadelphia to Paris, from Paris to Edinburgh and then back to Philly. In fact, he did this trip a few times and spent many a raucous and drunken night in Edinburgh, even discussing theories with Smith and Hume, but god knows why; these two weren't exactly proponents of republicanism. He also spent many wonderful days in …you've guessed it, St. Andrews, with his friend James Wilson and enjoyed his time so much that when writing to another old friend, Lord Kames, he said: "that if strong connections did not draw me elsewhere, Scotland would be the country in which I would choose to spend the remainder of my days."'

Brad wasn't in the mood anymore for providing mocking and derogatory thoughts. He was too busy now, wondering if Franklin's friend, James Wilson, was an ancestor of his boss.

'The relationship between St. Andrews and Franklin flourished,' continued Drew Wilson, 'as did the movement for American freedom and liberty. Moreover, the people of St. Andrews were so enamoured by the beliefs Franklin shared with them that the town bestowed on him the honour of Freeman of St. Andrews, an award of such high importance to both St. Andrews and Scotland they have given it to only one other American since, Robert Tyre Jones; more commonly known to you and me as Bobby Jones, the greatest living golfer in the history of the game.'

Brad was not so much shocked at these revelations but intrigued. And not because he didn't believe Drew Wilson, either -his boss was a stickler for the facts- but rather this was information he had never heard before.

'Scotland. Influence, power, control? No it couldn't be.

Surely we would have heard of all this by now?'

'Oh, it's out there Brad. You just have to look for it. The English, being the English, claim ownership and greatness in everything they touch. Take for example their subtle disregard in not giving the full recognition to Alfred Wallace for being an original pioneer of the Theory of Evolution, or their boast of their beloved Magna Carta. Hell, that document was written to protect property, not the rights of liberty and equality as per Scotland's Declaration of Arbroath. On the other hand, it's not in a Scot's nature to boast unless, of course, you mock him. Plus, let us not forget that Scotland's silence has been to its benefit. Just think of the power they yield today in business, politics and science. As I said, they're a crafty bunch.'

'But where is the goddamn connection with Atlanta?' pleaded Brad, wishing, and trying, to bring an end to his tutorial.

'Oh, Brad, I am disappointed, and you being a golfer as well. Bobby Jones came from Atlanta. What's more, he loved St. Andrews and he loved its people, and they loved him just as much back. In fact, when he was given the honour of Freeman he proclaimed through tears, and no doubt as a salutary nod in the direction of Franklin, "that you could take away all my life experiences except those here at St. Andrews and I would still have lived a rich and fulfilling life."

*

6.18 pm - Georgetown, Washington DC.

There was an eclectic mix of clientele surrounding Charlie. Politicians, journalists, tourists, lobbyists and students; not what he thought was your typical customer segmentation breakdown in a neighbourhood bar, and most certainly a far cry from some of the tribal gatherings found in the pubs back in Glasgow. The Merchant City full of young and confident profess-ionals, the West End noisy with students and media junkies called Kirtsy, the city-centre chains bars droned out by the mumblings of tourists, shoppers and conference delegates, and the housing scheme gang huts awash with blood, yellow wall-paper and Formica topped bars. Charlie chuckled and shook his head at the prospect of a rag-tag mix of drinkers coming together under the same Glasgow roof.

"*Ma man. Where do you belong tae?*"

"*Austin, Texas.*"

"*Hey boys, we've gote a Double U in wi' us the night.*"

"*Oh no. I'm a liberal; a rare Texas breed.*"

"*Ah, I get it. Any coo will do?*"

"*If it's girls you mean. Oh yeh.*"

"*Are you tellin' us yer boabie's as big as yer State?*"

"*Sorry. Didn't quite get that.*"

"*So, Buddy Holly ...lethally injected anyone lately?*"

"*Hell, no! I'm against the death penalty.*"

"*Yer a guid lad, Davy Crockett. Are ye havin a drink?*"

"*Ah, yes. That would be great. Scotch, no ice.*"

"*Come on ZZ. How about topping off your trip with one of our local brews? A White Lightening perhaps?*"

"*Ah well. When in Rome and all that.*"

"*There you go, Peggy Sue. Get that down yer gullet.*"

"*Mmm ...interesting flavour.*"

"*Hey boys. There goes George Senior. Sumbdy memmer tae pick him up off the flair. I'm off for a single fish.*"

Charlie Norton didn't look out of place in Georgetown. Having cut his surfer-dude, dirty blonde hair, it was now slicked back and across. He had also discarded the jeans and t-shirt, tonight wearing a tailored Hugo Boss suit from Buchanan Street, courtesy of Dixie's expense account, and a double cuffed shirt from Slaters. The shirt was open at the neck and he sat nursing a Macallan 18 year-old while reading the Washington Post. 'Oh yeh,' he thought. 'With all these hot looking students and PRs, let's hope Charlie-boy is on form.' All that, however, was for later; he had other priorities tonight. And taking some pics of a small, pheromone-free Jewish bloke was number one.

He had been trailing Zimmerman since flying in from Atlanta. According to Dixie's source in Washington, he was in Brad Zimmerman's favourite haunt: an old style mahogany and brass bar with dimmed lighting, good music and the best collection of beers and malt whiskies he had seen since he and Rory had been in Chookieburgh for one of those product launch jollies. Charlie let out a sigh and a smile, thanking God that tonight he wouldn't have to listen to Rory spouting on endlessly about ancient conspiracy theories!

He was here to follow up on his wee visit to Atlanta. It was a bit of a hunch but since Zimmerman was flying direct from meeting to meeting in quick succession, Charlie reckoned that Zimmerman was keen to finish whatever deal he was working on ASAP.

When Charlie saw Zimmerman walk in, he saw a man of confidence and of purpose, and fortunately, no Big Tony the bodyguard in tow. It was in Zimmerman's best interest to appear to be in control. He was The Fixer. He was the man. He made the deals, whatever it took, and if they just happened to include the odd breach of international law then so be it. Whatever the method used or outcome arrived at, he didn't care. He knew he was protected from way high up the chain of command.

Zimmerman often used this bar to discuss Hutchinson's strategies with lobbyists and politicians and, as he termed, to "incentivise and coax" members of the Senate to support various government initiatives. He didn't deal in political ideology, only huge gains for the group. This was where Zimmerman worked the floor. He was a man to avoid but also a man to be seen with. For politicians it was a gamble because meeting him could only mean one of three things: more cash in the off-shore bank, an increase in the popularity polls or horrendous abuse from constituents for not being suitably well-informed to secure a Defence contract and therefore thousands of jobs.

Charlie watched as Zimmerman took a seat in a booth at the far end of the noisy bar. It was close to seven o'clock and the decibel level was rising, as was the sexual tension. Springsteen's "Born in the USA" added a touch of irony to the setting, maybe a show of defiance from the bar staff, while the shrieks from the wet fanny contingent were drowning out the guffaws of the Ivy League's finest. Oh yes, the white teeth and luscious lips were certainly out-shining the quaffed hair and jutting jaw-lines. Life was exciting in DC. It was Central Traffic Control of the free world; with those in the bar believing that whatever was decided in Washington would have a ripple effect across the world. It was an awesome of amount of power to consider.

Charlie didn't have to wait much longer before two men of the well-over-fifty genre barged their way through the crowded bar. Zimmerman's drinking buddies. One was dressed in a suit while the other had apparently just stepped off the golf course. Either that or he had bought straight from the mannequin in Ralph's boutique. Charlie laughed. 'And surprise, surprise. No fucking socks with the loafers!'

When they sat down however, they did not grant upon Charlie an unobstructed view of their phizogs. They were sitting with their backs to him, which unfortunately meant that any snaps taken would have the aesthetically challenged Zimmerman as the only protagonist.

'Take it eeeasy, take it eee-eesy,' sang Charlie to himself as he pulled out his phone, hit the camera option and raised it to his ear. 'What? I can't hear you man!' shouted Charlie into the phone. 'Hold on a sec 'til I move away from the bar.' Standing up from his stool, Charlie headed towards the corner of the bar where an antique but still useable phone hung on the wall next to the restrooms. He now had his intended subjects at ninety degrees. He shouted, making sure he was close enough for Zimmerman and his cronies to look over with disdain. 'Yeh, dude,' bellowed Charlie in a mid-Atlantic accent, loud enough for Zimmerman to overhear. 'I'm in this cool bar in DC. Talk about beautiful women. All dressed up in their power suits and ready for a picking. What's that? …Yeh, I'm on my own. Pity I don't have you here as my aide-de-camp. I'm telling you, we could do some damage.'

Zimmerman turned to Charlie, who glanced back, raising his eyebrows and mouthing the word 'Sorry'. At the same time, Charlie pressed the capture button on his phone. He hit it once, waited, hit it again, waited, then hit it a third time to complete the portfolio. Zimmerman scornfully smiled back before turning to his associates and apologising. 'You think some people would show some common courtesy.'

Charlie was still shouting to Harvey on the phone. 'Yep, cool, dude. I'll see you in New York in a couple of days. And make sure you have these finance reports for me. Sure. See ya.'

Pretending to switch the phone off, Charlie stared down at the screen to check the pics. 'Yep, good enough.' Returning the phone to his pocket, he started back to his seat, casually leaning over Zimmerman's table on the way. 'Sorry about that, chaps. Now, if you don't mind, I think I'll return to some serious drinking and the chasing of the ladies.'

There was a slight acknowledgment from the table but Charlie didn't care. He was back at the bar in couple of seconds and planning his next move. Not work this time but sussing out which group of girls would be susceptible to his charms.

An hour had passed by the time Zimmerman's associates stood up to leave. All three shook hands. As the two older men headed for the door, Zimmerman sat back down, took a deep breath and a long sip on his drink. Browsing around the bar, he once again felt a pang of loneliness. 'Boy, after the week he had had,' he mumbled, 'I could do with a drink tonight.' Then he noticed the man with the phone.

'Hey dude, sorry about that phone call. I hate it myself when some arsehole is shouting down the phone.' said Charlie as Zimmerman became visible beside him.

'Hey, no need to worry, man,' replied the eager looking Zimmerman. 'Anyway, I couldn't help but overhear you were in town on your own. Well, so am I. How about a drink?'

'You're not a fucking faggot, are you?'

'Holy shit, man. No fuckin' way. Sure, people here care what they look like but as far as I can see, there ain't no tight-fitting vests, bulging muscles and a disproportionate amount of young men under the age of twenty pouting and twisting each other's nipples!'

'Yeh, fair play, dude. What ya having?'

Zimmerman was on the bar stool in a second. 'Bombay and Tonic. No lemon, only lime.'

'And you're sure you're not an arse bandit?'

'Just get me a drink. It's time I had a few. I'm Brad by the way,' said Zimmerman, offering his hand.

'Hi, Phil, please to meet you, dude,' replied Charlie.

Half an hour later and the two single men were giggling and joking, and admiring the local eye candy. Zimmerman was delighted, for here he stood, in a bar full of women, with a guy who so obviously knew how to play the "get the panties off" game. He was enjoying this rare moment of male bravado. Charlie shook his head slightly and smiled. Judging by the way Zimmerman talked about picking up women he was either a man who could drop a couple of thousand on sex and extras in a Berlin hotel or a desperate and pitiful loner who had been spanking his marmoset just a little too often for his own good.

'So, what brings you to DC, Phil?'

'Ah, not much, Brad. I'm in real estate and my boss reckoned there could have been an opportunity to invest in some of downtown's less respectable neighbourhoods. Bit of a wasted trip if you ask me. The do-gooders won't allow the ghettos to be sold off. I'm not surprised though, can you imagine the outrage if there were even more of the homeless bastards shooting up and begging in front of the White House?'

'Yeh, if I'd known you before now, I could have told you that. New York's the place to be, I'm afraid. It never sleeps and property prices never drop. Always a winner.'

'You're right there, pal. But it's out of our league now. Have to look elsewhere for our buck. Anyway, you from around here?'

'Chicago. After finishing Northwestern, I moved down here to work for a senator. A couple of jobs later and you know how it is. Ended up staying. Mind you, I do love it here.'

'Yeh, Georgetown and the Capitol are cool, but can't really say much for the rest of the city. It's a bit soulless. About as much fun as my home back in England: Leeds.'

'Leeds? Oh yes. Bit of a move into finance these past few years. How are things now over there now?'

'Don't really know, dude. Don't get back too often. But I

can't say I'm in a rush to get back there anytime soon.'

'Where do you live now?'

'New Jersey,' sighed Charlie.

'Which exit?'

Charlie shook his head at the nation's nauseating, and now very unfunny, homage to the Garden State.

It didn't take long for the alcohol to take effect, Brad soon suggesting they make a move on three girls at the end of the bar. Picking up his drink, he made to walk over but Charlie grabbed him by the arm. 'Nah, that's not how you do it, dude. You gotta go easy with these chicks. They work in DC, so the last thing they need is two pissed-up suits barging in and spoiling their night. You gotta test the water, first. ' Flicking a fifty on the bar, Charlie asked the barman to send over three drinks. 'Let's see their response and then we'll decide if we should move in or not.'

Fortunately, two of the girls raised their glasses and smiled across the bar. 'Okay Brad, we're in. Follow my lead.'

Picking up their drinks, Charlie and Brad shimmied over. Brad was beside himself. 'Oh yeh, baby. Here we go!'

'Calm down, dude, your cock's not in her mouth yet. Let's just play it cool. And be nice.'

'A-OK Maverick. I'm your wing man!'

Bloody Hell! Please don't grab a hold of the mic and introduce yourself as Goose. And please God, don't even think about screeching out "You've Lost That Loving Feeling".

'Hi,' smiled Charlie to the girls. 'I'm Phil. And this is my new best friend, Brad. Sorry for the intrusion but since I'm only in town for a couple of days I didn't want to waste an opportunity to acquaint myself with the local beauties. You guys just finished work?'

The most confident of the three girls took a provocative and drawn-out sip of her Grey Goose before speaking. 'Yeh, Mia's a senator's aide, Penny's in PR and I, Grace by the way, work at the Smithsonian. And you guys?'

'Oh, I'm a bit of a Mr. Insipid,' said Charlie. 'I'm in Real Estate. But Brad here works …yeh Brad, where do you work?'

119

'Oh …oh …I work in investments. Travel the world. Big money deals.'

'Please excuse my associate's vulgarity,' expressed a contrite Charlie. 'I'm afraid he doesn't get the meaning of crass. Anyway, Grace, you say you work at the Smithsonian. Believe it or not, I majored in Art History. Anything worth a visit at the moment?'

'There's always something to see at The Smithsonian,' flirted Grace with a beaming smile. 'Actually, there's a new exhibition on the First Nations of America -Native Americans or Indians to those not familiar with the term-, there's one on the tribes of Southern Russia and there's also a special retrospective on Scotland.'

'Wow,' exclaimed Brad, jumping into the conversation. 'My boss was just telling me about Scotland today. Interesting place. In fact, I was over just over there last week. Heading back on Wednesday. Weather sucks though.'

Charlie couldn't believe his luck. Not only the possibility of a lumber but now this.

Need to get on the phone quickly to Dixie. Bonus points for Charlie.

'Oh really?' enquired Grace, 'Anything exciting to look forward to?'

'Can't really say, I'm afraid,' said Brad, self importance oozing from his pores. 'We've a multi-billion dollar deal going through at the moment and I need to make sure our men over there are onside.'

'Sounds all very secretive,' mocked Grace.

Charlie didn't want Zimmerman feeling uncomfortable and quickly stepped in, 'Anyway, who's for another?'

Politeness reigned for a little while before they opened a tab and ordered another round of drinks. Preparing for a night of flirting and fun, Charlie would have no problem bedding one, or maybe two, of the girls. In contrast, Zimmerman didn't have the same inner-confidence. He was just praying the cast-off would be generously drunk enough to sleep with him. Nevertheless, he was anything but uncomfortable; he was loving it.

8

ravage the duplicitous bitterness
with a wee bit of porn and subterfuge

Monday 16th June

2.46 pm – Strathclyde Police HQ - Glasgow

DCI Paul Riley sat waiting in the office of his boss, Deputy Chief Constable Michael Hastie, having just received a text from him informing Paul that he would be another twenty minutes. Paul was relieved. His weekend had been one of deep contemplation. A couple of old issues had been bothering him.

Paul had been a loyal supporter of the DCC since his early days on the force and, in most part, it had been a good relationship. Hastie had encouraged Paul from when they first met, which to Paul had always been a wee bit disconcerting especially when he considered the humiliation delved out by Hastie to some of the other recruits. What's more, Hastie had been generous to Paul; watching him progress and, after Paul had shown promise, encouraging him to vary his roles. He had even been instrumental in getting Paul a sojourn with the highly respected SOCA, the Serious Organised Crime Agency, where Paul had excelled in bringing down some heavy hitters in the people-smuggling and money-laundering trades.

However, as much as he had gained some valuable experience in Scottish and International crime, and embarked on a rise up the career ladder, Paul had to take a back seat as Hastie's skills, both in catching the bad guys and in police politicking, catapulted his mentor even further up the chain, eventually leading him to the position of Scotland's top policeman. And that could only be good news for Paul. Sure, there were Chief Constables with greater powers than Hastie but these roles, nowadays, were merely ceremonial, and the real job of catching the baddies was headed up by the imperious Hastie; and in Glasgow, there were a lot of real bad bastards.

Glasgow cops danced close to the edge. It was a tough job. But whereas Paul's flirting with the legalities of his powers had been shorn out of necessity, Hastie's was not. He was just one nasty fucker. Renowned for his violent streak, Hastie was a ruthless operator who revelled in smashing skulls, drowning the occasional waster and shooting a few hard men at point blank range. Believe it, Hastie was a killer with the law on his side. What's more, it had surprised Paul that he himself had been persuaded by Hastie to become his right hand man. Not because he didn't fancy bearing witness to an evil deed or two but rather he had never been able to really trust Hastie. At first, Paul assumed this lack of faith could be attributed to the rumours of Hastie being a lapsed member of the Lodge -Orange variety- which, when translated into Scottish, meant he didn't like Catholics. Fortunately, Hastie hadn't revealed any incriminating evidence whatsoever that would have deemed him a disciple of the gay King Billy and his well-hung white steed. But times were changing, the old school prejudice not washing with the politicians any more and maybe that, thought Paul, was why the DCC had been so supportive. It certainly wouldn't have impressed the politicians if the top cop had a partial dislike for the Tims. However, when Paul analysed the relationship, he concluded that it might just be down to his own personal cynicism; just one of those things he tended to ponder over for too long. Anyway, he didn't have to like his boss. Nonetheless, Paul had been loyal and respected the job Hastie was doing. He was successful and Paul wanted some of that. And to be a successful policeman in Glasgow meant only one thing: you were one of the best. A metropolitan area of over two million people from all corners of the globe ensured that. There were drug lords preying on the deprived, Arms dealers selling to the protection mobsters and then there were the paramilitaries. Some old and almost forgotten like the IRA and UDA, and some who were new and infinitely more dangerous than any who had come before.

The constant changing of the international landscape had always been good for Scotland with several strains of immigrant having decided over the years that Scotland was the place for them. However, it soon became apparent that an extremely small section of the most recent immigrant cultures had brought with them not only a strange collection of stomach-churning criminal methods but also a very different ethos when it came to breaking the law. In fact, Paul concluded that some of those he dealt with recently had a much differing opinion than he on what the law actually stood for, if they believed it stood for anything at all. Soon Paul began to realise that policemen and policewomen were just a hindrance in some mobster's attempt to smuggle narcotics or a fundamentalist's insistence that he should obey, by setting fire to an airport and himself, his indoctrinated religious convictions. To Paul, and billions of others, religion meant peace and love but to a tiny few, it meant carnage. Nowadays, Paul and his fellow officers were now under some scary fucking pressure from this new breed of psycho with a jeep to crash; because not from poverty and religious egalitarianism did these people come but from a doctrine whose sense of destruction included all-in-one body bombs and quick-fire euthanasia, and to Paul that was a much more frightening prospect than anything the IRA or UDA had ever achieved.

Paul was thankful Scotland had escaped the terrors the UDA inflicted on Ireland and the IRA inflicted on both England and Ireland for no other reason, he believed, than the IRA and UDA thought their people had something in common with the Scots. Aye, right! The ancient celtic passion was there as were some ethnic similarities and traditions but fortunately, most people in Scotland seemed a wee bit more inclined to open-minded debate than planting devices that provided innocent people with the Hunter S. Thomson funeral treatment. What's more, the lack of the odd car bomb in places like Larkhall and

Castlemilk could also be attributed to the not so insignificant reason that one in nine Scots living in Scotland had an Irish heritage. Some were Protestant, like Hastie, but most were Catholic, like Paul, which in his earlier life wasn't exactly the best of social demographic when deciding on a career with the Police. However, Paul wasn't you typical Taig.

Paul's family had never bought into the plastic paddy mentality, immigrating to Scotland after his dad had seen enough of the social and moral destruction of last century's Ireland by the religious neo-con, Eamonn De Valera. After listening to his dad on walks through the park and late night discussions in the living room, Paul could never comprehend the wonderful old Ireland the minority still sang about. He had grown up in school with these chanters and played football with them, even going to Parkhead with the glorious green brigade. However, unlike some of the embittered few he knew, he had stopped short of refusing to go to Hampden to watch Scotland play. That was just too much. Okay, so the SFA hadn't exactly been accommodating but that hadn't prevented the parochialites from becoming as bigoted and evil as their foe. Moreover, as he matured, Paul could never quite come to terms with why they despised Scotland so much. Misguided and ignorant, there were even some of his kind who were more than willing to dip into their pockets and hand over their hard earned cash to the terrorist administration department passing round the explosives begging bowl in their pubs and clubs. They would get pished, sing a few Wolfe Tones' songs, in abject ignorance that Wolfe Tone himself was a Prod, and take great delight in learning of another poor unfortunate kid being liberated from a lifetime's use of her limbs by the Semtex they had chipped-in to buy. Furthermore, as Paul became distant from his community, integrating with the city at large, he began to pity them, realising that a relentless fascination with Ireland was not the answer. With his father and his family having been afforded the opportunity for a new beginning, it had been time to move on.

Paul's dad had been a bright man of insightful thought who cared about the future. He had persevered and overcome the bigotry, especially in some of the factories and shipyards whose prejudicial take on employment strategy had been influenced by a small band of wankers -descended from the repatriated Ulster Scots- who gloried in an extension of their Northern Irish bigotry and hatred of Irish Catholics in the west of Scotland. It was an inbred way of life for them: at their work, in their clubs, and in their churches.

"*What's your name and what school did you go to?*"

"*Riley. Sacred Heart.*"

"*Fuck off. There's no job for you here, pal. Ever!*"

Paul's dad, however, had always been quick to stress that prejudice could be reciprocal, often telling Paul of the Protestant workers in up in Coatbridge who had been refused jobs for the very reason they didn't kick with the left foot. It was a tragic… inexcusable …and vile take on community. To his dad, there was only one option and one way out of the slum: to defeat the hatred. And he did so by treating every man as an equal and by repeating over and over and over again that, "*We're all Jock Thamson's bairns.*" Moreover, having learned much from his dad, Paul was more than conscious of the wicked people found in all facets of life -he was a cop after all- and just because someone came from the same country or worshipped at the same church as he did, it didn't mean they were better than someone who did not. That was bigotry at its core. Nevertheless, he often reflected on the passage of those hundreds of thousands of Irish immigrants who had migrated to Scotland in the nineteenth and twentieth centuries, reminding himself of the conditions they had endured: the poverty, the hardship, the dirt and the vanquishing protests of the old Kirk of Scotland. He was more than sensitive to their suffering, sympathising with how they would miss their home and how they might have shed a tear when leaving. However, to live out their lives, twenty-four/seven, in a habitual fantasy of vicarious longing was self-defeating. Moreover, they rarely wanted to acknowledge that there had been others who also experienced great sorrow. Like the poor Highland Gaels who had been forced to migrate to the city after surviving horrendous famine and intolerable eviction from their burning homes; or the destitute Jews from Eastern Europe who ended up on these shores with nothing more than a suitcase and an education; or the political refugees from across the world who escaped disease and genocide by fleeing to Scotland? And yet, these many different tribes rarely felt self-pity -they never had the time- delighted were they at being given a second chance and more importantly, still alive! They had found their land of the free and embraced its very being. Sure, there had been minor conflicts on their arrival but they had managed to overcome the hurting through hard work. They had grasped their opportunity and rather than wallow in their own bitterness, had survived and flourished.

Nevertheless, a small number of his like were different. With the support of certain influential organisations, they had become advocates for a perverse agenda that ostensibly bound Irishness and Catholicism as a mutually exclusive entity in Scotland, consequently empowering them to engender their own brand of suffering or, as Philip Roth had once discussed, *"Irish Pity"*. Of course, they had imported their goodness of music and song, and of strong community, which blended warmly with Scotland's rich cultural and musical heritage, but also the rampant badness of an inbred psychosis of being hard done by and of feeling little love for the country that had given them a second chance. Moreover, this had gone a long way in creating a small but powerful lobby, which in its divisive desire to promote and engender its own insularities, had created separate schools, separate churches and separate fucking communities. It had been an almighty mistake, thought Paul; an erroneous ideology meant to protect their own when all it accomplished was a heightened mistrust within the indigenous population. They had refused to acknowledge the consequence of their isolationist empowerment strategy and in choosing to ignore the troubles of their recent ancestors had held Ireland up as some kind of ethnic and cultural Neverland. Paul laughed. Had they never read the inspirational Irish writers such as Wilde and Beckett and Joyce? Apart from the institutionalised bouts of blinkered protectionism and the sometimes jingoistic and unacceptable tolerance of their bigoted

126

and corruptible own, especially the country's current ruling political party and the Church, these people had little in common with the Ireland of today. There was a new generation over there willing to move on who were not only struggling against the property developers, they were also fighting the old guard to make amends for De Valera and the country's recent horrendous theocratic past. In most part, they had rid themselves of the engrained, embittered hatreds. They had confidence and were ready for the future. There was little to mope about!

That was when Paul really felt his dad's pain. He had been given one of life's raw deals but had stayed in the game long enough to overcome the loss and build a better life for his family. He had suffered; rejecting both the unthinkable abuse inflicted upon him by the Christian Brothers in Ireland and the bigotry in Scotland. A survivor, his dad saw through the evil and racism, often telling Paul, "That all the people in Scotland ask is that when others come to live here, they need to know they're in Scotland. Take it all, the good and the bad, and in most cases as you'll realise, it is more than good!" Paul smiled. This open-mindedness, he reasoned was why he had became life long friends with Johnnie Di Marco, as well, of course, as sharing a uniquely sardonic and twisted sense of humour throughout their teenage years.

Paul often thought about his best friend Johnnie and his family history, and of the thousands of Italians who had arrived in Scotland over the last hundred years. They had also suffered torment from the mouths and the hands and the feet of the exceptionally ignorant few. Seeing their houses burned and shop windows broken, they had even been ostracised because of said stupid bastards' misguided interpretation of their relationship with Mussolini. Nevertheless, in embracing Scotland, the Italian-Scots had flourished through toil and talent. They were now distinctly Scottish. Naturally, there were still loyalties to Italy but in reality, the community was an intrinsic part of Scottish life. Furthermore, Paul was heartened that many of Scotland's most famous sons and daughters were of Italian extraction. Like a few of his own kind, they were actors, lawyers, restauranteurs, musicians, singers, politicians, satirists, entrepreneurs, writers, footballers, rugby players, Indy Car drivers and much, much more. My God, thought Paul, even Scotland's Lord Advocate had Italian blood. And she was a woman.

Johnnie, like Paul, had a sense of worth about being a Scot. He loved the country, cherishing its contradictory nature, respecting its politics and treasuring its approach to education and the arts. What's more, this wasn't some "hopes and dreams" opinion, either. Having travelled and lived in other parts of the world, Johnnie knew that Scotland, with all its petty problems, was a fine place to come from and a fine place to live. The two of them had also become lifetime members of the growing band of younger Scots who, after witnessing the mentalists inflict bloodshed and carnage on the world, understood Scotland to be a well-thought of and respected land. Political corruption was minimal in comparison, the infrastructure was excellent and as much as the Scots could be opinionated and dogmatic, freedom of speech and common sense always prevailed. Regrettably however, and though Scots, as individuals, could be incredibly successful on the world stage, Paul and Johnnie both surmised that the people of Scotland required a collective confidence to re-energise their sense of worth in the nation. It was as if there was an urgent need for the Scots to rid themselves of their cultural pessimism before determining as a collective entity how they saw them-selves in the world. Moreover, to achieve this, and without sacrificing the inherent nature of the Scots to expect the best, there had to be a cultural shift towards being proud of the positive things happening in, and to, the country.

However, this didn't prevent the pair of them from taking the piss out of Scotland and its trivial insularities, flippantly e-mailing each other jokes about Weegies, Teuchters and the fucking city council. This dryness of humour was what made them feel Scottish. They reckoned it was inside every Scot: the irrational rationality. There was a conceit in their intelligence and an abrasiveness in their contempt but most of all there was an undying loyalty to what they believed made Scotland. They appreciated the constantly evolving nature of the place. It was their home. It was who they were. It was why, when glancing up at the Saltire floating in the wind, they saw just not the blue and white but much more. It was their emblem of enlightenment, of humanity and of humility. It was their Scotland.

Their aspirations, however, did not begin and end with a flag. For far too long they sensed a nation happy in itself to consistently knock and decry, and ridicule their own land. It angered them and on occasion when they had been on the batter, felt no shame in interrupting many a pub conversation between those numpty ne'er-do-wells who verbally abused their home. It was easy and cruel but it was fun, especially when said numpties had never set foot outside the city of Glasgow, let alone witness the majesty of the country. Johnnie recognised that the world had thousands of interesting and magnificent places and a whole host of kind-hearted people but what he couldn't understand in others, when they stood on their hustings in those small-minded pubs or clubs, moaning of "getting the fuck out of this country", was how they refused to acknowledge that other countries had bigger, uglier and more dangerous ghettos, far more corruptible politicians, and so-called democratic legislations who continued to make a mockery of human rights.

"You think the States is cool? The land of the free? Aye, right! More the land of the shut the fuck up or I'll lock you up in a fucking detention centre."

"France? Open-mined, tolerant, no racial issues? Aye, right! Try making it round a block in Northern Paris without feeling the burning sensation of Couscous's nine-inch blade!"

Nevertheless, Paul knew there were still a small number of psychos from all across Scotland who harboured their own brand of depression-filled hate: cleaners who detested the misogynistic CEO, employees who loathed the Human Resource Manager, punters who despised the Bookie and policemen who abhorred the NEDS. Paul laughed. Darts player and pool player. Gingers and Blondes. Wee car driver and big car driver. Big knob eejit and wee knob intellectual. The completely blind and the insufferable visually-impaired. The big-titted nymph and the wee-chested primary school teacher. Ramblers?! Scoffing at the prejudices, his own and those of others, Paul even remembered his primary school days when the local priest had warned the pair of them that they weren't to speak to the Prods on the way to lunch at the shared dining centre. Separate lives and opposing ideas. Kids who lived alongside each other but grew up without ever getting to know their neighbours. Same age, same address, different world. It was a madness that saw gangs formed to defend rights and swords drawn in underground car parks.

The insanity of it all!

Fortunately, in Johnnie, Paul had a friend whose dislike of the human race included only arseholes. Johnnie knew where he came from and knew where he was going. That was why Paul had grown to love him. Having first gone through twelve years of school together, Paul had followed Johnnie to the University of Glasgow. Not that he had any notion, of course, of partaking in the jabbing of Johnnie's jobbies. No, Johnnie was his friend, his best friend. And why the fuck not? After all, they had been there for each other for as long as he could remember and that was more than enough, wasn't it? What's more, no one would dare now criticise the unbreakable partnership; Paul being a successful policeman and Johnnie ...well ...the wanker was a fucking film star!

Fortunate to have families who used humour to vanquish the hateful stupidity, the two of them enjoyed their younger years for no other reason than laughing at the lunacy in the existence created for them. It was one of the great Scottish traits. Well, it was for those with a normal disposition. As kids, their religion and heritage meant little. They had their whole lives to think about. They had wonderful aspirations.

When they were younger, it had always been about how clever they were, or in the words of a few high school teachers, being a right wee pair of smart arses. They enjoyed being the rebels, albeit with a cause, and would have no fear in winding-up the learned ones. They had snogged each other in front of a nun during Classical Studies, before pleading, as they declared, homage to the Ancient Greeks. They even turned out for PE in the full Rangers kit: heavy blue cotton tops, ball-chaffing white nylon shorts, the famous black socks with red trim and, a la Derek Johnstone, huge black side-burns painted on their cheeks. Not the cleverest idea they ever conceived especially at a Catholic School in Glasgow but they enjoyed the attention that wee bit more than the black-eyes and bruised shins. However, it had been their opus -of seeking revenge on their French master who had inadvertently let slip in class one day that he wasn't an admirer of the Jewish Race- that eventually rendered their wee feet too big for their jimmies. Breaking into the spare science lab on the Language floor, the fearless pair had set to work linking all the Bunsen burner tubes together in one long tube before sliding it under the door of the adjoining and owner-occupied French lab. They ran. But not before jamming the door shut and turning on the gas ...and then being nabbed by the Jannie!

As a result of their consistent mischief making, they were due up in front of the headmaster, Father O'Rourke. It was to be the little bastards' comeuppance. They were sure their expulsion was on the agenda. Their parents had been asked to accompany them to the meeting and it hadn't been the best of times. It was all the fault of the French master they claimed, but Paul's mother was humiliated and Johnnie's father, furious. Excuses weren't listened to. *"They were to take their punishment and learn their lesson."* Their future was looking bleak, unless ...unless Paul's imaginatively brilliant but fucked-up modus of punishment avoidance and plight extrication succeeded.

Knowing that Father O'Rourke loved to referee the inter-house football matches, the two wee smart arses planned their bid for emancipation. Hiding beneath the Heedie's window as Father O'Rourke changed into his old leather boots and baggy black shorts, the boys listened and waited for the door to close and lock to be turned. Standing-up, Johnnie clasped his hands together. The window was a good six feet above the ground. Paul, as the lighter of the two, then placed his left foot into Johnnie's hands, pulling himself up to the window sill. Perched precariously on his honchos with his back to the window, Paul strained with his fingertips to lift the window-sash a few inches before wheeling round on his plimsoles, grabbing the window with both hands and pulling the window open a little more. There was just enough room for Paul to crawl through. He was in. Whispering for Johnnie to throw it up, Paul grabbed the wicked weapon of temptation with both hands before disappearing into the office. He was still giggling as he scrambled out of the window and back to the safety of terra-cinderdust. Resting against the wall, they burst into hysterics.

After dawdling out to the playing fields to watch the match, they returned to the window an hour and half later. As they waited, they hoped the Heedie wouldn't notice the small gap, between the window and sill, left open during the set-up. A few minutes later, they heard the keys jangle and the door open. The Heedie had returned. The priest sat down and threw off his boots, his breathing still hard from the exertion of the match. A few minutes later, the chair slid back as he stood to take off his shorts. Outside and down below, the boys held their noses as the snotters exploded from their noggins. And still they waited.

Inside the Heedie's den of officialdom, Father O'Rourke had changed back into his collar and cassock. He was sitting up at his desk and organising his syllabus reviews when he caught a glimpse of the September issue of Fornica Magazine in his file tray. Pulling it out while reaching for his specs, he examined the front cover. He focussed. Two naked brunettes bent over a pool table with cues in hand and nipples resting on four balls. After a quick gander and shudder, he swiped it off the desk, locking it in the drawer with the rest of his collection. He shook his head, wondering if it had been lying there all day. His arse was itching now. Scratching at his plooks and sticky dangleberries, he was distracted between screes and fault-lines and what might be revealed by the auspicious glossy. Choosing the former, he tried to concentrate but the earth's crust was farthest from his mind. Standing up sharply, he walked over the door and turned the key, quickly returning to his chair and unlocking the porn drawer. Out came Miss and Missy Fornica.

As Father O'Rourke opened the first page, he pulled his seat forward with his ankles until his legs, and cock, were under the desk. He flicked a page, then another, pressing his aging bulbous onion hard against the underside of the desk. Throbbing and pumping, he resisted its upsurge by firmly pressing it down with the ball of his right hand. For once, he ignored the readers' letters, perusing eight more pages until he found what he was looking for.

'Holy Mother of Jesus!'

The two brunettes were now employing the pool cues for anything other than playing billiards. On one page, a tongue was flicking a moist and eighties manicured clit while on the other, a cue was being rammed into a cute and peachy little arse. The Heedie grabbed his sweet potato.

'Oh, aye!'

Leaning back in his chair, the Priest lifted his cassock up and grabbed it between his teeth. Down below, his baby carrot was screaming for freedom behind his pish-stained Ys. In one swift move, he reached down with his fore and middle finger and pulled at the damp cotton. Light had been given to his elasticated half-a-parsnip. Strangling the vegetable with his right hand, he slid the mag closer to the edge of the desk with his left.

'Oh, aye! Oh, aye!'

He was lost in the moment, chugging away in peaceful ecstasy. His face reddened as his comb-over dangled in his eyes. He wanted to cum. His heart thumped faster.

'Oh, fuckin', aye!'

He was moaning, he was groaning. As the tickling sensation worked its way up his length, he stood up and pulled harder. He gasped, temporarily losing his vision as his load dribbled over the mag. He let out a breath. He smiled. And so did Paul and Johnnie! Seeing shapes in the window, Father O'Rourke turned sharply. He couldn't make them out. And then he was dazed by a flash. He was still holding his tadger in his hand as the cum continued to seep out from his mushroom. He looked up and reality struck. There stood Paul and Johnnie, balancing on the edge of the window sill and grinning from ear to ear. Johnnie was waving the camera in the air.

Johnnie and Paul were never expelled.

As Paul sat waiting for his boss, he considered the world's obsession with fundamental rights and protecting ways of life. It had all been so easy before. If somebody attacks, you defend. If somebody tries to lamp one on you, you fucking duck. Simple as. Now, however, the fundamentalists, wherever they were in the world, whether that was in North America, Britain or the Middle East, had become experts in indoctrination. It wasn't an acceptable strategy to just "defend" anymore; you had to take the battle to the enemy. It was always somebody else's fault or in the words of many an arsehole he had arrested, "It wasnae me!" Furthermore, recent times had sadly brought Blair and his WMDs, Bush and his stupidity, the IRA and UDA, Islam and Christianity and several cases of "my boys are bang on, and if you don't agree with me, and them, then I'll just have to blow you the fuck up! You, your children, your wife, you car, your house, your town, your country!" Simple as.

Paul, though, was not for believing in that nonsense. Disparate peoples could live together. All that was needed was something positive in which to believe, something to grab hold and run with. He also wondered if there would ever be someone strong enough to unify the world. He thought about Barrack Obama. He was a possibility but was America ready for a black president? More importantly, was the CIA and Washington ready for a "liberal" black President?

Paul had always thought Scotland, apart from the lunatic fringes of the Tims and Prods, was a fine example of hundreds of different tribes living together in peace -they had done for centuries, after all- however, with Scotland's association with Westminster, these good old days seemed to be drifting away. It also didn't matter that most people in Scotland didn't agree with London's foreign policy or with England's "broken society" theory because the faith his dad had taught him had already been stripped bare from within polarised communities down south and was now spread-ing north. What's more, this new strain of bomb-making fundamentalist certainly scared the shit out of Paul because these people weren't just content to sit and have a reasoned debate or even the odd fist fight over their beliefs;

these guys were prepared to strap a bomb to their torso, fill a car full of explosive gas and drive into an international airport terminal on a Saturday afternoon. 'Imagine that,' laughed Paul to himself. He even thought of an old bloke lying on the operating table, receiving a procedure on his piles, as the doctor poked and pinched and rubbed cream on his starfish while simultaneously deciding that gas canisters filled with nails and connected to a detonator and then mobile phone was most definitely the best way to murder a few hundred tourists. Who the fuck would have thought that then? Furthermore, now Dixie had been shot at, he knew things must be really fucking bad if the Yanks were now having a pop at a Scot in Scotland. And even worse if those guys in the Range Rover happened to be Yanks working for the Brits.

'So Pauly boy,' asked DCC Hastie as he marched into the office, 'what the fuck happened on Friday afternoon? After you dropped Dixie off, I called her wanting to make sure her protection team was on the ball and I'll tell you, the poor thing was badly shaken up, which is not surprising considering some idiot had just tried to blow her head off!'

'Well, after I called you on Friday, I sat down with Dixie and asked her if she knew of any reason why someone would want to have a pop at her. Obviously, she had no idea but she did tell me of the story she is working on regarding the usual "not so secret" shenanigans of the Hutchinson Group. However, all that is just standard practice for any political editor: an interview here, a photograph there, the odd Arms deal. Nothing special and certainly nothing to warrant this sort of response.'

'Do you think the Hutchinson Group was involved?'

'I don't think so. These guys have politicians and media groups from all over the world on their side, so in the long run they don't really care who finds out about what they do. Plus, what they get up to is generally within the law and as long as they can persuade their clients to sign on the dotted line without too much political turmoil and retaliation then they're as happy as jaikie with a bottle of Monkjuice. The general public might not like their MO but Hutchinson doesn't give a damn. In their eyes, if somebody has to do it then why not them. As long as the politicians and their fixers remain in the background, then it's a sunny day, everyday, on Pennsylvania Avenue.'

'And who did she meet at Loch Fyne?'

'No one of any note. Just an old friends' get-together. Elliot Walker, an old university buddy of ours. He and his wife were on their way up to see his folks in Fort William.'

'Has there been any trace of the Range Rover?'

'None at all. We had teams out on the Helensburgh road and the Dumbarton road, as well as the Stirling and Aberfoyle roads and the Loch Lomond road back north, but nothing, not a single sighting.'

'Any witnesses?'

'No one with any real information. A few drivers saw the Range Rover but it was going too damn fast for anyone to see the plates.'

'And why was there only one squad car on the scene? Why didn't you send two?'

'There was only one in the vicinity. The other two from Balloch were at a crash near Drymen and we couldn't wait. My priority was Dixie's safety.'

'Yes, good job. I would have done the same. Any news from Ballistics?'

'Aye, but we've only found two shells: one from the road and the other from Dixie's car. The guys are working on them now but early tests are telling us that they're either German or American.'

'Christ, that's just great, isn't it? Considering these two countries have sown up the hand gun industry, a needle and fucking haystack come to mind.'

'I know. It doesn't leave us with much, does it?

'No it bloody well doesn't, Paul!'

The two policemen sat in hardened silence, processing their thoughts.

'You know she had that wanker Charlie Norton dressed up as a golfer the other day at Gleneagles?' declared a direct and blunt Hastie.

'Yep, but he's always up to something. The guy thinks he's Lee Miller, albeit with a rampant cock. The great white hope of Scottish photographic art, eh?'

'I know. Does he really think we're that stupid?'

'Naw, I just think he enjoys the whole sleaze thing. Remember the time he got dressed up as a minister, trying to take a picture of that Right Reverend Mackenzie chappie and his bit on the side getting down and dirty at the back of the vestry. Bloody hell, have you ever seen a man of the cloth wearing flip flops, board shorts and a Snow Patrol t-shirt underneath his tunic? He may as well have walked straight in, caught the poor woman consecrating the Most Blessed Boabie and asked them to "just hold it there folks, I'm from Fornica Magazine!"'

'But the fact of the matter,' stated Hastie 'is that Dixie ordered Charlie Norton to go to Gleneagles and snoop around. We all knew Zimmerman was there so why all this hush-hush nonsense?'

'Maybe she knows something we don't. And maybe Zimmerman at Gleneagles is just part of the story. I reckon she has already built up a case file and is close to publication.'

'And have you any ideas what her piece might entail?'

'None at all but with Zimmerman and Hutchinson being American, it's not as if they pose an inherent danger to the grand scheme of things. In fact, we're normally in cahoots with the Yanks in just about everything we do. No, it's a strange one because it's not as if she'll come up with anything that we've not heard before, not unless she knows something we don't.'

'Ah Dixie, what do you know that you're not telling us?' asked the DCC out loud.

'Listen Boss, Dixie's intentions have always been commendable. A bit radical sometimes but worthy none the less. Why, do you think we should be worried?'

'Not really. But you mentioned the word radical and that word scares any policeman worth his silver buttons.'

'Come on, Sir. It's Dixie we're talking about here, not someone from the lunatic fringe.'

'I know, Paul but what we don't know could come back

and take a shark's bite out of our arse cheeks.'

'Jesus, Mike. The two of you had dinner only last week!'

'Listen, Riley. With something as serious as this, it's no use taking chances.'

'Bloody hell, Sir, she's been my friend since university and I would hate to see her or her job being compromised!'

'Riley, we're here to do a job as well by the way, and that is to protect the people. Therefore, if she knows something that could harm the Establishment in any way, then we need to find out what it is. Furthermore, she needs to fucking drop it.'

'I'm sure she'd be delighted to hear you say that when you next meet up for dinner at Fratelli Conti!'

'Don't push it, Paul. This is serious. And in case you've forgotten, this is the very same women who scooped the Loch Fyne meeting; and look at the shit the NSD threw at us for that.'

Paul decided he would let his protest drop. As long as Dixie's safety was ensured, that was all that mattered. However, he wasn't too sure about his boss's angle. Or his agenda. 'Sorry Sir. Point taken. So, what do you think?'

'I think we just sit back and watch closely. Her safety is paramount but so is the security of the country. Let's just see where she is going with this and then we'll decide.'

'Do you want me to bring her guys in?'

'No can do. They're not the ones breaking any laws. It's those idiots in the Range Rover who are doing that! Let's just make sure she's protected, okay?'

'Yes Sir. Will do.'

Paul left the room not knowing what to think. Regardless that Dixie was a good friend, she was a citizen who had been shot at. Furthermore, as well as questioning the DCC's handling of the situation, he also considered why his boss had inferred that she may have brought the shooting upon herself.

When his door closed, DCC Mike Hastie picked up his phone, dialled a number and waited. 'She knows something but I'm not sure how much. Maybe nothing, maybe everything.' The room was quiet as he listened. 'Okay. See you there.' The phone line went dead.

*

3.13 pm – Mayfair - London

Elliot hadn't slept well on his return from Scotland, which was not surprising considering he had willingly and foolishly agreed to help Dixie out with her wee assignment. Having repeatedly told Kirsten that Dixie had wanted to ask a couple of questions and nothing more, he had awoken in the middle of the night saturated in a stress-induced sweat. Kirsten had even given him the Stare but still he did not relent. Maybe he was cut out for this after all. He also wondered if Dixie should have taken the low road instead of the high road. His trepidation, however, was discriminating, which in turn did not prevent him from being fatalistic. Had he been followed up to Lochaber? Had they been watching his parent's house? Moreover, the inclination for what he was about to partake in came from God knows where because it sure as hell wasn't the most logical lifestyle choice he was making. He thought about Kirsten and their future together and wondered if he was putting it at risk. What a numpty, of course he bloody well was. He also thought about the consequences of someone not trained in the art of corporate espionage planning to record the conversations of one of the world's most powerful men, and he thought about his chances of success. 'Yeh, right,' he grimaced, 'about as much chance as the American Jewish Association asking a Mr. Melvin Gibson to be guest of honour at their annual convention.' Nevertheless, here he stood, outside a small electronic surveillance shop in Mayfair's Brook Street, not only thinking how best to explain why he had the need to buy a small and discreet bugging device but also choking in his own bullshit. He was a lawyer for goodness sake and not only was he dressed like one, he also sounded like one. Elliot shook his head. He was certain of only two things; that he didn't have the look of a cheap PI in to pick up recording equipment for another lurid case of some rage-infested misogynist's mission to discover who was shagging the wife; and neither did he have the expression, or the vocabulary, of a geek-hacker popping in to up-grade his IT capabilities which would allow the tapping of a government security system. *Oh, fuck!* Furthermore, there was no way he was going to announce to the wee man inside that, 'by the way, I was just thinking I'd like to eavesdrop on the chairman of one of the world's biggest companies for no other reason than I think he's a shifty bastard.' Nope, he was going to have to try something just as ridiculous. Heaving a large breath, Elliot opened the door.

'Good afternoon, Sir. How can I help you?'

Elliot wasn't wrong about the wee man. He could have been no taller than five feet and though a bit wobbly on his feet, Elliot sensed immediately he had seen and done it all before. 'Hi,' announced a sheepish and blushing Elliot. 'I was hoping you could help me out on a small matter of family pride.'

'I'll try my best, Sir,' replied the wee man.

'My request is a bit ridiculous and childish, I'm afraid,' struggled Elliot with a slight cough. 'You see, I'm the manager of the local football team and in a couple of weeks we have to play a very important match against the next village.' The wee man was professionally patient with Elliot's failure to convince. Remaining passive and engaged, he broke into a sympathetic smile before allowing the bumbling fool to continue. 'Naturally, I would like to win but unfortunately I'm not that good a coach; in fact, I'm pretty useless. To make matters worse, my father-in-law happens to be the manager of the opposition and he, to put it mildly, likes to gloat. Every bloody week. And it is driving me nuts. Not an admirable response I admit but I really don't think I could survive another twelve months of listening to his more than immodest drivel if his team happens to thrash us again.'

'So what you need Sir, I presume, is something to help you listen in to his tactics?'

'Exactly! I was hoping you would have some sort of device I can stick on his clothes, phone, briefcase or whatever. I know it's not cricket but if you knew my father-in-law then I'm sure you would understand my predicament.'

The wee man sensed that Elliot wasn't telling him the whole truth but what did he care. One look at Elliot was enough to confirm he wasn't exactly a master criminal. 'Ah well, I'm not sure it's legal, Sir, but since it's not industrial sabotage or a perilous and life threatening mission in the company of a certain

140

Mr. Bond then I think I can help you out.'

If only you knew. 'Fantastic, what do you have?'

The wee man pulled out a polished metal tray from under the sales counter, delicately placing it in front of Elliot. On it was an assortment of tiny boxes. 'Wow, they are small, aren't they?' offered a bamboozled Elliot.

'Well, Sir, the general idea is for concealment and not, as the more naïve amongst us would assume, for discovery.'

The wee man lifted two small grey boxes from the tray, his deftness of touch belying his years. Opening one, he slid a transmitter out. It was no wider than a couple of inches. 'This one is a little bit bulky but the quality is very good.' The other transmitter was the size of a shirt button and much easier to conceal. 'However, if you could insert this one into a pen or a mobile phone you'd be extremely safe from detection.'

Elliot could almost hear the old man chuckling at his ignorance and foolhardiness. A couple of seconds passed before the wee man looked up again and smiled. 'But that is easier said than done.' He waited while Elliot cleared his head, which by this point he was in way over. 'What do you think, Sir?'

'I haven't a clue. How do they actually work?'

'What you need is a recording device nearby to receive the transmission. Once you have uploaded its software, it will be able to pick up the signal vibrations, decode them, and then transfer the message to another device such as a laptop or an MP3 player. It uses technology similar to that of a mobile phone. He'll talk, your recording device will pick up the sound and you'll be at the other end listening in.' Observing the confusion in Elliot's eyes, the wee man sighed patiently. 'Just imagine someone has left their phone unlocked inside a pocket. All their moving around causes the call button to be pressed by mistake and it dials your number. You pick up your phone and all you hear is background noise like music playing or people talking. You can shout and scream as loud as you want and they still won't be able to hear you, whereas you, Sir, will be able to hear everything. Very simple but you need to remember to switch the transmitters on and that you are close by. No further than a hundred yards.'

'And do you have this thingy; this decoder and recording device? And remember, not too expensive now.'

'Of course I do, Sir. Do you have a laptop?'

As Elliot walked to the end of his garden, he struggled and fumbled with the two transmitters, a pair of headphones, the recording device and his laptop. The air was still and the smell of freshly cut grass drifted over his fence from his neighbour's garden. He turned to see the walls of his four-bedroom detached glistening in the early evening sun. The house looked well. All he needed now was some kids to make it a real family home.

Kirsten was off riding so he had time to work out which transmitter would be most effective. Walking back inside, he placed the bulkier one, the RFID X400, next to the television and the smaller one, the CSM A9, inside his pen on the coffee table. Closing the door behind him, he jogged to the end of the garden, -a good one hundred and twenty feet away- where he hooked up the USB cable for the recording device, plugged the headset in and began to listen. He had programmed the software for the RFID X400 first and couldn't believe the quality. There he was, over forty yards from the plasma screen, listening to Ken and Deirdre telling Blanche to fuck off. 'Bloody hell!' hissed Elliot. 'Unbelievable!' He then ran the software for the smaller CSM A9, and although the quality wasn't as good as the RFID X400, it was clear enough to hear Ashley whinging on about the price of butcher meat. He said the price of butcher meat!

Elliot downloaded the recordings to his laptop. Again, the quality differed but both were clear enough to make out. Step one completed. Unfortunately, that was the simple part of the exercise. Not only had he still to figure out how he was going to place one of these transmitters anywhere near Sir Alexander Lamont, he still had to find out when and where Lamont was going to meet these people Dixie had told him about.

'Oh Jesus, what in hell's name am I doing?'

9

oxygen required as the mountaintop beckons

Tuesday 17th June

7.27 am – Waverly Station - Edinburgh

Jamie had enjoyed the early morning breeze blowing up Leith Walk and on to Princes Street but now, as he briskly walked through Waverly Station on his way to Holyrood, he was breathing in the choking blend of warm summer air and diesel fumes from the trains. However, the suffocating odour was the least of his concerns; he had important business to deal with today. First, his daily strategic review with Andrew Drummond -the First Minister- and then a hush-hush meeting to administer between Drummond and Peter Buchanan, who was in town, officially at least, to meet with senior members of the Scottish Tory Party.

Full of confidence, Jamie strolled down the Royal Mile towards the Parliament. With the majority of people in Scotland alive to change, he could sense the mood of the nation swinging towards his dream. Nevertheless, his party still had to make sure they could administer affairs with competency, deliver on their manifesto and gain trust from those undecided. The Secession Referendum promised to the people was imminent and although the SNP was gaining in popularity, the team he led still had to remain vigilant as to avoid any dream destroying slip-ups and vote winning opportunities for the Opposition.

The Opposition, or the Scottish Political Establishment as Jamie preferred to call them, were incensed and intent on retribution. Their situation was not one it had planned for, nor come to expect, especially Labour, whose politicians would fight to the political death to ensure the Union, and therefore their jobs, remained in situ. The severity of the situation, however, still hadn't prevented Jamie from having a wee private chuckle and shaking his head at the Opposition jobs-worth's sitting agitated in the Holyrood chamber. They had no idea. They came from a Party whose priorities appeared to rest in ensuring any public amenity built to enhance the feelings of fun and laughter for three-year old kids slowly morphed into monolithic concrete monstrosities of Ukrainian proportions. Sometimes, though, Jamie had to tame his anger when dealing with the Labour Party. Not because they contested policy, for that was to be expected, but rather most of Labour's MSPs and MPs seemed to be in it for themselves. It was as if they were intent on building a career out of peddling poverty and of promoting fear of an independent Scotland while simultaneously blaming anyone bar themselves for the country's woes. Furthermore, if the rumours were to be believed, they had even been so low as to target the Catholic Church, hoping it would discreetly use its influence to spread trepidation among its congregation that an independent Scotland would marginalise Catholicism. It had become so ridiculous that when a former cabinet minister of the Westminster Government had been appointed chairman of a major football club, Jamie had thought it to be all part of a grander plan. Surely not? Then again, it was the football club, Jamie pondered, where a section of its supporters had been missing the point for years such was the ludicrous and ironic contradiction in singing songs support-ing the struggles of a free and republican Ireland while voting for a unionist party in the government of the institution they professed to despise. Mental? Oh yes, but such was the nature of Scotland's Jekyll and Hyde society. Jamie laughed. If it really was as simple as that, then it was a strategy of genius and had bloody well worked for over four generations!

Jamie was thankful he didn't have his own office in the

Parliament. He had freedom to think. And as much as he would often have to chair meetings in the building, he much preferred his discussions take place while strolling beneath the imposing Arthur's Seat and alongside the Queen's official residence in Scotland: Holyrood Palace. This morning, however, he didn't have time for philosophising. After a quick breakfast briefing with the Secretary for Business and Enterprise, he would be jumping into a cab and heading over to Charlotte Square to run over strategy for the Buchanan meeting with the First Minister at his official residence: Bute House.

Jamie was certain that Andrew Drummond had not only begun to reawaken the confidence lying for so long dormant in the people, he had also reinforced that confidence with some hope and some pride, so much of which had been eradicated by a political establishment expert in draining a nation's sense of itself. He had become a credible leader of the nation and behaved as such and unlike the many Scottish Secretaries who had preceded the new Parliament, Drummond's loyalties were to Scotland. Furthermore, by either an extraordinary stroke of good fortune or astonishing genius, Drummond now found himself in a position, which no leader of Scotland had been in for over 700 years.

Thanks to Jamie and his team, the Party was holding a considerable lead in the Scottish polls whereas in England, the Opposition was preparing itself for not only a landslide victory in the next UK election but also for Government. However, not even the ever eternal optimist Peter Buchanan could foresee a quick return of any consequential political influence for his Party in Scotland. With Buchanan's Party in control at Westminster, it would give Drummond the opportunity to go to the Referendum and the people of Scotland with guarded and rational optimism. And everyone knew why. Such would be the dearth of Tory MPs north of the border that the Scottish people just wouldn't accept another Tory Prime Minister with no mandate to rule Scotland. Furthermore, even if the Referendum did fail in its first attempt, Drummond would have long since secured enormous financial benefits from Westminster -to keep the "rebellious" Scots silent-that the voters in England would be beside themselves with rage. It was as if Drummond held all the aces and was the greatest counter of cards in the world. Jamie laughed. If Drummond had been in a Vegas casino, two big brutes going by the names of Felix and Billy-Bob would have quickly escorted him out the door. He couldn't lose. Win the Referendum and the Union would be finished. Narrowly lose out and Drummond, having secured incomparable advantages for Scotland, would still be a hero in the eyes of the voters. Furthermore, with those benefits on the table, the basic premise for a fair and equal United Kingdom of Great Britain and Northern Ireland would be over. Not because Scotland would have recouped the revenues stolen from it but rather the people in Westminster, without the North Sea, would no longer be in control, and that was something the British Establishment could just not contemplate. Whatsoever.

Drummond would often smile ruefully to himself while explaining to Jamie the hypocrisy of it all. Maddeningly, many commentators in England would consistently harp on about the "Sponging Scots" while simultaneously supporting the very organisations and institutions who were desperately trying to keep the country within the Union. If Scotland was a financial burden on the United Kingdom, asked Drummond, then why not let Scotland secede. Surely, it was the logical solution. But no, that just wouldn't be possible. Not with Scotland's geographical position as the gateway to the North Atlantic and not with billions of dollars worth of natural resources remaining deep in Scottish waters. And certainly not with lots more of the black stuff still to be discovered. Oh no! That would be unthinkable.

Drummond and his team had been working the world since coming to office, and in a significant move which saw him change the official name of the administration from the Scottish Executive to the Scottish Government, his cabinet ministers now held positions of Secretaries of State rather than non-descript titles not fit for a council leader let alone a senior government official. Moreover, his civil servants had worked the corridors of Brussels and Washington to a point where Scotland's secession was no longer a discussion topic but a fast approaching reality.

Jamie smiled. His strategies may have been working but they were also pissing some extremely powerful people off. As well as having an uncanny knack to aggravate a raw nerve or two, Andrew Drummond was, in the words of many a Westminster MP, a fucking arsehole. Nevertheless, this hadn't prevented his political foes from acknowledging that he was a brilliant negotiator who had managed to both out-manoeuvre even the best of politicians and woo the best of the business world. The Prime Minister could barely lift the phone to speak to him and the leader of the Labour Party in Scotland had been humiliated by him. Conversely, several leading businessmen had pledged support to him. In fact, the guy was so good that in his first few months of Office, he had already held several meetings with the Queen.

Jamie was never party to these meetings between the Queen and Andrew Drummond, tradition dictating that all such discussions remain in the private diaries of both individuals. Moreover, it was no secret that Scotland was her spiritual home, she loving the country so much, thought Jamie, it would come as no surprise to him that if she were ever to abdicate, she would probably be on the next train out of King's Cross in the morning, assuming, of course, her advisors were under lock and key in the Tower of London. However, in being republican by nature, the very thought of a Head of State being appointed by birthright appalled Jamie, not at all sitting favourably with his political conscience. As well as believing it was unfair, undemocratic and contradictory to all his underlying political principles, it also annoyed the shit out of him that many political commentators, in overlooking even the most basic of historical facts, couldn't even get her title correct. The Queen was Scotland's Head of State, just as she was in Wales, Northern Ireland and England but in Scotland, however, she was Queen Elizabeth I and not the "II" as generally thought, the more widely well-known Elizabeth I being the last ruling monarch of England before the union of the crowns in 1603.

Overtime, though, Jamie had grown to like the Queen, even coming to admire her, she having shown fortitude and resilience in rejecting the maniacal and self-deluding mass hysteria of the Paris underpass affair while valiantly with-standing the pressures of modern day media demands. She seemed to be a genuine and decent soul who had been good for Scotland, and if she was prepared to make time for Andrew Drummond then it was as helpful an endorsement the Party had ever received for its political aspirations. Furthermore, as much as the Monarchy was apolitical, in public at least, and as much as the thought of a constitutional monarchy abhorred Jamie, the fact that the Queen was Scotland's Head of State was infinitely a more workable solution than having a rogue political President, especially one as off the wall and easily influenced as an oil gimp from Texas.

*

8.31 am -- Bute House - Edinburgh
He stood alone in the Georgian magnificence of Bute House. He was at his desk and gazing over the beautiful New Town of Edinburgh and out across the wide expanse of the Firth of Forth. Without turning round, Andrew Drummond spoke. 'Isn't it just breathtaking, Jamie?'

'What is?'

'That,' said Drummond, pointing at the view. 'I don't ever want to tire of looking out this window.'

'Well, just along as long as we make sure these bastards don't bankrupt us, then I'm sure you never will.'

'Aye, Jamie, I can imagine there's nothing as frightening as the Westminster Establishment bearing its teeth. And if it's supported by a few unenlightened Scottish souls such as the Prime Minister then it will make our job just that wee bit more challenging.' Jamie nodded solemnly, and as if his boss could read his mind, Drummond spoke again. 'Listen Jamie, we may have a mandate, we may have a large amount of public support and we may have all the legitimacy in the world but when you're dealing with an institution as powerful as Westminster, we will have to be prepared for everything they throw at us: both of the legal and illegal varieties. People will suffer Jamie. Innocent people. And for what? To protect the jobs of a few Scottish MPs and the economy of London and South-East England, that's what. We have to grow up, Jamie. We have to go on our own. We have to put on our long troosers and be big boys once again.'

Jamie was impressed by Drummond's passion but also his pragmatism. Drummond knew that for all his publicly positive overtones, there was a political war to be fought. And if the opposition was going to get down and dirty then so was he. Drummond also believed in the Scottish people more so than any other modern day politician. In trusting the people to think for themselves, he was hoping they would vote for their aspirations instead of their fears. He was also hoping the other parties in Holyrood would share his vision, and praying they would support his Referendum Bill.

Drummond sat his plump gait at his desk. Although slightly overweight, his eyes still electrified. He could hypnotise, he could persuade, he could be tender and he could be ruthless. He was a leader. His thinning hairline and red face weren't what they called television friendly and neither was that horrendous Saltire tie but these slight imperfections were always a side show to what he said. Most of the people trusted Drummond and to Jamie that was half the battle.

'So Jamie, how did your meeting go with our man?'

'It went well. He tried his best with the bullying tactics but they didn't wash. I think he really believes in us.'

'Jamie, as much as you want to think that, you should always prepare for the worst. Don't be fooled. He is in his job to get the best deal possible for his shareholders and that means market share, market capital, increased dividends and bigger houses in the Caribbean.'

'I'm not. But he did offer us some pretty big incentives.'

'Oh really. Like what?'

Jamie didn't have the opportunity to explain; his phone was ringing again. 'Oliver! What's up?' As he listened, he turned his gaze on the First Minister. 'What? Now? ...Very well. See you shortly.' Jamie closed his phone and picked up the phone on the desk to call the Reception. 'Get the car ready, Joan. We'll be down in a second.'

Jamie turned to Drummond. 'That was Buchanan's man on the phone. We'll need to go. He's having to pull the meeting forward. Can we pick things up later regarding our discussions with our American friends?'

'Sure can,' smiled Drummond, grabbing his jacket and making for the door. 'And can we trust that what our American friend is offering is kosher?'

'Pretty much. I'm meeting him tomorrow to confirm our demands but I'd thought we'd wait and see what Buchanan has to offer first.'

'Drummond stopped and stared into Jamie's eyes. 'I'll ask you again, Jamie. Are you sure?'

Jamie didn't pause. 'Yes, Andrew. I'm more than sure.'

'And are we prepared for Buchanan?

'Yes Sir. Your papers are in this file. Our first demands are still as we discussed but we'll keep the other wish-list quiet until we need to bring out the artillery.'

'Excellent. Let's go meet our big man from Harrow shall we?'

*

8.52 am – St. Vincent Street - Glasgow

'Ahhh, now that's what I call a decent dose of caffeine. Two years I've been telling them to dispose of all that Fair Trade shite and go for the real stuff.'

'C'mon Rory, you know the benefits of Fair Trade. Have a heart, for Christ's sake,' replied a tired Dixie.

'Have a heart? Have a heart! It's pumping now, I tell you. Thunderously.'

As Dixie smiled and shook her head, Rory drifted into a bean induced trance. They were sitting in their Tuesday morning meeting place; a small Italian café owned by a cousin of Johnnie Di Marco. Monday was always the day when Dixie and Rory would discuss the major stories and political columnists in the

Sundays. Tuesday, however, was planning day: what leads they had uncovered, which angles to take and how to best cope with the policeman DCC Michael Hastie had assigned to look after her security. As Rory stretched back to enjoy the early morning sun, Dixie twitched, hoping the policeman wouldn't arrive for a few more minutes. She wanted time on her own with Rory who, as well as being a bit of a space-hopper, happened to be a first-rate backboard on whom to knock her ideas against. That's why Dixie had employed him as her assistant. He might have been a dreamer and occasionally misdirected when sticking to the point, but he always identified with the bigger picture.

'So, what did you get up to last night?' enquired Dixie. 'A threesome with two Ukrainian blondes? A good whipping at the hands of a hairy German sado-mas?' Dixie's eyes smiled mischievously. 'Or was it just a swift log-on to Porn Tube, out with your wee man and a *thunderous* five-knuckle shuffle?'

Rory feigned hurt. 'What is it with you, Dixie? Just because I don't have a girlfriend, please don't think I spend all my nights alone stuffing my face with white pudding suppers while splashing my jizz into an old sock. C'mon, some credit where it is deserved, please.'

'Don't play the pathetic bleeding heart with me, Rory. You haven't had a shag since last Christmas. Don't you think you should be getting out a bit more?'

'I would if I had anyone to go out with. You know, it's not easy working for you, Dixie. I never know where I'm going to be from one day to the next.'

'And don't you just love it, all the drama and suspense. However, if you're telling me you're unhappy, I can always have you transferred to Classifieds or Obituaries. That would be a dead exciting progression up the career ladder.'

'Bad joke, old joke. Very poor show from an acclaimed intellectual,' smirked Rory. 'If you really want to know, I was reading all night.'

Dixie couldn't be arsed to think of a decent retort for her unusual lack of wit. 'And?'

'And it was pretty interesting. I reckon there is a lot more to this ancient royal bloodline carry-on than meets the eye, much more.'

'Ach Rory, you're still not reading up on that bullshit, are you? There has to be more to life than becoming wrapped up in something you can't control, let alone believe. You know, Ian Hamilton once said to me that most people who find themselves caught up in that stuff are most probably nutters. I hope you're not one of them. As I said, how about reading up a wee bit more on the Hutchinson Group? Isn't that what I've asked you to do?'

'Yes, you did, and that's where I started and if you don't mind me telling you, things became a helluva more interesting the more I looked into Hutchinson and its history.'

Rory bowed his head before glancing up at Dixie from underneath his eyebrows. He was hoping for a reaction. Dixie could see his childish excitement but also knew it could be another half an hour before he would stop talking. 'Okay Rory, fifteen minutes. And it better have something to do with our story, do you hear?'

Sitting up in his chair, Rory was the wee boy about to tell his mum a story. 'Okay, so you know how some people believe there's a continuous bloodline from Jesus, and that some distant relations of the shaggy man on the cross may still be alive and kicking today. Well, I reckon they could be correct.'

'Ah Jesus, Rory. Not that old fucking crow on the wall,' moaned an exasperated Dixie. 'Get to the point.'

'I will. Just give me a minute.'

'Go on then,' demanded Dixie.

'Well, in researching Hutchinson's shareholders, my interest really perked up when not only did I discover that there have been a rather large number of politicians, royals and top businessmen who had held a seat on the Board, I also found out that many of them are Masons as well.'

'Christ, tell me something I don't know. Some of them openly admit to wearing the Apron.'

'I know, but it was the branch of Freemasonry to which they belonged that really got me going. And it's not what I would describe as your regular drinking fraternity who have a tendency to spend their Saturday afternoons in the Ibrox club lounge, either. Naw, these guys are members of a brotherhood that goes by the name of the Ancient Order of the Scottish Rite.'

Dixie stopped browsing her notes and cocked her head up sharply, her eyes piercing through Rory's. 'Did you say Scottish Rite. Who the fuck are they?'

After a slow sip of coffee, Rory grinned.

'Okay, smart arse, tell me more.'

'Well, it seems as if some of our men from this Scottish Rite, and therefore Hutchinson, have more than just a common interest in Scotland. I mean, this Order has had a whole host of esteemed brothers in its numbers over the years who have been, and I suppose still are, loyal to Scotland, and I reckon this loyalty goes back to when and how it was founded.' Rory looked across to his boss whose pretence of feigning interest was failing to have the desired effect. 'Any guesses? ...Thought not. The fourteenth century, just after Bannockburn. You see, Robert the Bruce was so delighted with his victory over the English that he used his winnings to pay for a wee building in Kilwinning that became the Masonic Lodge's spiritual home. Intriguingly, I also discovered that Bruce was a Templar Knight who believed in all that "take my heart back to Jerusalem" nonsense and, as far as I'm aware, he was the man who kicked it all off, or if not, kept this whole Church of Jerusalem thingy going or whatever hocus-pocus the Masons get their willies all stiff about.' Rory sucked in some more coffee before going on. 'Nonetheless, as much as all this ties in with our glorious past, I think there is whole lot more to this Masonic loyalty lark than just the Bruce's military prowess and the winning of Scotland's freedom. In other words, and maybe it's been deliberate, I think there is just as much ambiguity as there is indisputable fact in the information that is out there. I mean, Bruce was of Royal blood whereas the Order, in its workings, is pretty much a democratic organisation and if you ask me, that seems to be a rather important contradiction to take note of. However, to compound the matter even more, if Bruce's disciples and descendents were influential Templars or Masons or whatever, why did they disappear off the map for most of the seventeenth century while apparently distancing themselves from the ruling Stuart Dynasty? A dynasty, if I'm not mistaken, the Masonic Lodge pretty much controlled. That doesn't make sense. In fact, it has me flummoxed.'

Dixie sat up. 'Rory, I haven't got time for an unfinished history lesson. C'mon, I need real information. Like how about something that might actually help our story and how it relates to Hutchinson.' Her dismissive retort, however, was only a mask for her renewed interest. She was both listening and thinking. He had her attention.

Rory ignored her intransigence. He wasn't daft, either. 'Anyway, just after the Act of Union in 1707, when all the blow-hard, high-heid sell-outs in Scotland moved to London, the Lodge, or the Order, reappeared in the Scottish public domain. With less government and royal interference, it was pretty much free to set up the Apron-Fitting shop in Edinburgh and Glasgow, surprising all with its newly inducted and extremely influential brethren such as Robert Fergusson and James Beattie, and then over the years and centuries, by such luminaries as Benjamin Franklin, John Witherspoon and Robert Burns. Even Woodrow Wilson was an esteemed Brother, as well as an impressive list of US Presidents, Commonwealth Premieres and lest we forget, members of the Board of the Hutchinson Group. So, if you ask me again, that is one big and powerful goat-shagging lobby. What's more, when I read that the Order played the pivotal role in the success of the American Revolution, I really was about to reach for the old sock.'

'And?' asked an eager Dixie.

'Well, ever since the Colonials took control, I reckon the Order has been pulling the strings on both sides of the pond. Big business, politics, you name it.'

'No, no, Rory,' scoffed Dixie. 'That's ridiculous. There are far too many variables and indefinable factors for you to come to that conclusion. That's just as bad as saying there is a Judeo-Christian conspiracy seeking world domination. If you believe that then I'll be personally making a reservation for you at the Nut House.'

'Well, funny you should say that. Because I also read, though I'm not entirely convinced, that the Templar Knights were linked by birth to the Kaballah sect. You know: that ancient Jewish crew which is believed to have a direct and traceable bloodline to the elders and aristocracy of the Church of Jerusalem.' Rory glanced across sheepishly, looking for some sign that is was okay to continue, as well as hoping Dixie would be patient with his ramblings. 'I know it's all a bit far fetched but I really do think there's something to it all.'

He was misguided. Her deference had expired. 'Right, Rory,' hissed an impatient Dixie, 'I've just about had enough. I appreciate your endeavour but you're really not expecting me to be taken in by this shite?'

'I'm not asking you to believe me, Dixie. I'm just telling you what I found out. As I said, I'm still trying to put all the pieces together and in doing that, I just think there's a lot more to Hutchinson and its Masonic connection than first appears. Think about it. Whether it is an historic loyalty or a modern day pining, Hutchinson and the Order just have to have some association with Scotland, and every single thing I have read points to that. I'll tell you, as well as the Order controlling the destiny of the American Revolution, there have been some pretty strange coincidences. A Scotsman issued the first Presidential Oath to George Washington. Lincoln never went anywhere without his copy of Burns and even christened his son William Wallace Lincoln. Then there was the speech made by Woodrow Wilson's in which he declared that, "every line of strength in American History is a line covered with Scottish blood." The Declaration of Independence, no less, was written by Jefferson, who based it on the Declaration of Arbroath from way back in Bruce's time. What's more, of the US Declaration's fifty-six signatories, forty-two of them were either Scottish or of Scottish blood! Bloody hell, Dixie, the list goes on and on.'

Rory took a self-satisfied drink of coffee. 'Sorry Dixie but there are far too many coincidences. Even just taking a look at the small things, such as the Saltires some US states have adopted for their flags and the fact that nine out of the first thirteen colonial governors were Scottish, will allow you to see a correlation. Bloody hell, there are even statues of Burns and Scott in New York's Central Park, as well the US Library of Congress holding one of Burn's original manuscripts of "Auld Lang Syne". Come on, it's certainly worth considering?'

'Thanks for the history lesson Rory, but do you really think there could be a connection to our story?'

'Well, that's what I'm working on. I need to figure out why the Hutchinson Group or this Ancient Order for that matter, have been declaring more than a passing interest in Scottish affairs lately. However, when you realise how much shit hits the fan every time the political landscape changes in Scotland, you can't help but be intrigued.'

'Ach Rory, you can't prove the two are connected. In fact, I think you might be putting Rangers and Celtic together and coming up with cultural harmony. Come on, be realistic.'

'All I'm saying, Dixie, is that there are far too many variables making me wonder. But it's not enough yet. I need to know the why before I put it all together.'

'But more than that, Rory, as a journalist you need proof. Anything other is just circumspect shite.'

Dixie smiled. Inwardly she was delighted Rory had the same sniffer dog nose as she because what he had just told her might have some bearing on her story. Unfortunately, she didn't have time to discuss things further. Glancing down the street, she saw the huge lumbering man coming towards them. 'Time to go, Rory. You can update me later on your conspiracy theory. I think my chaperon is here.'

Picking up their coffees-to-go, Dixie and Rory started walking. Rory continued to talk but Dixie was having none of it. 'I said we'll talk later,' she stated firmly.

She turned to offer a scowling 'Good Morning' to the plain-clothed detective. Returning her gaze to the pavement in front, she smiled. He looked a lot like Kurt Broadhead who plays for the Teddy Bears.

Rory, non-plussed by Dixie's new bodyguard, thought it better to change the subject. 'So, did Charlie get the pictures we needed?' he whispered.

As they walked briskly down St. Vincent's street towards the office, Dixie's thoughts had drifted off elsewhere. Under orders from the DCC, she had been away from the office for over a week but time had been no healer as the thought of being an assassination target still hadn't given way to the " rug by the log fire, let's have hard core sex" feeling just yet. She was also thinking about Catriona and Lewis at her mother's house and hoping those who wanted her dead weren't so stupid as to go after her kids as well. If they were then they had better prepare for some Glaswegian retribution: a hack-saw to the scrotum, a taser gun to the arsehole and a long, slow sweep of a barber's chib across the throat!

'So, Dixie? Did you?'

'Did I what, Rory?'

'Did you get the pics from Charlie?'

'Yes I did,' snapped Dixie, 'but let's not discuss it here in front of Kurt Broadhead, shall we?'

Arriving at the office, the two of them checked in with the receptionist before moving over to the lift. 'You're not coming into fucking work with me as well,' she hissed at Kurt.

'Sorry Ma'am, but I'm under orders. DCC Hastie says I've to be with you at all times.'

'Did he, now.'

'Yes Ma'am. He did.'

'That was rhetorical, Detective,' snarled Dixie as she slapped the palm of her hand into the buttons at the side of the lift. 'And as much as I appreciate the security, I still have a job to do and I don't think it would be too profitable for our business if our readers suddenly discovered that the Fifth Estate is now being monitored by the Strathclyde Police, now would it?'

'That's not for me to comment on, Ma'am.'

'No, it's bloody well not.' sneered Dixie as she reached into her bag for her phone. 'Let's just give him a call, shall we?'

As she waited, Kurt's face reddened.

'Hi, Mike. It's Dixie.' There was short silence. 'No, I'm not okay. As much as I understand your concern, is there any chance your man here could lay off while I'm on the job. I'm sure he can keep looky-out from down here in Reception.'

Dixie handed Kurt the phone. 'Your boss wants a word.'

'Yes Sir. Certainly. I'll check on all visitors and keep my distance. Yes Sir. Roger that.'

Kurt handed the phone back. 'You're free to go Ma'am but please let me know if you decide to leave the office. I'll be down here.'

'Thanks. I'll do that. And Kurt, it's a mobile phone, not a walkie-talkie.'

As Dixie and Rory opened the doors to the third floor, the journalists already at work started falling off their chairs and hiding beneath their desks as Neil Jacobson, the sports editor, let fly with a toy cap gun borrowed from his son.

'A funny bunch of donkeys, so you are,' smiled Dixie, as she took a bow. 'Mind you, I'm surprised half of you sports guys aren't immune to this type of gratuitous violence considering you spend half your working life down at Ibrox.'

Jacobson walked over, giving Dixie a hug. 'Let's just say we're all delighted that we didn't have to take time off to buy a new suit for the funeral. And please excuse our childish humour, you being shot at was too good an opportunity.'

'Aye, very good Neil, but if you'll excuse us, I think we have to meet the wee man for a going over.' said Dixie, nodding her head towards the editor's office. 'I think he'll want an explanation. Don't you?'

'No doubt. And by the way, the boys here want the full run down on Loch Lomond when you have a chance. They love all this cowboy and indian carry-on.'

Dixie and Rory sat opposite Tom Gray, editor in chief of the paper. For a small and wiry man, he always appeared a little taller when sitting behind his desk. Rory reckoned he had the same model of chair as used by Alastair Saccharin in the TV series, "Unemployable Tyros Making a Cunt of Themselves". Rory smiled. 'Fuck me, if he sits any higher in that chair he'll be ending up with an attack of the vertigo!'

'First of all Dixie, I hope the nightmares have passed. Second, I hope Caty and Lewis are being looked after, and third, can you please tell me what the fuck is going on?'

Dixie had come to expect this from her boss. As much as he could be a wee shite with Napoleonic tendencies, he cared about his team. He was also an expert in some of the dangers posed in the world of broadsheet journalism, especially in the political world. Having covered Vietnam, the Miner's Strike and the Poll Tax Protests, Dixie knew he had experienced some intimidation in his time.

'Well, as you'll gather, Tom, this is no longer the chase of the wild goose as you once thought. Certain things have come to light and let's just say there are people out there hoping we don't switch on the Scumpool Illuminations.'

'Well?' demanded Tom Gray.

'Well, as you know, Rory and I have been working on this Hutchinson story and as much as it is a political hot tattie, I have a hunch that what Elliot Walker told me is somewhat related. Don't ask me why, I just do.'

Knowing how Dixie worked, Rory sat quietly. Her secret was to drip feed information, not divulge the entire story. She was doing it with DCC Hastie, she was doing it with Elliot Walker and now she was doing it with her boss. Wee Tom Gray might not like it but Dixie's four Journalist of the Year awards were enough for him to back off and give her some space.

'Listen Dixie, this is a wee bit more serious than some pathetic MP with a dodgy expense account and a rent-boy holed up in his South London flat. You were shot at, for Christ's sake. In other words, someone is trying to kill you. Kill you, Dixie. Do you hear?'

'I do Tom but ...'

'No, you fucking well don't. Listen, I've been in the mix during the Miners Strike and the Poll Tax Protests and there were some pretty bad bastards orchestrating trouble in there. And even though I was trying to cover the story from both sides, no one, and I mean fucking no one, ever had a go at topping me. They tapped the phones, they sent me hate mail, they even

159

ransacked the office but for fuck's sake, Dixie, no one ever tried shoot me in broad daylight on a Friday afternoon!'

Dixie sat in stubborn silence for a moment while Rory hoped Tom Gray wouldn't point his wee finger across the table and tell him he was fired. The office was quiet and Dixie could feel the eyes of her colleagues staring through the glass-partitioned office.

'I know, but as for now I only have wee bits and pieces, Tom. Furthermore, I don't know if the shooting is connected to Hutchinson or not and nor I am sure if what Elliot Walker told me is, either. All I know is that someone or some organisation is either trailing me or trailing Elliot and whoever they are knows we are pretty close to outing whatever it is they are hiding.'

'Well, what are they hiding, Dixie?'

'I don't know yet, Tom. I really don't.'

'Okay. I'm gonnae let you run with it for now. But two weeks, Dixie, that's all you have. In the meantime, I want this interview with Peter Buchanan ready for the Sunday edition, all right? Unfortunately, we'll still need to keep on pretending that the normalities of Scottish politics will carry on, which, in case you haven't noticed, help me to run this paper and therefore make some money, which, along with that ex husband of yours, pays for that lovely house of yours in the West End and your very fast and now very infamous BMW!'

10

embrace the ubiquitous revenge

Tuesday 17th June

9.29 am – Heathrow Airport - London

DCC Michael Hastie felt indestructible. He was the man: a man whose position of power permitted him the honour of being an untouchable and very much in with the top brass.

He swaggered quickly through Heathrow's new Terminal 5, sympathising with the BAA employees and the shit they were putting up with from the irate passengers. He felt even worse for the UK Airways staff whose love of their jobs with what was once renowned as the best airline in the world appeared to have been diminished by a chief executive's idea of good customer service -for hundreds of passengers waiting five hours for a flight to Melbourne- should only include a pitiful offer of a solitary bottle of water and a stale ploughman's. The incongruity of the company's plight wasn't lost on Hastie either, as its once famous service culture was now being compared to that of Blarney Air, possibly the airline with the worst customer service the industry had ever seen.

His driver was waiting for him at Arrivals. Standing to attention in grey uniform and ill-fitting cap, he was holding a hand-held sign with Hastie's name on it, the DCC abbreviation missing. Hastie knew why; the same reason he was wearing a suit rather than his uniform. Everything today was on the QT. But he loved coming to London. To him it was the centre of his existence, hoping that one day soon it would also be his new home. He smiled. It was also home to the Metropolitan Police Force he adored, the seat of government he had an undying loyalty to and, as he had planned for all his working life, the HQ of his future employer: the National Security Department. This was the town where major decisions were taken, really major decisions.

Hastie enjoyed a hot towel and fresh orange juice as the fully-loaded Merc drove off quietly towards the city. He was relaxed and prepared. He was also unaware of the innocuous black cab trundling along the M4 only one hundred yards behind him.

Paul Riley knew what he had been doing the previous day when he had logged onto his secure access connection to the international airline reservations system to run a quick check on his boss's movements for the week. This trip to London hadn't been on Hastie's agenda and having verified Hastie's flight times, Paul had headed home to book a seat on an earlier flight. He didn't usually suffer from nerves but his stomach was in knots. His best friend's life was taking precedence over his job.

Fifty minutes later, the cab shuddered to a halt in a narrow street behind Grosvenor Square. 'Fifty five quid?' he questioned the driver. These were certainly not Glasgow prices.

'Sorry mate. There's nothing we can do about it. It's the price of fuel nowadays.'

As he read the name plate on the building across the street, Paul handed the driver sixty quid and laughed. A few minutes later, after buying yet another newspaper, he took a window seat inside little a bistro opposite the building where DCC Michael Hastie had entered only a few minutes before.

Across that street and up a few floors, Elliot Walker was sitting at his desk and nursing a large whisky. Drinking at work was not something he espoused unless, of course, it was the odd drink pressed into his hand by a delighted Sir Alexander Lamont after another successful acquisition. This morning however, his need for a dram or two had been precipitated by the not so insignificant fact that he was shitting himself.

Before Elliot had moved companies to UKES plc and its fabled fourth floor, he had been a quiet operator renowned for his incisive and diligent approach to the legalities of the Energy business. However, having been fervently pursued by UKES, he had made the short-lived mistake of believing his own press. A rising star in the Oil business was how he had been described, leading him to conclude he could be also be a man about town. Only Kirsten had told him he hadn't a hope of living up to that reputation, telling him directly he would only end up making an arse of himself. Nevertheless, he did occasionally sample the Thursday and Friday nights in London's trendier bars, lap-dancing hovels and late night private clubs but had found his immersion into the "Power of London" not to his liking. There had been too much to risk. Kirsten had been correct. It just wasn't within him. As well as seeing associates come and go, he had also been witness to the odd wee mental breakdown or two in those people who, after becoming addicted to the wild partying scene, had found it impossible to escape their sinning ways. Earning huge sums of money, they snorted too much coke, fucked too many whores and found themselves on the wrong side of far too many influential people. Elliot was lucky. After moving in with Kirsten, he no longer had the need to excuse himself from the peer pressure. Not because he was an arse and his associates even bigger arses but rather his morning-after guilt had begun to last long into the following day. He had fallen in love with Kirsten and the fear of losing her soon outweighed the fear of not being one of the "aren't we just fucking great" gang. Now, however, he really was on the verge of losing Kirsten. The irony of it. If he were to be found out, she would definitely be packing her bags and leaving; he being either dead or spending a good twenty years in the slammer.

The whisky was a settler, as was the slight numbing of the senses. Though he was still trembling, he was hoping he had escaped detection. Half an hour earlier, he had bounced into the office blaming his lateness on Kirsten not feeling so well. He had also been a wee bit over enthusiastic in saying good morning to Marie, Sir Alexander's PA, and taking an unusually eager interest in her visit to the cinema the previous evening. 'Really? Clooney? Good film?'

Having collected his mail, he had walked towards his office but had turned after only a few feet. 'Marie, when's the big man in today? I need to pick up a couple of papers I had him sign for me.'

'He's in already. He's up in Strategy with the Director of North Sea Development. He should be back in about ten minutes but then he's only here for a short time before he heads over to his club for another meeting. Is there anything I can do to help?'

'Nah, you just stay where you are, Marie. I'll pop in and get them myself.'

Marie tilted her head to the side. 'Elliot, you know he doesn't like employees going into his office unannounced.'

'Okidoki. Any chance you could get them then. They need to be sent ASAP. I think they'll be in the file marked ...'

Marie interrupted him. 'Okay, make it quick.'

He had turned and blew out a silent, heavy breath while hoping that Marie hadn't noticed the beads of sweat dribbling on to his upper lip. Before going in, he had knocked on the office door for show. Working quickly, he took a pair of gloves from his briefcase then the bugging transmitters from inside his jacket pocket. Gently lifting up Sir Alexander's Faber-Castell from its display plinth, he unscrewed the top and slipped the smaller CSM A9 transmitter inside before giving the pen a slight dunt on the desk to secure the device. Returning the pen to the plinth, he had glanced at the desk clock. 9.58. 'Jesus!' He had been about to leave when he saw his boss's briefcase lying unopened on the floor by the desk. It was a cumbersome old floppy thing with the initials A.C.L. on the opening flap. He stared at the briefcase for a second, thinking he could double his chance of success if he placed the RFID X400 transmitter inside. He looked down at the transmitter in his hands, then to the briefcase and then to the door. He caught another glimpse of the time: 9.59. 'Naw, Elliot. Calm the heid.' Deciding rationality was a wee bit better for his health than just plain old fucking mental, he had pulled a document folder from his own briefcase and headed for the door. The risk had been too great. Coming out, he waved the folder at Marie before smiling and holding his fore-finger to his lips, intimating that his wee intrusion be kept between the two of them. 'Thanks, Marie. I'll have them ready in an hour or so. And can you call a courier, please? They're going to Henley.'

Back in the relative safety of his office, he had just collapsed in his chair when he heard the booming voice of his boss in the corridor outside.

'Any messages, Marie?'

'Yes, Sir Alex. A Michael Hastie called to say he'll be here around 10.30. I've also confirmed your meeting at the Club and they're expecting you.'

Elliot had squeezed the turtle's heid. Hastie was one of the guys Dixie mentioned to him at the airport. 'Fucking hell, I need a drink!'

Elliot could hear the strong Glaswegian accent chatting with Marie: small talk about flights and traffic. Michael Hastie was on time. A few minutes later, Marie pressed the intercom. 'Michael Hastie is here for you, Sir Alexander.'

Elliot listened as his boss's door opened, only a few yards from where he sat sweating and drinking and having a tussle with the reptile peeking out from his sphincter.

'Good morning, Hastie. Glad you could make it down at such short notice. Glasgow still treating you well?'

'The old town is still alive and kicking me where it hurts, Sir Alexander. Mind you, things have quietened down a wee bit since our friends decided to park their jeep in the main door of Glasgow Airport.'

'Ah yes, terrible goings on. Anyway, come in. I believe we've got some catching up to do. Marie, hold all my calls.'

Lamont and Hastie retired to the chairman's office while Elliot realised, that in all his untrained panic, he had forgotten to set up the recording device on his laptop. He quickly fumbled around for the various attachments, just managing to get the bloody thing working as Hastie soberly explained the shooting at Loch Lomond. 'Well, I don't think it sacred her off, Sir Alex.

She's a determined one, so she is. I even made an effort myself over dinner the other week but didn't have much luck, either. Unfortunately, we do think she is closing in and even though she has nothing on you as yet, it doesn't mean she won't have soon.'

'And just how do you figure that out?'

'Well, her photographer has been busy. I had him trailed to Gleneagles and without giving too much away I tried to warn her off.'

'Hmmph, I know this girl. There's not a hope in hell of her backing off. Anyway, what do you think her next move will be?'

'I'm not sure. But I do have a team ready to snatch her files and pull her evidence if need be.'

'But couldn't we just have arranged a little car crash for our photographer friend?'

'We could have Sir Alex, but until we know for certain that she has put you together with our man, I thought it better to hang back and not raise her already heightened suspicion. If we expose too much of our hand, she'll pull the story until a more suitable time. No, what I'm hoping is that she'll continue to think that Hutchinson is lobbying, through its usual corruptible methods, to increase the UK spend on the Faslane operation.'

'Sounds like the same old, same old and nothing to cause concern. '

'I agree. There isn't really. And if she ends up writing the typical conspiracy bullshit then all the better. I mean, your decision to have a Scottish military man meet with Zimmerman was a master stroke. Keeps all the credibility on our side. And anyway, if she does get too close then I'm sure our friends in the media can easily discredit her.'

'Oh yes, no problem there. And are you sure she knows nothing about the …how shall I say it …bigger picture?'

'None whatsoever. Impossible.'

'Good, because I don't need some lowly hack blowing this thing wide open. Furthermore, what I really don't need is that bastard Drummond finding out that London has decided to get serious. Especially with our little plan about to be put into action.'

'I don't think there's any chance of that. No one knows about it.'

Sir Alexander nodded his head slowly before standing up to straighten his suit. 'And Loch Fyne? Anyone interesting?'

'Nah, just an old friend and his wife. No one we should concern ourselves with.'

'Excellent,' grunted Lamont as he picked up his pen from the plinth and slid it into his jacket pocket. Moving for the door, he turned to Hastie. 'I think it's about time we made a start. Ever been to my club?'

'No, I can't say I have but I'm looking forward to it.'

'Fine wine and a damn good lunch. In fact, if all goes well Hastie, I might even propose you for membership.'

Elliot could hear the two antagonists laughing as they came out from Lamont's office. Hitting the "save" option on his laptop, he closed everything down. His hands were still shaking when he heard his boss tell Hastie to head down to the car. 'I'll be there in a minute. Just a couple of things to clear with Marie'

Having heard the lift doors open and close, Elliot creeped out to see Lamont. 'Sir, have you got a minute, I need to chat to you about Grangemouth. I'm sending those papers you asked me to review over to Henley and I just wanted to run a couple of things by you.'

'Sorry Walker, it'll have to wait. Send them over anyway then schedule a time with Marie for tomorrow.'

'Will do, Sir. Have a good day.'

Returning to his office, Elliot sat down, pulled a trash can between his legs and waited. Five gags later, up came his breakfast, his coffee and his whisky.

*

10.35 am – South Queensferry, Edinburgh

Peter Buchanan thought the Scarocca Hotel in South Queensferry was a bizarre choice of venue to hold a meeting of such importance. Nevertheless, he was prepared to go along with Andrew Drummond's suggestion; he had more pressing details to worry about than the location of a meeting. As he walked briskly into the room, he beamed at the First Minister. 'Mmm …very interesting, Andrew. Not quite the secure and intimate surroundings of my Belgravia club but smart all the same.'

'Ach, Peter my boy. I can't say I've ever had the pleasure of enjoying the hospitality of your London establishment but you're in the real Scotland now and where better to discuss our future than underneath these two magnificent structures.'

Their political stance may have been conflicting but each politician held a grudging admiration for the other. At ease and smiling, Buchanan sat next to Jamie while Drummond took a seat next Buchanan's advisor, Oliver Graham. Having recommended to Drummond that more could be achieved if the physical set-up of the meeting was inclusive and comfortable rather than exclusive and combatative, Jamie had reserved the private dining room: leather arm-chairs, mahogany coffee table and relaxed atmosphere. Buchanan took a seat and gazed out through the enormous window overlooking the broad, lumbering River Forth. Across the water, he could just about make out the roof tops of North Queensferry while to both his left and right stood the Forth Road Bridge and the inspirational Forth Bridge, the red-steeled wonder of the Victorian world.

'I thought you would enjoy the contradiction,' offered Drummond. 'A blend of the old and the new, if you'll pardon the expression.'

Buchanan chuckled. 'One down already, I fear?''

Knowing Buchanan was here to negotiate terms for Scotland after his predicted win at the next UK general election, Drummond asserted his control, 'So, Peter, my boy. What can you do for me this fine day?'

'I must say, Andrew, five gold stars for the psychological one-upmanship. Okay, we both know I'm new to the job and a little green but nevertheless, if I am to be Prime Minister, I feel I may have to be a little more abrasive, as we say. I also know that you have a lead on us but that doesn't mean I'm going to bend over and take one for the pack. I am here for the sole reason of protecting the Union and as much as I love Scotland, that is what

I'm going to do. I am also here knowing exactly what I'm prepared to offer to make that happen. Unfortunately, I've still not figured out what exactly you want.'

'Peter, its not a case of what Scotland wants, and I'm not being arrogant here, it's a case of what we're going to get. For far too long this country has pandered to our step-brother down south and it has to stop. Conversely, I don't want our sons and daughters embittered with these repetitive and, quite frankly, tedious drones of anti-English anger and frustration. I've listened long enough to the blame game, almost to the point where I'd like to shake half of the country out of its unacceptable and irreproachable depression. Scotland needs to grow up politically, and whether you like it or not, and with or without your help, that will be achieved.'

'Very noble of you Andrew but regardless of what you say, there are certain individuals and organisations who will do everything within their very substantial powers to keep hold of Scotland. Not very nice, I acknowledge, but that's the way it is.'

'What do you mean, "keep hold of Scotland". We're not some kind of prized possession, that's for sure!'

'I agree, it's not. But please realise there are many people with much to lose if Scotland secedes.'

'You mean the people of London and the South East of England whose banks and shares and jobs depend on Scotland?'

'Yes, that's exactly what I mean.'

'Well, you can fuck right off, Buchanan. I'm not here to grovel to London and the South East!'

'I know that, Andrew, but the two of us have to come to an agreement where you obtain what you think Scotland requires without incensing your opponents down South.'

'And how, exactly, are you going to suggest we do that, particularly without London employing financial threats?'

'At the moment, I don't want to use any financial threats. The Labour Party has done enough of that, don't you think. Their eight per cent reduction in the incremental block grant your administration received when it came to power says all that needs to be said about them.'

169

'Yes, I agree, but what about your friends in the City who have been short-selling WBOC shares for weeks. Don't tell me that isn't a threat. Christ almighty, there has even been some Labour MPs clapping their hands and jumping for joy at the news. Arseholes! But they're the least of my worries. What really concerns me is the motive of the Bank's CEO. I mean, he's not exactly been crying in his porridge over the share price. In fact, the aggressive SOB who should have stuck to selling turnips and tatties instead of turning his hand to banking. Sadly, Peter, something about the whole affair really stinks, so please don't sit here and tell me you won't threaten Scotland when it's clear you don't have to. Canary Wharf is doing the job for you!'

'Andrew, we know it hasn't been good and to be quite candid, even I think it has all been rather peculiar; and to say I am as infuriated as you is a major understatement. Nevertheless, please believe me when I tell you that I will get to the underlying cause of it. In fact, I've already had some strong words with my contacts in the City to bolster support for the WBOC Group. All I hope is that the awful mess won't transpire into anything more debilitating.'

Drummond remained firm while Buchanan took a sip of water. Jamie struggled with his agitation. There was no way Buchanan could be as angry as he and Drummond. No way!

'But you must listen to me, Andrew. I could just as easily defend Westminster and like many others, revel in how it could make Scotland suffer. As well as being unproductive, however, that is not my way of getting things done. Furthermore, as much as it frustrates me to be sitting here at all, I'd much prefer to focus my energies on something a little more positive; like saving the Union and everything good about it. But before I can move forward, I need to know how much I will have to relinquish to make that happen.'

Although he didn't show it, Jamie was surprised. Peter Buchanan had been smart, turning the conversation away from the idea of Separation and on to negotiating terms for Scotland remaining within the Union. He didn't seem to care how much Westminster would have to give away. Drummond, however, was also prepared. Being a man for the gee-gees, he hadn't forgotten whose horse was still leading by a head. 'Ach, you're not such a bad politician, Peter. Very good indeed. But from where I'm sitting, the view is a deep shade of very rosy, in more ways than one. So don't come up here and pretend you don't know what we want. It's pretty fucking clear. What's more, it appears as if we are going to achieve our objectives, regardless of how much Westminster attempts to manipulate the situation. The EU will support us, as will the United Nations and that will only relinquish one outcome: Scotland controlling the oil. Come on, you know as well as I do that Westminster has been at it for years, and I mean to bring an end to it. Think about it. It re-registered UKES plc as an English company when it relocated from Glasgow and now it has just sold EGB Nuclear to the French. I mean, how much longer do you think the people of Scotland will suffer this orchestrated crippling of our economy? No, Peter, it has to stop. Westminster has left Scotland with absolutely no alternative because it has failed to offer genuine equality.'

Drummond leaned back and smiled, hoping Buchanan would relax a little more before he pounced. 'What I really think we should be discussing, Peter, is how Scotland and England will work together after the Union is dissolved. That to me would be progressive politics, wouldn't you agree. I'm also sure you wouldn't want to be remembered as the man who oversaw the acrimonious break up of the Union. Surely it is better for you to make a deal where both Scotland and England win. That would undoubtedly be the measure, and the legacy, of a fine politician.' Drummond smiled again, this time deciding to throw Buchanan a teaser. 'I mean, we'll still have the same Head of State, won't we?'

'I bloody well hope so,' snapped Buchanan. 'England has no intentions of allowing the Queen to fill out an application for a change to her official residence anytime soon.'

'I couldn't agree more,' laughed Drummond. 'See, now we're getting somewhere.'

Peter Buchanan smiled ruefully in return, just stopping

short of calling his adversary a supercilious son of a bitch. 'I'm not at all sure what line we should take,' he pondered. 'I know you have us at your mercy, Andrew, and for that I congratulate you, but bigger things are at stake.'

'Like a nation with a sense of itself and recognised at the highest table in the land. Yes, England can have that if it so desires. We will have no complaints up here.'

The Tory leader laughed out loud.

'Listen Peter,' continued a more diplomatic Drummond. Hunching up his trousers, he sat forward in his chair and leaned across the table with his palms held out as if to say that this was how things were going to be. 'You know how we feel. In fact, I'm damn sure you feel it as well, Peter, and though your Harrowfied accent could contradict my assumption, you're as Scottish as they come. Surely, for everyone's sake, a peaceful separation agreement is the only way forward. England is big enough to look after itself and we, as its nearest and dearest friend, will endeavour to ensure a healthy, open and progressive relationship. What's more, and this is very important from your perspective, if you allow Scotland and England to separate with all this bitterness in the air then you'll be finished because of your links to Scotland. Not only will you take it up the arse from the pack, you also get a good rogering from the scrum-half and the replacements. In fact, your only option after the Referendum is to push for a peaceful settlement. History will remember you for that, Peter; it really will. Don't and we'll squeeze London, and you, until you really do scream for mercy.'

'Okay Andrew, I get the point,' sighed an exasperated Buchanan. 'But don't you think we should be negotiating two agreements. One should be post-Secession and the other,' smiled the Tory leader across the table, 'just in case you don't win the Referendum, should be based on my proposed constitutional amendments. Whatever, the agreements will have to satisfy both institutions. 'All I ask is that you don't become too greedy.'

'Greedy? Och no, Peter. I think you'll find that is Westminster's problem, not Scotland's.'

11

to the dancer belongs the truth

Tuesday 17th June

10.45 am – Grosvenor Square - London

Paul Riley lowered his head as DCC Michael Hastie and Sir Alexander Lamont emerged from the main door of UKES's headquarters. A few seconds later, after they both took a seat in the back of another chauffer driven Mercedes, Paul took one last gulp of his latte, picked up his Guardian and headed for the door. The Mercedes had just driven away when Paul pulled open the door of the café and hailed a cab from the other side of the road.

'I know this is going to sound a wee bit weird, pal, but any chance you could follow that car?' asked Paul of the driver. 'Not too close but don't lose sight of it, okay.'

The cab driver grabbed tightly at the wheel then shook his shoulders. 'Blow me, squire. I've been working these streets for close on thirty years and not once has this happened.'

'Well, there's always a first time for everything but how about we keep it to ourselves, shall we?'

'Yes Siree!'

From the outside, it looked like any other black London Hackney but inside was a clichéd and personal tribute to the driver's domestic bliss. With the Black Watch picnic rug pricking at his arse, Paul studied the array of lucky charms hanging from the rear-view mirror: a tiny silver horseshoe, Rosary Beads, a West Ham pendant and a heart-shaped necklace with a picture of who Paul presumed to be the driver's wife. Stuck on the dashboard was a little silver framed family snap of the driver and his extended clones enjoying themselves somewhere down on the Med. Thinking of the thousands like it across London, Paul smiled at the family portrait. The driver and his wife standing centre, he resplendent in a West Ham t-shirt and recently purchased pair of multi-pocketed white shorts and she in a linen gypsy skirt (again in white), flip flops and a cotton vest framed by freckles. The three sons and spouses stood on the wings with arms around one another and wide glowing smiles on their faces. Not dissimilarly dressed from their old man, the sons were wearing "Official" West Ham Replica shirts while two of the daughters-in-law had squeezed into shorts that had no doubt caused two of the sons to be liberal with the truth when asked if certain bums looked big in these. The other daughter-in-law sat on the sand holding a baby while the other five grand children (two boys, three girls) sat alongside laughing, sticking out their thumbs and kicking their legs in the air. With the kids togged up in the complete kit of top, shorts and socks, West Ham was playing a stormer. Christ, thought Paul, even the baby's all-in-one was claret and blue.

Paul couldn't help but look on in admiration, not only at this man's financial contribution to West Ham United Football Club but also at the pride so evident in the grandparents' smiles. Granted, their heads, faces and limbs might have been bordering on the skin cancer side of red but there was a genuine feeling of fulfilment. And Paul wasn't scoffing in any way. Apart from a difference in footballing loyalties -the Bully Wee instead of the Hammers- his own mother had a much similar picture on the mantelpiece at home. Farther along the dust-free dashboard, a clip-board and flyer hung beside the air vent. It was asking for sponsorship for a local children's home away-day to Southend. What was it with London taxi drivers and their love affair with Southend, asked Paul to himself. He had been there once before and once had been enough. Why not take the kids to Brighton or the New Forest for heaven's sake. Nevertheless, the commitment some of these drivers put in to helping kids far outweighed the shitty aesthetics of the away-day destination. He must be a good man. However, as Paul was thinking of his next move, he and the driver caught each other's eye in the rear view mirror. Paul didn't want to react but he was thankful the driver wasn't a Mike Reid wannabe. Today, of all days, was not the day for being given the runaround!

The Mercedes in front travelled down the narrow Upper Grosvenor Street before taking a left into Park Lane. Gliding elegantly down the famous road, it was soon passing The Dorchester before slowing down as it approached Hyde Park Corner. Sweeping right at Wellington's Arch, then left at The Lanesbourough, it continued on for a few hundred yards. A couple of minutes later, it was turning left off Knightsbridge and into a quiet street in Belgravia: the neighbourhood of five star hotels exclusive residencies, private members clubs and the extraordinarily wealthy. This was where the elite of London shopped, shagged, shit and socialised, where acquaintances opened doors, where middle-eastern oil barons kept their three mistresses, where A-listers took cover from the paparazzi and where an old school tie most certainly secured a position with a multi-national company. As the Mercedes drew to a halt outside a grand building, Paul ordered the driver to drive on to the end of the street. Before the taxi pulled up, Paul handed the driver the fare plus an extra tenner for the children's trip to Southend.

'Cheers Guv. I won't say another word about you Jocks being tight-fisted bastards; I promise.'

Paul smiled back before hopping out and into a doorway a few doors along from where Hastie and Lamont had been set down. Opening the newspaper, he waited a few minutes until he was sure the two men had disappeared inside the building before taking a wee dander alongside. Passing quickly, his eyes shifted for a mini-second to the plaque by the front door. 'I don't fucking believe it. The Alba Club!' He carried on walking, doing a quick recce across the street for a suitably secreted vantage point from where to view proceedings and from where he could secure another cup of decent coffee.

Sitting a couple of seats back from the window of the

café and enjoying a bloody good latte, Paul speculated on how London was changing. As money poured in from across the globe, it had become the world's number one financial centre, and such was the magnetic pull of London's cash, many of the industry's top bankers had even reversed the Manhattan-bound migration trend. Nevertheless, thought Paul, the City hadn't been the cheeriest places of late. The bankers were edgy. Something more ominous was flying in from New York. What's more, as London continued to expand, it had once again become a major terrorist target. Like Glasgow, immigrants had long come to London to begin a new life but with a new intake from countries in the Middle East and beyond, the city's task of coping with a multi-cultural society was becoming increasingly dangerous. Paul pinched his lips; Glasgow's troubles were a playground spat compared to this place. There were now countless neighbourhoods throughout the city where English was not the first language, where racism was on the up and where gangland murders had taken a disastrous turn for the worse as youngsters thought a great night out involved sticking one of their mum's kitchen utensils into more than the odd passer-by. And Paul didn't think the situation was going to get any better, what with the new mayor now in office. Who would have thought, he mused, that the numpty of the highest order, otherwise known as the former public schoolboy and Tory MP, Archie Robert Steven Edwards, would be mayor of this great city. For here was a man, who in banning public drinking on the Tube one week, had defended a group of alcoholically-challenged bankers the next by depicting them as being anthropologically misunderstood after their arrest for holding a cocktail party on the Piccadilly Line. Mind you, thought Paul, you have to give it to the man; he had balls!

Five minutes later, another cab pulled up just along from the Alba Club. Out-stepped Elliot Walker, sheepishly twisting his head one way then the other. He was nervous. Deciding to jog in the opposite direction from the club, Elliot crossed the street before disappearing into a department store at the junction with the main road. He climbed the escalators quickly, heading for the café on the third floor. Having grabbed a bottle of water en route, he took a seat at a window overlooking the Alba Club. He pulled out his laptop and logged on, hastily plugging the recording device into its USB socket while taking care to place the device out of sight on the far side of the table. Delicately inserting the earpieces into his ears, he pretended to read a newspaper while nodding his head in fake acknowledgment to music that was most definitely not booming out from his music folder. A few seconds later, the receiver was picking up a signal from inside Lamont's pen. The clarity was far from ideal but considering he was over thirty yards away on the other side of the street, Elliot could make out everything being said. He hit the record button. He was well inside the barrel of shit now; not quite up to his neck but if the name Walker was inadvertently dropped into the conversation by Hastie, he would be scrambling over to the self-service counter pronto and grabbing more than a few curly straws for which to breathe before he drowned in an ugly tub of dirty brown jobbies.

He also considered, while thinking about Dixie and her tendency for inviting trouble and her all too frequent habit of finding herself rebuked and then censored by various figures of authority, if the time had passed to extricate himself from this deed. Remembering Dixie at university, he could do no more than shake his head. They might have been good friends but even he couldn't defend some of her protests; such as the time when Dixie's determination to hang hundreds of "Down with Thatcher" posters throughout the library during exam time had resulted in a couple of hundred pissed-off students and, such was her DIY ignorance over the differing adhesive qualities of BlueTac and a roll of industrial-strength masking tape, the destruction of several areas of the three-hundred year old wood-work. That stunt had led to her first suspension; the second coming about after she and the pipe major of the university pipe band thought it a hilarious act of political sabotage to disrupt an awards ceremony in Bute Hall -whose guest of honour was a senior member of Thatcher's government- by marching gleefully down the aisle and launching into a rendition of The Red Flag. If it hadn't have been so funny, it would have been tragic, the only thing saving Dixie from expulsion being her role as the star player on the world championship debating team!

However, had his loyalty to Dixie gone too far this time? These were not the days of protests and shouting obscenities, they were days for protecting yourself, your family and your job. Times had changed and this was serious stuff both she and he were getting into, very serious. What's more, he had been the instigator. He was the one who had heard Lamont shouting at Peter Buchanan, and he had been the one to run and tell tales. Apart from his days at high school when he had clyped to the rector of the bullying tactics of Mad Mungo Munro, he couldn't really fathom why his psychological needs had seen him arrive at this ridiculous, current predicament. Maybe it was the destruction of the local economy in Lochaber when the paper mill shut down, maybe he despised men who could get away with destroying people's lives, maybe he just couldn't stand by and let that happen, regardless that he was part of the problem, or maybe he was just a good bloke who, when pushed to the limit of subjugation, had told himself enough was enough. Worryingly, though, the punishment for being discovered in the middle of this nonsense certainly surpassed the loss his two front teeth and having his head flushed down the lavvy courtesy of the Mad Mungo!

Elliot closed his eyes and focussed his attention on the small talk from the other side of the street. He was in deep concentration, so to say he shit his pants when he re-opened them was a tad on the understated side. Elliot couldn't speak; mouth wide open, tongue out and a slow appearing sense of fear washing across his already burning cheeks.

'Well, if it isn't Bonnie Prince fucking Charlie himself! I hope you've got some good tunes on that lap-top of yours.'

'Paul, what the hell are you doing here? More to the point, how the hell did you know where to find me?'

'Oh, just by chance. It's what I do you know. A hobby of sorts. Take a day off work, jump on a plane, stroll the streets of London hoping I bump into an old friend. Just a normal Tuesday

178

for me.' Paul stared into Elliot's eyes. 'What the fuck do you think I'm doing here, you arse-witted, Highland sheep-fucker?'

'I've no idea,' mumbled a wary Elliot. 'But it's bloody good to see you. I just thought I'd clear my head of the damn refinery negotiation for a couple of hours and here you appear. Wow. Coincidence or what? Anyway, how are things?'

'Elliot, you can dispose of the haggis right now. I know why you're here. Picking up a good reception are we?'

'What do you mean? I'm only listening to some tunes.'

'Aye, Elliot, you're a right wee Edith Bowman so you are. Who's playing? Belle and Sebastian? Jack Bruce? Please don't tell me it's fucking Depeche Mode.' Paul's expression hardened. 'Listen Runrig, you can remove your tongue from the bull's colon right now. I'm a cop for fuck's sake. I can see what you're up to so you may as well let me have a wee go on these cans.'

As Paul reached across to take the earpieces from Elliot's ears, Elliot pulled away.

'Don't even think about, Ellie Macfuckingpherson.'

'You ...c-c-can't,' stuttered Elliot, hesitantly reaching for the earphones. 'I've ...I've already turned off the programme and it'll take too long to re-launch.'

'Christ, for a man with such well-regarded negotiating skills, you're not so fucking competent at blawin' the stoor up someone's arse, are you?'

'Lying about what exactly?' stammered Elliot again, now shaking with fear.

'Well, Uisge-Breath, how about I requisition that laptop of yours and we'll see?'

'You can't do that. Not without a warrant.'

'Oh Elliot, shut the fuck up.'

Having been rumbled by his old college friend, Elliot sat still for a moment, not knowing what to say or where to turn.

'Look Paul, it's not what you think. Really!'

'It's exactly what I think, Elliot. You see, I've had a wee ...,' Paul broke off sharply, holding his hand to Elliot's mouth. 'Shoosh!'

Turning his gaze to the imposing door of the club, Paul looked on as another Mercedes pulled up and out stepped two men in pin-stripped suits. 'What the fuck?' He double checked with Elliot to make sure he was still recording.

Elliot was still playing it safe. 'What do you mean, "recording"? I've told you, I was only listening to some tunes.'

Paul ignored the weak protest and swung the laptop across the table. 'Good.' Lifting one earpiece to his right ear, he winked as he returned the other to Elliot. 'Okay, let's listen to what these arseholes have to say to each other.'

'Paul, can you please tell me what's going on'?'

'What's going on, Nessie, is exactly what I'm down here to find out and if you weren't such a smart wee bastard, the job, if it wasn't already, would have been a wee bit more of the problematical sort. So, if you'll indulge me, may I offer my sincere thanks to your fine Highland education.'

'What job? What do you mean?'

'Elliot, for fuck's sake! I'm here for the very same reason you're here. To find out why my boss -DCC Michael Hastie, Sir Alexander Lamont and by the looks of it, Alain DeWitt and Sir Myles Turner, are meeting in the Alba Club this very day.'

'You mean the heads of both TFW Newspapers and the British Television Corporation are in on this as well?'

'Well, I don't think they've turned up for a Bagpipe convention, do you?'

'Jesus Paul, I met that guy DeWitt when I was hunting with Lamont a while back. He was with a man called ...let me think ...yes, a Sir Peter Milligan.'

'You're kidding me, right? Milligan is the Government's Permanent Secretary! What the hell is going on?'

'And here was me thinking you were going to nick me.'

'Count yourself lucky, Elliot. Considering this amateur set up you've got going on, I'm surprised Sean Connery himself hasn't turned up and, for crimes against the noble pursuit of espionage, punched you square on the coupon. You couldn't be more suspicious if you turned up with a long hairy beard and a bomb strapped across your belly!'

12

hell hath no fury like a fat bastard scorned

Tuesday 17th June

11.15am – Belgravia - London

It was a throw back to the days of the Empire, a private establishment for London's Scottish elite. It was where drinks were served in luxurious old world elegance, where a member could get a bed for the night and where hands were shaken on big money deals. Sir Alexander Lamont adored the Alba Club.

Founded as a haven for the Scottish Victorian gentry visiting London, the Alba Club quickly transformed into a discreet meeting place for prime ministers, royalty and super rich merchants keen to advance their own interests. However, unlike the other, more famous, private Scottish establishment in Belgravia -The Caledonian Club- the Alba Club allowed Sir Alexander to scoff at the ideology of what most Scots thought to be Scottishness. Treating the club as his own personal kingdom, he had been the first member to hold the post of president three times and been instrumental in creating many of the club's more recent policies, such as ensuring prospective members held the appropriate lineage and insisting on a presidential veto. But more than that, Sir Alexander used the Alba Club to re-enforce his already potent authority. This was the place where he would often set his agendas for making Britain stronger and, of course, to further increase his standing in society. It was here where he would impart on everyone he met that he stood for London and for Britain. It was here where he became greatest fixer of them all and to hell with what they thought of him and his family.

It was in the club over thirty years ago that Sir Alexander had insisted to the then Prime Minister that the McCrone Report -a government paper commissioned to discuss the economic impact of the oil and gas discoveries in the North Sea, which highlighted Scotland's potential, if it voted for Secession, to be twenty three percent better off that England and Wales- be shelved under the Official Secrets Act. It was here that he arranged for four of the North Sea pipelines to be redirected to English refineries. It was here that he demanded the Barnett Formula be kept in place unchanged. It was here that he ensured the oil and gas revenues be taken out of Scotland's GDP periodic measurements. It was here where he met three influential hedge fund CEOs to discuss the destabilising and short-selling of the share price of Wakefield Bank of Caledonia. And it was here where he had persuaded the Press to begin its indiscreet and subversive campaign to mislead the voting public on Scotland's expenditure deficit. He knew Scotland contributed more to the Treasury than what most people believed. He just had to make sure no one found out. That way he could enjoy his status as London's most powerful man.

Keep them needing me.

He chuckled to himself. Only last week he had held a meeting with the Secretary for Enterprise to make certain there would be no official sanction for Scotland to share its electrical capabilities with Norway. Another little victory. Craving the power, he could get anything he wanted. He was the Chairman of UKES and without UKES, the economy would be in a shambles. He needed to be in control: for his family, for himself and for his legacy, his lasting reputation uppermost in his thoughts. Moreover, he used his position within UKES to ensure there was no chance of said reputation ever being compromised by the nation he had come to loathe. He was the most ruthless operator of all, and regardless that Scotland had a legitimate claim on 95% of the North Sea's resources, he would be the instigator to prevent Scotland, by any means necessary, from getting its grubby appendages on the oil and gas. There was too much at stake.

He also reasoned with himself as to Britain's needs. Yes, he despised Scotland for personal reasons but there had to be a public justification for Westminster controlling the UK's fossil fuel market. Therefore, for him and his supporters, there had been the delivery of a consistent message that Scotland had done "reasonably well" with the public being regularly told that the industry up there employed thousands. This, in turn, would keep most Scots with rebellious inclinations passive. So what if the majority of the energy jobs were in England, Scotland still profited. Moreover, Britain was stronger for it. But it wasn't just the oil. Privately, the oil boom had been conveniently under-played by both Healy and Thatcher thus preventing the Scots from realising its full potential. Publicly, what happened under Thatcher had been necessary for Britain's economic recovery and if Scotland happened to suffer in the process then it was only a minor irritant in the bigger scheme of things. Her handbag-waving strategy, in making the country economically stronger, had been to concentrate exclusively on the South East. What's more, Lamont thought the trickle-down effect had been successful. Of course, London had enjoyed the vast majority of the new found wealth and by creating thousands of jobs in the South-East it had been assumed the strategy would create thousands more in the rest of the country. Yet, he still retained a hatred for the traitorous disposition of Scotland. Why had it been so disloyal to the Union when the Union served it so well? Okay, he sniggered, Scotland might be a little miffed that their oil revenues had been used to subvert the miners, destroy heavy industry and pay social security to those laid-off, but wasn't that a fair swap for the new industry that subsequently evolved in the following years. Of course it was. In his eyes, Scotland's North Sea Oil had saved England but England had then saved Scotland.

Now, inside one of the great old members' rooms of the Alba Club, Sir Alexander Lamont was holding court. He sat at a large round oak table above a dark blue tartan carpet. In the centre of the table stood two crystal decanters, one filled with an

Islay malt and the other a Stathspey. To his right, a gold framed Raeburn hung above a gaping stone fireplace while in front of him, heavy silk curtains, again in tartan, guarded the long thin windows. He felt alive in his chair, his imperious glare filling the room, and like many who had come before, felt that so-called superior intelligence of the Scots. It was an embarrassingly shameful trait but one which some Scots were renowned for. Furthermore, with England's class-system and its squabbles with Society's pecking order long since holding it back, it was Scots such as his great-grandfather who stepped into the void, taking control of business and politics.

Sir Alexander's gruff, no nonsense approach appealed to the English, whose niceties didn't reach as far as telling someone they were bloody useless at their job, more intent were they at sliding a fine piece of sharp Sheffield steel into someone's shoulder blades. Nevertheless, there was the more than the odd dissenter in London who made it his mission to whinge in the right-wing press at the MacMafia's failings but as long as he delivered, Sir Alexander was King. Of course, when the country was being well-governed, his selective Scottishness and the characteristics of prudence, sharp legal wit and operational excellence was a show of strength for the Union, but when the economy took a turn for the worse, the whingers came out in force with appeals to free the country from the marauders from the North. It was how the Union worked. As long as the Scots embraced the Union then all was well in the land of the rose and the three lions. And Sir Alexander's success proved that.

DCC Michael Hastie, on the other hand, had never been intimidated by the likes of Sir Alexander Lamont. He had too much information on them. Nevertheless, in working his way to the top, Hastie knew who was in charge. He needed them but in return, they needed him. That was why he didn't flinch when introduced to the other men in the room. Sitting down to the right of Sir Alexander, he waited.

The room slowly filled up with a small group of men whose influence spread much wider than their public remit. In other words, they were regarded as some of the most powerful in

Britain. On Sir Alexander's left sat the quiet and unassuming but influential Sir Peter Milligan -Permanent Secretary to her Majesty's government. Next to Hastie sat Alain DeWitt, the media mogul and owner of TFW Newspapers who as well as owning several daily publications throughout the UK and across the world, also had a successful satellite television enterprise. To the right of DeWitt sat Sir James Montague, the long standing head of the National Security Department and next to him sat Sir Myles Turner, the newly appointed chief executive of the British Television Corporation. Hunched and slight detached on the far side of the table sat Cardinal John Kelly, the ambitious leader of the Catholic Church in Scotland.

Milligan, twitching with his tie, had been one of the early arrivals along with DeWitt and Turner. Cardinal Kelly and Sir James Montague, however, had been smuggled in through a side door by aides now sitting outside in the ante room alongside several hefty security men who had already swept the place for bugging devices.

DCC Hastie watched and listened carefully, observing how the men didn't speak much to each other. There was no room in their worlds for small talk. He had met and worked with them all before, sometimes abusing his powers to support their various strategies. Today, however, the others didn't matter, it was Lamont and Sir James Montague of the NSD whom he needed to impress. Hastie had been down in London a few times to discuss policing strategy with Montague but, frustratingly, the NSD didn't want him just yet, just his information, and regardless that he was already highly thought of and regardless that he had received many congratulatory calls from Montague after several of his operational successes, Hastie saw this operation as his opportunity to finally dismiss any doubters that he, indeed, was Britain's best policeman. If things transpired as he hoped and planned, he would be well on his way to becoming the top man under Montague within the NSD. Yep, this was big time.

Sir Alexander, meanwhile, didn't have the energy or the spirit for politeness when it came to business. It was one of the many characteristics that made him feared. He knew it, and so did these men around the table. Money, reputations and power, when men wanted all three, Sir Alexander knew how to inspire and knew how to manipulate.

The ice in the whisky tumblers clinked softly as the club butler left the room. The regal Sir Alexander began. 'Let me thank you, gentlemen, for meeting this morning at such short notice. Furthermore, we've all known for many years that this moment would come but even I have been taken aback by the speed of change. However, that is not to say I have been tardy in my scheduling; in fact, the lack of time may be to our advantage. It will save us procrastinating. Therefore, before we begin, and since we only have one objective at hand, may I suggest that we all try to keep to the point. And that includes you, Cardinal.'

As Sir Alexander sneered, Hastie recognised the evil. The ensuing silence from the table hinted the others sensed it as well. The only man in whom Hastie could sense unease was the Cardinal. Hastie was unsure of the clergyman's agenda and unsure that he should be here at all. Now it was Hastie's time to sneer, firing a fierce look across the table. Cardinal Kelly responded by mumbling a few expletives before falling silent as Sir Alexander continued. 'I also expect that what is discussed today will remain of a strict confidential nature and any such discussions on the matter, which take place outwith this room, be kept to a minimum. However, if you do have to talk, which I'm sure you won't, make sure you do so in the most private and secure of locations. After our meeting, it will be impossible for us all to meet up again.'

As Sir Alexander took a sip of Islay, some of the others removed their jackets and slipped them over their chairs.

'Gents, we are meeting here today to discuss the future of the United Kingdom: an institution very close to our hearts, an institution we wish to protect and an institution in which we all hold a large personal stake. Let us not be fooled, gentlemen, the state of the Union is at crisis point and if Scotland was to secede from the Union it would reduce all of us, and hundreds of thousands more, to extreme and dire circumstance. The political situation in which Britain presently finds itself is far from encouraging. The Government is in turmoil, the economic climate is worsening by the day and, if things continue as is, it seems to be a foregone conclusion that Peter Buchanan and the Tory Party will be in Downing Street after the next election. Furthermore, with the demise of Labour's influence, both down here and in Scotland, the Scottish Nationalists have seized power in Edinburgh and, worryingly, as long as Labour continues to self-destruct, the Nationalists' share of the vote will continue to rise. Therefore, when the Tories do gain control of Westminster, we will once again see the return of that old familiar imbalance of power. And such is Scotland's scorn for the Tories -Margaret Thatcher having seen to that- we will see a Tory Government with, once again, only two or three MPs from Scotland within their ranks. Consequently, and this is the most disturbing scenario, the door will be wide open for the Nationalists to go to the people of Scotland with the utmost confidence of winning the Secession Referendum.'

DCC Hastie eyed the men around the table with intent. He was searching for weakness but could see none. This was where he wanted to be, at the centre of truly big decisions. He turned back to Sir Alexander and listened some more.

'And let us be perfectly clear about one thing. When the Council of Europe published their directives on the Rights of National Minorities, everything changed. And as much as we abhorred signing up to that bureaucratic garbage, we didn't have an option. It was either sign or face up to the UK being thrown out of Europe. We had to allow Scotland have its own Government and that, I'm afraid, has negated somewhat our ability to be surreptitiously coercive with the appropriation of certain funds.'

Sir Alexander laughed while the others guffawed at his sarcasm. The looming change in the political landscape may have been a serious cause for concern but it wasn't going to prevent him from enjoying his description of economic slavery. As the table settled down, he quickly cut the joviality dead. 'However, when the Tories do win the next election, the people of Scotland are likely to seize upon the Referendum to change the current state of affairs or, indeed, demand a much greater portion of the crumble. Either way, we will all lose out down here. The United Kingdom will dissolve or be in such a position of economic and cultural crisis that favourable policies will have to be given up to the Scottish Government. Therefore, all hell will break loose in London, and when I mean hell, it will make Black Wednesday feel like a walk on the beach during a Cayman Island sunset.'

Slipping his pen from his jacket pocket, Sir Alexander glanced down at the leather folder in front of him. 'Gents, I have in front of me a list that highlights, and not to understate the matter, the cataclysmic effects of the Nationalists increasing their already sizeable share of the vote and the possibility of an independent Scotland becoming a reality.'

Hastie listened as the chairs shuffled. His eyes glanced across to Milligan, the Permanent Secretary. Being the Civil Service's most senior employee and the man who actually ran the government from the inside, Hastie knew Milligan had been considering the consequences for a long time, especially since he had served for seventeen years alongside three Prime Ministers. Hastie also knew that the dissolution of the Union was the most critical issue on the Cabinet table at any time during Milligan's tenure; much more so than the Saddam and Iraq, the economy, or weekend trips to Paris with extortionately priced hookers. What's more, given that both the main parties were in favour of the Union, government policy was always the same; the Union must survive at all costs, regardless of whichever Party was in power. Milligan's strategy, therefore, was simple. He was to ensure the government never made a big deal about Secession, especially in London. It was one of those issues that was always there, even though it was rarely discussed in public.

DeWitt, however, as a private entrepreneur, didn't have anyone to answer to. In fact, he held almost as much power as Lamont. Nevertheless, having recently withstood mass Union demonstrations and endured some tough negotiations concerning his near monopoly in private sector broadcasting, he felt an obligation to Lamont, Montague and Milligan for the "encouragement" they had provided in his struggles. Furthermore, if he wished to continue the expansion of his media empire, he would most definitely require the NSD and the Permanent Secretary's assistance once again. He also understood that an end to the Union would have severe implications on his many businesses, having to, amongst other things, not only renegotiate his broadcasting and publishing rights with two countries but also have to deal with the ensuing protracted complications and delays. More important to Alain DeWitt, however, was his knowing that if he were to utilise his organisation to influence events about to be discussed in this room, he would have a substantial file of personal data on some extremely influential and powerful men. Hastie grimaced. DeWitt was most definitely a man with whom he dare not mess.

Across the table, Cardinal Kelly harrumphed in his seat. Hastie had known the old cleric for many years. He was a shrewd politician. Mind you, thought Hastie, any man who had risen through the Church as fast as Kelly would be well-versed in how to work the system. Hastie had met him on numerous occasions, mostly at police and community conferences but also in his office at HQ. There was an unease in their relationship: first initiated by Hastie's "nine in a row" jibes, continued by the Cardinal's mocking of the financial situation down at Ibrox, then brought to a near collapse by both of them and their indefensible protection of a couple of sinister organisations. Time, however, had been a so-so healer and the Cardinal and Hastie had grown to respect each other's position. There was still a wariness but they both had to survive. And the Cardinal was exceedingly good at that. Accustomed though he was to holding an almighty power over his constituents, he found this meeting both a hindrance and an affront to his self-declared position in Scottish society. To be on equal terms with these six other men at this table was not what he had campaigned for during his time with the Church. He believed he was answerable only to the Holy Father and not at all to these men of lesser standing.

Montague -the head of the NSD- was also apprehensive: not from a financial standpoint but from a much more threatening stance. Montague was in charge of Britain's internal security and any matter that could disrupt, or worse still, destroy his plans, was most distressing. Britain's strategic position and its relationships with security services from other states and major international objectives were at stake. What's more, Hastie knew that an independent Scotland would rip Montague's office apart. There would be two new states to deal with and with that, a re-alignment of funds, new policies to be negotiated and a loss of several key stakeholders, like Hastie, to either side. There would have to be a re-structuring of the UK National Security Department from its present state, as well as the creation of a new Scottish Security Service over which he could expect to exert no influence. Key initiatives would have to be re-drawn and above all else, he would have an administrative nightmare with which to contend. Hastie, sycophantic as always had offered sympathy, imparting on Montague that he under-stood the predicament he now faced.

After permitting his colleagues to contemplate the outcome, Sir Alexander continued. 'Do we all understand?' he demanded. The silence was the answer he was looking for.

'First and foremost, and please ignore the official and published stats while we're at it, the United Kingdom, or should I say Scotland, is the eleventh biggest oil producer in the world from whom the UK Treasury has received direct revenues worth over £350 billion and hundreds of billions more indirectly, which, to put it gently, has kick-started and propped up the economy down here for over thirty years. For a long time, we have managed to deceive the Scots into believing that what they receive more from the Treasury is far more than what they give. In other words, just like our official stats, what we tell them is a complete fabrication. Scotland, without exception, is the biggest contributor to the Treasury outside London. And that excludes the oil revenues. In fact, every year the Treasury has a net gain courtesy of Scotland, with it receiving about £40 billion less than it should. Furthermore, with Scotland's untimely secession, it is acutely possible that up to 95% of those oil revenues will disappear from the Treasury's balance sheet, and with the price of oil and gas expected to rise again over the next few years, that is a source of revenue the government desperately needs to hold on to. Not just for the sake of investors and infrastructure development but for the jobs that rely on it. Make no mistaken assumptions, the oil and natural gas revenues are not just an incremental bonus, they are fundamental to Britain's economic development. All these lies we have been touting about the oil running out have been fairly successful but if the Scottish public ever discover that there could be up to a hundred years of oil left, there will be carnage.'

Sir Alexander paused to take another sip of the Islay.

'And let us not forget the energy the North Sea already supplies to the country in the form of oil and gas. The public is already rattling its monkey bars at the increase in utilities prices, so if an independent Scotland feels the economic need to sell to the highest bidder then the rest of the UK will not just suffer a deep recession but an almighty fucking depression. Not only will the Russians' UK loan book be substantially fatter, we will also be in hoc to Drummond and his boys. What's more, if, for any reason, Holyrood decides to increase its export and incremental energy taxes sometime in the near future, then those costs will not be endured by Scotland but by England, Wales and Northern Ireland. Consequently, our blue-chip manufacturers will see their orders disappear because they cannot afford the additional costs, and energy companies such as UKES will see a massive, if not devastating, loss in profits. Shares will plummet, public spending will be non-existent and, eventually, jobs down here will have to go, or worse still, be relocated to Scotland. So please, gents, let us not have any doubts, what we are talking about is Scotland having a slush fund the size of Norway's and a bigger say in the international oil market than Kuwait. And look how much trouble that place created for us.'

DCC Hastie was surprised at Sir Alexander's knowledge and understanding. He might be a ruthless son of a bitch, but he knew his stuff. On the other hand, Sir James Montague of the NSD wasn't quite in agreement with Sir Alexander.

'No, no, no, Sir Alexander. Don't you think you could be

overestimating the threat, dear boy? It's not as if the oil revenues are really that significant, it's only £15 billion or so per year. It might be a pain in the rear end from an administrative point of view but London's economy is so big it would easily withstand the fall-out. In fact, we've been subsidising the Jocks for years so I'm sure it will be they who suffers. No more English tax payers' money to fund their free gratis public services, no long lines of English customers for their banks, no welfare benefit to keep those Glaswegian junkies happy. And on top of all that, we can add some extra import costs for our goods and services. Oh no, Sir Alexander, I think your playing this up a bit too much, wouldn't you say?'

Sir Alexander's stared down at the table. He breathed in deeply. 'Are you really that fucking naive?' roared the infuriated chairman. 'Really, are you? Surely not? Or are have you just been existing in some parallel universe and believing our own press? In case you are unaware, the £15 billion is our figure, not the reality. So let me put you straight.

'When the Devolution Bill was settled with Scotland, Westminster reclaimed six thousand square miles of the North Sea, and the Scottish oil and gas fields within, and renamed the area as an Extra-Regis Territory. This means that they don't officially belong to Scotland when it comes to working out the financial contribution Scotland makes to the Treasury. However, that won't stop the UN and the international community from taking Scotland's side in a secession agreement. But what it does mean, at the moment, is that companies like mine, who re-registered themselves as English companies rather than Scottish, and who derive a large percentage of our revenue from the North Sea, can pay the much needed taxes, if it so requires, into an English based Treasury. In other words, the UK Government has fixed the economic viability figures in England's favour. But if that were ever to change, and the complete revenues streams such as petroleum revenue tax, corporation tax, excise, stamp duty, hydrocarbon tax and the incremental taxes such as VAT and exploration charges, and not to mention the billions in income tax paid by those employed in the industry, were to go to a Scottish Exchequer, it would create an unholy catastrophe. In other words, there'll be no more money left down here!'

Sir Alexander slurped back the saliva brought on by his frustration. But he hadn't finished.

'And just where do you think our beloved England is going to supplement these lost revenues when no one is fucking working because companies can't afford to trade and we can't afford to pay for our public services? Furthermore, if the price of exporting the oil and gas is ramped up by an independent Scotland, where do you think we will find the spare cash to balance the books? How will we pay for the Defence Orders? How will we produce goods for export if the manufacturers can't afford to manufacture because energy costs have gone through the roof? Jesus Christ, don't you fucking understand, you stupid bastard! The Scottish economy will be in surplus to the tune of forty billion, while we down here will have the collection tin out. All this nonsense about the spend per head and Scotland receiving more than its fair share is just that: fucking nonsense! And let me guess; you didn't know that the oil and natural gas underwrites the country's debt? And how do you think the hedge funds and investment firms will continue to generate their already enormous profits if half the companies in the country have gone to the wall? Moreover, how will we replace the billions the banks contribute in corporation tax? And how do you think we will continue to finance London and its entire infrastructure? Don't you get any of it? The funds we used for the Jubilee Line, the Channel Tunnel and the Cross Rail didn't come, as most people think, from London or English money but from British money derived in a rather large portion from the North Sea. And while we're at it, who the hell is going to pay for those bloody Olympics?

'All of these funds come from a British Treasury in what the UK Government has declared as Unidentified Expenditure for Projects of National Importance. In other words, the billions of dollars we have conveniently omitted from the Barnett Formula, the Block Grants and the GERS report! And before you ask: yes, we have fixed these reports in our favour as well because what Scotland receives is a direct percentage of what England, as a single entity, officially spends, which, as you'll no doubt now be aware, does not include Britain and its projects of national fucking importance!

'Listen; there are five hundred thousand, yes, half a million, directly related oil and gas jobs in the UK. Scotland only has 90,000 of them so that leaves England and Wales with the rest. That means 410,000 men and women in England who need that business to survive. Of that number, 240,000 are directly employed by the oil and gas corporations, 80,000 employed by its economic activity and a further 90,000 employed in exports. And those figures don't include the spin off industries that are reliant on the oil and gas like finance, manufacturing and the thousands of small suppliers. So, if you'll pardon my expression, it's not all about London, that's for sure.

'We could be talking about millions of people here …millions! And let me advise you that one doesn't require a degree in fucking economics to figure that out.'

As he finished, Montague sat in silence, cheeks flushed and head down. Hastie shook his head. That'll teach him, he thought. Sir Alexander breathed again while the other men in the room shuffled in their chairs with their glazed eyes set on the table. There was tension. But Sir Alexander didn't care.

'And if you would kindly let me continue, James, I might be able to impart some fucking sense into that empty Oxbridge head of yours. Do you hear?'

The room fell silent once again as Sir Alexander calmed himself with another large Islay. Staring at Sir James Montague, he let his words linger. He picked up his glass and stared at the peat-induced liquid. He also thought about the two billion in tax revenues the Whisky Industry gives to the Treasury every year but that was for another day. A couple of minutes later and he was ready to go again. No apology required. This was business.

'Number Two: The finance industry and the supposedly indefatigable Scottish banks and corporation tax.'

The others were well aware, now, of the economy's potential meltdown. Sitting up, they set their gaze on Lamont.

This, indeed, was very serious.

'The good news is that I've already made sure one bank will be taken over. In fact, I've been working on it for a couple of years now and the deal is almost there. Okay, so it might be taken over by a group who has its world HQ in Edinburgh but let us not forget that once this deal goes through, the organisation will come under the sole charge of LBST's English company. Therefore, if some of the undecided voters are seriously thinking of breaking away, they will be sure to think twice, especially if they know that one of their oldest banks would be paying its tax dollars into an English Treasury down here rather than one in Edinburgh. All we have to do, now, is ensure the other one will join it.

'The big two up there, three if you include the LBST Group, are among the top five contributors of corporation tax in the UK, bar none. Fortunately, there will only be two remaining in a few months, one of which will be controlled by London. However, let's not get complacent because the one that remains is still one of the biggest banks in the world. Moreover, as much as we enjoy having it down here, it will be extremely difficult to make the Royal Caledonian Bank relocate from its Edinburgh HQ. Alone it contributes over billions in tax and invests big numbers into new business development, as well as providing thousands of jobs here, in the States and across the world. And as much as I can't ever see it wanting to lose London's business, neither does the Treasury want to lose its tax dollars.'

The men at the table didn't flinch. The state of people's lives was not on the agenda

'So as well as the oil changing hands and causing a mass exodus north and over the border, we have to consider Andrew Drummond's plan to reduce Scotland's corporation tax rate as having the same effect. Scotland is already the ninth largest financial centre in the world and Edinburgh has the healthiest economy in the UK, so it's not as if it couldn't cope with finance companies flying out of London and up the M6.'

The other men at the table were furiously writing notes. They were calculating the potential losses.

'Number Three: The UK has thousands of companies that have quite rightly, because of the population demographic in the South East, located their head offices and logistics operations down here. If Scotland becomes independent, the administrative nightmare of opening additional international headquarters up there could be too much to bear, almost as much as relocating members of staff; if they decide to move that is. If they don't then it's another long line of people at the welfare office waiting for a cheque we can't provide because Scotland has taken all the oil revenues and the incremental business that comes with it! Think about it gents. Does the word chaos come to mind yet?'

Sir Alexander was just beginning. He could sense his words having the galvanising effect he desired. He needed to scare the men into action. This was how he always acquired what he required, such as the deal he made with the UN over land rights in the North Sea. He smiled as he remembered how he had persuaded energy officials in New York to back down. They became flustered, they were on the phone to Washington, and they disappeared to the toilet once too often. That was the extent of his power.

The room was warm. Sir Alexander stood to open a window. The sash creaked and the paint cracked. He breathed in. Turning round to face the meeting once more, Sir Alexander remained standing. Clasping his hands behind his back, he began to circle the table, his table.

'Number Four, gents: Defence. Think of all the Defence contracts that provide investment and jobs and national security to the country. Unfortunately, said Defence Strategy requires close on £40 billion of annual government funding. Admittedly, there could be a saving if Scotland goes AWOL from our Armed Forces but that would put our relationship with NATO at risk. Not that they will throw the UK out anytime soon, but it would concern them greatly if its North Atlantic location at Faslane is placed in jeopardy. The whole relationship would have to be re-negotiated with both the UK and with Scotland, and because of the geographical requirements required for our subs, we would struggle to find a suitably prepared base in England or Wales.

That, therefore, would bring us even more trouble from our American cousins who, like us, have invested billions in our Nuclear Defence Regeneration Programme and who, I'm damn sure, will not want to see their cash drifting down the Clyde as well. Typically, Drummond has indicated his opposition to Trident but that doesn't mean he won't renegotiate with NATO and the Yanks, and more importantly, their investors. In other words, if Scotland secedes then bang goes our position as the gateway to the North Atlantic and therefore the investment and jobs that come with it.

'Then, on a more simpler matter in relation to Defence, we will have to consider Scotland's military capabilities and the impending security and financial risks if Scotland was to secede. Will we have cross-border agreements on Island defence? Do we still fight together overseas? Can we rely on Scotland to support our international initiatives in the Middle East and beyond? Will Scotland continue with our suppliers? What's more, the logistics companies who support the Forces will, like others, have to renegotiate their current agreements with both the Scots and ourselves. Prices will go up and, once again, without the oil business and related revenues, we could be facing a collection of extreme cut backs.'

Hastie glanced across to Sir Alexander standing at the other side of the table. Here was a man at the height of his powers. Creeping around the table, he was the old headmaster spreading fear amongst his pupils.

'Number Five: Energy. With the world heading towards a more environmentally friendly culture, we in the South have had to make contingencies. With the price of oil as volatile as it is, we are now finding we are spending a small fortune in the research of more cost-efficient renewables. We're not quite there yet but we will be soon. However, I'm offering no cuddly toys for guessing where we've planned for most of that energy to come from. Oh, yes. With wind and water being the prime resources, Scotland has over twenty-five percent of Europe's renewable energy, which, England, Wales and, to an extent, Northern Ireland, will have to import from Scotland, who, once a-fuckin-gain, will be only too willing to sell to the highest bidder.

'Number Six: Our Assets. Or should I say our shared assets. As we know, Britain's assets are almost incomparable and fortunately, as the world goes into meltdown, those assets have permitted us some breathing space. Regrettably, to divide those up with Scotland would be an economical and logistical nightmare. Our gold reserves, bank reserves, and their effect on the value of Sterling; our seats on NATO, the UN Security Council and the G8; our military bases, our military capabilities, our military agreements; and even our bloody Embassies. Think of Paris and Washington and Moscow. Christ, what in hell would we do with them? Have one door for the United Kingdom and another door for Scotland! And let us not ever, ever, forget our Commonwealth Dominions and god help us, the Caymans and our Overseas Territories, in which we all know safeguard eighty percent of the world's hedge funds, 1.44 trillion dollars in banking assets and 29 trillion dollars in insurance assets!'

Sir Alexander deliberately raised his voice to emphasise his point. He wanted them to feel the severity of the situation. He needed them to agree with him but most of all he wanted to feel their anger, their fear and the insult to their power. If he could feel that then he would win. Again!

'Number Seven: the Yanks. They have always been more than supportive of Scotland, gents. Just think of the power and influence across that continent. And we're not talking about the odd immigrant construction company here. We're talking about men of influence in the highest seats in the land. So don't you think for one minute they won't support an independent Scotland if it is going to line their pockets?'

Lamont, in hammering home his point, could almost hear the six minds working in unison. But he had them. 'Listen, gents, we're fucked if we don't do something about this!' They were on board, each one thinking how to reverse the situation. But Lamont also knew that each one would be safeguarding his own position. And he was ready for that. He sat back down and before permitting anyone to speak; offered one final treacherous scenario. 'And number eight, chaps: Our Head of State.'

The men all turned towards Sir Alexander, reeling from what they already knew to be a distinct possibility.

'As we have witnessed, with his peacock-like posturing, Drummond has become one of her best buddies. How and why this has happened, God only knows. Unfortunately, and as much as we would like to turn the clock back, we have to accept that she is just as much Scottish as she is English. In other words, she has become a right royal pain in the arse of this country and one wrong move in the next couple of years could see her packing up court and heading to Holyrood. Yes, I know you're thinking I'm being a traitorous son of a bitch but I'm nowhere near as bad as she. Just look at how she reacted when that girl hit the crash-barrier for the last time. For weeks she was nowhere to be seen. Up there chasing fucking deer and sitting on her arse watching hairy men in kilts chucking logs around a field. And although what we are discussing today is bigger than the Monarchy, it won't stop the people screaming for blood if the houses on the Mall suddenly become a home for her annual vacation. The public already despise the Prime Minister and they're not too keen on Peter Buchanan's Scottish heritage, so the last thing they need is to see old Queenie walking her corgies up the Royal Mile for six months of the year. Christ, she's even the leader of the Church of England. What's more, don't even think we can pressgang Drummond, or her for that matter, into giving up on Scotland's right to a Head of State. Of course, and yes, we will need to put pressure on her but we will have to be careful. Sadly, I still have no idea what is going on inside the royal mind. There's something, that's for sure, and I know it involves Scotland, I just don't know what. And if I don't know, then it becomes a liability, a very large and uncontrollable liability.'

Sir Alexander took a moment to gather his thoughts, his eyes burning into those around him. He could not only sense their concern, but also their own agendas and ambitions pissing in a Scottish breeze. As yet, he was not expecting any response; they were too busy thinking of their own position. This was the moment for them to understand they were all in this together. He was ready to attack the table. 'Gents, I think I have achieved my aim of detailing the horrendous outcomes if Scotland secedes, but, as is my want, I now need to know what each of you may be thinking. However, I will warn you not to make any plans to go out on your own, and for two or three of you, no running straight to Drummond's door. As powerful and influential as we appear to be, we cannot fully exercise that power without unity and cooperation.'

Sir Alexander's aim was to return the Union friendly Labour Party and its self-aggrandising MSPs to power in Holyrood. If he could achieve that, the opportunity for Secession would be gone forever. And he would do it, by whatever means at his disposal. 'Have no doubts, gentlemen, having considered the consequences if Scotland secedes from the United Kingdom, it is therefore imperative we devise an appropriate plan of action to prevent it happening.'

He circled the table, planning to attack the least susceptible first. 'Let's look at what's at stake for you, Cardinal. Scotland has always been in favour of a secular society so I can just imagine Brown Shirt Benedict's response when Holyrood announces that your school system is to be non-denominational. Bang will go your exclusive control over one million people, as well your very achievable ambitions of becoming Pope.

'And Hastie, as much as you imitate otherwise, you are just like us: a slimy bastard. Rest assured, the NSD would only be a distant dream for your career aspirations.

'And as for you Monsieur DeWitt: If this whole affair goes breasts-up you can also be assured that the government will come down on your monopoly quicker than you can sell those hotels of yours on Mayfair and Park Lane!

'Leaving us, of course it does, with the British Television Corporation and the NSD.' Sir Alexander didn't even bother to look at the two men heading up those organisations. 'Let's just say that if this debacle is not sorted out soon, then Sir Myles and Sir James will be retiring to the West Country with nothing with which to remember their careers except for being known as a couple of useless bastards!'

The room fell silent and eerie. Sir Alexander had not described a propitious outlook. It was doom and gloom whichever way they turned. And it wasn't just their arses on the line; it was thousands, maybe millions of others, as well. 'So, are we all wondering what we are going to do? Well, I have a few ideas but first I want to hear from you chaps. You know, all for one and all that. And something constructive if you please?'

Sir James Montague, head of the NSD, was first to speak. 'Well, first of all, we certainly don't want to go offside with the Americans. They have invested heavily in this country as well as being our brethren on our commitment to international security. And with both jurisdictions wishing to continue as is, it is imperative Scotland stays within the Union.'

'For heaven's sake, Montague,' shouted Sir Alexander. 'We already know that. What we need to figure out is what we are going to do about it.'

Hastie coughed in readiness for his offering. 'As much as we consider the consequences, we have to consider where the success of the Nationalists is coming from. Even if I do disagree with his politics, Andrew Drummond is a brilliant politician. Not only has he been the driving force behind this movement, it is his political nous that has taken us to the perilous stage we are at now. However, and this is pertinent, they can be a bit of a one man band. Take out the king and the kingdom will fall.'

'That's a bit hastie, Hastie, if you'll excuse and pardon the expression,' grunted Sir Alexander. 'Taking someone out like Drummond creates a martyr, does it not?'

'Not if it's by accident, it doesn't.'

'Paris was meant to be a bloody accident and look at the trouble that caused the State. Christ, it led to the housewife's revolution which nearly brought down the monarchy.'

'But it didn't Sir Alex, did it? Time is a great healer and now look at the public. Their love of the monarchy is now stronger than ever.'

'Good point,' interjected DeWitt, 'and I made a fortune from it, even if yours truly did shoulder most of the blame. And I'm sure, with Sir Myles manipulating the BTC in our favour,

Drummond's accidental death could easily be played down in the international arena.'

'Maybe not,' pondered Sir Peter Milligan, the Permanent Secretary. 'The girl Drummond has as his second in command is a shrewd operator. She also has excellent support at grassroots level, as well as having certain sections of the Scottish media behind her.'

'But you're overlooking the fact that DeWitt and Sir Myles control the media, including Scotland's,' chortled Sir Alexander. 'A firm word with some top reporters and broadsheet editors and her credibility could fall rather quickly. How many titles do you have in Scotland, Alain?'

'Most of the broadsheets in Glasgow, Edinburgh, Dundee and Aberdeen and though I don't have the Tribune yet, I do have three of the Red Tops in Glasgow.'

'That's a possibility, gents, but apart from knocking the First Minister off, what do we have?' asked Sir Alexander.

Hastie wasn't shocked by the matter-of-factness of the discussion. Here these men sat, discussing the assassination of a national leader, and not one soulless body flinched. This was all business.

'Well, my flock will be sure to listen to me,' boasted Cardinal Kelly. 'And I can also have a word with those within my football club. They're a powerful lobbying group, you know, and I'm sure my message will have the desired effect.'

'Your football club?' sniggered a surprised DCC Hastie.

'Yes; *my* football club. We already have the chairman onside so replacing the old chip back on the shoulders of the masses shouldn't be a problem. If we can create fear in an ostracised community, they'll vote whichever way I tell them. If the Church has to be saved from inside the Union then I'll make sure they vote Labour.'

Hastie, however, was quick to point out that the Cardinal had been playing for both sides. 'But Cardinal, didn't one of your Archbishops come out in favour of the SNP last year? I wouldn't say that was one of your better moments?'

The Cardinal stared angrily back. 'Listen Hastie, my

loyalty is to the Vatican, not Britain or Scotland or even the Orkney Islands. I do what I have to, and if that means providing more benefits for my congregation then so be it.' The Cardinal threw his pen on the table and took a swift drink.

'Jesus Christ, Cardinal, if you'll excuse that expression.' blasted Hastie, 'your only loyalty is to yourself so don't give us that old shepherd bullshit. Can't you see that the SNP are just playing you for votes? If they win, there is no way the people of Scotland will stand for your shite if secession happens.'

'I have had assurances from Andrew Drummond on my requirements. What's more, it is being written into the statute books as we speak. Oh no, he won't go back on his word.'

'Please tell me you're not as dumb as you look?' shouted Hastie. 'If Scotland separates then they can tear up the fucking statute book. Surely you can't be so naïve?'

The Cardinal fell silent, reverting to contemplation. Sir Alexander smiled, patting Hastie lightly on the shoulder. This was the very reason he had brought Hastie him down here: to highlight to the old bead rattler what could happen.

That's my boy. More votes for Scottish Labour.

'And what about you, Montague?' asked Sir Alexander. 'What can the National Security Department do for us?'

'What we always do best.' Sir James Montague sat back in his chair with nonchalant arrogance. 'Destroy from within. We at the NSD will organise dissent, maybe violent, from within the Unions against Drummond's administration because every once in while a strike is needed to destabalise confidence. We can also feed Mr. DeWitt's newspapers with fabricated stories regarding the weakening Scottish economy, as well as closing down these bloody online comments threads. We'll also have our experts appear on television with some well thought-out and balanced opinions denouncing the SNP. You know: the drip-drip strategy. Scare the hell out of the voters. And with our men down here working their magic to destroy the Scottish banks, it shouldn't take much to have the Scots rushing to us in fright. I'll also have a word with our chaps in the Civil Service. Have them interfere and destabilise the workings of the Scottish Office.

Then we'll find some dirt on some Nationalist MSPs that we'll release to the Press. If we can't find anything substantially and scandalously newsworthy, we will make something up. But we'll go for the jugular; some serious crime, whose evidence, I'm sure, will be willingly supplied and corroborated by the DCC.'

'Quick and decisive. Excellent work, gents,' laughed Sir Alexander. 'And what about you Sir Myles? What's the take from the BTC?' Sir Alexander looked on intently. The BTC was fundamental to his strategy. Without its support, his strategy would have absolutely no chance of success.

'It should be quite simple really. With the top BTC jobs in Scotland already taken by Labour supporters, I'll order the producers, directors and editors to take a tough line on any pro-Secession issues, as well as ensuring our side of the debate is strongly if subtly endorsed by our *experts* keen to spread fear amongst the voters about Secession. Furthermore, our presenters will be harried by the programme directors to give Nationalist politicians a rough ride by contradicting their policies with negative analysis regarding Secession; the usual stuff like the oil running out, higher taxes, less investment, job losses. And we'll keep any news on the McCrone Report to a minimum. What's more, I'll also make plans to use the girl who does our late-night news programme more frequently. As well as the influence she wields in the industry, she's also powerful in political circles up there. As for here in London, we will project Scotland within the Union as a positive move for both countries, banning all comm-entary on the 'Sponging Scots' while highlighting Scotland's contribution to the United Kingdom. I'll also plan for some more Scottish-based programming so we'll move a few productions up to Glasgow. Historical dramas, documentaries, investigative reporting; all highlighting how good Scotland can be. That strategy, along with bolstering the Prime Minister's Scottish profile, should go a long way to appeasing both the whingers down here and the undecided voters up there. All in all, it should certainly have a lot more of them voting Labour.'

'Good stuff indeed, Myles. But just watch how you do it.

The way that girl of yours handled Drummond on News Line caused uproar, losing Labour more support than it gained. And keep any news on UKES's new oil discoveries out of the news as well. I would hate to think of the backlash if they found out about the new Gorrie and Carmichael oil fields. Just make sure you paint the Labour Party as the bright future of Scotland.'

'And can I ask?' interjected Milligan, the Permanent Secretary. 'You mentioned RCB earlier. How do you intend to weaken its position? They are a much bigger proposition than Wakefield Bank of Caledonia, certainly too big for another bank to take over.'

'Yes,' pondered Sir Alexander. 'I've been thinking about that. The RCB situation won't be easy but the City is much smaller than people realise. Like any other small town, it listens to rumours, its grapevine is rife with speculation and it doesn't take long for it to react, whether that is with confidence or with panic. Just look at how all those idiots bought up shares in the Dot-Com revolution. Bloody hell, they were buying stock without ever reading a balance sheet. Nevertheless, with the help my man's scaremongering, they are the very same people who are off-loading WBOC stock as we speak. All it takes is a crisis of confidence and the brokers are off and running.'

Sir Alexander smiled viciously.

'It also helps that the man at the top of WBOC is on our side. He's well aware of what's at stake and won't need much persuading to make a deal with Llewellyn-SBT, especially when he's offered a two million pound pay-off.'

Sir Peter Milligan, though, wasn't buying the idea that Sir Alexander could do to RCB what he was doing to Wakefield Bank of Caledonia. 'But you've still not answered the question. RCB is much bigger than WBOC. And in case you've forgotten, the LSBT Group is still a Scottish registered company.'

'Yes, tell me something I don't know, Milligan,' groaned Sir Alexander. 'However, with the economic situation worsening every day, we should be able to hitch a ride on the back of the international crisis without anyone pointing the finger at us, or the Government. We will, however, have to recruit more of these scum sucking speculators to our side. And as some of you know, I've already begun to further exaggerate the stories about RCB's exposure to the US Sub-Prime mortgage market and as much as we all know that Fannie Mae and Freddie Mac, and Wall Street, are most likely to blame for the mess, it won't take long for my men to further strip the City of its already decreasing confidence in RCB and LSBT. If they can, I reckon it will only be a matter of months, maybe weeks. Nevertheless, to add even more weight to my strategy, I think it's about time I had another word with my chap in the City. Get him to force through a reduction of RCB's credit rating. That'll more than scare the hell out of the market. Then maybe Milligan here can persuade the Government to take a stake in the banks. That would be the real answer. Remember, we don't want their banks to go to the wall but if the British Government procures a large share in the Scottish Banks then it would make it almost impossible for Scotland to secede. Moreover, if the Government can create an English registered holding company in which we control the taxpayer's interest in the Scottish banks then an independent Scottish Government, with RCB and LSBT as the major players in a new Scottish stock exchange, would have to buy the bank debts back from the English taxpayer. And that, I'm afraid,' sneered Sir Alexander, 'is something Scotland could never afford.'

Sir Alexander was scathing with his contempt. 'What a hoard of really stupid bastards they are. It'll be like Darien and Culloden all over again! And instead of London, it will be Edinburgh we will see in chaos, especially with the thousands of job losses it will have to endure in its financial sector. However, if all that transpires in the negative, I have our man Buchanan already lining up his cronies in JMCB for a take over. Oh yes, Jacob's Son no more!'

'But are you really that sure about Buchanan?' asked Milligan. 'He's already indicated that Scotland could go it alone. In fact, isn't he the wild card in all of this? He is, for all intent and purpose, a Scot himself.'

'In case you've forgotten, Milligan, so is the DCC here. But that doesn't mean jack shit when you believe in the Union.

And besides, I've already had a word with Buchanan and he's onside already. He knows on which side his croissant is buttered. Nevertheless, if you're still concerned, I'm sure the DCC will be vigilant of what Buchanan gets up to, and whom he meets, when he's in Scotland. More to the point, Milligan, I need you to be focusing your energies on things a little closer to home, such as imparting your influence on the government to pass the word that if Scotland breaks away it will have to shoulder some of the National Debt. Believe me; that should certainly inspire some of those tight-fisted bastards to come running down here for cover. Oh, yes. We'll make them pay, just like they do with Trident!'

Sir Alexander laughed as he snapped his folder shut. Sliding his pen back in his jacket pocket, he stared imperiously around the room, extremely satisfied with his morning's work.

'Right, gents, let us first attack the SNP's credibility and increase the fear factor. We'll keep the other plan for Drummond on the back-burner as our contingency. In the meantime let's get to work and make this happen.'

Paul and Elliot couldn't talk for a few minutes such was the shock at what they had just listened to. They sat there in silence, shaking their heads and choking to find the words. The disbelief ran through their bodies to the very depth of their beings. This was the kind of thing they usually only experienced while munching on a large bucket of popcorn and sucking on a Coke extra-grande as Tom Cruise and Daniel Craig were being tortured by some evil bastard with fucked-up facial features deep inside a Mongolian volcano. These things just didn't happen here: not in a gloomy cafeteria, on the third floor of a department store, in the middle of London, on a damp Tuesday morning.

'I …I …I …Jesus Christ!' whispered Paul.

Elliot remained still, eyes burning and ears disbelieving. This was heart attack stuff.

He had been instrumental in pulling off some brilliant negotiations during his tenure at UKES. He had even devised his own strategies to ensure UKES would come out on top. He also knew how tough and single-minded Sir Alexander Lamont could be. Nonetheless, Elliot's successes were usually restricted to an unwavering and professional commitment to due diligence on potential legal complications. What he just heard was maybe still business to Lamont but to Elliot it was treason, it was conspiracy and it was what most people would call a coup. If this had been Africa, there would be civil war and an international outcry. This kind of thing just did not happen in Britain. This was a despot and revolutionary problem.

'Holy Mary, Mother of all Gods,' whispered Paul as he stared deep into Elliot's eyes. 'Did we just hear what we thought we just heard?' He pressed his thumb and forefinger against his temples before squeezing the side of his eyes and letting his hand come to rest over his open mouth.

Elliot shook his head, this time with more than a hint of defiance. 'I'm afraid so, Paul. As clear as the day by the side of the Bannock Burn.'

'For fuck's sake, Elliot,' whispered Paul, trying to keep the volume of his anger and his fear to a minimum. 'This is not some fucking epic movie we're talking about here. That,' said Paul, pointing to the laptop, 'that is fucking real! These bastards are planning to bring down the Scottish Government and I don't care whom you vote for, this is undermining something we both dearly love. And I'll tell you something else for nothing, their plan is a helluva lot more than a slight on the people of Scotland, it is akin to depositing each and every one of us in San Quentin and throwing away the key. But not before they take a seat in the stalls and enjoy the muscle-bound chieftains of the Aryan race ripping off our pish-stained breeks and inserting their not-so-tender tadgers into our copper cracks. These wankers across the street are fuckers, Elliot: a group of self-serving, despicable fuckers!'

'I take it then that we're going to do something about it? You know: our Diehard, Bruce Willis, retribution moment,' smirked Elliot, trying to add some levity to the conversation.

Paul was not in the mood for smiling. 'No, Elliot. You and I will destroy the file. Then we'll go home, live quietly, play with our beautiful children, have lunch at the golf club on

Sundays and wait 'til those beautiful children pack us off to die in some old folks' home in Perthshire.' He paused. 'Of course we're going to do something about!'

'Any ideas?'

'Elliot, I understand you're a lawyer and emotion doesn't come high on your list of priorities but I don't think you nor me is in a position to think of a plan right at this minute; not when we've just heard some extremely powerful men hatch a plan to destroy our country. No Elliot, we need to get the fuck out of here, calm down and have a wee think. In fact, I don't think the dinner ladies over there are feeling too comfortable with our presence, either. I think the sweat, the whispering and our look of bewilderment may have something to do with it. Come on, pack that thing up and let's go!'

The two bitterly shaken men walked outside, turned left and quickly shuttled away.

'Where are we going?' asked Elliot.

'I've absolutely no fucking idea. But hopefully as far away from here as possible. There's no telling who's about. Just keep moving and follow me.'

Paul led the way, glancing over his shoulder and turning corners at every opportunity. As Elliot struggled to keep up, his steps became shorter and shorter until he started into a jog.

Paul could see the baby steps out the side of his eye. 'Calm down, Elliot. Just keep walking.'

'I will if you'd just slow down. My feet are going so fast I feel as if I'm in some Buster Keating movie.'

'Well let's just hope we don't end up on top of some scaffolding with your arse hanging over the side.'

'Ah, you're a funny bastard, so you are. But, seriously, have you any idea?'

'Not yet but let's keep moving and we'll grab a cab in a bit.' They hustled briskly for another five minutes before Paul thought it safe to take a taxi. Hailing one down just off the Kings Road, they both jumped in. 'Regents Park Plaza, please?'

'Well, well. Would you Adam and Eve it?' chuckled West Ham's finest as Paul and Elliot took a seat on the Black

Watch rug. 'Twice in one day, Jock. Friendly wouldn't you say? Anyway, how's all the cloak and dagger stuff going? And do I have to put me foot down?' mocked the cab driver.

'Aw, for fuck's sake.' muttered Paul. 'Of all the cabbies in all of London, I have to get fucking Sid James …again.'

'What's going on, Paul?' asked a frightened Elliot.

'Nothing. Leave it to me,' whispered Paul as he engaged the driver. 'All right, pal. What are the odds, eh?'

'I'd say about 25,000 to one, Guvnor. Who's this you've got with you now?'

'This, my dear driver, is the man I've been looking for. We're flying out to Vegas tonight for his Stag but the dirty bugger couldn't wait. He decided on an early start. Didn't come home last night.'

'I hope she was worth it, mate,' said the driver. 'You only get married for the first time once. Me, I remember my Stag night well. Forty years ago this year. Got trollied down the supporter's club before heading up the West End to see some strippers. Dirty slappers so they were. Mind you, never got my end away, not like Dirk Diggler here. Ah well, not to worry. I've got three kids and five grandkids now. See this picture. Last year down in the Algarve. Great time so it was and the food was all right. None of your foreign shit for me.'

Paul, deciding he wasn't in the mood for a quick chat, waited for the driver to continue.

'Anyway, how's your football up in Scotland these days? These two teams still kicking the shit out of each other? Never understood all that Catholic and Protestant nonsense. Now, Pakis and Northerners, they're a different kettle, but religion? All fucking nuts if you ask me. Anyway, I'm down at West Ham so I am. Had a few of your guys over the years. Like Frankie boy. What's he doing now then?'

There was tense silence in the back. 'Hey Sweaty, what's MacAvennie up to now?'

'I think he's doing some TV work,' said Paul.

'Really? We loved Frank down Upton Park.'

Knees up mother fucking Brown!

Elliot and Paul indulged the driver until they arrived at the hotel. The cab drove into the courtyard where a concierge was sharp on the uptake in grabbing the door. Paul gave the driver the fare and ordered Elliot into the hotel lobby. 'Thanks mate. Hope the Hammers do well next year. All the best.'

'Cheers Jock. And you make sure you look after Dirk there when you arrive in Vegas. I heard the Yankee birds don't take no prisoners.'

Sitting in the hotel lobby, Paul and Elliot were trying to relax. Not a hope.

'Settle down, Elliot. You're making me fucking nervous. In fact, give me the laptop and go get some coffee.'

'Settle down?' shrieked Elliot.' How in hell can I settle down when I've got this thing in my hands?'

'Well, as I said, give it to me and go get some coffee.'

When Elliot returned, Paul had the laptop open on the table in front of him.

'The coffees will be over in a minute or two. And what are you going to do with that?' asked Elliot.

'It's not what I'm going to do with it, Ellie. It's what you're going to do with it. First, I want you to send the file to Dixie using a Yahoo or Hotmail or GMail or whatever fucking account you want to set up. But whatever you do, don't register in your own name. Ask Dixie to save the file then copy it to a USB memory stick. Once she's done that, tell her to hide the memory stick in a safe place, preferably a safety deposit box. Tell her not to open nor listen to it until I'm back in Glasgow. And tell her not to call me; I'll be in touch. Don't tell her why; just tell her to do it. As for you, Elliot, I don't want you using your phone to call Kirsten or Dixie, or anyone else for that matter. No doubt Dixie's phone, and maybe yours as well now, will be tapped so no more calls from your mobile. Got that? From here, we will go to Euston where you will buy two tickets, cash, for the Fort William Sleeper tonight. Then you will grab your cahonas and head back to the office. When you're there, copy the file. Keep one copy on memory stick for yourself then send another to my Glasgow office marked private and confidential. Then you'll call Kirsten and tell her your mother's taken unwell and that the two of you will have to go to Scotland tonight. Tell her to book two plane tickets from Heathrow to Inverness then to pack a bag and come and collect you. When you arrive in Glasgow, change trains for Edinburgh and head straight for the Kelso Hotel on the North Bridge. Once there, you'll get a room, whatever the price, but don't use your credit or debit cards and register under a false name. Riley will do. In fact, here's my credit card. Use it for the reservation but pay cash. And stay there until you here from me.'

'But...'

'No buts, Elliot. This is not a game of snakes and ladders we're playing here. Just do it. In the meantime, I'm off to make a couple of calls.'

When Paul returned, he checked the email to make sure it was fine. 'Alright, send it!'

Elliot hit the *send* option and waited patiently till the email went through. After and age, the corner of the screen eventually read *send/receive completed.*

'Who were you calling?' asked Elliot.

'Tom Gray at the Tribune. I wanted to find out where Dixie is. She's in Edinburgh interviewing the right honourable Peter Buchanan. The fucking irony of it, eh?'

'You didn't tell him about the Alba Club, did you?'

'Don't be stupid. I know he is a stand up guy and all that but this is too big a story to tell anyone we don't trust just yet.'

'And what about you, Paul. What's your plan?'

'Don't you worry about me, Elliot. Just make sure you look after yourself because I don't think it'll be too long before Hastie and Lamont have a wee chat and your name pops up in the conversation. Just make sure you're on that train tonight but most of all, don't panic. At the moment they have nothing on us but that's not to say they won't have soon, hence why I need to make your whereabouts secure and to make sure this is one story Dixie gets published. Either that or we'll all be taking a long lie down at the Necropolis and wishing each other good night and good luck for many years to come.'

13

the lothian chronicles

Tuesday 17th June

12.22 pm – The M8 - Livingston

Dixie was delighted she was on the road and heading for Edinburgh; not only because she was looking forward to her afternoon's assignment but also because she had coaxed her boss into persuading the Chief Constable of Strathclyde to withdraw the services of her bodyguard for the rest of the day. She was free, at least for a few hours. She was also quietly pleased that Rory was with her in the car as well. If there was to be any assassination attempt, she thankfully had someone to hold her hand, even if it was only Rory. As they passed Livingston, Dixie turned to her companion. 'Okay, I know you're just itching.'

'Me?' mocked Rory. 'Nah, it can wait.'

'No it can't and you don't want it to. So out with it or forever please with your eternal silence.'

She had deliberately waited until now to let him speak. They were only twenty minutes from Edinburgh and that was more than enough time to squander on Rory's glorified historical recollections.

'Well,' started Rory, 'You know how I said there could be some Scottish tie-in between the Masons, Robert the Bruce, and the Templars?'

'Christ, Rory, it was only this morning. Please don't treat me as some doddery old biddy. Not yet anyway.'

'And you know how there could be some tie-in, which leads all the way back to Jesus and the Church of Jerusalem?'

'Do I? That's strange. I could have sworn I'd kept my mouth shut during your last wee spiel. Anyway, please continue my Wee Wise One. But be careful when you quote someone, mistakes like that will get you into trouble one day.'

'Really? It's never stopped you before.'

'Rory,' sighed Dixie. 'In case you've forgotten, this wee discussion is on your time.'

'Point taken, boss. Anyway, as I was saying ... Yes, so I reckon there is some long-standing connection.'

'Yeeess,' said Dixie, prolonging her reply while faking a yawn. 'Go on.'

Rory was bordering on the cocky. He didn't even turn to talk. 'Well, when I was reading up on the Templar Knights, I discovered they were the back-room movers and shakers of Europe. Lots of secret deals and investments and shit loads of cash and influence. In fact, they were a bit like the Hutchinson Group of their time.'

'Ooooohh ...spooky!'

Rory ignored the ridicule. 'Anyway, within the Templar ranks there was this guy called Hughes de Payens.'

'What kind of fucking name is that?' snorted Dixie.

Rory didn't rise to her mock contempt. 'Well, this guy, de Payens, ends up marrying a Scottish bird by the name of Catherine St.Clair, sometime, I think, in the twelfth century. As you will gather, she was one of the Rosslyn crew, who at that time, and maybe even today, were an essential branch of the big knob and fancy party brigade otherwise known as the Scottish nobility. You know: making money, stealing land, exploring the world, that kind of thing. Funnily enough, I even read that one of the St.Clairs discovered America way back in the twelfth century as well.'

'Fuck off, Rory. Now you really are talking pish!'

'No, seriously. Someone not so long ago found a pile of old scrolls and navigational maps in an Orkney Masonic Lodge. I checked up on it and there's an old stone lighthouse on Rhode

Island, which is an exact copy of one near Kirkwall.'

Rory grinned at his own glorified pomposity. 'Sorry, Dixie, the arsehole in me is digressing.'

'Well how about nipping your bumhole and telling me something that's not?'

'Anyway, as I was saying, the St.Clairs were extremely close to the Scottish Royal Family. In other words, they were officially aide-de-camps to the High Stewards of Scotland.'

'Are you saying the St.Clairs were a bunch of lachies?'

'Yes, some of them were. However, it may be salient to note that one or two of Caty and Hughie's descendants were already into the more senior line of work.'

'Ah yes, the High Stewards. And who the hell were they when they weren't at home shagging their cousins?'

'Well they weren't exactly the Monarchy but they were pretty high up the pecking order, a bit like the Army Chief of Staff or the Head of the National Security Department. As well as having the King's confidence, they were the top brass who actually protected and advised him. And to say they were influential could well be an understatement, especially when you consider the boardroom shenanigans going on back then.'

'Fair point, but their veins weren't exactly flowing with Royal blood.'

'Funny you should say that,' laughed Rory. He was enjoying this alone time with his boss.

And as much as she was enjoying taking the piss, she was intrigued by his theory. 'Well, don't keep me hanging.'

'Well, amongst the jigs and the reels, and after the Bruce had defeated the English at Bannockburn and royally pissed-off Edward the King of England, much of the Scottish nobility, including the Bruce, were excommunicated from the Church for being Templars. It also didn't help that Edward had the ear of the Pope who, in already having a long-held beef with the Templars, had no qualms about signing the Excommunication Order.'

Dixie's eyes were open wide. She pinched her lips then wondered at the validity of Rory's research -she also knew her

215

history. However, she didn't need a debate or a discussion at this moment in time. It was better just to let him continue.

'So in trying to raise Scotland's profile in Europe, the Bruce found himself in a wee bit of an ecumenical stooshie. He had battles still to fight and land still to acquire but to be successful in those endeavours he knew he had to develop his international relationships. Fortunately, there was no better way to achieve his objectives than to utilise his off-springs and their subsequent inter-monarchy marriages. I mean, if he required some additional support in times of war or the occasional need to add to his burgeoning property portfolio then why not sell off the kids. Fair trade, wouldn't you agree? Unfortunately, there was no way in hell he was going to get his way if Scotland was regarded to be outwith the patronage of the pointy-hat brigade in Rome. Come on, who would want their child hitched to a pagan infidel from the land north of Hadrian's breeze blocks.

'Bruce needed help, so who better than his well educated High Stewards and their aide-de-camps to turn to for some much needed assistance in constitutional and international diplomacy, and in trying to regain the favour of Rome. Beginning with the exchange of lands and the occasional persuasive offering of the odd child or cousin, it ended with a document very close to all Scottish hearts: the Declaration of Arbroath. However, the Bruce and his nobles, in deciding that the bartering of the horticultural and mortal matter may just about have generated the required softening of attitudes within the European elite, decided to push both their luck, and Scotland's eternal independence, by including in the Declaration one extremely famous passage:

"...for as long as but a hundred of us remain alive, never will we on any conditions be brought under English rule. It is in truth not for glory, nor riches, nor honours that we are fighting, but for freedom - for that alone, which no honest man gives up but with life itself." '

'Christ, Rory. Will you ever give it up with all that patriotic shite,' exclaimed Dixie.

He let out a mischievous grin, knowing Dixie wasn't into the whole national pride thingy. Well, at least not in public she wasn't. 'Anyway, it was world's first declaration exuding the virtues of the rights of man, and for the notion that the people could dispose of the King if he didn't take care of his subjects, or in the real world, if he became too big for his pixie boots.'

'Rory,' moaned Dixie. 'Stick to the fucking story.'

'Well, the Declaration's main aim was a direct appeal by the Nobles for Scotland to be brought back under the tutelage of the rulers absolute in the Vatican. Furthermore, considering it was written in the early fourteenth century, it was an impressive piece of work, so it was. And by the way, it worked. The great big pudding of a pontiff took it on board and declared Scotland a Nation State once again.'

Dixie blew hard. She was still listening but the car was rapidly approaching Edinburgh.

Rory picked up on her impatience. 'Are you still with me?'

'Yes Rory, but make it quick.'

'Well, for the first few years after Bannockburn, all seemed well again in the parish, for the time being at least. What's more, the High Stewards, for their fine work on the Declaration, were much in vogue with the Crown. They were the boy wonders of the nation, the Grand Slam championees. So when I discovered what happened next, and if you'll excuse my choice of words, you could have sucked me dry with a Dyson.'

'Thanks Rory, but I'll give it a miss.'

'Well, didn't one of Catherine St.Clair's great, great, great, great grandsons -whose name was Walter and who just so happened to be the High Steward of Scotland- end up marrying Marjorie, the daughter of Robert the Bruce.'

Dixie took her foot off the accelerator and turned to Rory. 'You're fucking kidding me?'

'No, not at all. And what's more, when David, Robert the Bruce's son by the way, passed away, the throne was passed on to Wattie and Maj's offspring, Robert II. And ding-a-ling-a-ding-dong, this is the first we know of the Stewarts as the Kings of Scotland. Or as we know them to be in our old Scots tongue, the Stuarts!'

Dixie shook her head, trying to suppress an excitable and childish giggle.

'However,' continued Rory, 'the real bonus feature was yours truly discovering the deference they held for their ancient past and their supposed loyalty to the Church of Jerusalem. That homage appeared in the public domain a generation later when the couple's grandchild became Scotland's first King Jimmy.'

Dixie had thought she could get way with planning her interview while she was driving. That plan had long gone.

'And in case you're wondering,' Rory continued, 'James is the old Scot's translation for Jacob. So as far as I know, this is when the Stuart Dynasty - latterly Jacobean - began in Scotland.'

It was an interesting theory and it was emotive. She was also delighted with Rory's investigative skills. Nevertheless, it was still just a theory and besides, she needed to return her attention to this afternoon's assignment. 'Brilliant deduction, my wee Rory. All you need now is some undisputed truth, some hard facts or evidence, as they say. Find that and I'll defer to your greater knowledge.' She glanced over at Rory again. 'But there's bugger all chance of that ever happening, is there?' She grinned. 'And that I believe is a wham-bam-thank-you-ma'am!'

Dixie and Rory hurried into the five-star Lothian Hotel at one o'clock looking more than a little windswept. The rain was not so much pouring down, as being blown in from the sea at forty-five degrees. It wasn't heavy or drenching rain, just the typical Scottish summer precipitation, which prevented the sun from shining for any longer than three or four hours at a time. Dixie looked upwards. The sky was awash with the whispy cloud formations that seemed to envelope the country from time to time.

They had been on time when they arrived in Edinburgh but since their technical competencies did not reach as far as persuading the gate of the hotel's underground car park to move in an upward direction, they had been forced to circle back round and park in the multi-storey on Castle Terrace. As they jogged across Lothian Road they passed yet another pro-biotic yoghurt sponsored event on the hotel plaza. Rory was miffed. He would have enjoyed watching the middle-aged female tourists bending over some exercise ball while having their flexibility tested by an agile and nubile blonde-haired promotional girl who appeared to be anything but unattractive in her arse-hugging green hot pants and nipple-sucking yellow vest.

Peter Buchanan's aide was on the wrong side of agitated when Dixie and Rory came bursting through the door.

'I'm so sorry we're late, Pippa. Goddamn parking again. I hope he's not too pissed off?'

'He's not, but I am,' responded Pippa in a tooth drilling, whinging and aristocratic accent more attuned to auctioning off paintings and furniture on behalf of the recently impoverished or deceased wealthy than wiping the arse and running the daily affairs for a leading politician. 'He's down here with Oliver in one of the private dining rooms and you'll have until two before he heads off to Dundee. He has to be there at four for a presentation to the University's Rector regarding some Life Science gobbledegook. So, regardless that you might be one of his favourite journos Dixie, there will be no going over your time limit.'

'Yes Ma'am,' spat Dixie.

As Pippa gently opened the door to where Buchanan was munching away, Dixie turned to the PA. 'Pippa, you weren't by any chance the Head Girl of your school, were you?'

'Actually I …'

'Thanks Pippa. See you in an hour. Don't worry, Rory here will get the door.'

'Mzz Armstrong,' grinned Peter Buchanan, rising from behind a large rectangular table strewn with a bigger selection of cold cuts, cheese, fresh bread and red wine than the Valvona and Crolla delivery van.

'I'm still a Mrs, Mr Buchanan,' said Dixie flirtatiously, 'at least until the Divorce papers come through.'

Dixie had always thought Peter Buchanan to be what they call in Glasgow, a handsome bastard. He had a muscular build, a sharp jaw line, friendly eyes and a good head of light brown hair, his only down side to being a super hunk being those puffed up and healthy rosy cheeks, which seemed to belong in the private domain of someone who attended an exclusive public school. Maybe, thought Dixie, the rosy cheeks enigma could be attributed to the early morning runs in the freezing cold; either that or a late night sperm facial from one of the second form fags. Anyway, it didn't really matter. He was married now and a fling with a journalist was way off his limits.

'So, according to the Fifth Estate, how are things in the world of Scottish politics?' asked Buchanan.

'I don't know, Peter. How about you tell me? I wasn't invited to the meeting with the First Minister today.'

'Oh Dixie, this country is just too damn small sometimes. Can't even have a quiet and confidential chat these days without someone knowing about it.'

'Ah, that depends on which quiet and confidential chat you're talking about.'

Buchanan fixed his eyes on Dixie for a second too long. And he knew it. He paused, reassuring himself that there was no way on earth she could know about his meeting with Sir Alexander Lamont. Impossible. 'Dixie, when you're in my position, there are many important meetings to be had.'

'Planning for the future, are we?'

'Someone has to and who better than Peter Buchanan.'

The verbal innuendo would go on all day if Rory hadn't alerted them with a slight cough and a glance at his watch. 'Yes, Rory,' snapped Dixie, 'time is of Pippa's essence.'

'You know Ollie Graham, don't you? My chief advisor. But I don't know this young man.' said Buchanan as he offered his hand to Rory.

'I never knew your last name was Graham,' interjected Dixie with an impish grin. 'I hope your ancestors came from this side of the border and not the other? By the way, Peter, this is Rory Hamilton, my only advisor. But only on time-keeping issues and certainly not on parking facilities.'

As they all sat down, Dixie pulled out her Blackberry. 'You don't mind if we record this today? I left my Dictaphone in the car and I think I might be in need of a reliable back up for my ailing shorthand.'

'No, not at all, fire away.'

As Dixie made to switch on the voice recording option on her phone, she noticed the email from Elliot. She read it once, took a couple of seconds to compose herself, then glanced over to Rory and then to Buchanan. She tried to disguise her concern.

'Everything all right?' enquired Buchanan.

'Yes. Yes. Catriona, my two year old. Not too well at the moment. But not to worry, that's what grannies are for. Anyway, where were we? Yes. Let's begin, shall we?' Dixie regained her focus. 'So, you met with Andrew Drummond today. Is there anything from that meeting you would like to comment on?'

Buchanan made himself comfortable and checked with Oliver Graham. His advisor nodded.

'We had an extremely constructive meeting, Dixie. As we stand, we are both conscious and concerned of the challenges facing both Westminster and Holyrood in the coming years. Fortunately, we also agree that the UK Government and the Scottish Government must realign and improve communication channels to ensure a better working relationship. Unfortunately, Mr. Drummond thinks that all future communication be handled by two independent governments and not the one.'

Dixie could already sense the difference between the language Buchanan was using and that of the current Prime Minister. Dixie smiled; not that the PM used such language when dealing with Andrew Drummond, more a case of spitting blood. Buchanan's rhetoric, however, was inclusive. Very clever, thought Dixie

'Conversely,' continued Buchanan, 'and being of fine Scottish blood myself, I believe that Scotland is best served within the Union. However, there is far too much animosity at the moment especially from the Labour Party and though I find it amusing that they have brought it upon themselves, I do agree with the Prime Minister when he says that all four countries within the Union should be learning from each other. What's more, I'm sick of all the sniping especially from those little

Englanders down south and the anti-English campaign up here. It's not healthy and it's not constructive. Fortunately, I also believe in the settled will of the Scottish People. If they choose to vote for Independence then who am I to stop them. I would, however, strongly advise against it. Because in times of trouble, and there is much ahead, I believe we should be pooling our strengths.'

Buchanan sat back and relaxed. He had rehearsed these words a thousand times.

Dixie's mouth, as well as Rory's, seemed to be locked open in suspended animation. *What the hell?*

'Look Dixie, Westminster has to stop turning a blind eye to Scotland, hoping this issue of separation will go away. We all know the people of Scotland are big enough to decide for themselves, but nevertheless, I just hope they decide to stay in the Union because I'm sure, that in the long run, it will be better for all of us.'

She was more than a little taken aback, his words nothing like she expected. Certainly not after what Elliot had told her about Buchanan's meeting with Sir Alexander Lamont. Were these words really coming from the mouth of a Tory leader, she asked herself. He has to have another agenda. Or is it just his way of feeding the people what they want? Saying nothing and everything at the same time. 'Is this new rhetoric,' enquired a perplexed Dixie, 'emanating from the fear of losing out on the oil and natural gas revenues?'

'We all know about those revenues, Dixie, and all the benefits they bring, but high priced oil always comes at a cost. Higher energy costs, higher transports cost, higher production costs, which are always met by the consumer. I just believe the United Kingdom, with all its combined and shared resources, is better placed to negotiate on future energy issues, especially the growing might of Russia.'

'Are you telling me then, because of the other states' reliance on the oil and gas, that the last thing Westminster needs is for Scotland to secede?'

'Look Dixie, the rest of Britain will survive whether

Scotland secedes or not. Things might be difficult for a while down South but not as bad as they will be for Scotland if the oil price falls again.'

Dixie raised her eyebrows. 'But even if that does happen in the short term, prices will soon be on the rise …again?'

'You never know. OPEC and the G8 countries have been discussing this for some time now and once the speculators have come to their senses, I've no doubt the price will be kept at a standard rate.'

'Maybe so, but many of the eminent scientists in the field have been discussing the effects of Peak Oil. You know, when demand outstrips supply and the price just keeps on rising.'

'Yes, I'm well aware of Peak Oil but there is more oil out there; the world just has to find a way to get at it.'

'Is that why some of the companies down south, who are reliant on the oil and gas in the North Sea, been pressuring you to preserve the Union?'

Ollie Graham coughed, an indication that Buchanan was giving too much away. Buchanan was slightly bewildered. *No, she couldn't possibly know about my meeting with Lamont.*

Dixie grinned. 'You can ignore my last question if you want but, just to let you know, I'll be keeping it in my wee file of secrets until times need.'

Dixie glanced at her notes again as Buchanan fixed his tie. Rory shifted his eyes towards Ollie Graham. The advisor was about to shit himself. Rory tried not to laugh.

'Obviously, there was much more than the oil to discuss with Mr. Drummond this morning?' asked Dixie. 'Trident and Faslane on the agenda by any chance?'

'Yes, we did talk about Defence but as yet we couldn't arrive at a consensus. Of course, we both understand the benefits of the Nuclear Programme to the economy, and to our national security objectives, but in relation to Defence, no, we couldn't agree on a solution acceptable to both sides moving forward.'

'If the two of you can't agree on such issues as Defence and the North Sea, surely you must be considering a move towards the federal option of government?'

'Absolutely not. The United Kingdom wasn't devised in such a way. For a start, it would create even more problems than we have now and several scenarios which would be detrimental to our system of constitutional monarchy; not to mention the increased animosity it would encourage between our individual states

'You mean like Scotland's oil revenues being used as a safety net for England?'

'Ah Dixie, you're a trier that's for sure. No, a federal system would create isolationism and self-preservation. Because of the larger voting community in England, the leader of this new federal institution would almost exclusively be English. And we all know that that wouldn't be fair, whatsoever. No, culturally and economically it would be a disaster. Moreover, where would the constitution stand? How would it work with the Monarchy? No. I think we have enough tiers of government without adding anymore.'

'So, in which way do you think the political framework would work best?'

'The devolved government in Scotland administers practically everything in Scotland bar the Treasury, Defence, Social Security, State Broadcasting and Corporation Tax. It has slightly more power than Wales and Northern Ireland but less than Westminster. The major issue we have to solve, between Scotland and England, lies somewhere between greater fiscal autonomy for Holyrood versus Scottish MPs debating and voting on matters exclusively for England. Personally, I think they have been the two biggest mistakes of the Devolution Bill. Furthermore, Andrew Drummond and I are both in agreement that the present arrangement shouldn't continue in its current state, not for any political gain but for democracy itself. It's an absolutely crazy situation in which we find ourselves. What's more, it frustrates many of the people in both Scotland and England, and rightly so.'

'But these five departments are pretty much what makes a country tick.' offered Dixie. 'And yet they are still controlled by Westminster. Not entirely fair, is it? And plus, if you are an advocate for increased fiscal autonomy for Holyrood, surely that will eventually lead to the Treasury having to relinquish the oil revenues back to Scotland? And if that happens there will only be one outcome.'

Buchanan leaned forward, fixing a stare on Dixie through steel blue eyes. 'Listen Dixie, I have my thoughts on what to do regarding the oil revenues and greater fiscal autonomy but you're not going to hear them today. It's just that things are …how do you say …complicated at the moment.'

Buchanan let what he said hang in the air for a second. 'However, if you do think I'm going to make a commitment on the matter, you've got another thing coming. I might be new to the job but I'm certainly not stupid.'

Dixie decided she would drop the subject of oil. She wasn't getting anywhere with that line today. However, a wee dig at the heart of the constitutional set-up wouldn't go amiss. 'But if Scottish Westminster MPs withdraw from voting on English matters, it will surely play into Tory hands? After all, most of them are Labour at the moment.'

'Of course it does … at the moment, but it would be up to Labour, or any other party for that matter, to work harder in persuading the voters in England and Wales to vote for them. That is the way democracy works.'

'But you know that after the next Westminster election, half of these Labour MP's will be gone. I mean, the SNP could win up to thirty or forty seats, and that's a pretty big mandate for them and even better news for you, cos as we stand, Drummond has publicly declared that his party won't vote on matters that are exclusive to England.'

'Look Dixie, it's not my fault the Labour Party is in such a mess and that Drummond has come up with this strategy. Yes, of course, it is good for the Conservatives but it's not good news for the state of the Union. I mean, with all those SNP members not voting, it's pretty much like sticking two fingers up to the system.'

Dixie was puzzled. *Where is he going with this?*

'So you're wondering what I am going to do about it?'

225

challenged Buchanan. 'Move to bring the SNP onside, that's what. Yes, it might mean change but if it saves the Union then that is what I'm prepared to do.'

She hadn't been prepared for Buchanan and was clearly flustered by what he was saying. She needed time to think. She was also conscious of the time. Flicking a couple of pages back and forth on her note pad, she recomposed herself.

Buchanan looked over and smiled. *Keep them wanting more.*

'Moving on,' said Dixie. 'How do you intend to advise your Scottish MSPs when dealing with the SNP and the notion of Secession?'

'The Tory Party within Holyrood must do everything in its power to support the people of Scotland, whether that be in Education, Health or Policing. That is the reason they are there. They have not been elected to benefit England or Wales or Northern Ireland but to help Scotland move forward, and I will support them in any way I can. But what I told them this morning, and it's what they believe in, is that Scotland is better served within the Union and not out of it.'

'So does that mean, if you win the next Westminster election that is, that you will consider giving more powers to Holyrood to further improve the lives of people in Scotland?'

Buchanan was rueful. He felt he was trying to pacify a goddamn Highland Terrier. 'Andrew Drummond and I had a very frank discussion today and that is all I can say on the matter. We discussed a variety of issues, including playing golf sometime, but as the future is concerned, we don't know what is going to happen.'

'But if you win a landslide at the next election, it will give the SNP a mandate to go to the people with a referendum they could possibly win?'

'And that is the very reason we in the Conservative Party will be trying our utmost to encourage the people of Scotland to stay in the Union. I mean, think of all the benefits we will bring to the table when we're in power.'

14

whisky makes it all so clear

Tuesday 17th June

1.58 pm – St James Square - London

Elliot was back at the UKES head office only half an hour after Paul had given him five hundred pounds in cash and jumping on a train back to Glasgow. He had taken a cab and sat passively in the back, running over Paul's instructions again and again.

When the cab dropped him off, he darted up the steps and through the main door, making sure to avoid eye contact with any of the reception and security staff. As he stepped into the lift, he began to hope that his boss was still out of the office and praying that DCC Michael Hastie was still with him. The lift doors opened. It was quiet, the only sound being Marie's light fingers on a keyboard.

'My goodness, Elliot, you're ashen faced. Is everything all right?'

'Yes,' offered Elliot with a fake languidness, 'But my mother has taken unwell. The doctor says she felt palpitations in her heart so they've taken her into hospital. I'm going to have to take a couple of days off, head up to see her and look after Dad. Kirsten has already booked a flight for later today and she's going to pick me up before we go to the airport.'

Elliot was hoping Marie believed him. He didn't need her to be asking any awkward questions. 'I'm just going to finish up what I was working on this morning, make some calls and pull some work together to do on the plane.'

'Oh, Elliot, I'm so sorry. Is there anything I can do?'

'No, you're grand, Marie, but thanks anyway. I'm sure everything will be fine. More to the point, do you know when the Boss will be back?'

'No, sorry. You know him and his meetings. They can easily, and usually do, turn into a long lunch so I've no idea. He might not even be back in today. Who knows?'

'Ah well, I'll be in my office if anybody needs me.'

Elliot faked a sorrowful walk to his office. Once inside, he locked the door, took a seat at his desk and immediately opened his laptop. He set to work copying the file.

He was in a daze and beginning to sweat again, the stress squeezing his body. He was tight, his heart thumping and his head pounding. He just wanted out of there but knew he had to follow Paul's instructions. When the file was copied to the memory sticks, he laid one on the desk beside him and the others he slipped into his wallet. He picked up the phone and called Kirsten.

'Hi honey, I've got some bad news. Mum's taken ill.' He listened while Kirsten talked through her shock before telling her what to do. 'Honey, can you book two seats tonight, anytime after seven, to Glasgow or Inverness; either will do. And can you then pack a bag and come pick me up at the office as soon as you can?'

'But Elliot, wouldn't it be better if I just met you at the airport?'

'No honey, I'd prefer you collect me.'

'Okay darling, if that's what you want. I should be there about fourish. And are you sure you're all right? In fact, why don't you just come home now?'

'The doctor says Mum is fine, Kirsten. It's not a matter of life and death.'

'But she's seventy-six, Elliot. You never know.'

'Thanks honey, but you're just making things worse. As I said, just pick me as soon as you can. And don't bother calling

Dad. He's with Mum at the hospital.'

'Okay, I'll be there as soon as I can.'

Elliot quietly put the phone down, stumbled clumsily over to his drinks cabinet and poured himself his second large whisky of the day. Turning towards the window, he held his glass in the air and offered a toast to the city. He stood silently for a short time, thinking about his time in the London and wondering if he would ever see it again. He couldn't believe that even in his distressed state he could be so melancholic. 'Come on, Elliot, get a bloody grip of yourself,' he muttered. Again he stood motionless for a few minutes before a small smile passed his lips. 'What the hell, it will certainly make life a wee bit more interesting than deciphering UK tax law!'

Sitting back down, he pulled out a non-logoed, white envelope. His hand was quivering as he wrote the address on the front. He also composed a small note before picking up the memory stick, wrapping it in paper and slipping it into the envelope. There would be a post box at the train station. He licked the envelope closed but it wouldn't stick down properly, deciding to wrap Sellotape around the top for extra security. After locking it in his laptop case and placing the case on his desk, he waited.

Elliot was almost drunk by the time Kirsten called him back at five to four. For a couple of hours, he had been stoking his adrenalin with the whisky. He was exhausted. Packing up his things, he headed out the door, saying goodbye to Marie on the way and telling her he didn't know when he'd be back but he'd be sure to call her as soon as he knew.

As the lift opened on the ground floor, Elliot's tired eyes strained to see out through the main doors. He was checking to see where Kirsten had parked the car. Keeping his head down, he made to leave: attention was the last thing he needed. However, as he raised his arm to push open the door, he saw a black Mercedes pulling up behind Kirsten. He stood frozen, watching in horror as Lamont and Hastie stepped on to the pavement.

Oh, Kirsten, please don't jump out and say hello!

He made an excuse to the doorman that he'd better take a pee. Turning swiftly to his right, he disappeared into the toilets behind the waiting area. He locked himself inside a cubicle and listened as the echo of the two men's chatter bounced off the high ceiling of the atrium. He would wait until he heard the lift doors closing before leaving. In a matter of seconds, he was through the main doors and down the steps to the waiting car.

'Hi honey,' said Kirsten with a sympathetic smile. 'I have us booked onto the eight-fifty to Glasgow. Are you wanting to go back home first, or would you rather go somewhere for a bite to eat?'

'I don't really know how to tell you this, Kirsten, but we won't be taking the plane, we'll be going on the Sleeper.'

While Elliot waited in his office, he had contemplated telling Kirsten nothing of the day's events but couldn't bring himself to lie to her. Not only because he loved her, but also for the unfortunate truth that he was a bloody awful liar.

'What do you mean "we're not taking the plane"? Do you know how much these tickets cost me?'

'Yes, I know, Kirsten, but I had to ask you to book the flights for a reason. I've not had the best of days at work, honey. Quite the opposite, in fact.'

'Elliot, what the bloody hell is going on?'

'Nothing yet. It's just that something could happen and I'm just playing it safe. But for the moment, just drive. Head for the Plaza Hotel on Regents Park and I'll explain on the way. We can park the car there and take a cab to Euston.'

As Kirsten turned the ignition and started to drive, she swivelled her head and scowled. 'Okay, Buster. Start talking.'

Sir Alexander Lamont and DCC Michael Hastie had indeed taken the long lunch Marie had suggested. Laughing and joking as they came into the Reception, Marie shook her head and tutted like the mother she was. 'Boys will be boys.'

'Oh Marie, we're only enjoying a wee private joke,' stuttered Lamont in an affected Scottish accent.

Marie thought the Scottish accent was strong enough at

the best of times but after Lamont had had a couple of drinks, her translation skills could be severely tested. 'So I take it lunch was more enjoyable than the meeting?' she asked with a smile intended for couple of four year olds and not for two of the most powerful men in the country.

'Actually Marie, I'm not sure which of the two was the more enjoyable,' smirked Lamont as he turned to Hastie and winked. 'Anyway, any messages for me?'

'Yes, there are a few. Do you need me to come into the office?'

'No, you're fine, unless there is anything of an urgent matter, that is. Otherwise, we can do it tomorrow. Anyway, I'm just going to have one last chat with Hastie here and then I'll head home.'

'Oh, I nearly forgot. Elliot had to leave the office early. His mother has taken unwell so he's heading up to Scotland to see her. He's taken some work with him and said he'll be in touch.'

'That's a pity. Walker's a good man.'

'Though he did say she should be fine and he'd be back in a couple of days.'

Hastie furrowed his brow when he heard the name. He was trying to recollect where he had heard it mentioned before but couldn't think where. 'Did you say "Walker", Sir Alex?'

'Why? Do you know him?' asked an indifferent Lamont.

'I do, but I can't think where from.'

'Don't worry, old boy. I'm sure if it's important it'll come back to you. Anyway, how about one for the road? And Marie? Hold all calls for ten minutes, will you.'

They two men turned to walk the few feet towards Lamont's office but as Lamont opened the door, Hastie came to a sudden stop. 'Elliot Walker. I knew it.'

Without seeming to pay attention, Lamont moved through the door. However, as he made to take his jacket off, he spoke. 'Hope he wasn't the one shafting that ex-wife of yours. What an unfortunate turn of events that would be.'

Hastie ignored the snide remark. 'Does he work for you,

231

Sir Alex?'

'Yes, of course. He's my Chief Litigator. And a damn good sort he is, too.'

'Can we go inside, Sir Alex?' asked Hastie as he gently guided the older man into the office. Closing the door behind him, Hastie asked Lamont to sit down. 'We need to talk.'

Lamont was beginning to look more like a scorned and cheeky child with every passing second. 'Why, is something up, Hastie?'

'I hope not but I do need to ask you a few questions?'

'Sure, go ahead.'

'Is this Elliot Walker by any chance Scottish?'

'Oh yes. Fort William, I think?'

'And how long has he been working for you?'

'About four years. Helped me through some tricky and difficult negotiations.'

'And before that?'

'The Dutch bastards. Was with them, I think, since university.'

Hastie was agitated but his intuition told him he already knew the answer to his next question. 'Let me guess, University of Glasgow?'

'Yes, I think so. Smart little bugger. Finished top of his class. Magna Cum Laude.'

Hastie didn't give a damn about the honours. 'And where is his office?'

'Two doors along from here. I need to have him close by so he can run over various strategies from a legal point of view.'

'What do you mean?'

'A and M, tax, employee relations. Look Hastie, where are you going with this?'

Hastie wasn't for listening. 'And have you ever discussed politics with him?'

'Not really. He doesn't do politics. No, all he's ever mentioned is that he's not a supporter of Andrew Drummond which, considering all my rants about the SNP was a bloody good thing to hear.'

'And would you consider him to be a loyal employee?'

'Of course. Very much so. Very dedicated and diligent.'

'And does he have access to your office, at all?'

'Not really. But I trust him implicitly. He'll pop in for the odd paper when I'm out but Marie is always here.'

'And you've never left anything in here in relation to our wee meeting today?'

'Absolutely not! I have no evidence of that sort in here whatsoever. I wouldn't be that foolish.'

'And have you ever discussed anything in here in relation to your wee operation. You know; something which could be connected to what we are planning?'

'No, nothing at all. The only time I've even remotely discussed the matter was the other week when young Buchanan was in. I had to give him a good talking to about the implications of the Scottish Problem but there was no mention of the meeting today, or our plans.' Lamont sat up indignantly. 'Look Hastie, what the hell is all this about?'

Hastie didn't respond. He needed information quickly. 'And when you gave your man Buchanan this "talking to", you didn't by any chance raise your voice or shout at the man?'

'Hastie, I'm always shouting in here. No one takes any notice. C'mon, boy. What are you trying to say?'

'What I am saying, Sir Alex,' forced Hastie, 'is that the "nobody" Dixie Armstrong met up with at Loch Fyne was none other than Elliot fucking Walker!'

Hastie picked up a paperweight from Lamont's desk and lashed it at the door, throwing it with such force that it left a dent in the panelling. Lamont sat in passive silence, hoping his worst fear wasn't about to become a reality.

There was a knock on the door. 'Is everything all right Sir Alexander?' enquired a sheepish Marie.

'Yes, everything's fine,' snapped Lamont. 'Just get back to work.'

Lamont turned to Hastie. 'You're not actually implying that Walker listened in on my conversation with Buchanan, put two and two together, called this journalist friend of his and headed up to Scotland to tell her what he heard?'

'That's exactly what I'm implying, Sir Alexander. I'm a cop for Christ's sake. It's my job to deduce things.'

'No, it can't be so. Walker would never to that. It would ruin his career. Oh no, no, no, no. Impossible.'

'Well, in case you didn't know, he and Armstrong are old friends from university. Loyalty runs deep, Sir Alex.'

'Yes, but he couldn't have. It's just not in his nature.'

'Who cares about his fucking nature!' Hastie's voice was notching up the decibels. 'If you hear someone bawling out one of the country's leading politicians on a matter as delicate as this you're not exactly going to go home, forget about it then bugger off on a picnic with the wife. Are you?'

'Listen Hastie, just calm down. In fact, I'm sure there is nothing to worry about, at all.'

'Yes, you could be correct, Sir Alex, but something tells me otherwise'

'But I can't believe that Walker would do such a thing. Not to me anyway.'

'Oh really? Well how very fucking convenient for us that on the very day I come down for this meeting, he just happens to fuck off to Scotland because his mother has taken ill. C'mon, Sir Alex, think about it.'

Lamont didn't wait. He hit the intercom. 'Marie, can you come in, please?'

As Marie timidly opened the door, Lamont was hoping she hadn't heard the recent conversation with Hastie. 'Nothing much to worry about, Marie. Just a couple of questions.'

'Yes Sir.'

'Take a seat,' offered Lamont as he indicated for Hastie to give Marie his chair. 'Marie, how was Elliot today?'

'He seemed fine, Sir Alex. He came in late. About nine-thirty, nine-forty-five. Said Kirsten wasn't feeling too well.'

'Bloody hell, has this boy caught some infectious virus. All his family seem to have taken ill on the same bloody day. And then what?'

'Well, we chatted about nothing really. Movies and stuff.

But he did ask me if he could come in here and pick up those papers you signed for him.'

'What papers?'

'I don't know, Sir. He didn't say. All he said was that he had to have them couriered over to Henley on Thames.'

'And you let him come in here?'

'Yes, Sir Alex. It was Elliot,' implored Marie, wearing an expression that it was an acceptable course of action to take.

'And how long was he in here?'

'I really don't know. A minute, maybe two.'

'And where was I?'

'You were upstairs with North Sea Development.'

'And was he in the building when DCC Hastie arrived?'

'Yes. He was in his office.'

'And after we left, was he in all day?'

'No, he popped out shortly after you left, saying he had a meeting with Finance.'

'And when did he return?'

'Just after two. He told me about his mother and then he told me Kirsten was picking him up to go to the airport. I think he said he was flying up tonight. In fact, he left at four, just minutes before you got back.'

Lamont glanced over at Hastie standing by the window. Hastie shook his head, indicating he had heard enough.

'Thanks, Marie. That's all'

When the door closed, Lamont turned to Hastie. 'Call yourself a policeman? And a DCC at that. And you couldn't even deduce that Dixie Armstrong, an award winning journalist, fucking old friend and well known adversary of mine just so happened to have a hush-hush meeting with a man who works less than forty feet from my office! Christ, Hastie. Are you really that stupid or just an arrogant bastard!'

'Okay, I think we've both fucked up here, Sir Alex, but it's not as if Walker has anything on us. No, Armstrong is the problem here. She also has the brains to take the information and delve deeper. We'll need to find out what she knows.'

'Can't you just search her house, office, computer, phone

records and the like? Surely, *you* can fix that, Hastie?'

'I can but I need to know specifically what, if anything, she has found out. As I said this morning, if we go digging and she discovers we are on to her, she'll shut everything down immediately and that'll make our job almost impossible.'

'So what do you suggest, Mr. Deputy Chief Constable?'

Ignoring the sarcasm, Hastie moved slowly to the edge of the desk, 'First, I need you to check on Walker's story about meeting Finance. Then have the papers he sent over to Henley brought back here so we can find out what they are, though I'd suggest they have bugger all significance. As for me, I'll call Montague at the NSD and have him put a trace out on Walker, as well as all calls he's made today and in the last few days. I'll also, if you don't mind, have Montague send over his Tech Security to sweep this office for any bugs.'

Hastie was pacing the room, occasionally stopping at the window to glower over the city.

Lamont meanwhile didn't know where to look. 'And then what?' he demanded

'Then we'll find him and bring him in.'

Hastie was thinking on his feet. He was good at that. Quick decisions made him who he was. 'All five airports in London fly to Scotland, so we'll order BAA Security to run a check on his possible flights. We should be able to grab him before he even steps on a plane. If not, I'll have teams waiting at the airports in Scotland and we'll get him when he lands. I'll also call my guy at the Met and ask him to put a call out to the cab firms. We need to find out if anyone picked up a man of Walker's description this morning; both here and where the drop-off point was.'

Hastie moved swiftly round to Lamont's side of the desk, picked up the phone and before he started dialling, turned to Lamont. 'Don't worry, Sir Alex. We'll nab him before he does any damage. But we need to work fast.'

Fifteen minutes later, after Hastie made all his calls, the once confident men sat waiting. There was an agitated silence in the room; impatience was now getting the better of them. They both twitched when the phone rang.

'Call for Mr. Hastie, Sir,' said Marie.

'It's for you,' growled Lamont as he passed the phone to Hastie.

Hastie grabbed the receiver and listened. After he put it down, he sighed a breath of relief before turning to Lamont and smiling. 'Walker and his wife are booked on the eight-fifty to from Heathrow to Glasgow. That should give us enough time to alert BAA Security and have him brought in.'

Lamont paused momentarily. Hastie could see the old man recomposing himself.

'Well, Sir Alex, looks like I have the pleasure of another night in the capital.'

'Thank goodness for that. But may I ask what you're going to do with him. He hasn't exactly broken any laws?'

'Sir Alex, as most of us in the security services know, there is a long line of people throughout history who have never broken the law but have ended up either being silenced or better still, made to disappear. Just as there have been many who have broken the law and walked away Scot-free.'

'No pun intended, I hope?'

Hastie smiled. 'However, think about it. There was the NSD's involvement in the Miners' Strike, the Munich Terrorists and Mossad, and the Mafia and the JFK assassination. It's the way things work. And it's for that very reason that Britain is what it is today: a rather large and powerful bastard! Anyway, you should know about that, Sir Alexander; look at what we're doing, for heaven's sake.'

Lamont stood up, fixed his jacket and reached for the drinks cabinet. 'Time for a single malt, Hastie?'

'Now there's a good idea.'

After ten minutes of gloating and of toasting their power, there was a knock on the door. In came Marie. 'There are two men from a Sir James Montague's office to see you, Sir. Shall I send them in?'

'Yes, yes, right away.'

As the two dark-suited men from NSD Tech Security

walked in, nothing much was discussed. One was carrying a large briefcase and two laptops while the other struggled with a black, high-security boxed container about twelve by twelve. Lamont didn't care what they had brought with them; his only concern was to introduce Hastie. 'This is DCC Hastie from Strathclyde. You're here under his orders. Now, what do you need to do?'

'Sir, we just have to set up the laptops, the control screen and scanner. It'll sweep the office and pick up any transmitter within fifty feet. But don't worry, it shouldn't take long.'

As the two NSD operatives began to calibrate and programme their equipment, Lamont turned to Hastie. 'Now then, I'm thinking about my supper. Any preferences, Hastie? The Holly Restaurant, perhaps?'

'Sounds good but is it not a bit late for a reservation?'

'Mike, dear boy, you're forgetting who I am.'

The confidence had returned, as had the sparkle in the eyes of both men. Their pomposity, however, wasn't missed by the NSD operatives who were raising their eyes to each other in silent mockery.

One operative remained at the control screen while the other took what looked like a miniature light sabre and began to sweep the room. Lamont and Hastie sat in smug silence, scoffing any suggestion there could be some sort of bugging device in the office. Ten minutes later, the operative with the scanner turned to Lamont. 'The place is clean. No trace of any receivers in any of the light fittings, phones, appliances or behind the wall. Just have to check the two of you now.'

Hastie stood erect as the Operative waved the scanner up and down and around his frame. Nothing. He sat back down. Lamont, however, was enjoying what he thought to be a frivolous matter and was quickly off his chair. Holding out his arms as if he was being searched at the airport, he giggled. The operative held the wand at Lamont's feet before moving it slowly up and around his legs.

'Don't get too close, boy. We don't need anyone talking out of turn, do we?'

The operative tendered no response. The scanner had just reached Lamont's stomach when the other operative, sombre at the control screen, asked the other to stop. 'Can you go over that area again, please?'

'Do these chaps not have names?' chuckled Lamont at the apparent childishness of it all. 'What is it? Have you found some device that Captain Kirk dropped off the other day?'

'No Sir. But there's definitely something here. Its small but we can't place it as yet. Would you mind slipping your off your jacket, please?'

The giggling came to an abrupt halt. Lamont turned to Hastie as if to ask him what was happening.

'Just take it off, Sir Alex,' ordered Hastie.

Lamont removed his jacket, draping it over the desk. The operative performed another full body scan on Lamont. Nothing. Unfortunately for Lamont, as the operative swept the scanner over the left breast of the jacket, a strong beeping sound erupted from the control panel.

'Sir, can I ask you to empty the pockets, please?'

Lamont did so in a flustered hurry, taking out his wallet, his comb and his pen and throwing them on his desk. The operative swept the items. The beep was now constant.

'Can I?' asked the operative of Lamont as he emptied the wallet and handed the contents of the wallet to his partner. He handed over the comb and the pen shortly after.

The other operative picked up the black security box and took out a device which looked like a high-tech, two-tiered personal printer. A high powered light shone brightly from beneath the glass examination plate while above, a laser scanner hummed continuously. He began to place the items one by one on the examination plate. There was a negative response from the wallet, its contents and the comb. However, when he placed the pen on the glass, the machine omitted four elongated beeps while two green lights flashed on the side of the device.

'What the hell is this?' demanded Lamont.

'We don't know yet, Sir, but if you give us a second we should be able to tell you.'

The operative picked up the Faber-Castell, twisting and unscrewing the refill before shining a small torch into the pen's casing. Nothing. He did the same with the top-half of the pen before offering a rueful smile to his colleague. He flipped it over and gave the pen a slight dunt on the desk. As a small transmitter fell out, the operative held it up. 'Ah, the infamous CSM A9. How predictable. Sorry Sir, but I do believe that someone has been listening into your conversations. The clarity of reception may not have been that good but they would have heard you all the same.'

Lamont was stunned.

'Is there anything else we can do for you, Sir?'

'No,' interrupted Hastie before standing up and grabbing the small transmitter from a laid-back and unperturbed operative. He examined it for about thirty seconds, spinning it in his fingers and taking a lingering look at the model and serial number. He turned to the NSD operatives, handed it back and shook his head. 'No, that will be all. And boys, keep this to yourselves, will you?'

As the two operatives packed up and left the room, Hastie walked slowly towards the window where he stood in silence, looking out across the cityscape. He was attempting to find clarity in the predicament he had now found himself in. 'Sir Alex, I have to ask you again, and you know how critical it is for you to remember: Did you disclose anything to Peter Buchanan, anything at all, which could implicate you in what we have been planning?'

'No, absolutely nothing. No one is aware of the meeting today except those who were there. I didn't even have direct contact with any of them. That was done by Montague's people. I never sent any emails, either. It was all done in the manner Montague suggested. The only thing I asked of Buchanan was that he and his team should hurry up and formulate a Scottish strategy for when he takes control. But as for the bigger picture, I can assure you no one knows.'

'Okay,' pondered Hastie, 'the rest of us should be in the clear. Nevertheless, if Walker has overheard your wee talk with

Buchanan and has told Dixie Armstrong, then you had better get your press guys on the case right now. If she goes public then you'll have to be prepared to explain yourself, which, judging by your past cameos in front of the cameras should be no problem at all.'

'What is that supposed to mean?'

'What it means is that you will offer a standard rebuttal. You know: security as one nation, job losses in Scotland and England, unity and strength going forward in today's difficult economy. I mean, you're the top oil man in the UK so having a wee discussion with a future Prime Minister is nothing out of the ordinary, is it?'

'No, no. I disagree, Hastie.'

Now it was Lamont's turn to call the shots. He wanted to remind Hastie who the boss was. As he put his jacket back on, the old man looked up and stared intensely into Hastie's eyes 'We have to stop the Tribune, or anyone else for that matter, from printing anything that connects any of us to my meeting with Buchanan, or God forbid, to the Alba Club. Oh no, there is far too much at stake for it to be brushed under the carpet in a haze of spin.' As he fixed his tie, his eyes opened wide. Dixie Armstrong's grilling at Aberdeen was still fresh in his mind. 'I've a better idea. We shall eliminate Walker and Armstrong, and the recording.'

As Hastie grinned, and nodded in agreement with the ruthlessness of Lamont, the phone rang. He picked it up and listened before lifting his eyes and staring without expression at Lamont. Lamont frowned back in anticipation.

'Yes,' said Hastie quietly, 'I understand.'

Hastie returned the phone and shook his head at Lamont. 'Well, Sir Alexander. It's not just you that seems to be in the shit now. That was the Met. A cab company has just got back to them. They say a man with Walker's description was picked up today at eleven-fifteen from just around the corner.'

'And?' asked Lamont.

'And you don't need me to tell you where exactly he was dropped off.'

Lamont offered no response as Hastie let the answer wait for a second. He sat down and rubbed his eyes before turning to Lamont and informing him of the exceptionally bad news.

'The Alba Club!'

15

"na... na-na, na-na, na-na – angus!"

Tuesday 17th June

3.30 pm - Dundee

The east coast city of Dundee appeared on the horizon as the silver M3 approached the Tay Bridge. Rory had been flying. Earlier, though, he had been both concerned and overjoyed when Dixie had asked him to follow Peter Buchanan on his visit to Dundee: concerned that Dixie had asked him to not only cover Buchanan's presentation but also to keep an eye on the Tory Leader's movements that night and the following day, but overjoyed at being given this not very often opportunity of an unaccompanied road trip in his boss's beloved car.

His nervous spasms, brought on by being at the controls of such a fuck-off quick machine, had disappeared by the time he dropped Dixie off at Haymarket. She was going to catch the train back to Glasgow. Nevertheless, he was still a wee bit perplexed that his debut drive included stopping off at PC World for Dixie to pick up a couple of memory sticks then parking outside an internet café in Gorgie as she disappeared inside to check up on some emails. She did have a Blackberry, after all. But what did he care. He had just driven up the M90 with the roof down and The View blasting out from the sixteen high-performance speakers. While they were thinking about trying on some new jeans, he was feeling like Jim Clark on an away day!

Rory was one of the few non-Dundonians who actually

had a soft spot for Dundee, not at all fussed was he with the city's image of not being the most aesthetically pleasing of urban centres. He had been a student there only a few years before and having witnessed the city's make-over from post industrial cess-pit to scientific centre of excellence, he was pretty sure that the people of this old city would have the last laugh. He also knew that back in the nineteenth century, Dundee just happened to be one of the richest cities in the world. It was the centre of the Empire's jute industry and home to the pioneers of modern journalism. That was why Rory's father insisted he attend the university. It was also the world's oil capital back then. Unfortunately, mused Rory, the oil in question did not come from deep inside the earth's crust but from the blubber of a few hundred thousand disposable whales. In fact, the city had been so wealthy that the financially well-endowed citizens of Dundee had once owned an enormous chunk of the North American land mass; bought under an ambitious project known as the Collective Scottish Investment Vehicle. However, like many cities of that century, the wealth was short lived. Dundee began to wilt as technology overtook heavy industry, leaving its people behind to suck up the dregs. And boy, did they have a couple of oceans worth of flat beer to dispose of. The shift in the economic landscape had left the city in despair and hanging over the edge of an abyss full of shite. The place had been in bad shape, the self respect of its citizens well below zero, and as company after company pulled out, the public ridicule had endured well into the nineties. The city had contorted into a large pile of industrial neglect. It had become infested with kettle-boilers and windae-hingers. Politicians shunned it and tourists only ended up there by mistake. The city's demise hadn't escaped its unfortunate citizens, either. They more than understood, shamefully, how others perceived the city, for whenever a Dundonian enjoyed the hospitality of another city, they avoided, at all costs, of making any reference to their current abode. What's more, if they did make that instantly regrettable slip they were sure the reply would always include the same old, same old; 'Sorry pal, nae luck!'

Even the people of Aberdeen got in on the act. Bolstered by having a recession-free economy, courtesy of the other more profitable oil from the waters of the North Sea, Aberdonians, in their unashamed arrogance, decided it would be a fine idea to create their own city game of Monopoly. As well as having an obnoxious need to tell the world of their financial success, they also wanted to rub the "snot-ridden" Dundonian faces into the dirt. Rory laughed aloud as he remembered the outcry when it was proposed the "Go to Jail" square be replaced with "Go to Dundee". Jesus, how far could the city fall, he thought.

However, he had also been well aware of Dundee's phoenix-like transformation. While the educational institutions were still among the best in the world, the reliance on the sea and on textiles had been replaced by successful endeavours into Life Sciences and IT. Boosted by investment from Holyrood and by a community fed up of being on life's scrapheap, the city was now catching up with Aberdeen's success by being the world leader in cancer and biogenetic research, as well as creating a new generation of young entrepreneurs who were rocking the world in such specialist fields as Pharmaceutical IT and CGI. Top researchers and scientists were rushing to Dundee to work in state of the art facilities amongst a culture of enterprise and invention while young programmers were buying up the city's top properties as they set about designing videogames such as *Grand Theft Auto*. Good for them, thought Rory, the city was on the up. It had even been nominated as the most intelligent city in the world by UNESCO! And Rory, in both his support and his kind-hearted derision, couldn't believe the revolution. Yes, in time he would be proud of his alumnus status.

Rory was thinking that Peter Buchanan had impressed in his interview with Dixie. Even if he was a flirtatious wanker, he had been ready for Dixie and had ensured she had kept her claws inside her paws. Buchanan spoke with the conviction of a man who not only expected to be the next PM but actually thought he deserved it. The all inclusive rhetoric, the "let's make Britain great again" nonsense, "the power as one" bullshit, Buchanan had it all. But what impressed Rory most was Buchanan's nonaggressive approach towards the SNP. This was new in cross border politics, certainly in Rory's short working life. Buchanan had short-sided Dixie, indicating he was prepared to work with the Nationalists, even negotiate better terms for Scotland. What was Buchanan's agenda, thought Rory. He couldn't be a closet nationalist, could he? This, Rory pondered, was certainly a different approach from the miserable and non-communicative attitude espoused by the present incumbent. He chuckled to himself. And certainly no surprise considering the current PM came from the land of the entrenched view point. The land of *"ye hoor, sir. Wur no changin' fir nae bastart!"* The land of *"wur prood of oor ane unemployed lads signing up fir Hur Maajestae's Furces and bein broucht hame in a boadae bag."* The land of *"wur happy tae live in relative povert-ae and still vote Leeboor."* The land more commonly known as south central Fife.

Rory parked the car in a far off bay in the underground university car park, still petrified that a scratch would render his position with the Tribune untenable. Twice checking the car was locked, he nervously glanced back three times to make sure the alarm light was flashing. As he made his to way the presentation, he gave himself a reminder to have his wee Rafa Nadal problem checked out.

Peter Buchanan would be speaking in the new Life Science building, much to the dismay of his advisors who had tried and failed to have the presentation held in the Caird Hall, Dundee's most famous building. Rory shook his head. That would have been unbearably painful in the sanctimonious stakes. "Buchanan sings his own tune in the Caird Hall" would have run the headline. 'Fuck me. And to think Sinatra once graced that famous stage.'

After Buchanan's speech congratulating the university on its successes in the field of science, Rory rushed over to the small room where the press conference would be held. Placing his Dictaphone alongside the microphones, he decided on a seat at the back of the room. Dixie had already bagged the exclusive earlier so unless Buchanan was going to shock the political world by dropping his trousers and wildly shaking his cock in the faces of the country's political commentators while screaming, 'How do you like the look of this big boy?' then Rory could sit back and relax.

After the press conference, at which he made no attempt to ask a question, Rory dashed back to the car, hoping that some NED would have had the decency not to drag the keys to his boarded-up heroin den across the bonnet. He was also hoping he could be out on the road before Buchanan's, now single-vehicle, motorcade got going. The schedule, released by Pippa, would see Buchanan staying overnight at a family friend's estate in Argyll where he was to enjoy some fishing and shooting before heading to Glasgow the following day for another official engagement.

Rory didn't have a clue what he was meant to do in the meantime but knowing Dixie could always sniff a good story, he was prepared to hang around to see if anything arose, regardless that Buchanan might be having some private down-time in the company of friends on the other side of the fucking country.

He was fumbling with the Sat-Nav and trying to type Lochgilphead into the contraption when Buchanan's car came swinging onto the road. Quickly giving up on the technology, Rory decided to take his chances and trail Buchanan by sight. With only one major road heading west, he was confident even someone as geographically-challenged as he couldn't get lost. However, as Buchanan approached the large roundabout on the western side of the city, his car, instead of taking the motorway towards Perth, bore right and began to make its way north towards Aberdeen. 'Mmm …What's the fuck's going on here then?' asked Rory.

The M3 was a dream to drive, much better than his dilapidated green machine, and possibly the reason, he thought, why he had never got used to Sat Nav. He would also have much preferred to be the owner of a Golf GTI but since he was on a salary that permitted him only two white pudding suppers a week rather than his preferred four then driving Dixie's car for the day was as good as it was going to get.

Rory kept a safe distance as the two cars drove around Dundee on the Kingsway. Thinking Buchanan was on his way to Aberdeen, Rory got comfortable. However, Europe's oil capital was apparently not on the itinerary as a few minutes later the car in front took a quick left turn off the motorway and on to the road sign-posted for Kirriemuir.

'Kirriemuir!' groaned an exacerbated Rory. 'Who the fuck goes to Kirriemuir?'

Kirriemuir was a small town a few miles north-west of Dundee. It was also the birthplace of two very famous but very different characters in the world of entertainment. The irony was not lost on Rory as he considered the talents of both JM Barrie and Bon Scott: one who wrote delightful plays and fairytales about small people and big, hairy dogs, while the other regularly tripped-out on delightfully hallucinogenic sub-matter, played a goddamn mean guitar and hung around with big, hairy people.

Apart from those two guys and the odd statue, there was not much else to see in Kirriemuir. He had been there only once before; at the behest of the most ridiculous of suggestions only a wired and delusional flat mate of Rory's could make.

"Why don't we to go to Kirrie for the day and pay our respects to AC/DC? Not only that, how about we christen the trip 'Our Sunday Afternoon Highway to Hell' then get well and truly blotto on the Monkjuice!"

Rory continued to follow at a safe distance, negotiating a few dangerous curves as the road descended into the floor of a small glen. However, as he turned into the last corner before the road straightened out, Rory looked on confounded as the Tory Leader's car turned slowly off to the right. Rory continued on, passing where Buchanan's car had left the road. He dare not be spotted. No, he wasn't going to let that happen on his watch.

As Buchanan's car disappeared through huge gates set into an enormous and very long stone wall, Rory decided he'd better find somewhere to kip down for the night. But not before he took note of where, and with whom, Buchanan would be enjoying this evening's hospitality.

16

illusions

Wednesday 18th June

3.49 am – Milngavie - Glasgow

Dixie lay on the bed cuddling her two sleeping children as the early morning sun rose above the sandstone and concrete of Glasgow and shone through a narrow gap in the thick curtains of her childhood bedroom. She was spending the night at her parent's Milngavie home, a Victorian terraced house with a double whammy view: the Highlands and the Campsie Hills.

She had been frustratingly trying to nod off but there was little darkness in a Scottish summer. With the light barely fading around eleven before re-emerging around three, the senses were exposed to a never-ending sunrise. No sooner had the summer sun dipped its head beneath the horizon than it was up again and chapping on the window, and reminding her that life was indeed worth living.

Dixie often thought how the climate shaped the psyche of the nation. Long summer days offering hope and happiness while the short, dark days of winter driving people into despair. No wonder there were so many parties over the winter months. With Hogmanay and its five days of excessiveness and Burns Night and its long night of celebration and contemplation, they were the release valves of the nation. She also reflected as to why Scotland was a country of the all or nothing. All for those prepared to face up to life's challenges but nothing for the few

249

neighbourhoods of extreme poverty speckled across the country where unemployment had become a profession, robbing old ladies a pastime and dying before you were sixty a lifelong certainty. The people living in these dreary pits had long since lost hope. Thatcher would be smiling; they were her greatest invention, and her greatest legacy. Like the long winters, there seemed to be no end to the darkness for Maggie's chosen ones.

When she first listened to the recording of the meeting in the Alba Club, Dixie had been shocked and bewildered. Now, as she twisted and turned in her bed, she was so fucking angry.

How distressing, thought Dixie, how ironic, that this rich potential source of a nation's wealth had been employed to destroy hope and prosperity for thousands. How tragic for those isolated communities who had dissolved into a loch of scarce social cohesion. How frightening that the great working class spirit of the shipyards and coal mines had mutated into ghettos of sombre neglect and compassionate remembrance. This was not Scotland, not the one she really knew. This was the Scotland others had fashioned to secure votes and readers. Those like the short-sighted councils and their lap-dog tabloids in Glasgow who shaped society for the masses and whose media ambitions for Glasgow included the infectious and relentless portrayal of desolate landscapes and the establishment of an acceptance culture that Scotland's place was not at the top table. It was as if they felt no shame in strangling the very last breath of aspiration, even pushing Irvine Welsh to become their literary hero with the provocative "It's shite being Scottish" line, thus creating an excuse for thousands of young men to drink Monkjuice and wallow in abandon, and to be in ignorant awe of a satirical sitcom which portrayed two men coming to terms with old age, poverty and social deficiency in a bleak Glaswegian tower block. If the Forgotten had long since accepted that this is how their life was meant to be, then the purveyors of that life had achieved their aims.

This god forsaken artistry created a spurious image of Scotland: where poverty ruled supreme, where reliance on the State was a given and where any desire for self-improvement was stripped from deep inside the soul by an establishment only too willing to install fear and deprive ambition. This was definitely the Scotland others wanted.

Dixie rued the audacity of the London controlled media. Furthermore, she wondered of how often did she ever watch a drama or TV special set in Scotland, which did not include murder, unemployment, violent crime and drug abuse? Not very! On the contrary, it had been year after year of English period dramas rammed down the throat. The same jowled actresses dressed up in the same black dress and the same white skull cap. The same fat actors waving the same old walking sticks and tapping the same old buckled shoes in deepest Yorkshire and Victorian London. Oh yes, Bronte and Dickens were good and Shakespeare was genius. Yet, wasn't that the case with Burns and MacDiarmid, and Scott and Byron and Stevenson? Of course it was. But Scotland was a special case for the major broadcasters. All they ever had to show for Scottish culture was production after production of dilapidated, grey and miserable housing schemes. It was as if that what Scotland was; one enormous set ready for a secret millionaire. No sitcoms about normal life in Scotland, no middle-class dramas, no blockbuster mini-series on Scottish History, no high-financed documentaries on Scottish Invention, no positive news about business and community initiatives and very few Sunday night exclusives which shone a light on the amazing landscape. And specifically no Tam O'Shanter, Sunset Song and A Blind Man Looks at a Thistle! It was a disgrace.

Nevertheless, there *was* light for those prepared to leave the past behind. Scotland had been given hope by the new Parliament in Edinburgh. Times were changing and for those who longed to live the three-bedroom, two car, two holiday lifestyle like the vast majority of Scottish citizens, there was opportunity. Unfortunately, Glasgow and some of its outlying towns and villages were now the problem. Once the driving force behind the Scottish economy, the rest of Scotland was now desperately seeking to drag them out of their loathsome, willing indifference. People were incensed by the region's crime, its mortality rates and its loyalty to the old ways, and exhausted by the culture of stubborn and bitter self-indulgency; that life was harder and sadder than everyone else's, that poverty was accepted to be the agreeable solution, that many of its citizens had morphed into their own caricatures and that they took their own self-deprecation to a new level of pathetic parody. It was as if the people of Scotland were screaming for the wind to blow them onto another course, onto another ship, so gripped were they by the exasperation of seeing some of their compatriots in first class while others were dispensed to languish in the darkness of steerage.

Dixie thought there had to be many like her who could see the benefits of a new Scotland. Sure, times would be difficult but Aberdeen was thriving, Dundee reborn and Edinburgh one of the key financial cities in the world. Surely it was Glasgow's time again? Take large parts of the deprivation in Glasgow and its surrounding areas out of the economic equation and Scotland was one of the wealthiest and healthiest nations in the world. Furthermore, investors viewed Scotland as a reliable source of return and exiles were keen on returning home. Living standards were good, roads well-maintained, education still the nation's right and confidence all too evident.

But you couldn't take Glasgow out of the loop. It was Scotland's biggest city and whether people liked it or not, it was an intrinsic part of Scotland. It was the unofficial boss man. And more importantly, Dixie was a Weegie herself. She was just as proud of her city with its beautiful neighbourhoods, its status as a World City of Music, its humour, its millions of good citizens and of its enlightened heritage as she was ashamed of its divides, its abominations, its violent bigotry and its misplaced arrogance. Glasgow was ready, she felt, for a real change and not another pointless PR campaign boasting of its wonderful shopping, great museums and fantastic art scene when behind every other gum-infested corner lay a moronically designed concrete monstrosity and some drunken NED ready to fleece you for a fiver. Like the other great cities of the world, it was ready to be united. It was ready to take its pride back.

Drifting in and out of sleep for most of the night, she thought about her beautiful kids lying beside her and of all the other kids waking up this morning around her city. It was time for a change.

She opened her eyes just before seven, and quickly had to pull her head back as Lewis's smiling eyes bore into her from above, his wee runny nose only a couple of inches from hers. Catriona was still sleeping, sucking her thumb in oblivious contentment. Dixie beamed as her older child started jumping up and down on her wearisome body. As she lifted him off, there was knock on the door and in came her father carrying the sweet morning godsend of a cup of tea.

'Come on Lewis, time to get up and let your mum get dressed,' said her Dad. Lewis didn't need asking twice, charging downstairs and screaming like a banshee with his Spiderman pyjama legs dragging beneath his feet.

'Is PC Clump still with us?' Dixie asked her Dad.

'Of course he is, Dixie. Poor man's been standing outside all night. Remember, he's here for you and the kids. It might not be nice and it might be a wee bit intrusive but better the devil you know.'

Oh Dad, if only you knew.

Having taken a wee detour in Edinburgh the previous afternoon to listen to Elliot's recording in full, Dixie had been railroaded by what she heard. She had also expected a little time on her own to digest the information of the file. Unfortunately, on her return to Queen Street station Kurt Broadhead had been impatiently waiting to drive her back to Milngavie in an unmarked police car. Pissed off, she had afforded herself some light relief as she played on his strict adherence to protocol, stopping first at the office to check in with her boss for a de-briefing on the Peter Buchanan interview, then having Kurt pull up at an off-licence so she could buy some wine. After the off-licence, she had decided it was time to push him even closer to the edge, dragging poor Kurt around the supermarket while taking an inordinately long time to deliberate on the pro and cons of buying 100 percent virgin olive oil. Having arrived, finally, at her parent's house around seven, she had laughed out loud as she slammed the door in the policeman's face.

After breakfast, Dixie gave a warm hug to her kids while saying goodbye to her parents, giving no indication as to when she would be home. As she opened the front door, the fresh morning air engulfed her lungs. Turning to the uniformed PC Clump standing guard, she offered her not so sympathetic condolences to the poor chap about not getting any sleep. He didn't offer much in return; a weak smile that Dixie could only describe as a "C'est La Vie" grin. Walking down the steps to the road, Dixie whistled to Kurt. She was ready to go. The detective, who had been waiting for nearly an hour, folded his Daily News on top of the dashboard, took a sip of coffee and fixed his tie before jumping out to open the back door.

'Morning Kurt, how's life at the sharp end?'

'Please Ma'am. I'd be grateful if you didn't call me Kurt. It's George. And I'm a rugby player not a footballer. Can't stand the game myself.'

'Just like Kurt Broadhead then!'

Arriving at the office just after eight, Kurt took a seat in the Reception area and continued to read his paper. Dixie meanwhile, strolled over to the desk to check for any messages. There was only one. Picking up the note from the receptionist, she read it as she waited for the lift.

'I'll be in Special Collections (floor 12 in case you've forgotten) of the University Library. Meet me there at ten. Tell your bodyguard buddy that you need to look up some historical piece about a story you are working on. If he needs to know more, tell him it's none of his fucking business and he'd be too stupid to understand!'

Dixie's eyes smiled as she read the note. Kurt didn't appear interested, the sports news evidently more entertaining.

An hour later, Dixie and Kurt struggled for conversation as they drove across town. Fortunately, she felt her phone vibrate.

'Hey, mien Fuhrer. Performing any tricks last night?'

'Ah, good to hear from you but make it quick.' "Make it quick" being the phrase she used when she had that bowel churning premonition her phone was being tapped.

'Not to worry. It's a pay-as-you-go,' declared Charlie.

'Mine isn't, so you know the drill.'

'Anyway, since the sun is shining bright this fine morn, I thought I'd be into taking a little drive. Will be in touch when I've something to report.'

'Thanks for the update. I'll be over at the university if you need me. Have to do some research. Speak soon.'

She was playing up to Kurt, trying not to give too much away. She was also hoping he wouldn't have anything to report back to DCC Hastie with.

The ancient university's spire came into view as the car reached the top of the hill at the West End.

Oh, to be back there now.

Dixie had many happy memories of life at university and often smiled with fondness at some of the things she and her three best friends got up to. Though she studied hard alongside Elliot in the Reading Room, there were far too many late night parties with Paul and Johnnie. She also smoked too many joints and had too many one night stands with a selection of extremely able and finely-racked freshmen. It was a life of constant excess: excessive work loads, excessive fun and excessive beliefs. She sighed, wondering if she would be prepared for the excessive danger she might face this day.

As they arrived at the Gibson Street entrance of the university library, Dixie jumped out of the car leaving Kurt at the wheel. She sauntered off telling him she was fine and that he could stay where he was. Unfortunately, Kurt was having none of her antics today. 'Ma'am, I've already had a very tired DCC Hastie on to me this morning with orders not to let you out of my sight at any time. So, I'm sorry, I don't think me being flexible with your movements would be appreciated. In fact, he's just off the first flight from London and not exactly in the best of moods.'

'Is he, now? Well, poor wee Kurt. As you're probably unaware, my boss has been speaking to Hastie's boss -old friends by the way- and I've been told that if I don't want or need you around then that is my prerogative. What's more, if you're not for believing me, we can always double check. In fact, why don't I call the Chief Constable right now so the two of you can have a wee chat?'

Kurt's face reddened. He knew she would do it.

Dixie sensed she had won yet another small battle. 'But you know, and I know, that your career prospects might be in for a wee battering if you were to disobey the Chief Constable. Therefore, Kurt, if you are personally willing to jeopardise the long-standing relationship between the Glasgow Tribune and the Strathclyde Force, then please, come hither and talk to the man.' Dixie walked towards Kurt, holding his eyes with an unyielding glare. 'However, judging by the look of fear on your coupon, I don't think you're all that keen.'

The detective didn't have much capacity for decision-making, and when the realisation dawned on him that he was caught between his two superiors, his frustration began to show. 'Okay, I'll be right here. But just to let you know, I'm calling for back up to keep an eye on you.'

'Listen, George,' stared an angry Dixie, 'you are here to protect me, not keep me on a fucking leash. So, if I were you I would have a tendency to keep things hunky-dory with the Chief Constable, if you know what I mean. If he says I can have space then that's what I'm going to have. In the meantime you can do whatever you fucking well want!'

The detective stood shaken. Yet again he was suffering humiliation as another door closed in his face. 'Fuck you, bitch,' he shouted as he slammed the ball of his hand into the car ceiling and unclipped the car radio to call for back up.

Dixie was still giggling as the elevator door opened onto the twelfth floor of this very special place: a library holding extraordinary papers, precious books and ancient manuscripts taken from a long list of exceptional scientists, philosophers and economists. A priority pass had to be obtained for entry to this floor but since Dixie was the chief political editor of the Tribune, as well as being one of the university's better known daughters, the normal rules did not apply.

As she walked slowly down the aisles reminiscing of her college days, she recognised the familiar dark brown hair and broad shoulders. He was sitting behind a reading desk partly obscured by a floor to ceiling shelving unit.

'Glad you could make it. Mind you, I do wish it was in a slightly more life enhancing situation?'

'Ah, Paul, what's life without a bit of fun, eh?'

'A helluva lot better than the state we're in now, that's for sure.'

Dixie knew instantly that Paul was in one of his "don't fuck with me moods". She sat down quietly, deciding to keep her wise-cracking and bombastic comments to a minimum. 'So, what do you think?'

'What I think …Dixie …is that your insatiable need for the big story knows no bounds. Fuck me! Of all the people in the world you could have asked, you thought, in your wisdom, that Elliot Walker would be the man for the job.'

'But Paul, he was… '

'To hell with your reasoned defence, Dixie. If you had seen him yesterday, shitting himself in that department store cafeteria, with me having to guide him through procedures not in the "how to be an upstanding member of the legal community manual", then I think you'll get the picture of how fucking angry I was. He's a bloody tax lawyer for fuck's sake, Dixie. Not wee Tom Cruise on some impossible mission. Christ, Elliot couldn't have been more exposed if you had asked him to run around Leicester Square with a ferret sticking out of his arse!'

'I know, Paul. But after I explained what I needed to find out, he was insistent. And when I pointed out the risks, and the serious repercussions if he was exposed, he was even more determined.' Dixie was still trying to defend her actions when she realised she had forgot to ask the obvious. 'Anyway, what the hell were you doing down there?'

Paul had allowed Dixie to see how naive she had been.

Now it was time to talk business. 'Let's just say I had one of your hunches. After speaking to the DCC about the shooting at Loch Lomond, I figured out pretty quickly that he wasn't being the most supportive of your predicament.'

'Interesting, I got the same feeling at dinner last week.'

'Ah yes. Sorry about that. Next time a policeman treats you to dinner I'll make sure it's at Big Jake's Burger Joint!'

'Big Jakes? I'd be delighted. Would sure as hell beat the less appealing culinary option of having a hungry family of maggots crawling inside my big gob when I'm six feet under!'

'Anyway, I take it that you never heeded my specific instructions,' started Paul. 'You've listened to the file?'

Dixie nodded.

'But you've made a copy and hidden the memory stick?'

She nodded again, deciding it wasn't the best time to tell Paul she only had the one copy and it was on her now. However, instead of behaving like a chastised child, Dixie could sense the dangers she had not only brought upon herself but to Elliot as well.

What a selfish bitch.

Paul continued. 'As things stand, and as much as I can permit myself to surmise, Hastie will reckon it is only you and Elliot who are in on this. Fortunately, he doesn't have a clue where Elliot is hiding. Unfortunately, you'll be his next target. He also doesn't know that I know about the file but that doesn't mean he won't find out. At the moment, he is using me to get to you, calling on the pathetic excuse that you're in danger. In fact, he was on the phone to me late last night, wanting me to bring you in. He didn't say why but I managed to force the issue of a citizen's right to freedom of movement to a point where he couldn't justify bringing you in without revealing what he was up to in London. He then used the Hutchinson story as an excuse but since you and your guys weren't breaking any laws he was up shit creak without the proverbial. However, we can have no doubts that Hastie and his men will be keeping pretty close tabs on your movements until they have definitive proof of what you now know.'

Dixie could only stare. She was already thinking of an escape plan.

'The man is on the warpath,' continued Paul, 'and it's too far gone for him to just bugger off to the pub and forget about it all. He now knows he's in trouble and he'll use all his available resources to find you. And when he does …and he will … he'll be hell bent on getting his hands on the recording.'

'And what do you suppose all this means to us?' asked Dixie, beginning to fear the inevitable.

'C'mon Dixie, you know what this means. I reckon this mob have already tried it once at Loch Lomond and you didn't know about the recording then. I think that was just a rouse to scare you off the Hutchinson story and any ties it may have to Sir Alexander Lamont and his wee plot. It means they are out to kill you Dixie, whatever it takes!'

As the possibilities were considered, the library fell even more silent than its normal acoustics would allow. Sensing Dixie was thinking about her children, Paul grabbed her hand. 'It's okay, Dixie, the kids will be fine.'

'I really don't know, Paul. This is beyond the safety of a family. In the minds of Hastie and Lamont, everything is at stake here: oil, tax revenues, the control, the economy, millions of peoples' livelihoods. Admittedly, they might not all be living in Scotland but they're normal people just like you and me. And I don't care if they're English or not, nobody deserves to face the fall out.'

'But Dixie, if the Tribune doesn't produce the evidence and publish the story, it could be disastrous for Scotland.'

'I know, and that means we're going to make sure we do get the fucking story published. Nevertheless, we have to be certain that the people know it is the Establishment at work and not the people of England.'

Paul wasn't in the mood for kind-hearted neighbourly affections. 'I disagree. They're the very same fuckwits who have been harping on for years about the Scots and how we receive more than our fair share, so why should we play the pragmatic diplomat when some of their very own are trying to screw us? If that's how they feel then let's see how they cope when Scotland goes its own way. In fact, I've had it up to here with their petty racism. It's rampant in the security forces, the arts, the media and the political world. It might not be in our faces but just like fucking herpes, it's always there. Why the fuck do you think Blair and Brown have never discussed the irrefutable fact that they are Scottish? I'll tell you, shall I? Because they have always known that deep down within the psyche of their glorious Middle England, it doesn't sit well that a Scot is in the top job. Sure, no one has ever had the balls to say it publicly but behind all the PC bullshit, that's what they think. In other words, when it comes down to it, their complete existence revolves around London. So no way, Dixie, I say fuck them!'

'Listen Paul, I'm as pissed off as you but it won't do anyone any good by making the ordinary punter in England suffer. It's not their fault. In fact, they've never known any better because the Press down there have never told them what's really going on and, because of the Westminster agenda, nor do they want it to. But Scotland shouldn't be the antagonist. We're still going to have to live next to each other, work with each other and marry each other. That will go on.'

Distracted by the possible political scenarios for a few moments, Dixie had ignored the urgency of their meeting. She has been trying to piece everything together and decide on a strategy when she glanced up at Paul and realised he was waiting for her to continue. 'They're not in on the Hutchinson deal as well are they?' she asked.

'I don't know yet. As you will have heard, there was no mention of a deal with Hutchinson in the Alba Club meeting, but that doesn't mean there isn't a connection. In fact, who knows with these guys, they *are* the fucking Establishment. So it wouldn't surprise me if there was some tie-in with Hutchinson. Furthermore, I think they have slightly more important matters to concern themselves with at the moment. If their little plan is exposed, there could be an economic tsunami in the South of England, as well as it having a disastrous knock-on effect around the world. Worse still, not only could its exposure more than

260

sour the already volatile relationship between Scotland and England, it could harm them forever. Like it or not, Dixie, the disclosure of the Alba Club meeting *will* destroy the Union.'

They sat in silence for a few minutes more before Paul continued. 'Okay, Dixie. It's your call. What do you want to do?'

'Well, I'm going to get this story is published, whatever it takes. You can be damn sure of that. But first I have to make sure the kids are alright. In fact, I'll call the Chief Constable now to put extra security on the house. Maybe tell Dad to take them out for the day. And Jesus, I nearly forgot, we also have Elliot and Kirsten to take care of.' Dixie glanced up in anticipation. 'Can we do that, Paul?'

'I don't know, Dixie. Half the Scottish Police Force is out there looking for them.'

'Paul, we have to find a way. In the meantime I have to get in touch with a couple of people.'

'And who might they be?'

'I'll tell you when we're in your car but first we have to get the fuck out of here without Strathclyde's finest finding out. Surely there's another way out?'

'When you're a former student who just happens to be a DCI, there's always a way. Follow me if you please, Miss Dixie of the rotund arse.'

'What the fuck do you mean, "we've lost her",' screamed DCC Michael Hastie into the police radio. 'Christ, she can't just have disappeared. She only went in there twenty minutes ago.' He didn't even have to think. 'Get your arses in there …now! I want that place searched from back to front.'

Hastie had arrived just minutes earlier having stopped off en route to meet with his Tech team at HQ. He had needed to prepare them for a possible operation later in the day. He had also been canny, leaving out, for now, Dixie and Elliot's names from the operation's intended targets list and re-iterating the point that any orders the Team received would only come from him or the NSD in London. And absolutely no one else.

He was sitting with two NSD spooks in an unmarked car, two blocks away on Bank Street. Having decided to remain in London overnight to direct operations with Sir Alexander Lamont from the UKES office, he had arrived in Glasgow to find his usual regal demeanour replaced by one of shaggy hair, pungent breath, deep red eyes and vile temper. Moreover, his conceit had quickly disappeared when he learned that the various teams he had in place around Britain had still to discover the whereabouts of Elliot Walker.

The Walkers hadn't checked in for their reserved flight to Glasgow and after sending out images of the couple to all of the London airports, the search had produced no more than a few apologies and the occasional misleading identification. The security teams at the Scottish airports had also been prone to misfortune, with no sighting of the Walkers disembarking from any London flight after six pm. It had been a frustrating time, leaving Hastie and Sir Alexander Lamont with no more than a sleepless night and a cancelled reservation at the Holly.

Twelve hours later, and not only had he no information as to how and where he could find Elliot Walker, Hastie had also lost Dixie Armstrong. More importantly, he still had no idea how many copies of the Alba Club recording they had. Sitting in the back of the car, he began to think of the personal implications if the file was ever released into the public realm. The entire Establishment would be held accountable, the country would go into meltdown and his precious career would most certainly be taking a nice long boat trip down the Suwannee.

Hastie waited impatiently for another twenty minutes as the library was searched. News soon came back that the place had been turned over and still no sign. 'Here,' he demanded of the NSD spook sitting in the front passenger seat. 'Let me speak to whoever is in charge in there.' The man handed Hastie the radio. 'What's the fucking story?' He waited only seconds.

'Nothing, Sir. Nada.'

'Has she checked out?'

'No Sir. There's actually no record of her coming in here, at all.'

Hastie violently threw the radio back into the front of the car. 'Fucking useless bastards!' A tense silence ensued before he spoke again, this time to one of his spooks. 'Okay, let's trace her phone.'

'We've already tried that, Sir. And it's off.'

'Fuck it. Right, I want her car traced, her house searched, her parents' house staked-out and her credit cards checked. I also want teams at all train and bus stations and one at the airport.'

'But we'll need to have signed warrants for the house search, Sir, and that could take a bit of time.'

'Listen boys and listen carefully. I own this city and I can do whatever the fuck I want. Just get it done. Print off a false warrant, anything. Don't worry, I'll look after the fall-out if there's any, but let's just find the bitch. And one more thing. Somebody organise a uniform fitting for that shit for brains, Broadhead. I want him back on the beat in the morning.'

The DCC was now calling on all his experience of the criminal world; skills that not only made him feared but had fast-tracked him into the position he now held. 'But we still need to find Walker. Okay, I want his picture and description sent to every police force in the country, even fucking Cornwall, and then I need a special bulletin on every radio station, television station and news website in the country, stating we are looking for a man who could be armed and dangerous. I also want his phone and cards traced, his parents house in Fort William searched and while were at it, put out an alert to all our airport teams. The last thing we need is for him to skip the fucking country.'

Rather than use the lift, Paul led Dixie down the fire exit stairs and out through a back door. They walked slowly into the Hunterian Art Gallery then out again on the far side, passing the Scottish History department before running through the Adam Smith Building. Dixie chuckled at the irony.

'Would you care to enlighten me as to why you think this is so hilarious?' demanded Paul.

'Och, Paul. Look at the names of the buildings. Even you

have to see the funny side to it all.'

Paul didn't have time to think. 'Eh?'

'Never mind, I'll tell you later.'

Rounding the wildlife garden, they ran down the wee lane next to the building of Social History before darting across the street and down a side alley to where Paul had parked his car. Driving calmly and silently up Great George Street, Paul took a left into Kersland Street and finally on to the Great Western Road.

Ten minutes later and Hastie knew he had lost her. Deep in thought in the back of the car, he was sipping on a cold coffee while staring out the window and occasionally tapping the radio on his teeth. However, in a sudden involuntary spasm, his eyes opened wide. As he ordered the driver to head back to HQ, he took out his phone and hit the dial button. 'Paul, it's Mike.'

'Sir, how are things this fine morning?' replied Paul. Putting the phone on speaker, he mouthed silently for Dixie to keep quiet.

'Not good, Paul. Not good at all. We really need to find Dixie as soon as we can. Our boys in International Security have discovered it could be the Hutchinson Group who is trying to kill her, after all. The problem is we don't know where she is.'

'Can't they get on the blower to Langley and put a stop to it?'

'Fuckin' hell, Paul, it might be the CIA who is trying to pull the trigger.'

'Sir, it is Dixie we're talking about here. Surely we have to protect her?'

'Paul, I think they might have bigger things to worry about than what the effects of Dixie Armstrong's death will be. And remember, these guys will stop at nothing to get to her. No, we need to bring her in and take her to a safe house as soon as possible.'

'Are you saying then that Hutchinson is in bed with the CIA? And whatever story Dixie is working on could mean big trouble for them?'

'Of course it bloody well could. If weapons sales are on the agenda, it's not necessarily some poor fucker in Africa who first gets the bullet.'

'But Sir, Dixie is working on a story about Scotland, not Africa,' said Paul, trying to disguise his chortling.

'I know that, Paul,' cried an exasperated Hastie. 'I'm just using it as an example. Anyway, that's not the point. We need to find her soon before we find her dead. Where are you now?'

Paul, instead of telling Hastie the truth by saying he was on the M8 and heading for Edinburgh, lied. 'I had a tip off about the black Range Rover and I'm driving up to Helensburgh to ask some questions.'

'Helensburgh, what the hell are you going up there for?'

'Well, I've a theory the Range Rover could be from the submarine base up there. It did disappear out of thin air after it turned off the road at Loch Lomond, so where better to hide it than somewhere with close ties to the US Defence Services and strangely enough, somewhere outwith our jurisdiction.'

'Listen Paul,' said Hastie, knowing the order to kill Dixie didn't come from Faslane. 'Don't you go rocking the boat there, son. You'll create more trouble than you can deal with.'

'Well, it's not so much as rocking the boat, Sir. More like rocking the submarine!'

'Paul,' shouted Hastie, 'this is not the time for you to be fucking around. Get your arse back to the office as soon as possible so you can help me trace Dixie.'

'But if someone stationed up at the base is intent on killing Dixie then maybe I can scare them off.'

'No Paul, I want you back here ASAP. Got it?'

As the phone went dead, Paul turned to Dixie. 'You are one very popular lady, so you are.'

'Too popular, I reckon. What are you going to do, Paul? You'll need to get back.'

'Ach, he'll be fine,' said Paul with a mischievous grin. 'He just wants me close at hand in case you call him from your very secret location next to me. Unfortunately, he knows his arse is well and truly on the line here, Dixie. And anyway, he'll have all his bases covered and when he gets this serious, it will mean trouble for everyone. Thankfully, we still have one last saving grace: as long as he remains clueless to my involvement, we should be in grand shape.'

'And what about my kids?'

'They'll be fine, Dixie. In fact, your dad will already be packing their lunch for a long drive through the Highlands and they'll be dancing round the house singing "Ye cannae shove yer Grannie off the bus!"

17

ancient blood

Wednesday 18th June

9. 39 am - Glasgow International Airport

After demolishing a costly and unimpressive breakfast, Charlie Norton walked out of the terminal and across the road to collect a car from the rental car park. Now he was waiting. Anytime soon, Brad Zimmerman and his ubiquitous guardian, Tony, would appear on the concourse with their driver.

His trip to the US had been a success, and after sending the images of Zimmerman and his various cohorts back to Glasgow, and before jumping on a plane for home, Charlie had enjoyed a stroll around America's capital city.

Many before him had compared DC to Rome and as he walked, he wondered if, in centuries to come, there would be tour guides offering trips to the dilapidated Lincoln Memorial and the ruins of the Senate. Being a lover of both ancient and modern art, Charlie contemplated the comparisons between the two cities and DC's impending fall from grace, and considered if another dark age was on its way and who or what would take control of the world. Something like the Church of Rome? Surely not? He even imagined if it would be those nutters known as the Creationists and their not so intelligent design, and wondered if they would do it in six days and have a rest on the seventh. Oh, Christ. No! Nah, it would probably be China and its unstoppable and brazen ascent to world dominance, or worse still, Brussels and its endless corridors of shuffling and whistling bureaucrats.

Charlie strolled with learned and eager purpose amid the architectural majesty and contradictions of Washington DC. Set carefully amid wide open spaces of green grass, the glistening stone of classical monuments and government buildings paid homage to the empire. However, it wasn't all imperious grandeur. 'Ah, the great hypocrisy,' he said. 'Here I stand amidst this wonderful Ionic, Doric and Corinthian architecture when only a few blocks away, deprivation and crime rampage through the city in a wave of homeless shelters, soup kitchens and hypo-dermic needles.'

What a fucking joke!

Charlie took in the Lincoln Memorial and thought of Gettysburg and old Abe himself, and of Martin Luther King. A short time later, he was strolling around The Ellipse and passing the White House, and remembering with fondness the great and not so great Presidents whose enduring time in the Oval Office had seen wars declared, New Deals imagined, missile crises avoided, offices' impeached, human rights abused and the odd blow job provided.

After touring the many seats of power, Charlie chortled as he glanced east towards Pennsylvania Avenue and the offices of the Hutchinson Group. He shook his head and smiled ruefully at the company's surreptitiousness before crossing the road to see the famous New York Avenue Presbyterian Church. It was here where Presidents searched for redemption and prayed for forgiveness, and where Peter Marshall, the controversial Scottish minister, conducted his services as the Chaplain to the Senate.

Charlie continued north, revelling in both the French influenced architecture and the deference to ancient Rome. He was trying to identify the year of construction and design styles of certain buildings when after a few blocks on Sixteenth Street his attention was abruptly commandeered by an astonishing building more akin to an ancient temple than a nineteenth century church. This was far too good to miss. Out came the camera. Set high on a colossal plinth of granite, the building was surrounded by a row of classical pillars and protected by a pair of magnificent sphinxes he later learned represented wisdom and power. Taking a closer look, he approached the imposing structure and smiled. 'Fuck me! Is there anything in this world those damn Scots haven't had their mucky mitts on?'

The Temple of the Scottish Rite, home to the Supreme Council of the Ancient Order of the Scottish Rite, was a truly sublime building and one that not only impressed Charlie's knowledge of architecture but also appealed to his sense of history. He had to know more.

Once inside, and after discovering the Temple had been designed by the ironically named John Russell Pope whose drawings had been based on the tomb of King Mausolus at Halicarnassus, one of the seven wonders of the ancient world, Charlie doffed his imaginary Yorkshire cap to a group of men of extraordinary vision. It was a remarkable piece of architecture. The rooms (the ones Charlie was permitted to view) were wonderful and joyous and ingratiated with a sensational décor of Masonic symbolism. Nevertheless, it was in the library where Charlie truly understood the magnificence of achievement. As he lightly gasped for air, he found himself in a library which just so happened to house one of the world's largest collections of works by Robert Burns. This was an array of works on or by Burns, which took even Charlie Norton by surprise. There were thousands of publications. Furthermore, as Charlie wondered at this fantastic tribute to the national bard, he began to understand why Burns was held in such high esteem by the Brotherhood. All he had to do was read the Ancient Order's motto: *"Human progress is our cause; liberty of thought our supreme wish; freedom of conscience our mission; and the guarantee of equal rights to all people everywhere our ultimate goal."*

He smiled. 'That'll be me off the membership list.'

His mind was just as creative as he enjoyed the relaxing flight home from Dulles to Heathrow. It was a quiet journey that afforded him some sleep and the opportunity to acquire a phone number or two from the female cabin crew. He even thought of the possibility of a third visit to the Mile High Club but damn it, had some wanker in Washington not insisted on implementing the new security regulations. Bummer, especially as he had the morning after the night before, dose of the horn. For about three hours, his libidinous mind worked overtime as he thought of the many frolicking mornings he loved so much. He thought about Grace from the Smithsonian. Now he couldn't sleep. He was so horny. As he slipped his seat back, he reminisced. Frustratingly, knew it wasn't the best of subjects to think about on a flight. He even tried to read a book and watch an in-flight movie but fuck, it was always the best sex. He thought about Grace once more.

The morning before, his cock had been throbbing as its wee head peeked up with an eager eye. The damn thing was trying to awaken him from his sexual unconscious state. It was succeeding. He squeezed the wee man a couple of times between his fingers before pulling at his balls until they hurt. He had lain face down, pressing his hydraulic, organic sperm pump into the bed, and even contemplated nipping to the loo for a ham shank. Then he had stared into the abyss for a couple of minutes before giggling and saying to hell with this for a game of soldiers.

There had been no time for foreplay. Too much trouble. He rolled over gently, carefully spooning the fortunate curator dosing beside him. Wrapping his arm around her waist, he went straight for the flower -no time for the nips. He pushed his hand into the moist allotment of pleasure and tickled her flaps. He squeezed his stonker between her butt cheeks as he listened to her muffled groans. As she opened her eyes, he produced a bloodshot grin. She sleepily smiled back. He turned her onto her belly. She parked her ass in the air. He struggled to his knees and glared down at his champion. He shook his head to freshen his mind. He breathed out deeply. He was sweating ten pints. As he slid his boabie up, he tried not to piss himself laughing. She groaned again as he fumbled around with his bell-end before finally parking his big, bad, red Ducati inside her garage. Vrooooom! Vrooooom! Oh fuck, it was good. Oh yes, it had been really fucking good. In fact, the-morning-after sex was undoubtedly the best sex he could have. No coy innuendo, no sweet talkin', no apology necessary. Just sober enough to enjoy

270

every moment, just lucid enough to feel every sensation but still drunk enough not to give a damn about how ridiculous he might appear as he thrashed away woof-woof style inside Grace's hot, wet and gushing punani! It's just a pity his fortune did not afford him an audience to her blowing the old trombone!

He also had a good night, surprisingly, with Zimmerman. Though the man turned out to be an imbecilic thoroughbred with women, it hadn't stopped Charlie from enjoying his company. Ungracious, ignorant and obnoxious, Zimmerman was fantastically oblivious to how hilarious he was and it never pissed Charlie off when guys were like that. One look on a woman's face while she listened to people like Zimmerman was damn good entertainment in itself and absolutely no threat whatsoever to one's chances. In fact, he should make a concerted effort to hang around arseholes like Zimmerman more often.

Charlie had flown into Glasgow on an earlier flight from Heathrow after Zimmerman advertently boasted about the first class service he would receive on the flight from Dulles to Glasgow. Charlie had thought about catching the same flight but the chance of bumping into Zimmerman at the airport would have been too great, deciding on an earlier flight to London then the Shuttle up to Scotland. Barring any screw-ups at Heathrow, he would be touching down in Glasgow three hours ahead of Zimmerman, and in plenty of time for a rest.

As Zimmerman's car pulled out, Charlie prepared to follow in the family hatchback, which in Charlie's mind wasn't exactly the sexiest of cars in which to carry out the task of being the number one trail dog. And that annoyed him. He had wanted to take his Ducati but he had taken too great a risk in Atlanta. If big Tony noticed another motorbike madman on his tail on the much quieter roads of Scotland then it was over.

Through Glasgow the two cars drove, over the Kingston Bridge and down through the tunnel below Charlie's favourite building, the Mitchell Library. As the motorway wound its way east of the city centre, Charlie sighed. Each and every time he drove on this road, he became infuriated at the town planners of yesteryear; the beautiful buildings of Glasgow obscured by drab concrete while high up above the motorway on the left, eyesores masquerading as residential properties drowned the skyline. 'How on earth,' muttered Charlie, 'in such an artistic city that produced the likes of Mackintosh and 'Greek' Thomson, could the planners get it so wrong?' But Charlie did note that it was a functional city and the infrastructure was excellent, and as much as commuters complained, Glasgow never suffered the massive log jams like other major cities. However, regardless of how relatively good the M8 was for drivers, he still thought it a dreadful fuck up by the planners, at least in an aesthetic manner, and one which no doubt brought tears to the impassive eyes of those bureaucratic numpties who promoted Scottish tourism. Nevertheless, this was Glasgow and Glasgow always did things its own way.

Zimmerman's car passed the massive gas containers on the left before taking the Stirling exit and the M80 north. As they flew out of Glasgow, the two cars passed Scotland's "wonder" cities. Charlie laughed. 'What's it called? Cumbernauld!' Built in the sixties to accommodate the overflow from the city slums, Charlie had read that Cumbernauld had been considered a wonderful success back then, resulting in the city being awarded numerous accolades on the living conditions of the future. Thousands of design experts and students from across the world had flocked with eager anticipation to Cumbernauld to marvel at the sensational town planning and lavish it with praise. Until, that was, someone asked one very important question; where are all these people going to work and shop and play? Charlie smiled again. He didn't think there would be a rush of town-planning students flying in for a gander anytime soon.

Fortunately, for Charlie, as he left the M80 to join the M9, the traffic volume decreased. Not only would he now find it easier to trail Zimmerman, he now had an opportunity to enjoy the countryside. As he passed Stirling, he had a wee chuckle to himself at the history between Scotland and England. As an Englishman, Charlie didn't really care much for the many battles between the two countries but could understand the Scots' point of view. If someone had attempted to invade his country, he would have been mightily pissed-off as well. As long as his people could keep York and the Dales then the invader was welcome to the rest of it, and, of course, Bradford! He was now driving through sacred Scottish land. With Bannockburn and Stirling Castle on his right and Wallace's Monument in the distance, this was the land where Scotland under Wallace and then Bruce, had finally kicked the English out. He smirked. He loved winding up his Scottish friends about the wars and how it all appeared to be for nothing when the parliament dissolved and moved to Westminster some four hundred years later. He knew it pissed them off but what the hell; it was all part of the fun.

As the cars continued north past Dunblane, Charlie began to think that another trip to Gleneagles was on the agenda. However, when they passed the exit for Gleneagles, and then Perth, Charlie cursed, 'Aw, for fuck's sake, don't tell me he's going to fucking Dundee!'

Charlie breathed a sigh of relief as Zimmerman's car bypassed Dundee before taking a turn-off for a place Charlie thought to be Kirrie something. 'Jesus, what is it with the Scots and their language? Every bloody word seems to have an 'ae' at the end of it? Cannae, winnae, dinnae, couldnae, shouldnae! Will they ever learn to speak properly?'

Keeping a safe distance, Charlie slowed. He also questioned the choice of location. When Zimmerman's car turned off again, the saw the familiar BMW M3 parked a few metres up the road in a small village. Charlie paused for thought. Apart from his cock, something big was up. He drove by Dixie's car and parked beside a shop just outside the castle gates. Creeping back along the verge, he thumped the window with his fist to startle Rory out of his mid-morning slumber.

'What the fuck?' screamed Rory.

As Charlie's glazed and crazed eyes appeared on the other side of the glass, he gestured for Rory to open the door. 'Holy fuck, dinnae dae that again ya fuckin' arsehole,' moaned Rory. Coming to his senses, he moaned again. 'You'll gimmie a bloody heart attack, for fuck's sake. Anyway, what the hell are you doing here?'

Charlie took a seat while taking a swig of Rory's cold coffee. He left the door ajar. The car needed some air. 'Just following our man Zimmerman. Strange place for him to come, may I add. And you, Badger Balls?'

'Buchanan's here. Has been all night. I've been ordered to keep tabs.'

'So, what is this place?'

'Glamis Castle, childhood home of our late, beloved Queen Mother. It's also the none too shabby bidey-in of Lord Strathmore, a famous landowner in these parts.'

'Interesting times indeed,' said Charlie to Rory, both still oblivious to the previous day's events down in London. 'I take it then that Buchanan and Zimmerman are being introduced as we speak.'

'It appears that way. Any chance you could get a pic?'

'I don't know. If these two are meeting then I presume it won't be in front of the Blue Rinse Brigade and the Viagra Veterans here for a day out. More likely they'll be heading out to somewhere on the estate. However, that doesn't stop us parking our car, paying our entrance money and having a wee goose at the aristocratic grandeur. What's more, I've heard it's pretty unbelievable.'

'You're joking, aren't you? There's no fucking way I'm going in there. We'll be spotted.'

'Have you seen the size of the bloody place, Rory? It's enormous. Not a hope of being seen, and remember, these guys don't mix with the peasants. C'mon, let's go.'

Rory remained in his seat as Charlie pulled his door closed. 'Did you hear me, Rory? I said, let's go.'

'Are you sure, Charlie? It's a wee bit risky.'

'Listen Donkey-Breath, its one of the busiest tourist destinations in the country. There'll be hundreds of people in there taking snaps and the last thing Buchanan needs while he's munching on his croissants is to be bothered by a crowd of nosey fucking tourists. Oh no, he'll be off hiding somewhere.'

'Okay, Charlie, but on your head be it.'

'I just love it when you talk all regal. How appropriate.'

As Rory and Charlie drove down the tree-lined driveway towards Glamis Castle, they both stared in awe at its majesty. It created both a sense of excitement and trepidation. The driveway itself was long and straight, and lingered through grass fields littered with magnificent old trees, cattle and deer fences. In the distance, the massive corner towers of the castle stood erect, guarding the estate. The castle was so imperious that the main door seemed uncomfortably small amidst the grandeur. It also became clear to Charlie that the design of the castle intimated it was both a home and an ancient seat of power. Furthermore, such were the contradictions in its architecture, it was difficult to pin down the era in which it was built. Maybe, Charlie thought, the castle had been added to over the years because there would certainly have been enough political turmoil to justify the odd extension or two.

As the car swung left in front of the main door, Charlie laughed out loud. 'Bloody Hell, Rory, even the aristocracy think they're Retail magnets! Look at that, a bloody shop, a restaurant and a mini-garden centre. Next thing we'll see is the FT running a story on the latest blue-chip take-over. Imagine the headlines - "Tesco to buy medieval castle in bid to further increase market share".'

The contradiction of history was not lost on Rory, either, as he pulled into the car park. Rows of tour buses stood idle on the gravel as their drivers smoked cigarettes and discussed the merits of the attraction's commission payments. To the right of the buses, over two hundred cars were neatly parked: some with the odd barking dog inside and most with a tartan rug lying neatly folded in the back window.

'Well, Chic,' said Rory, 'it seems as if we'll be putting the demographics and visitor survey out of sync today. Not only will we be the youngest here, we'll also be the only two with our own hair!'

'Ah Rory, you disappoint me. There will always be the odd bus or two of foreign students at places like this. I mean, they're not all up in the Highlands jumping into waterfalls and falling down mountains while their bikes lie twisted in some wee burn. Oh no, I can sniff them from here.'

'You are one dirty bastard, Norton. Is there anything in this world that enhances your pathetic life other than motorbikes and sex?'

'Of course there are but I'm afraid they're nowhere near as much fun!'

Rory smiled and shook his head as he parked the car. 'Okay, what now?'

'Well, there's a restaurant and shop over there. How about a coffee, a key ring and a cuddly Highland Cow?'

'Seriously Charlie, what's the plan?'

'I suggest you wait here while I become the dumb-wit tourist who inadvertently gets lost in the grounds with my camera. In fact, why don't you have a wee wander around the castle? It'll be good for you; all that history. And you'll have all these old ladies to look after you as well.'

'Nah, I think I'll just wait in the café, Scab-Nads. But you'll be wasting your time. It's not as if Peter Buchanan and Zimmerman will be having brunch on the lawn.'

'No they won't, but it might be interesting to see if it's just the two of them having a wee chat or if our other friend from Gleneagles is still in on the Hutchinson deal. Anyway, please yourself, but keep your phone on. If I get made, we're outa here.'

As Charlie set off on his safari, Rory took a mosey round the immediate grounds. The place was busy and Rory was surprised at the public's interest in the castle. It was staggering what Royal connections could do to please the manager of a private bank. Furthermore, with hundreds wandering inside the castle, eating lunch, buying gifts and coming to enjoy the odd concert, Rory knew it was making more than a few extra bob, this was a fully functioning business; and all without adding the farming revenue. Yes, thought Rory, it really is amazing what royal connections can do for the old bank account.

As Rory sat drinking a coffee and munching into an onion bridie, he considered the history of the castle, and more importantly, its location. Not only were there many Pictish

276

crosses dotted in the fields throughout the area, Rory also knew that Glamis was only a few miles from the famous battlefield of Dunnichen where, in the seventh century, the Picts had given the Angle and Saxon invaders from England a right going over. After the Romans a few hundred years earlier, it was the second and last time the ancient tribe had overcome invasion from the south. Rory smiled at how this oft forgotten period had been omitted from the many books on Scottish history. He smiled even more when he thought of how success in this bloody battle created the foundations for Scotland to exist as a nation. Had the Saxons been victorious, Scotland as he knew it, with all its tribes and customs, and languages and cultures, would never have existed. It was just as important to Scotland as Bannockburn was. Furthermore, and surely by no coincidence, he also knew that one of Robert the Bruce's beloved sons, Prince John, was buried nearby at the Priory of Restenneth.

Today, however, Glamis meant more to others than just its location and much more than what the Picts had achieved. The olden estate was the ancestral home of the Queen Mother, the glorious matriarch and lover of gin, and one of the most influential Royal figures in the last three centuries.

Rory ruefully shook his head. He knew the family at Glamis had enjoyed an incredible stroke of luck, or bad-luck, back in the nineteen-thirties. In fact, he wondered if they danced in aristocratic ecstasy when they learned of Teddy's abdication, brought on by his unyielding love of an American commoner. For not only would their very own blood become the wife of a king, she would also become Queen Consort and be given the responsibility for both providing an heiress and for grooming the next monarch: Queen Elizabeth I of Scotland.

Rory was well aware of the Queen Mother's appreciation of all things Scottish. He had heard that she had her children cared for and educated by a Scotswomen, their health monitored by a Scottish doctor and as often as she could, brought the girls here on vacation. Seemingly, she had wanted to engender and empower the kids in the culture of her ancestors. She was a distinctly Scottish Queen who wanted nothing more than to leave a lasting legacy where Scotland was just as much home for her family as London was. Moreover, after her husband died and the present Queen anointed, the Queen Mum did not drift into obscurity. She drove her family to become at one with the people and opened the doors to the Monarchy in a way that no one had ever seen before. She made them more human, she made them serve the people and she became, de facto, the Head of the Royal Family.

Rory contemplated the power this woman held. How did she do it? Where did it come from and who supported her? It wasn't all coincidence, was it? In the world of the aristocracy, the only rules by which they played were reserved for politics and birth rights. Heirs and spares. Furthermore, it appeared as if it was their raison d'etre. And if the Queen Mother had known this, she had been extremely wise. She had positioned herself at the very top.

'You're joking, eight pounds? That's a bit much for a mooch around an old castle,' questioned Rory as he handed a tenner to an elderly male member of staff.

'Ach, laddie! For a young man like yourself, it's a good bargain.'

'What do you mean "a bargain"? This mob has taken far more than eight pounds from me in the past. In fact, they should be paying me to come and visit.'

Rory grinned, letting the man see his impudence.

'If you only knew what the Family has done for you.'

'Aye, if only!'

The old man produced a grin even more mischievous than his. He was a wee bit taken aback.

'Is there anything else I can do for you, young man?'

'Aye. My change and a receipt!'

'Certainly. Here's your map. Just follow the directions.'

The employees of Glamis Castle were wonderfully friendly and polite. Walking briskly through the building, they ensured the flow of traffic kept moving while meticulously attending to business and making every attempt to make the visitor's experience a memorable one. Wearing white blouses or fleeces, well shone shoes and short hair, they were an army of devoted subjects whose pleasant demeanour exuded enjoyment and loyalty. They were incredibly supportive of the Family. It was as if they had accepted their position in life and trusted the word of their boss implicitly. It was also hilarious, chuckled Rory, that they all spoke in that broad Angus accent; where pies were *pez* and onions were *ingings*.

Bouncing up the old stone staircase, passing the various health and safety certificates and tourism awards, he was soon in a large and elegant dining room full of antique furniture and heraldic crests. Gazing around indifferently, Rory listened as a guide explained the significance of the room and its items to a group of Canadian tourists. "The Queen Mother used to sit on this chair as a child and gaze out across the estate," and "the Princesses used to play just outside there during the war." Rory giggled at the ironic and gentle portrayal of supposedly normal life within this great family.

Tagging on to the Canucks, and his new complimentary tour guide, Rory made his way through the castle. It was as he expected -the dining room, the stags' heads, ancient living quarters and bedrooms. He loved history but not this stuff. Yes, it was beautiful and astonishingly well-preserved, if all a bit predictable.

And then he entered the portrait room.

This windowless room must have been twenty metres long with huge portraits from centuries gone-by fixed high on the pink walls. Down below, badly typed signs warned off the ambitious tourist from touching the works of arts. Rory breathed out and let his eyes wander. Courtesy of Charlie, he had read a little Art History but having only ever seen the odd masterpiece before, most notably a hung-over visit to see "The Titians", he found himself surprised by his sudden interest. These paintings were something else. Within the massive gilt frames of intricate Italian mouldings, the light and movement in each subject was astonishing. Rory gasped as he took a closer look. The portraits themselves varied in size from four feet by three, to an enormous one that was six foot in height and ten foot in width. With more than twenty of them hanging on the silent walls, the room was an intimidating place to be. Rory felt small and insignificant as the eyes of the Earls pierced into his. Holding their heads high in a backward tilt, a haughty expression dripped indignantly from their pointed noses and pouting lips. They wanted Rory to know they held an almighty power. Transfixed as the guide's words drifted off into a distant murmur, Rory was a little boy lost in an artistic cavern of fear. These men were kings and leaders of men whose deity told all. They weren't to be messed with.

The reality of this chance encounter with history sent Rory's mind into inquisitive turmoil. Sensing there was more to learn, he shook himself into the present as the guide began to explain who each subject was, what their historical achievements were and what significance they held in the Family's history. As Rory listened and toiled in vain to focus his mind, the guide continued to talk about the various Earls. One had lost an important battle against the English somewhere in the Borders, another was hailed by a Tsar as being an inspirational leader in the Russian Wars while several of them had been awarded high-ranking commissions in various armies across Europe. One had even been a friend of Benjamin Franklin during the American movement for Independence. However, not until Rory quizzed the guide, who in turn revealed that most of the Earls had been loyal supporters of the Stuart Dynasty and the Jacobite Cause, did Rory feel a rattle in his file of obsessive scholarship.

Just the other night, he had read that the Stuart Dynasty had apparently long since died out. Humiliated, they had become pretty insignificant to the world-at-large.

He glanced up again at the portraits, studying each one carefully. His body twitched, a weird feeling telling him there was more to discover. As he tapped his foot on the floor, his eyes flicked involuntarily up to his left. 'What the fuck is it?' he whispered. He was full of frustration. He closed his eyes and thought deeply for a few seconds more. When his brain finally stirred, his eyes, and mouth, opened gently. 'Okay, so the Earls each have a genetic similarity in how they look,' stated Rory.

'Nah. Too simple and far too obvious, and besides, they're all from the same family.' He continued to stare, searching for some clue to questions and answers he did not yet know. 'Of course, it's not in their uncanny resemblance to each other; it's in the pose in which they are captured. It couldn't be a coincidence.'

The guide was telling the group that the style adopted by the artists was similar to that of the great Regal Masters: lots of emotion and narrative, and golds and reds and whites. Moreover, the artists were teasing Rory to see more than just a face. Glaring into the ancient eyes looking down at him, Rory could feel their power. He studied their appearance. 'But their hair is long and their complexions pale,' he mumbled. He knew they wanted to say more. They wanted Rory to know who they really were.

Rory looked down. He shook his head. He smiled.

At first glance, the pose adopted by each Earl displayed a slight arrogance but as Rory focussed on the subjects' eyes once more, he could feel sadness. He felt they had a need to tell the world something more meaningful. Then it hit him. He gazed at the empty fields and deserted mounds that made up two or three of the portraits' backgrounds. He sympathised with their agony. He believed their pain. He felt their suffering. Then he noticed how one of them was dressed. Rory took a couple of shaky steps back and glared open mouthed. The Earl in a painting in the far corner was not kitted-out, as one would expect, in ceremonial attire with medals and gowns and swords, but simply dressed in a single, white loin cloth wrapped around a frail body. He wore very little else. His arms were tense as he held out his palm. Was he pleading for help? He was arching his back in an anguished curve while exposing his bare and shallow chest to the darkened sky. He wore an expression of proud despair. He held a pose very much like that of Jesus Christ at the Crucifixion!

Rory could feel his legs weaken. They were shaking. He squeezed his eyes between his thumb and forefinger, seeing only tiny and blurry white stars. Taking a deep breath, he thought for a moment before whispering again. 'But why? This is only my interpretation, and I have been hankering to see something like this for a long time now. What's more, I needed a place like this to back up my theories. Maybe I'm just trying too hard to prove something to Dixie.'

Taking a seat on a long sofa, Rory grappled with what he felt in this room and what he had read the other night. He was craving to discover some kind of correlation. 'All this must have something to do with the Stuart Dynasty.' Moments later, he was talking through his rationale with himself.

Before they were exiled, the Stuarts had reigned over Scotland for close on four hundred years and such was their belief in being on this earth as direct descendents of the God Almighty, they had long since believed they had been given a divine right to rule. Rory knew it was far fetched but he also knew that cultures and philosophies were extremely different back then. Furthermore, when Knox and Calvin appeared on the scene, the political and religious landscape changed forever; not that it hindered the Stuarts' continued desire to rule Scotland, and neither did it prevent them from having a pop at taking over the English throne as well. Nevertheless, they did feel their hold on power slipping away, and with that possibility on the royal horizon, they began to play the politics game: first with the Covenanters and then with Cromwell. Rory laughed. 'Not a good move for the health!' But still the Stuarts persevered with their belief in the Divine Right. Unfortunately, they had no idea this Divine Right would be instrumental in their dynastic demise which, catastrophically, included a wee bit of foreign exile, the odd public decapitation and a serious arse-kicking by William of Orange at the Battle of the Boyne. Only then were they forced to relinquish all power to the new kids in the palace: the Hanovers.

Rory continued to think back to his research, searching for some parallel between the portraits and his learnings. He knew the Stuarts, before taking over both crowns, had long since portrayed themselves as loyal subjects of Rome but some of the portraits in this castle seemed to dispel any loyalty to the great Holy See. If truth were told, these portraits would have been considered blasphemous. 'Maybe,' Rory mumbled, 'before adopting Episcopalianism, the Stuarts wanted to give the impression they were trusted subjects of the wee man of the papal tiara

Maybe it was the politics of the day that brought about the sham. Maybe this false homage was their way of seeking French support for their claim to the Scottish and English thrones. Whatever the hell it was, it certainly pissed-off the Hanovers just enough for the new Dutch masters to offer no fucking quarter whatsoever during the Old Chevalier's Rebellion in 1715 and Bonnie Prince Charlie's in 1745!'

Rory lifted his head and glared into a void. His mind may have been full of theories but he had to find reason in all of what he was witnessing. Moments later, he was looking down at the floor while resting his elbows on his knees and cupping his hands beneath his chin. He knew there was more to the Earls he still needed to uncover. He pondered over his ideas for a few seconds more before raising his head again. 'Could the Earls be related to the Stuarts?' he said inquisitively and with surprise. 'The Stuarts were Jacobites after all, and not just any old kilted highlander but the founding fathers of the entire Dynasty!' For a moment, Rory didn't breathe. 'Of course they bloody well could,' he answered aloud. 'Inter-family marriage was common place back then. And Christ, it certainly wasn't by chance that Robert the Bruce's nephew, King Robert II, granted the castle and estate to the Lyons Clan in 1372. In fact, why shouldn't they be? And to think this is the ancestral home of the Queen and her good old mama!'

Rory was trying to answer too many questions. He knew he was on to something, but what? He just didn't have enough information yet. It was, as Dixie said, all circumspect shite!

His hands were sweating and his head thumping. He thought about all these lonely hours in his apartment as he read up on his historical theories. He thought about his inability to substantiate his findings. He thought about the Ancient Order of the Scottish Rite. He thought about the Hutchinson Group.

Rory took one last look around before pinching his lips and shrugging his shoulders. Despondently, he shoved his hands into his pockets and strolled absent-mindedly on with his tour de free gratis. As much as he craved answers, he reckoned he would have to wait.

A few uninspiring bedrooms later, he stood in a wood-panelled room, which at first glance resembled a small chapel. He was correct.

'And now, ladies and gents, this is the private chapel of the Earls,' explained the guide. He also warned the group of the Grey Lady ghost who had been known to haunt the castle. The tourists giggled.

Rory shook his head. 'Aye, right. Pull the other testicle.'

However, Rory's disparaging lack of faith in the spirit world became alarmingly irrelevant when he began to survey his surroundings. He nearly fucking collapsed, coincidence and self-theorising quickly eliminated by fascination and intrigue as he struggled to take in what he was seeing. The chapel was small. No bigger than thirty square metres, its walls were adorned with paintings of Jesus and the apostles!

Feeling the need to sit down in a pew, Rory reached out behind. Facing the altar, he studied the paintings with wide eyes. He was trying to remember all of the apostles' names. He was also surprised to note that although the painting behind the altar was, as one would expect, of Jesus, there also appeared to be just as much importance given to his brother James, known back then as Jacob. This was especially disconcerting because not only was James one of the largest paintings, it also appeared as if Jesus had been demoted to second-in-command, his portrait hanging, as if inconsequential, on the wall to the right of where Rory sat. It was just beside the door. Taking out his notebook, Rory searched for clarity.

The paintings of the other disciples and apostles were similar in size than those of James and Jesus. In counting them, Rory became perplexed. One was missing. He began to write them down. Philip, Peter, John, Andrew…, twice running his pen over his list before realising what a stupid bastard he was. 'Of course, Paul's not here,' he whispered. 'And why am I not surprised? He was the one who purportedly betrayed James when James became the leader of the Church of Jerusalem. In fact, was it not Paul who fed the rumours of Jesus' reincarnation to the Romans, first becoming their lachie then standing back as

James was thrown over the wall at the Temple Mount?'

Rory stretched back against the ancient wooden bench. His thoughts were becoming more lucid now. 'The lack of any reference to Paul in this chapel can only mean one thing and I'm certain of it,' he whispered. 'The Earls, and maybe the Stuarts, had no loyalty to Rome whatsoever. However, if that was the case and they weren't full-on Christians then what the bloody hell were they?'

Rory scribbled furiously in his note pad, writing names and dates and drawing lines between his ideas. He was trying to find that elusive truth. He could almost touch it. He began to giggle to himself as his wide eyes drifted around the small chapel. He was in the zone, ignoring the tourists shuffling and chattering between the pews. He twiddled his pen between his fingers as he continued to stare at the picture of James. Moments later, the pen was in the corner of his mouth and he was gnawing at the top. He began to slurp and then to whisper. 'And with all this deference to James, maybe it explains why the Earls were loyal to the Jacobites. It could also explain why the Stuart Dynasty gave eight of their Kings the name of James. Did they know that James, and not Jesus, was the true leader of the Church of Jerusalem?'

Frowning in frustration, Rory knew he was very close to discovering what he was searching for. Furthermore, he was almost sure the Earls were related to the Stuarts. And then, as if he knew he was about to shit himself, concern spread across his face. 'Maybe there really is some ancient power held by this family.'

Tilting his head back and closing his eyes, he felt dizzy as the blood rushed to his head. He thought of the relationships between the Earls, the Stuarts, and the several conveniently named King James of Scotland, as well as the association with the Queen and the Monarchy of today. He also considered the correlation between the religiously inclined portraits in the Portrait Room and the order of importance placed on the paintings in this chapel. 'Holy shit! This is too much! This is Mr. Brown on steroids!'

When he opened his eyes, he quickly realised it was more than that. It was a goddamn concoction of ephedrine, caffeine and the big red bull. His head shuddered, he blinked and he looked up again. His mouth fell open and the pen dropped to the floor. In glaring up at the ornately designed ceiling, Rory didn't seem to care he was allowing his thoughts to vocalise, and he didn't care who was listening. 'You've got to be kidding me. No way! You have got to be fucking kidding me.'

The other visitors turned in both shock and amusement at the young man swearing to himself. Mouthing an apology, he returned his eyes towards the ceiling and the individual wooden panels above. Rory's neck jolted back. Standing up to take a closer look, he almost lost his balance, so transfixed by what he could now see: more than forty beautiful and intricately painted biblical images and a handful of symbols and one specific symbol ...a Masonic Symbol. The All-Seeing Eye!

Feeling for the edge of the pew, he sat back down. He was hypnotised with his discoveries while trying to put them all together in some meaningful explanation. Though the logical journalist inside of him knew what to do, he first had to calm down. Unfortunately, he was still mesmerised.

Breathe.

'Fuck me, it all makes perfect sense,' he whispered. 'If the Earls used this chapel to worship James, the true leader of the Church of Jerusalem, they must, and without question, be Jacobites. Hence why they were such fervent supporters of the Stuarts, who, incidentally, believed they were direct descendants of the God Almighty. If that is the case, then it could explain why some portraits in the Portrait room were painted in that pseudo-religious style.' Rory twitched his head. 'And maybe that could point to the Earls holding the same beliefs as the Stuarts!

'And then there is the Masonic connection to consider. Obviously, some of the Earls must be Masons, most probably holders of senior degrees, to boot. Hence the relationship with Benjamin Franklyn, hence the powerful commissions in European armies and hence why they happened to be high-ranking commanders in the rebellions and wars of the eighteenth century.'

Rory was shaking his head in disbelief and wonderment. He was also delighted he was getting a result. Nevertheless, as he began to expand on his thoughts, he became a wee bit jumpy. In knowing how his mind worked, there was no way he could prevent what he would ask himself next. 'If these guys were members of the Masonic brotherhood, which they most probably were, is it possible they were Templar Knights? And if they are Templar Knights, could there be a bloodline that stretches all the way back to the Church of Jerusalem?'

He was chortling now and smiling at his own audacity in even thinking this. He had proved that some portraits in the other room, and now this chapel, did reveal an exceptional devotion to James and the Stuarts. Thinking some more, he reasoned that if the Earls weren't related by some sort of ancient bloodline to James and Jesus then what he had witnessed was an extremely perverse and self-obsessed display of loyalty and devotion. 'C'mon,' he asked. 'Who the fuck gets dressed up in a loin cloth and open shroud and pretends to be the Lord God Almighty just so they can have their picture taken?'

He was still coming to terms with his discoveries when another thought came to him. And it was as *out there* as he had ever thought before. This time he decided not to snigger. 'Holy Fuck! If this is all true, and the Earls are related to the Stuarts,' Rory paused and opened his mouth in disbelief, 'could the Queen and the Queen Mother be direct descendents of the biblical James? Or even Jesus Christ?'

Rory couldn't believe he had stumbled upon this kind of information. Astonished at the various relationships, he sat down and tried to compose both his mind and his heart beat. And then, as if the possibility that the Queen could be related to Jesus and James wasn't alarming enough, he thought about the Hutchinson Group and its role in all of this. As well as many of its Board members having belonged to the Ancient Order of the Scottish Rite over the years, Hutchinson is the reason Zimmerman is here. More to the point, why else would the Fixer from the world's most powerful private equity group and the future British Prime Minister come here for a meeting?

Ten minutes later, after running through the evidence repeatedly, and coming to the same conclusion, Rory began to chuckle. Smiling and laughing out loud, he clapped his hands and listened as the echo reverberated among the hushed voices of the castle. Tourists smiled and guides shook their heads. But what the fuck did he care? He had proof.

Rory was still rolling his head as he sauntered past the exit sign and down a back stair case. He glanced to his left and out through a window. The light shone through. He laughed. 'The Light? I'll show you the fucking light!'

Behind him, at the foot of the stairs, stood a door marked, *"Private: Staff and Family Members Only"*. Rory wanted to learn more of Glamis Castle but it would have been a step too far to take an illegal peeky-boo around the private quarters. He would come back another day and do a one-to-one with the head of the house. He had discovered enough today. However, as he made to leave the castle at the point he had come in, he noticed a small and simple drawing hanging on the wall at the foot of the stairs. Stopping to look, his eyes contracted as he leaned in a little further. He smiled. It was a hand-made linear diagram of the family tree of the Monarchs of Scotland dating back over a millennium. Rory took out his pen to use as a guide to follow the marriages and deaths and births. The Queen's children were at the bottom right, a few inches along from the Glamis family. Moving the pen up to the Queen Mother, Rory began taking mental notes of the varying branches of family. His eyes followed the pen as the branches of the tree began to intertwine with the marriages of various historical figures. He stopped when he saw a direct link to King James VI whose name sat proud and centre. 'Well, bugger me with the crown and sceptre.'

Rory felt cocky. And why the hell not? As he carried on upwards, he noted that some of the past King James' of Scotland were related by marriage to the family here at Glamis. As his heart began to tremble, his smirk slowly faded. And when his eyes reached a name he couldn't quite believe he was seeing, he had to grab the wall for support. 'My God, not only could the Queen be related to James or Jesus, she is also a direct fucking descendant of Robert the Bruce!'

Rory's head did a quick swivel to see if anyone was looking. Out came his notebook to record that the daughter of King Robert II married the first Earl of Glamis, four years after the estate was bequeathed to the Family by the King himself, and four years after he became the first ever Stuart King of Scotland. Rory wrote quickly and as he did so, repeated to himself what he already knew. 'Not only was Robert II the first Stuart king, he was also the nephew of King Robert the Bruce: the King who kicked English arse, the King who signed the Declaration of Arbroath, the King who was a Templar Knight and the King who was a founding father of the Masonic Lodge!'

Rory's hands were shaking and his eyes were leaping from their sockets. He was gasping for breath. 'Oh yes, Dixie. Take that! This is the proof I was after.'

He was now smiling broadly. Dixie had mocked him, even taunted him but now he had the answer. 'Jacob, Jesus, the Templars, Robert the Bruce, the Stuarts, the Ancient Order, the Monarchy, the Hutchinson Group. Holy Fuck!'

Rory was standing outside the shop when Charlie came running round from behind the castle wall. Rory didn't see him; too busy was he, thinking of the implications if what he had discovered were ever to go public, especially during times like this with the governments in Holyrood and Westminster at each other's throats and especially with Peter Buchanan, the future Prime Minister, meeting the Hutchinson Group on these very grounds. 'Fuck me, the repercussions could be seismic!'

'Right, Cock-a-leekie. Time to go. I've been rumbled.'

'Eh? What?'

'I said it's time to go, Rory. The security team spotted me taking pictures of Zimmerman's wee get-together and they're on my tail.'

'Bloody hell, Charlie. I thought you were going to be

careful!' gasped Rory as they began to jog towards the car.

'I was. They were outside a lodge over two hundred yards away and if it wasn't for that prick of a bodyguard having a wee play around with the binoculars, I would have been grand. Unfortunately, the big fucker knew how to use them. He even had them turned the right way round. And that was it. I was made. So it's all feet to the gravel and all hands to the steering wheel, my boy. I think we'd better get the car started. You drive; I'll hide in the back.'

As Rory drove slowly out, he could see two men running into the car park, their eyes darting in every direction. They both stared at Rory as he passed. He returned the favour with a smile and a wave.

'It's fine now. You're safe. But don't get up just yet. They're still looking at the back of the car.'

Once they were out of sight of the two security men, Charlie climbed over to the front seat and Rory relaxed. Ignoring the exit sign, Rory took a road that was much less romantic than the one they came in on. Rory didn't care. He had found what he was looking for. However, as the car reached an exit, which would bring them to the centre of Glamis Village, Rory saw a small church on the left, set back from the road in its own grounds. He slowed down to take a closer look and as he passed, almost drove onto the grass verge. Having just seen a large gate leading to a graveyard, he hit the brakes.

'What the fuck are you doing?' screamed Charlie. 'Let's get the fuck out of here now.'

'Just a second,' hissed Rory as he jumped out of the car. He couldn't believe it. His eyes popped for the sixth time that morning. On top of the gate were two symbols, one above the other. The one on top was a beautifully crafted, golden Christian cross. However, as he glanced down at the other, Rory shook his head in disbelief …again! This time he had no words and no thoughts. He stood alone, glaring at the simple wrought-iron design. He was looking at a six pointed star. He was staring at the Star of David!

18

come and relax in our fabulous...

Wednesday 18th June

12.12 pm - Kelso Hotel – North Bridge - Edinburgh

Despite the inclement Scottish weather, Edinburgh was a tourist mecca and a 24/7, 365 days a year destination. From the hundreds of thousands of revellers celebrating Hogmanay, to the millions who came to be entertained and enlightened by its many festivals, to those who came to marvel and learn of its turbulent history and to those who came to lord it up with champagne at its many international conferences, it was a town where being in the tourism business meant having a licence to print money. And in realising this, the Kelso hadn't been reticent in spreading the ink over the Gutenberg. Though it overlooked shops and offices, some of its rooms did have a partial view of Princes Street and the North Bridge. What's more, the Kelso was only yards from the World Heritage Site of the Old Town; no surprise then that it had an established reputation as one of the best known in the city. It was also an old style Scottish hotel servicing the needs of those who wanted to experience the tartan, the castles and the bagpipes. However, like most chain hotels in Edinburgh, the influx of workers from Eastern Europe had diluted the famous Scottish hospitality somewhat. Not that it was worse, just different, and in some cases, better. Nevertheless, for those who did complain at the dearth of local accents, there was always the whisky bar, the plaid upholstery and the concierge dressed in navy tartan waist-coats always at the ready to compliment one of the many different faces of the city.

Elliot and Kirsten Walker had never been exposed to the treats of the Kelso, more inclined were they to stay in some of the city's trendier boutique hotels. But this was not a visit to see friends and to spend a fortune shopping on George Street, this was a wee bit more serious. What's more, it didn't excuse the room they had been allocated and in having a difference of opinion with Elliot on the standards expected, Kirsten hated it.

Soulless and mundane, and lacking any nous in design ingenuity and recent capital investment, it was the kind of room to be found in most hotels across the world. With its typical wee basket of toiletries from some upmarket brand like Mouldy Crown sitting alongside two glasses covered with branded paper coasters on the artificial marble sink, the ensuite was an aesthetic disaster. When they had arrived early that morning, Kirsten had looked around and groaned, not in snobbery but in desperate castigation. The toilet paper was rolled-up neatly with the end turned into a little V, fooling only the very stupid that it was just out of the packaging while behind the thin and greying shower curtain, the ridiculous message from the general manager had informed her that she would be an environmental saviour if reused the towels. 'Oh yeh, sure,' moaned Kirsten. 'What he really means to say is that his hotel is too bloody tight to wash the towels, preferring instead I dry myself in the morning with the defiled and very same, skid-mark ridden piece of cloth!'

When she had wandered back into the main body of the room, the television stood encased in an enormous fake walnut unit. The minibar was underneath. There was a desk and chair to the right of the television and a further two uncomfortable looking lounge chairs beneath the window. On top of the desk lay the fake, leather-covered, hotel handbook filled with all the useless information she would not require, as well as a couple of bottles of own-brand water and a room service menu offering Caesar salads, 100% burgers and club sandwiches. Fortunately, it wasn't that bad a hotel; it didn't offer frozen pizza. The room service charge was discreet in small print at the bottom. On either side of the queen-sized bed, covered with a bedbug infested bed-spread, stood two bedside tables, each with a heavy brass lamp on top. Kirsten had smiled, wondering how long it would take for Elliot to figure out how to switch them both off at the same time. The television hummed with a "Welcome, Mr. Riley" message on the screen while up above, the plastic encased price-list for movies had been delighted to inform her that the invoice for porn would not be mentioned on her bill. Again, she had scoffed. 'The cheek hotels have in calling it porn. Okay, so there might be moans and groans, and writhing in naked ecstasy but never had the couple going at it ever considered the idea of full penetration!'

Kirsten had been seething, her frustration teeming out at the apparent stupidity of her husband in becoming mixed-up in this affair. Now she was taking it out on the room, the hotel and the people in the hotel, loathing the constant embellishment of all things shit and why too many hotel companies thought their patrons to be of an incredibly gullible disposition. What's more, she hated the insincere service culture first thought of by hotel directors before obediently being adopted by "need the money" employees. A wee bit of Highland honesty, she thought, would never go amiss.

'Ah, Good afternoon, Sir ...Madam (big cheesy smile). Welcome to Sunny Scotland and the Happy Highland Inn (big cheesy smile). My name is Shona and I am your part-time-Duty-Assistant-Receptionist-Manager (big cheesy smile). How can I be of assistance? (big cheesy smile). Yes, I do have a reservation under that name (big cheesy smile). And how many nights will you be staying with us? (big cheesy smile). Seven? Excellent! (big cheesy smile). If I can just have your credit card for our records, that would fine. I know we usually say that we won't process it until you have finished your stay with us but you know and I know that that is just a lie. Your room bill will be on your card by this afternoon (big cheesy smile). Anyway, just leave your bags here and although they won't be in your room in the next hour or so, Dwight, our most incompetent concierge, should have them with you by tomorrow (big cheesy smile). Breakfast is *served between seven and nine but try to make it down before eight as we have a group in from Arkansas who'll be sure to demolish the buffet in the one sitting (big cheesy smile). Lunch is served all day in our shitty bars, both in the hotel and by the pool. Tips are discretionary (big cheesy smile). And would you like me to reserve a table in our Cheap Car Rental Company, Two Rosette, Bog and Bothy Restaurant? (big cheesy smile). If you book now, we will give you a ten percent reduction from the price of our nerve-end destroying house wine (big cheesy smile). I think that's about all but if you require any further help, please feel free to call Reception at anytime and although there'll be no one here, please wait on the line for I'm sure someone will get round to answering the phone ...eventually (big cheesy smile). Here's your room card: room 582. I won't tell you anything about inserting it into the keycard holder because I'm sure that will only confuse you both: especially you, Sir (big cheesy smile). Anyway, just follow the corridor here to my right for about 300 metres. As the elevator isn't working, use the stairs to go up five floors and follow another corridor round for a further ten minutes until you see your door. I hope you enjoy your stay with us at Happy Highland Hotel (big cheesy smile).'*

'Listen Kirsten, I've said I am sorry a hundred times for dragging you into all of this but please believe me when I say it's for your own good. The kind of people we are dealing with here will stop at nothing to find me. And if that means getting to you so they can get to me, then that is what they'll do.'

'But Elliot,' snarled Kirsten, 'you could have pretended you heard nothing, told Dixie nothing and we could have been quietly getting on with our lives. Not held up in this dismal hotel with only room service and bad television to keep us happy.'

'Honey, I've listened to Lamont's bullshit for four years now and witnessed at first hand what a bad bastard he can be. Worse still, I've even been instrumental in some of the things he and UKES has orchestrated. So I'm sorry, I just snapped, and because this could affect the country, our country by the way, it seemed the right thing to do at the time.'

'My poor wee Elliot,' sneered Kirsten, oozing sarcasm. 'I never thought you could be so noble and proud and patriotic. You really are pathetic, aren't you? In case you haven't realised, this bullshit that Lamont is trying to pull off has been fashioned from that very same instinct. Protect the old country, protect our way of life, protect out culture. I mean, wasn't it Oscar Wilde who said that patriotism is the virtue of the vicious? If that is the case, which I'm sure it is, then why the hell are we here?'

'I disagree, Kirsten. Sure, I love my country and I love what it stands for but what I've done has not been prompted by some blinkered and teary-eyed view of patriotism, anything but. I am in this mess because I have finally realised, after keeping my mouth, and my mind, closed for years, that there has been a coordinated stripping and crippling of Scotland's resources, its aspiration and its soul, all so it can satisfy the needs of the so-called privileged view who have never given a damn about the ever-lasting consequences their greed has imposed on my country. I see what I have done as not a result of my viciousness but of a privilege given to me by my culture and my intellect. We are here, Kirsten, because the multi-nationals and the politicians, who continue to abuse their power, have been kept in their position by people like me. So no more; I've had enough.'

'Enough to put our lives in danger?'

'I'm sorry but yes. Either that or I end up going nuts because I failed to do anything about it.'

Kirsten, in knowing she wasn't going to persuade him otherwise, moved towards him with a sympathetic smile. 'Okay, I might not consent to your stupid and oh so, honourable bravery but unfortunately I married you and, God help me, it now means I'll have to stick by you. All I ask, Elliot, is that we get through this in one piece. I couldn't bear to see you suffer.'

The couple held each other for what seemed like an age. As they made to part, the old cream coloured phone sitting on the bedside table shook and rang. Kirsten continued to hold one of Elliot's hands as he picked up the receiver with his other.

'Mr. Riley? There's a Mrs. Armstrong here to see you.'

'Thanks, can you send her up, please?'

A few minutes later, there was a delicate knock on the door. Elliot waited nervously out of sight as Kirsten went to open it.

'Room service for a Mr. and Mrs. Sheep Shagger of the fine clan of Shinty Shaggers!' announced Paul as he sauntered into the room, quickly followed by Dixie.

'Jesus, Riley. Another visit to the Kenny Everett School of Comedy, was it?

'Aw! Big, tough Elliot from Teuchterland is not a happy haggis. Hi Kirsten, how's life being married to the most wanted man in Scotland?'

'Paul,' answered Kirsten, 'give it a rest will you. We're not exactly the shiniest of happy people at the moment. And Dixie, I can't believe you have the gall to show up here. Look at what you've caused.'

'I know that tensions are a bit high folks but I'm just trying to brighten things up,' reasoned Paul. 'Anyway, how are the both of you? And before you go off on one Kirsten, we're here to help, by the way.'

'Not bad, considering,' droned Elliot. 'Though we'd like to know what the plan is.'

'Well, we've been having a wee think about that and as yet, we don't have one; not until Dixie speaks to her buddy here in Edinburgh.'

'And who might he or she be, Dixie?' asked Elliot

Before she spoke, Dixie walked over to the desk and picked up a bottle of sparkling water. 'Elliot, you don't need to know. And because there is still some negotiating to do first, I'm afraid you can't go anywhere, either. Paul wasn't being funny when he said you are the most wanted man in Scotland. Hastie has put your face and description on every television and radio station in the bloody country with a warning that you may be armed and dangerous. And while we all know that would be impossible, considering your past record of shiteing it, even from wee old ladies in the Offie, the public don't and they'll be on the phone sharpish reporting a sighting of anyone who even remotely looks like you. Nope, at the moment you're staying put. Nevertheless, and this is the good news, if it all works out how I hope it works out then we won't be moving you far.'

'Jesus, you mean to say I'm all over the News?'

'That's right, my boy.' smiled Paul. 'Please accept my apologies on behalf of my soon to be ex boss, DCC Hastie, and the Strathclyde Constabulary.'

'The bastard. Just a fucking bastard!' shouted Elliot.

'All righty, let's keep the noise down. This is going to be tough enough without you scaring the shit out of the old couple in the next room. We know what Hastie is up to, Elliot. We just needed to make sure you and Dixie were safe before deciding on anything else.'

'What do you mean "anything else"?' asked Kirsten.

'What we mean, Kirsten, is that you, Dixie, and your numpty of a husband here, have to be in a secure location before we can decide on how we are going to publish the story.'

'You mean you don't even know what you're going to do with it yet. Bloody hell, what are you guys playing at?'

'Well, for the story to have the full effect, we have to ensure it is printed and the recording made available through the Tribune. For some reason, once it's in the paper the readers take it as gospel. That's why we decided we couldn't put it on-line just yet; we've no back up. All the NSD has to do when they see it online is deny the whole thing and infer that anti-establishment protesters have concocted it to cause unrest. Even worse than that, the NSD can use their powers to pull any website they wish, including the Tribune's. If things transpire how they wish, they'll know the story will soon die out. Nope, the paper is our most logical means. But once it is in the newspaper. it can be substantiated beyond doubt with editorial and pictures, and scientific evidence proving the voices on the file match those who were in on the Alba Club meeting. Follow that up with a few glaring headlines and the obligatory discussion and opinion, and it will be more than credible.'

'Why can't we just contact the Tribune now?'

'It's not as easy as that. Hastie has the NSD involved and they'll have surveillance on the Tribune's office, its IT systems and its printing plant. And if that isn't enough they'll have teams at your house, at Dixie's house and the editor's house. They'll even be tracking our e-mails and, as I said, have the Tribune's website ready to be pulled if needs be. If they have their way, you and Elliot will be dead, Dixie will be dead and so will the story. And they won't stop until their job is finished. Therefore, we need to make sure we are one step ahead and we can only do that by having a reliable source of people willing and ready to support us.'

'Why don't we contact the other Scottish papers? Surely they'll be desperate to print something like this?'

'There's no chance of that because Alain DeWitt owns the other papers. And he was in the Alba meeting.'

*

12.19 pm – M90 – Perth

Rory and Charlie had swapped cars outside Glamis under the premise that with Charlie being the better driver, the BMW's V8 engine could be handled a wee bit better with Charlie at the wheel. Rory hadn't complained; Zimmerman's security hadn't seen Charlie's rental. Rory had waited for Buchanan on a slip road a few miles north of Dundee and was now back on the M90 and heading south, trailing the Tory leader's car from only a few hundred yards further back.

Rory, having been unable to contact Dixie, had just had an enlightening conversation with an old friend of his whose business was lecturing History to first year students at St. Andrews. Rory's ear was still ringing. What his friend had told him about Glamis and the history of the family didn't surprise him. What's more, as well as his friend indicating that it was no coincidence that some of the Queen's children, and latterly grandchildren, had been educated at schools and universities in close proximity to Glamis, the info on the Freemasons and the Ancient Order of the Scottish Rite was the real flashing puggy purler, especially the unheralded homage to James, the true leader of the Church of Jerusalem. Rory had never noticed it

298

before and no one he knew had ever discussed it, but he now realised that wherever he had been in Scotland or England, or Ireland for that matter, there had been un-noted references to James everywhere: St. James's Palace, St. James's Hospital, St. James Brewery, St. James's Park. Everywhere!

Rory was also aware of Peter Buchanan's own family history. The large estate near Inverness, the role played in the colonisation of the Far East by Buchanan's great grandfather and the connection to Jamieson and Marshall, the old and extremely influential financial group from which JMCB, one of the world's biggest banks and past distributors of opium, arose from early in the last century. What he could not figure out, however, was whether or not Buchanan was Freemason, because Buchanan's sympathetic approach to Scottish politics was certainly new in the dialogue dimension, especially from a Tory leader, and what's more, if Buchanan was planning some strategic manoeuvre in favour of Scotland, it was certainly in direct contradiction to what he inferred to Dixie in the Lothian Hotel yesterday,

Rory hadn't driven much further when his phone was at it again. He didn't recognise the number.

'Hi. Rory Hamilton.'

'Rory, it's Paul Riley.'

'Paul, how's it going?'

'Listen Rory, I don't have much time. Dixie needs to know where you are.'

'Can't the good-for-nothing lazy bitch pick up phone and call me herself?'

'No Rory, she can't. We think her phone is bugged. So, if you don't mind, where the fuck are you?'

'Just passing Kinross. Looks like Buchanan is… Hey, why the sudden interest from you?'

'Listen Rory; just tell me what's going on.'

'No can do, Paul. Dixie would happy-slap my baw-bag.'

To his surprise, Dixie came on to the phone. 'Rory, just tell me the fucking story and make it quick.'

Rory sat up sharpish, straightening his back. 'Buchanan

didn't go to Lochgilphead last night. After Dundee, he went straight to Glamis Castle. You know the place: where the Queen Mum was from. He did an overnighter, and this morning had a meeting in some lodge on the estate with Brad Zimmerman and, believe it or not, General Sir James Urquhart.'

'How do you know that?'

'Well, it just so happened that Charlie was trailing our wee fat American friend. When he arrived on the scene, Charlie and I got busy.'

There was silence on the other end of the line as Dixie and Paul struggled to figure out what the hell was going on.

'Dixie …Dixie? Are you still there?'

'Yes Rory. Just give me a second. …So, where is our gorgeous Buchanan now?'

'Just a couple of hundred yards in front of me. Looks like he's heading back to Edinburgh.'

'Okay, Rory. Stay with him.'

'But Dixie, I've come up trumps on up some crucial info regarding the Queen and Glamis Castle, and its connection to Hutchinson. In fact, you'll never fucking believe me!'

'Rory, I don't have time for your bloody conspiracy theories right now.'

Bringing the phone round to in front of his mouth, Rory repeated Dixie's words in silent mockery. *Rory, I don't have time for your bloody conspiracy theories right now: blah-di, blah-di, blah!'*

'Listen,' said Dixie, 'when Peter Buchanan arrives in Edinburgh, call this number.' As Rory flaffed around in his pocket for his pen, Dixie read out the number and told him that when it was answered, he was to ask for Mr. Riley's room; no other names. 'And for god's sake use a public phone, not your mobile.'

As the car continued to struggle, Rory wondered if it would be able keep pace with Buchanan. He dare not lose him such was the wrath his boss could unleash. Pushing the rev counter close to the 4000 mark, Rory passed Loch Leven and mumbled to himself in adolescent self-pity. He also smiled as he caught a glimpse of one of the many castles where Mary, Queen of Scots had been held captive. It was a ruin.

He drove on with a renewed and smug self-satisfaction. He would gloat to everyone of his investigative skills. Sure, wasn't that why Dixie had hired him? However, so engrossed was he in the noble and bloody history of Scotland and his own self-worth, he failed to notice the unmarked police car joining the motorway at Dunfermline.

Rory had no idea that DCC Michael Hastie and two spooks from the NSD were in the car. And he had no idea that Hastie had put a trace out on Rory's phone after the police tech room picked up his signal just outside Dundee. Hastie had been shrewd. He had been cruising around Glasgow, tapping his radio in frustration and waiting for some info on Dixie and Elliot, when he had decided to chance his luck by tracing Charlie's and Rory's phones as well. Charlie's was off so it was by sheer good fortune and some pretty outrageous driving that he caught up with Rory's signal on the M90.

As Rory's car flew by, Hastie turned to the driver. 'There he is. Now have someone check to see if he has been using his phone. He has to have been on to Dixie Armstrong at some point.'

The three cars drove into Edinburgh on the Queensferry Road, all unaware of the situation unfolding in front and to the rear. Buchanan had no idea that Rory was following just a hundred metres behind, Rory had no clue that Hastie was trailing him from fifty metres further back and Hastie, as well as having no idea that Peter Buchanan was leading the procession, was oblivious to Dixie's M3, with Charlie at its wheel, cruising a further hundred metres back.

The four cars motored swiftly through Blackhall, slowing down as they approached Learmonth. To his right stood the famous old Stewarts Melville School while down to his left, Fettes, the imposing childhood learning institution of the previous Prime Minister, stood as imperious and intimidating as ever. 'Ooooohh ...spooky!' paraphrased Rory.

The motorcade continued over the Dean Bridge before

turning left into the cobbled streets of Randolph Crescent. Arriving in the city centre on Queen Street, just below Charlotte Square and Bute House, Buchanan's car carried on before veering right onto Hanover Street and up across George Street. The car pulled up abruptly, just outside the Royal Society. As Buchanan and his advisor, Ollie Graham, stepped out, Rory took a sharp turn left onto George Street before pulling into a motorcycle parking bay in the middle of the street. Hastie's car, meanwhile, carried on past Rory's Focus before stopping just short of St. Andrews Square. Leaping out, Hastie made his way over to the Pan-European Hotel while his driver continued, rounding the square and returning to park on the other side of George Street. Charlie, cautious of Dixie's car being seen by Hastie and his spooks, took a sharp right passed Buchanan's car before stopping a few metres up the street, just outside the Freemason's Hall.

As Rory locked the car and made his way over to the public phone box standing outside an old bank turned upmarket bar, he was unaware of Hastie keeping tabs on his movements from the hotel across the street. As Rory picked up the receiver to call Paul, Hastie's phone vibrated on the table in front of him.

'Hastie speaking?'

'Sir, we've traced two calls to and from Rory Hamilton. It's not good. One number matches a professor at St.Andrews while the other matches that of a DCI Paul Riley. What's more, the call came from Edinburgh. We don't exactly know where but it's somewhere in the central district.'

Hastie's face turned a paler shade of drawn and washed-out. He stared down at the phone and across to Rory talking in the phone box. He made a decision. 'Okay. Bring the wee scrote in. Let's find out what he knows.'

'Where shall we take him, Sir?'

'Over here, for fuck's sake! We haven't got time to take him to a station.'

The two spooks slithered out of their car, moving slowly towards the phone box. As Rory pulled a couple of coins from his pocket, he was suddenly and violently grabbed from behind, dragged across the pavement and down a side alley. 'What the fuck!' grunted Rory as bewildered pedestrians looked on.

Charlie was walking quickly towards Rory when he saw the struggle. 'What the...!' Charlie started into a run, preparing for a rammy, but as Rory was escorted from the alley and man-handled across the street, Charlie caught sight of DCC Hastie waiting by the door of the hotel. Charlie froze. He was boiling with anger inside. He scowled, at not only the unfortunate timing of it all, but also at the wanker Hastie who was standing tall, legs apart and smiling broadly.

'Who have we here then?' gloated the DCC. 'I do hope you've something to tell us about the whereabouts of your boss. If not, then it could be cheerio for Rory Hamilton.' Hastie glanced at the two spooks and nodded. 'Right, get him off the street and in here. In fact, take him out the back.'

Charlie didn't know what to do. He couldn't leave Rory in Hastie's hands; the guy would destroy him. He then thought about barging his way in and demanding to know what the fuck Hastie was doing with Rory, but because Dixie needed to see him ASAP, he knew that approach could fuck everything up. He decided on going to see Dixie, concluding that if he didn't know what the hell was going on then neither would Rory. Rory's ignorance would save him.

Keeping his head down as he walked over to the phone box, Charlie briefly let his eyes wander inside and saw nothing apart from a number on a scrap of paper. Snatching it quickly, he stuffed it in his pocket before retreating and making his way quickly down towards Princes Street. Crossing the street at Scott's Monument, he jogged quickly alongside the Gardens and the Balmoral Hotel before taking a right across the North Bridge. By the time he made it to the Kelso Hotel, he was tired and very fucking angry.

Rory, meanwhile, stood helpless in a darkened courtyard at the back of the Pan-European Hotel. As the two spooks each took a grip of an arm, Hastie hovered, demanding to know where Dixie was.

'I don't know,' hissed Rory. 'I was told to call her when

I arrived but you guys never had the sense to wait until I spoke, let alone wait until I was finished. So in other words, I've no fucking idea!'

'And where is the number?' growled Hastie.

'Well excuse me if I didn't have time to pick it up when I was being accosted by Johnson and Dallaglio here.'

'Fuck me,' shouted Hastie at his two lachies. 'Could you not have fucking checked? One of you arseholes go and see if it's still there …Now!'

Hastie moved his imposing face in on Rory's. He could smell the fear. 'Listen you self-satisfied, little prick. If you can't give me anything substantial then you'll be living out the rest of your days being hoisted into taxi cabs while you sit vegetised in a fucking wheel chair.'

'Vegetised? Very clever! Your command of the language is mind blowing. Did you just make that word up?'

Hastie didn't see the funny side, a quick and thunderous Glasgow kiss putting an end to Rory's mockery. 'Where the hell is she, Hamilton?' he roared.

Blowing blood from his nose, Rory attempted a retort. 'Is there something up with your ears as well as your fucking brain? I've already told you that I've no idea where she is, as well as having no idea what the fuck's going on. However, even if I did know something, there is no way in hell I would divulge it to a retarded lump of shit prone to emptying his sack in the well-worn arses of Kelvingrove rent boys!'

Hastie turned his back slowly before rotating a sweeping hand back across Rory's face. Rory fell to the ground, his head thumping on the concrete and knocking him unconscious. As Rory lay there, Hastie kicked him hard in the stomach before spitefully dripping some whisky induced, dirty, green phlegm on Rory's face.

The arrogant DCC recomposed himself. Fixing his hair and wiping the sweat from his neck, he turned to the impervious spooks standing by his side. 'Right, I want this town locked down. Road blocks on all roads leaving the city centre. And get rid of him. Immediately!'

19

the americans

1.31 pm – George Street - Edinburgh

Drew Wilson, chief executive officer of the Hutchinson Group, sat pondering the street names of the New Town. Thistle, Queen, Castle, Rose, Hanover, George and Frederick; all named in recognition of the Union between the Kingdoms of Scotland and England. He had just sat down after a meandering morning stroll to see Abraham Lincoln standing proud over David Hume on Calton Hill. He was tired but relaxed and from a large first floor room inside the Royal Society he was now admiring the statue of James Clerk Maxwell on George Street. When Peter Buchanan walked into the room, Wilson rose from his seat by the bay window and offered his hand.

'Thanks, Ollie. You can leave us now,' said Buchanan to his advisor. Ollie Graham shuffled away, making no attempt to mask his indignity. As the door closed, Wilson and Buchanan shook hands lightly. Only four fingers of each hand clasped as they placed their thumbs into each other's knuckles between the index and middle finger. Wilson, being a 32 degree Master of the Royal Secret, and thinking Buchanan was also a Mason, placed his left hand on top of Buchanan's to cement the greeting.

As they sat down on the antique lounge chairs, Wilson poured tea from a silver teapot before scooping an enormous spoonful of sugar and stirring it into his drink. They both smiled.

'In need of some energy?' asked Buchanan.

'I sure am, son,' said Wilson, 'just flew in from Andrews Air Force Base this morning and I'm feeling a little jaded.'

'Ah, private jet I presume?'

'You bet ya. I gave up on commercial airlines after 9/11. Too much hassle. And plus, I don't think I could have handled sitting next to Zimmerman for seven hours.'

'Yes, your man can talk.'

'Well, that's what we pay him for, as well as bringing people around a table, of course.'

'Of course,' said Buchanan taking a sip of tea.

Wilson took in the view of the grand street stretching out below. 'Sure is a beautiful city they have here, Peter. Or should I say *you* have here?'

'That depends on how things turn out, of course.'

Wilson ignored the opportunity to begin with the official business. 'You been in this building before, Peter?'

'No, I can't say I have.'

'No, I suppose you wouldn't have had the pleasure, what with you spending most of your life across the border. Amazing history it has. You know, Adam Smith was a founder member and more's the pity the bankers hadn't read him in a little more depth. Anyway, just to sit here makes it an honour to have this ancient heritage in my veins. Wouldn't you agree?'

'I've just as much pride in my heritage as you have Mr. Wilson but as things stand, I'm more concerned about the future; the immediate future to be exact.'

'Oh Peter, there will be plenty of time to talk business today. Let me just enjoy the moment. And please, call me Drew. And while I'm at it, don't think for one minute I'm not aware of your own national pride. You're as Scottish as they come.'

'Being Scottish is not a nationality, Drew. It is a state of mind.'

'Ah, you quote Herman from the Smithsonian; such a wonderful historian and writer. Did you know, Peter,' stated Wilson as he stared across the rooftops, 'that Edinburgh was the world's first City of Literature? Think about all the great men, and women now, from this small country who have penned some of the finest works of the modern era. Hogg, Byron, Scott, Stevenson, Barrie, Gibbon, Sorley MacLean, Spark, Rowling, Kelman, even good old Hugh MacDiarmid himself. And of course, let us not forget the greatest of them all, Robert Burns.'

'Yes,' groaned an increasingly frustrated Buchanan, 'I'm fully aware of Scotland's writers but in case you haven't noticed, I'm on a bit of a schedule.'

'Schedules schedules, time means money, a rolling stone. Yes, I'm alert to your requirements, Peter, but please don't fret, you'll be outa here in good time.' Wilson took another sip of Makaibari tea while turning and fixing Buchanan with a steely and penetrating glare. Ever read MacDiarmid, Peter?'

'No. As you can probably gather, he wasn't exactly a curriculum favourite at Harrow.'

'No ...I expect not, but one day you should. You know, he once said that England destroyed nations not by conquest but by pretending they didn't exist.' Wilson let the quotation hang in the air for a moment as Buchanan stared back, eyes glistening with deep-rooted melancholy. 'Yep, its England's way, it's the Westminster way. Always has been I'm afraid, and a darn good method of keeping control, wouldn't you say?' Hell, we across the Atlantic are at it as well, though not quite as covertly may I add. It's as if we can do whatever we please and not because we have to, but because we can. However,' Wilson paused, flicking specks of dust from his trousers, 'when it comes to this small country whose hospitality we are enjoying right now, things are little different. We owe something to Scotland, Peter. In fact, we owe it a helluva lot. I mean, where would you and I, and North America for that matter, be today if it weren't for our ancestors? I'll tell you; much worse off. Like some of the poorer immigrant nations who long for love and acceptance from the modern world yet are unwilling to give anything back. Goodness, can you imagine a world like that? Scotsmen and Scotswomen didn't just build the modern world, Peter, they invented it: political and economic philosophies, legislatures, countries, banking systems and many a great company, and most of those great souls who did so sat and studied at one time or another within one square mile of where we sit right now. Look around. Less than four hundred yards from where we sit, you will find the original headquarters of Principal Life Assurance, RCB, Encyclopaedia Britannica, Bank of Caledonia, and The Royal College of Surgeons. In fact, wasn't it the great Winston Churchill who once said, "That of all the nations of this earth, perhaps only the ancient Greeks surpass the Scots in their contribution to mankind."

'Nonetheless,' continued Wilson, 'as proud as we maybe both are of Scotland's past, what is of more significant concern to me is why a country as successful and influential as Scotland can also be riddled with so much self-doubt and defeatism. Why? Because Westminster has made it that way. Yep, it makes me sad to think that Scotland can develop such things as its own Hydro-Electric power then is coerced into not only giving most of away to its neighbours but also selling the power back to itself at inflated prices. It then creates the world's greatest broadcaster and watches as it ridicules and condemns the country of its founder. And then it discovers oil, only to stand back and watch it pumped down south. No, it's just not an equitable solution and it's about time we let Scotland see what it's been missing out on. Think about it, Peter. We owe this country more than just a debt of gratitude, we owe it our world!'

Peter Buchanan was beginning to realise he was being outflanked at every turn: first Sir Alexander Lamont, then Dixie Armstrong and Andrew Drummond, and now Wilson. He was close to losing it. 'Since when did the Hutchinson Group become all teary-eyed over Scotland?' he asked. 'Come on, you guys have never really cared about nationality. With you, it's all about the influence, the money and the power.'

'Some of it, yes,' beamed Wilson. 'But don't you think there might be something more to our involvement?'

'I'm not sure what you're implying, Drew. And nor do I care. Anyway, I thought I made things perfectly clear to your man Zimmerman at Glamis Castle this morning.'

'Well, you should care. Furthermore, what you did make

perfectly clear, Peter, is that you are vociferously loyal to one team while pretending to support the other. Your option of building a suitable submarine base for the new generation of nuclear subs in Wales or England just won't work. We've had your options checked out. The locations suggested imply that no one would be entirely happy, especially those who use Faslane as a political foil. And then we would have to concern ourselves with the job losses in Scotland. That won't work with us, either. Sorry Peter, but there are too many people in DC not prepared to sit back and do nothing anymore while Scotland suffers yet again at the hands of Westminster. Nope, Faslane stays open.'

'But what if Scotland secedes? The people here won't allow Faslane to remain open.'

'Oh, they'll allow it, Peter, especially if the US suddenly begins to up its inward investment and Scotland agrees to a shared and united island defence strategy with Westminster. It'll be a fair trade-off. You see, with the banking system hitting the skids and massive public expenditure both expected and required to keep the world afloat, everyone is now looking longer term. What's more, we at Hutchinson and the US government are well aware of that and it would be negligent, and crazy, if we weren't to grab a piece of the increased business that will come with both the rise in energy costs and national public spending.'

'And where would that leave the rest of the UK? Without the North Sea and all its associated revenues, Westminster will never be able to afford to continue its spending on Defence. I mean, I want as much for Scotland as you do Drew, but there will be carnage down south and I'll be the one who will have to deal with it. Lord Almighty, we are talking about the destruction of a rather large section of the English economy here.'

'Listen Peter, the boys in DC and Langley are fully aware of the predicament facing Westminster, but consider who has the upper hand. Not London, that's for sure. But be patient, all is not lost. The Defence orders we will continue to place in England, though may I add that England might have to borrow the money from us to pay for the production, but hey, that's life. We will also continue to share our resources with Westminster on our joint initiatives on International Security and such like, but nevertheless, you are absolutely correct; the oil is the key. And if Scotland secedes, I will have to keep Drummond onside. Think about it, Peter. You win the Westminster election, of which that is almost certain, then you will have to create a whole raft of special agreements, including shared defence capabilities, with Scotland. Otherwise, the Union is over. In fact, even if you do agree to special conditions, the voters down south will never accept it. So, in reality, the Union is over anyway. But I'm sure you know that, hence why you are here. Nope, it's all about the oil. You know it, I know it, the US, Canadian and Dutch companies, who have invested billions of dollars, know it, and, more importantly, the people know it! Even that asshole Lamont knows it. And as much as he has tried to hood-wink us into believing that he is the major influence in Westminster, he has failed to understand the level of support for Scotland in DC and more critically, failed to understand that my men have been watching the political situation in Scotland for years. We're not that daft either, as the Scots would say, when it comes to protecting our investments and yet …and yet his arrogance still knows no bounds. That's why he tried to scare off that journalist with the shooting at Loch Lomond, and why he hopes that Hutchinson will take the blame; once again making certain that any undue attention his grand plans receive is passed-off as someone else's agenda. It is also why he continues to spout off his lies about there being no further oil and gas discoveries in the North Sea. Hell, it's clear to everyone, including the academics and the scientists, that there is a shit lot more oil to be found. One just has to look at the prolonged and continued investment into research technology at Aberdeen to figure that one out.'

Drew Wilson intensified his stare across the small table. 'But don't get me wrong, this is not all about some petty love for the old country. Sure, there are political sympathies but this has always been about business and ensuring that my investors are reliably and substantially informed to make the decisions that will provide them with a healthy return. And make no mistake, Scotland, when it secedes, will certainly provide that. Nope, it's all but over and if I were you, Buchanan, I'd rather be a politician in a country with hope than one in meltdown.'

Peter Buchanan was stunned. Not so much at the political implications but more for his political ambitions. Would they be wasted on a United Kingdom that did not include Scotland? Would the South East revert to chaos? 'But what about General Urquhart?' he asked. 'He gave me the impression he was in favour of the Union?'

'He is, but not the political union you're thinking of. You see, he is one of the most prominent members of the Lodge and most loyal to the brotherhood and the Queen. As long as she continues to reign over Scotland then why should he care about the political infrastructure? Hell, his family have always been sniffing around the power plays. What's more, to those of us who make the decisions, having him and The Lost Tribe of Israel on our side is a darn good bargaining tool to have at our disposal, as well, of course, as them being the Masonic Lodge's and Ancient Order's founding fathers!'

'The Lost Tribe? The Ancient Order?' Buchanan was confused. Here was one of the few times in his life when he had absolutely no idea what was going on.

Back across the table, Wilson took another sip of tea and grinned, readying himself to deliver yet another history lesson. Pausing for breath, he turned his gaze to the window and out across the magnificent city. He began to talk.

'Did you know, Peter, that the ancestors of the Lost Tribe were said to be elders of the Church of Jerusalem who, after being hounded out of Israel by the Romans, set up shop in Northern France. Once settled, they kept together most of the time. Lots of inbreeding and secret rituals but most of all, lots of cash. Not only that, they were also quite brilliant; only starting to call themselves Templar Knights when, a millennium after their ancestors had been kicked out of Israel by the Romans, they decided it would be a good idea, in their guise as saviours of Christianity, to return on a crusade or two to the Holy Land. Or to be more precise, the Temples of Solomon and Herod. Once in Jerusalem though, religion got the bullet; more concerned were they in retrieving their ancient treasure and artefacts left behind when they did a runner. Anyway, just like in Israel, the Tribe wasn't too popular in France either, eventually being driven out of there as well. So in their wisdom, and to avoid the odd family wipe out, they thought they would move as far away from the centre of the world as they could. And there are no prizes for guessing where that was. Nevertheless, although they arrived to Scotland in large numbers, there are still very few people who want to discuss why the Templars ended up here, how they came to play a significant role in the Scottish Wars of Independence and more importantly, why the Tribe and the Order is so keen on helping and protecting Scotland today.

'You see, by the early fourteenth century, the Vatican and, by association, France and England, had grown to despise the Templars' covert wealth and influence. What's more, reason decided it wouldn't be long before one of the Big Three finally snapped. And when they did, it would be horrendous. Unfortunately for the Templars, it would be the King of France who would be first to exact revenge, and on none other than the Templar leader himself, Jacques De Molay. It was at a time when the King of France and the Pope were having their little *contra tent* about who had the biggest pair of balls and it is said, that after De Molay had refused to financially support the French King in his punch-up with the Mitred One, Molay was tortured on the island of Notre Dame. The King demanded to know where he had stashed the cash. Silly boy never told him. It was brutal. The King, in his perverted twist on the Lost Tribe's initiation rituals, sat him on a chair, wrapped him in a blanket and beat the shit out of him for days until, in deciding the poor guy still hadn't had enough, escorted him outside and roasted him alive! What's more, some claim the torture blanket is the Turin Shroud, and the image on the Shroud is not of Jesus but actually our very own Jacques de Molay. Strange coincidence, wouldn't you say?'

Buchanan stared wide-eyed across the table, wondering how all of this related to his rapidly disintegrating, Union-saving strategy.

'Anyway,' continued Wilson, 'while that was happening, a few of the Templars decided another runner was in order. So it was over the water and into the safety of an old friend and fellow Templar: Robert the Bruce. Once in Scotland, they set up camp at a little town called Kilwinning where a relieved Bruce set them to work immediately, using their skills to train his troops in readiness for another showdown with the aggressors from across the border. In fact, as the Scots tore down the hill to kick some serious English ass at Bannockburn, De Molay's coat of arms flew in the wind alongside the Scottish flag of the victorious Scottish Army. Bruce was delighted -who wouldn't be- returning to Kilwinning where, in celebration of his victory, he established the Masonic of Heredum de Kilwinning, otherwise known as the Mother Lodge of all Brotherhoods. Soon after, the Templars were being seen as an intrinsic element of the Scottish fabric and in being welcomed all over Scotland, some of them decided to relocate from Kilwinning, with most of them, funnily enough, moving to Edinburgh and Rosslyn. There they ingratiated themselves to an elated Scottish Nobility who not only heralded their arrival because of the helping hand given at Bannockburn but also because one of their very own had a maternal ancestor who had married the first ever Templar Leader way back in the twelfth century. However, what very few people know is that this great, great, great, great grandson of Hugh de Payens and Catherine St.Clair was also a fellow Templar Knight and a High-Steward of Scotland who just happened to get real lucky in the matrimonial stakes …real lucky. For didn't the most fortunate Walter Steward end up marrying a certain Marjorie Bruce, the much sought after daughter of King Robert himself.'

Buchanan's head was buzzing now. These historical tales was getting him nowhere.

'What's more, after the resounding defeat of the English and having played a pivotal role in the reclamation of Scotland's liberty, the Templars became national heroes. More than that, they now had influence. They were also to be forever grateful for the kindness offered to them by the people of Scotland, demonstrating their appreciation by expanding the Lodge and sharing the secrets of their education with the ordinary man. And that was that. The Templars, as we knew of them then, ceased to exist in the public domain. The Lodge and the Brotherhood was now in control.

'But you know what made the Templars and the Lodge, and latterly the Order, so damn important, Peter? Enlightenment, that's what. And they brought ship loads of it, as well as shit loads of cash and skills in war unseen in this part of the world before. Hell, is it any wonder the Scots welcomed them, for there's not much more a country at war needs than money, battled hardened men and a little nod from a supreme being upstairs. So over time, and in becoming aide-de-camps to the King, the Lodge pretty much became the unofficial government of sorts and very much trusted by the Scottish establishment. And with trade being financed and education encouraged, it also came as no surprise that Scotland once again became a leading nation in the royal courts of Europe. You see, with the Lodge and the Order, it has always been about three things: liberty, education and truth, and that, ultimately, is where its power comes from. All this shit about Rosslyn Chapel is just the tip of a large chunk of floating ice.

'So, the Lodge, fortunately, ended up running Scotland's affairs. Okay, so it wasn't always peachy, considering they were paying false homage to Rome with one gauntlet while protecting their investments from England and the Pope with the other. Nevertheless, with Scotland being so distant from Rome, the Lodge flourished, as did its influence and knowledge among the Scottish nobles and merchant classes. It was all quite brilliant. And when England's throne found itself without an heir in 1603, in stepped the Lodge with James VI of Scotland to save the day. The Stuarts, the astute and devious bastards, and therefore the Lodge, now had two kingdoms under their control.'

Buchanan could only sit and listen in bewilderment. *What the Hell?*

'However, all this political manoeuvring quickly brought about the real riotous turmoil. Naturally, the English elite, angry at losing control to a Scottish King, became dis-enamoured with

314

the Stuarts. What's more, so did the Lodge.

'The Stuarts, who were never going to relinquish their self-proclaimed God given right to Absolute Rule, had become a liability, such was their arrogance in dismissing their loyal advisors just once too often. So the Lodge, in sensing a massive betrayal, made plans to move on, with or without the Stuarts. Sure, in knowing the Stuarts were key figures in their strategy to maintain control, the Lodge tried valiantly to keep their men on the throne but alas, England was too big to take on and London too far away, and eventually the Hanovers took over the throne. The Lodge was losing out big time and if things weren't bad enough, there was also the unfortunate Darien Adventure and the consequential political union between Scotland and England.

'However, it is important to note that the Lodge didn't throw its toys out of the baby-walker when it came to its association with the Stuarts. With the Lodge ensuring the Stuarts acknowledged their own arrogant failings, the Stuarts were forced into taking a back seat. And as difficult as that may have been, considering their belief in their Divine Right, they did remain loyal to the premise and beliefs of the Lodge. Maybe because they sensed they would have a second coming sometime in the future or maybe because they didn't want to be cast out in the Scottish cold. The Lodge wasn't dumb, either. Knowing the Stuarts still wielded some influence in Europe, the Lodge was able to manipulate their influence in the century that followed. Hell, I certainly don't think it was a coincidence that the French supported the US in its drive for Independence, and it is certainly no coincidence that the Stuarts and descendents there of, now dance to the Lodge's jig.

'And so to 1707, and under pressure from the newly empowered Hanovers, the English and Scottish Governments amalgamated, which, in a ridiculous twist of fate and fortune, indirectly paved the way for what was to become the Lodge's finest century. Such was Westminster's concern with its ongoing wars with France and of clearing the Highlands of their wretched enemy -the Jacobite Clans- Scotland took its opportunity and flourished. Universities and trade grew at such as terrific rate that money poured into the country, giving the Lodge its long awaited opportunity to finally rid itself of feudal loyalties and to create a republic of their very own.

'The Lodge, as ever, was shrewd. Having its own men as officers in both the American Colonial Army as well as the King's Army, it was the Lodge, or the Ancient Order as they became, who conveniently arranged for the King's men to tactically screw-up during the American Revolution, as well as having men of influence like Benjamin Franklin working both sides of a stormy Atlantic persuading the French Monarchy -who had ancient connections with the Stuarts, most notably Mary Queen of Scots- to support the American cause. Therefore, when the British decided enough was enough and couldn't afford to fight protracted wars on two fronts, a new country, The United States, was born. The finance was in place, the educated men had garnered intellectual support and the infrastructure had been planned, designed and built. It was easy. Fait accomplis!'

Peter Buchanan gazed across the table, beginning now to understand Wilson's emotional and economical allegiance to Scotland. What Drew Wilson had told him went much deeper than the "distant ancestors and friends across the water" nonsense. This was about protecting a culture and a way of life that had given hope and opportunity to billions. This was an acknow-ledgement of everything dear to America's heart. He shook his head slightly as a smile came over the pale lips of the older man.

'You see, Peter, you can have an Italian-American, an Irish American and an African-American but you know what you shall never have? I'll tell you, shall I? What you cannot, and will never, have, is a Scottish-American. Why? Because it was the Scots who became the Americans! It is they who invented our Constitution, the American psyche and the American way of life as we know it. It is they who we turned to for guidance in our pursuit of practical idealism. It is they who led the way. It is they, unequivocally, who are America's founding fathers.

'Oh yes, It's been a long road home, Peter, and if I was you, I suggest you buy a ticket soon and come join the party.'

20

no time for being a feartie

1.46 pm – Kelso Hotel – North Bridge - Edinburgh

As Charlie Norton took a seat in the atrium of the Kelso Hotel, his scowling face didn't endear him to the staff at the Reception. Whispering under their breath, they were discussing who he was and what his problem was. Charlie didn't give a fuck! His close friend had just been accosted by two spooks from the NSD while he stood by and let it happen.

What a useless bastard!

Sixty minutes earlier, he had been making his way back to Glasgow. Happy because he had just snapped Buchanan, Zimmerman and General Urquhart together, and delighted one of his girlie friends had sent him a text to let him know she would be free later that night. However, as he had been passing Perth, his pager beeped. It was Dixie. Knowing that a message to his pager meant no mobiles, Charlie pulled into the Cherrybank Pub to make a phone call to the Kelso. After she explained some of what was happening, he was soon back in her car, doubling back and making his way to Edinburgh, sharpish.

Once on the M90 and just before Bridge of Earn, he slapped the car into sixth and slammed the gas. Ten minutes later, he spotted the rented black Focus up ahead. He wanted to call Rory to give him an update but that was out of bounds. It also began to dawn on him that Dixie was in a whole lot of

317

trouble. As much as he was well versed in the art of dodginess, the National Security Department was not a fellowship guild he had a desire to strike up an association with any time soon. He would have to get to the capital fast. Unless he was there to watch her back, Dixie wouldn't stand a chance.

The British Government and the NSD played to win. Bar the occasional victories by the CIA, and the surprising populist wins by the rank outsiders, Ghandi and Michael Collins, the Brits had held the title of World Security Champions for the past two hundred years. Losing was not a consideration. That is why they had access to surveillance equipment that MIT hadn't even thought off yet and a communication network, which put the combined technological might of Google, IBM and Microsoft to shame. However, what petrified Charlie more than anything else was the ruthlessness of how the agents of the NSD did their job: with the minimum of hullabaloo and a super quick clean-up process. They did exactly what it said on the tin. There were even operations of which Charlie had heard that had ruined national economies and installed "elected" despots. Yet still no one suspected good old GB. Charlie smiled ruefully. The spooks of the NSD were devoid of conscience. They were the dirtiest of dirty fuckers in a world full of dirt-bags!

As he sat waiting, Charlie wondered if he had taken the wrong decision on George Street. Rather than save Rory from Hastie, he had held back, deciding he would look after his little buddy from a distance. He should have known. Fuck it! He really should have known. When Hastie's car pulled out from the Dunfermline exit as Rory drove passed, Charlie should have confirmed his fears there and then. This time the National Security Department was playing for keeps.

Although Rory hadn't been long in the newspaper game, Charlie and he had grown close. Charlie adored his audacity, and his cheek. He made him laugh and made him feel young again, and regardless Rory thought it was an obligatory requirement to compel Dixie into declaring insanity, he was also good at his job. He was sharp, loyal and understood, unambiguously, the consequential nature of what that job entailed. Unlike others,

Rory *got* it!

Charlie had always treated Rory as the younger brother he never had; not only someone he could laugh at but also someone he could laugh with. Charlie shook his head as he imagined Rory heading for Edinburgh in the small black car. Hunched over the steering wheel, Rory would have been taking the piss out of Buchanan. With his cheeks puffed out and face contorted, Rory would have been haughtiness personified as he mimicked the RP accent, the droopy eyes and the pinched lips. Charlie smiled. He was hoping Rory would write his memoirs one day, especially if they included the incident with the overweight BTC Political Editor down at Holyrood.

He and Rory had been waiting for the First Minister to finish an interview with the fat BTC Voice-Piece when out the corner of his eye he saw Rory mimic the choke-inducing art of shagging the BTC fatty up the arse. No one could see him apart from the camera man, Charlie and the First Minister's chief advisor. Their giggling was light at first but it wasn't long before stomachs ached and tears flowed. And not because Rory was being ridiculously childish. Oh no! And neither was it that funny that it just happened to be a major league correspondent who was the fall guy. Oh no! What brought on the hysterics was the sight of Rory imitating the act of penetration while employing a half-eaten and freshly battered white pudding as his cock.

Now Charlie was beginning to regret not wading into Hastie's spooks. He had been one minute too late and two minutes short of decisive action. His friend was in trouble and he was determined to help. However, he first had to find out what the hell was going on.

'At least one of my favourite boys has made it,' grinned Dixie as she popped her head out of the staircase door. 'Any chance you would like to join me in my bedroom?'

Charlie rose from his chair and glared over at two old ladies enjoying an afternoon pot of tea. They had been dissing him for the past five minutes. It was two in the afternoon, he was tired and he was pissed off. As the two old ladies whispered their disgust, Charlie marched towards the door and winked. 'It's all right, ladies. She pays well but I'm worth it.'

He followed Dixie up the well-worn carpeted stairs and down a glass walled hallway with an obscured view of the old Royal High School. A couple of turns and a dimly corridor later, they stood outside Room 316. Checking with Charlie to make sure he had removed the battery from his phone, Dixie knocked on the door four times. They waited a few seconds for Paul to open the door.

Dixie went first, followed by Charlie who smiled as he inspected the congregation. Elliot and Kirsten were sitting up on the bed. 'You know,' said Charlie, 'I've never been adverse to the odd orgy or two but I think I'll give it a miss today. Not, of course, because you two ladies aren't stunningly beautiful but I'd rather not have Paul's two scotch eggs dangling anywhere near my sniff and suck apparatus!'

Charlie sauntered passed Paul, plonking his arse on one of the lounge chairs to the far side of the room while Dixie took her stance against between the bed and the window. Paul remained standing, leaning against the television unit.

There was some slight shuffling and an uncomfortable silence. Dixie snatched another of the green bottles of spring water sitting on the table. The seal cracked. As Dixie gulped down the water, Kirsten looked over and tutted. She had been in the room all day and was irritable. She wanted to know what was happening.

Paul coughed as he took the floor. Kirsten stared with angry indignity while Elliot bowed his head and scratched his knuckles. Charlie grabbed the corner of the curtain pole and baton-twirled the end between his fingers. Dixie leaned back with arms folded and one eye on Kirsten. Everyone was tense.

'Right folks, I'm not going to bullshit anyone,' opened Paul, catching everyone's eyes except Elliot's. 'I'm afraid we're not in the best of situations. Far from it. In fact, we're in deep shit. All the same, that is not to say there is no way out. Elliot and Dixie are fifty miles from where Hastie thinks they are so not only do we have some space, we also have some time.'

320

Charlie coughed. 'Nah, don't think so, Paul. I think your personal Sat Nav could be on the blink today.'

All eyes, including Elliot's, turned on Charlie.

'And what the hell is that supposed to mean?' demanded Dixie.

'Hastie and his men hooked Rory in George Street and if it wasn't for my fucking indecision, I could have helped the poor bastard.'

'You mean to say Hastie is in the city?' gasped Kirsten.

'Fraid so,' stated Charlie. 'And so is Peter Buchanan.'

'And what about Rory?' asked Dixie. She slammed the wall with her hand. 'What was I thinking, getting him involved?'

'My thoughts exactly, Dixie,' moaned an increasingly frustrated Charlie. 'He's only a kid, for goodness sake, and now he's in the hands of a fucking lunatic.' Grabbing tightly on the curtain pole, Charlie flicked it violently against the glass. 'In fact, I want to go back down there right now.'

As Charlie pushed himself up from the chair and made a move for the door, Paul stepped out to block his path. 'Hold on, Charlie. Rory doesn't know a thing so he'll be of no use whatso-ever to Hastie. And I know Hastie. He might knock him around a bit but that will be all.'

Charlie stood impassively for a second. 'I hope you're right, Paul. But remember, this is not a case of P.C. Murdoch slapping Oor Wullie across the lughole.'

Paul and Dixie glanced at each other, both realising at once that their plan would have to change. Dixie tapped the small bottle against her palm as Paul folded his arms against the television unit and placed his chin on top of his hands. Charlie sat back down, resting his elbows on his knees. Kirsten and Elliot looked at each other and then at their three motionless saviours-to-be.

'Well?' demanded Kirsten, 'What the hell are we going to do?'

Without turning his head, Paul lifted his left hand. 'Just give us a minute, Kirsten. I need some time to think.'

'In case you haven't noticed, Paul, Hastie is already in

Edinburgh so we haven't got time to think. And even a poor wee house-wife like me can figure out it won't be long before the big bad policeman comes knocking on the door.'

'And there'll be no club sandwich and a Coke with him either.' sighed Dixie.

Paul glanced across to Dixie, asking the silent question. Dixie knew what he wanted to do and nodded in return. Charlie looked up sharply. He was about to say something but Paul held out a hand, asking Charlie to give him a little more time. Charlie then looked across to Dixie. He knew what they wanted to do as well. He had to speak.

'No way, Paul. We won't have a fucking snowball's.'

Knowing that Charlie would more than disagree with the plan, Paul responded quickly. 'We'll discuss what we're going to do shortly, Charlie. First we have to make sure everyone at least has an understanding of what has been going on and who is involved.'

'For fuck's sake, Paul! You do know what you are asking everyone to do, don't you?'

Paul couldn't let fear and panic engulf the room. He had to build confidence. He had to give Elliot and Kirsten some hope. 'For fuck's sake, Charlie, I said we'll discuss our plan in a minute.'

Kirsten wasn't for waiting. She sat up sharply. 'What the hell are you planning to do, Paul? Or more importantly, what is one woman well versed in being shot at, one man who spends most of his life hiding from well-trained security teams while taking pictures of powerful politicians and multi-industrialists, and one man who on a daily basis stares down the threats of mobsters, gangsters and international drug cartels, going to ask a happily married, mortgage free, horse owning suburban couple whose only brush with danger is avoiding the rush hour stampede on the Tube, fucking well what to do?'

Dixie and Charlie raised their eyebrows while sneaking a peak at each other. They both looked across to the couple on the bed. Elliot was putting an arm around his wife. She was shrugging him off.

'Well?' she screamed.

'Kirsten,' reassured Paul. 'Everyone is going to be fine; including you and Elliot.'

Paul dare not glance over at Dixie now. The last thing he needed was for Kirsten to sense that even he wasn't too sure about the plan.

Kirsten glared at Paul for a few seconds more, deliberating on whether to pursue her demands. Her silence was his cue.

This time it was Paul's turn for a swig of water. Opening the door to the mini-bar, he took out a bottle before kicking the door shut with his feet. 'What we have is a recording of seven of the most powerful men in the country holding a private meeting in the Alba Club in London. The aim of that meeting was to devise a multi-faceted and covert plan to ensure the United Kingdom, as we know it as a political entity, remains in tact. In other words, they want to stifle all hope the SNP has of winning the Secession Referendum, which, if successful, will see Westminster kissing a big and slurpy goodbye to the oil and gas revenues.

'And if anyone is wondering how we know this, our brave Elliot has made a recording, which is now saved on his laptop and on four other memory sticks. Elliot has one, I should have one waiting for me at my office and Dixie has two, one of which, I hope Dixie, is in a secure location.'

No one looked up, especially Dixie. For the second time today she reckoned now was not the time to tell Paul she only had one copy, and it was on her as he spoke.

'And just in case you're wondering why these guys are planning all of this, let's just assume that the implications and repercussions of the Nats winning the Referendum has them petrified. Make no mistake, the whole goddamn shebang is on the line here: their businesses, the government, and the economy of London and the South East. In other words, if the people of Scotland vote for secession, there is a whole host of influential businessmen and government officials out there who are going to be pretty much shafted.

'Their strategy, hatched at the Alba Club, involves an orchestrated and vicious propaganda campaign by Sir Alexander Lamont, Sir James Montague -the head of the NSD-, TFW Worldwide Media and the British Television Corporation. Their main aim, amongst other things, is to discredit Scotland's First Minister and the SNP. In other words, they desperately need to increase the popularity of the Scottish Labour Party before the Referendum takes place in 2010. To achieve that however, they are planning, at every opportunity, to indoctrinate the public psyche with stacks of negative press surrounding the SNP while at the same time increasing the amount of positive spin that Labour receives.

'Meanwhile Lamont, that wanker of a chairman at UKES plc, has already moved to destabalise the Scottish banks, as well as making plans to launch a PR campaign based around the so-called depletion of oil reserves in the North Sea. While Lamont is at that, the NSD will move to plant criminal evidence on a small but unfortunate group of SNP politicians that will lead to their arrest on charges of corruption and financial irregularities, which then, of course, will be investigated and corroborated by DCC Michael Hastie of the Strathclyde Force who, incidentally, has his heart set on a top job with the NSD. Furthermore, to make certain he has all his bases covered, Lamont has also increased the pressure on our future PM, Peter Buchanan, to engender support for Scotland within the Union and to meet with the US private equity firm Hutchinson to re-enforce the point that Westminster has no plans to allow Scotland to secede.'

As Kirsten sat open-mouthed, Charlie shook his head in disbelief. He had an inclination this was the reason he was now in hiding in an Edinburgh hotel. Unfortunately, he had no idea as to the severity of it.

'Also in on this fucking coup de tat,' continued Paul, 'is Sir Peter Milligan, the Permanent Secretary in Westminster. He will work the Treasury to push through proposals with regard to the squeezing of Scotland's finances and the Holyrood Budget.'

Paul finished off the bottle of water and took out another. Standing back, he indicated for Dixie to speak. She hardly moved, aware now that everyone knew of the trouble they were in. 'The idea,' she said, 'is to engender a greater public trust in both the workings of the Union Kingdom and therefore by default, Labour's credibility in Scotland. This, they think, will defuse the potential inclination for some of Scotland's citizens to vote for separation. In other words, they aim to spread fear among the undecided poor while increasing the self-respect among the undecided middle-class.'

'But unfortunately that may not be the end of it,' interrupted Paul. 'These guys are some of the most ruthless bastards you will never want to meet, and who will stop at nothing to achieve their objectives. And when I say stopping at nothing, it also includes the planned elimination of Andrew Drummond.' Paul let the information settle. 'And that doesn't mean setting him up in some tawdry corruption scandal; it means ending his tenure as First Minister by cutting off his air supply!'

Dixie caught Paul's eye, letting him know she wanted to speak. 'However, before we go public with this story there are a few things we need to be doing first.' Since no questions were forthcoming, she handed over to Paul again.

'Our first priority,' stated Paul 'is to guarantee that we are secure from Hastie and his spooks. As far as we can gather, DCC Michael Hastie is Lamont's major henchman. And because of his ambition of being top NSD spook, he sees himself as the main man to clear up this mess. If he can do that, he knows he will be off to London in the morning and gazing out across the Thames from a rather large and well-equipped office, and a healthy sum of cash in the bank. Therefore, nothing will prevent him from removing any obstacles …and anyone else for that matter who just happens to get in his way!'

'Just like Rory,' objected Charlie.

'Okay Charlie,' continued Paul, 'We know it's a real fuck up that Rory's been nabbed and that Hastie is in town but if you'll please just give me a moment to finish.' Paul was eager to get moving but he was determined for everyone to understand the entire story. 'On top of all this, Dixie was shot at last week, we think, by a team working for Sir Alexander Lamont. His objective is to pin the shooting on the Hutchinson Group, hoping it will detract from any meddling involvement he has in government affairs. And if that wasn't enough to single him out as a ruthless bastard, he has also been exerting some London and DC pressure on Hutchinson's main fixer, Brad Zimmerman, who is in Scotland trying to obtain a guarantee, we think, that the submarine base at Faslane remains operational and continues to host the covert operations of the US Navy. However, we think Lamont may have been blind-sided by Hutchinson because Zimmerman has been working both sides, keeping all his options open. Not only has he been negotiating with Westminster, he has also been negotiating terms with the SNP, hoping to ensure, if Scotland were ever to secede, that the investment and research will continue into the Nuclear Missile Programme under an independent Scottish government. Thanks to Charlie's opportunism, we know that Zimmerman has met once with Peter Buchanan this morning and three times now with General Sir James Urquhart, Chief of Staff of the Royal Caledonian Regiment: last week at Gleneagles and St. Andrews, and again today at Glamis.

Charlie's head snapped upwards. 'While we're at it, Paul, what *exactly* is the Chief of Staff's role in all of this? I presumed he's working for Westminster and is on side with Lamont?'

Dixie smiled. 'For once, Charlie, your presumptions are misplaced. That's what they may think in Whitehall, but he's not in with Lamont and the Alba Club crew at all: anything but.'

'And what makes you so sure of that?'

'Let's just say I have my contacts.'

Charlie shook his head. 'Any chance you could enlighten us then?'

'I will,' said Dixie '…but later.'

'Wow, nothing much to worry about, is there?' muttered Charlie, unaware of what else might be going on in Dixie's mind and also unaware of what Rory discovered on his tour of Glamis Castle.

Paul was becoming impatient. He knew time was against them. 'What we think is that Hutchinson doesn't really care what happens to the United Kingdom, it just has to ensure Dobbie and

McGregor keep manufacturing in Atlanta and Aldermaston. If that continues, Hutchinson's investments will be secure and its investors happy to have a wee bit more cash in the bank. And whatever the cost or political implications, that can only happen if Faslane remains open and operational.

'As you know, Zimmerman also met with the President of Dobbie and McGregor in Atlanta, as well with the leader of the Senate Defence Spending Committee and some high heid yin from the CIA in Washington. We figure it's the usual murky shenanigans that Hutchinson is prone to adopting but Faslane is their aim. There could be some shady political manoeuvring on Holyrood's part but let's be under no fucking illusion, Faslane is what Hutchinson want.'

Paul looked around the room before raising his eyes to the ceiling. 'However, there's still one aspect we haven't figured out yet; why on earth Glamis was chosen as a meeting venue. That, I'm afraid, is still a mystery.'

It was the last unsolved piece to Dixie's story. She was presuming there was some sort of tie-in with Peter Buchanan. 'Charlie, I don't suppose you know who Buchanan was meeting in the Royal Society?' she asked.

Charlie shook his head. Silence.

Kirsten, however, having kept her peace for long enough, couldn't keep quiet any longer. 'Look, I appreciate that you guys are trying to put some reasoning to all of this but let's not forget that Elliot is still the most wanted man in the country and I, personally, would be of a much happier disposition if he was in slightly less of a health threatening situation than he is right now.'

Knowing he had everyone's attention, Paul stood up straight. 'I know, Kirsten. That's why you are going to have to listen very carefully.' As Paul began to explain the escape plan, the sounds of police sirens echoed around the city. And it wasn't just one cop car chasing some drug infuelled waster, it sounded as if the entire Lothians' police force was on the tail of a terrorist bomb squad!

*

2.07 pm - Melville Place – Edinburgh

The Georgian townhouse where Brad Zimmerman sat munching on the best club sandwich he had enjoyed in months was four blocks away from the ear-splitting commotion in the city centre. It was a beautifully designed building and one of many in the city whose owners had decided that persuading guests to pay for the privilege of staying overnight was infinitely more profitable than forking out on Friday night dinner parties and long Sunday lunches for the cream of Edinburgh society.

The Strathearn was the most exclusive of a small chain of three boutique hotels located in Edinburgh's New Town, where personal butler service, American sized beds and superb food enticed what the marketers described as the discerning traveller to part with much more than the city's average rack rate. It offered privacy, excellent service and a touch of class not always afforded by the five-star multiples. This hotel was where Zimmerman deserved to be.

'Jeez, Houston, I thought this place provided "tranquillity in the city",' imitated Brad with his imaginary quotation marks. 'Hell, it sounds like 9/11 outside. And here was me thinking Edinburgh was such a peaceful little town.'

'Yes,' offered a cautious Jamie, 'I can't really think what could be happening because crime in the city centre is almost zero. I wouldn't worry, though. I suspect the local constabulary have just decided to give their cars a run out. Most likely just some old lady caught shoplifting in Jenners.'

Jamie was in no mood at all for Zimmerman's pseudo Ivy League posturing. He had far more important things to worry about. Furthermore, when his uncle, General Sir James Urquhart, had laughed with derision when telling him of his day with Zimmerman at Gleneagles, Jamie could only smile in pity. Not only because Zimmerman thought a round of golf should take as long as it did on the PGA Tour but rather Zimmerman had deemed it legal to take a preferred lie at every opportunity and forgot the odd stroke every now and then while declaring on most tees that someone called Mulligan had conferred on him the option of playing another ball. All that whilst conveniently ignoring the two stroke penalty for knocking half a dozen balls six miles left of Timbuktu!

Cheating, thought Jamie, was a way of life for many in Zimmerman's business: sometimes blatant, sometimes taking on the life of a finely-crafted illusion. Nonetheless, Jamie could understand the prestige afforded by the outcome. In politics and international business, the only game that mattered was the end game and the plays in between just a means to securing the ultimate prize: money and power. And here Jamie sat with a man who knew how to achieve those objectives, who knew how to work the players in the game and who invariably came out on top. He felt he was drinking with the Devil.

'You know, Jamie,' pondered Zimmerman, 'Peace, I'm afraid, is just another word, or an excuse for that matter, to make a small number of people even wealthier than they are now. In public, they use the word alongside the other great stalwarts such as Freedom, Opportunity and Hope while behind closed doors in DC, they scoff at Peace. In fact, it is ridiculed and abused.'

Zimmerman was sitting back. Pigeon-chested, with one arm outstretched along the back of the large sofa, he had his legs crossed, one leg lifted over the other and parallel to the floor. It was his tough guy posture. When Jamie didn't respond, he continued. And why the hell not, he thought. He was the one calling the shots, wasn't he? 'Where is the Peace in an African Civil War, Jamie? Where is the Peace in an airliner crashing into the World Trade Centre? To most there is none but to the select few, Peace comes along all too frequently in the guise of up-state mansions and beach houses in the Hamptons. It's just a game, Jamie. Maybe a very expensive game but these guys, including me, don't ever play to lose.'

Jamie sat reflecting on the deal he was making with this arsehole and his masters in the Hutchinson Group. The Trident Programme was a reminder of Scotland's contradictory position within the world elite, where the country ensured the financial benefits of association found its way north while attempting to make certain the terrorist atrocities suffered by other countries remained in far off places. Well, it seemed that way, considered

Jamie, until they arrived on the country's doorstep with the attack on Glasgow Airport.

The locating of the Trident nuclear submarine base and the nuclear warhead storage facility only thirty miles from Scotland's biggest city rankled with many not conversant with international politics. And in most respects, they were correct. Scotland, who held no spite for most nations in the world, had been drawn into many, many wars but more recently it had first experienced the Cold War and now it was suffering another Middle East debacle. And it infuriated him. If the Ministry of Defence had wanted a base for their nuclear submarines during their wee spat with the Russians, or to flaunt their powerful arsenal to NATO and the world, then why not build it near Liverpool or London. Why did it have to be Glasgow? The answer, like most issues in politics, was not the most lucid.

Scotland, however, had much to gain from the Nuclear Defence Programme, both in economic terms and in her relationships with both North America and Westminster. And whether people agreed with it or not, Scotland was part of the international political dream team: a left back or right winger maybe but she wore the same colours. Knowing most observers didn't realise it was Scotland's blue painted on both the Stars and Stripes and the Union Jack, Jamie smiled. It would have annoyed him before, especially the North American connection, but now he was thankful no one really knew, because who in the modern world wanted to be associated with these icons of imperialistic freedom now readily abused by some recent inter-national shysters and their version of political and economic gain? Additionally, who enjoyed seeing their fellow countrymen and women die for a political philosophy far removed from what most people in North America, Britain and the rest of the world thought it to be?

Nevertheless, as much as present day events pained him, and as much as Scotland could be associated with empire building, Scotland's record in international development was a record Jamie was content to be associated with, and after some rational and reasoned reflection, justifiably removed from the gratuitous slaughter normally allied to international land-grabbing.

Most historians talked about the British Empire but those in the know knew it for what it really was: The Scottish Empire. Backed by the muscle of England, it was Scots with the Scottish mind-set who created and developed the New World as it came into being. Indeed, Scotland had produced some star players who shone in the Great Emergence and who were very much a source of pride: Australia and McQuarrie, New Zealand with Morrison and McLeod, Jardine and Matheson in the Far East, Israel had Balfour, MacDonald being appointed as the first Prime Minister of Canada and Witherspoon, Wilson and Hamilton in the US. However, there was also the shame; most notably the indelible and guilt-ridden role Scottish merchants played in the notorious slave trade to the Americas.

With most of Scotland's history, there was just as much suffering as there was glory. Jamie described it as the Trade-off. In other words, it was a hypocritical yet equitable outcome. In proudly belonging to that rarest of rarest Scottish breeds, the optimist, he also tried to lessen the human cost of Scotland's gains by stating that Scotland's great travelling heroes had endeavoured to develop the Scottish psyche of believing in the Rights of Man whilst engendering and promoting a culture of equality and liberty. McQuade reformed convicts, McLeod made peace with the Maoris, Jardine and Matheson reinvested millions into the Far Eastern economy, MacDonald was the first Prime Minister of Canada and Witherspoon, Hamilton and Wilson had signed the Declaration of Independence.

But in choosing to sleep in that bed, Jamie wondered if it had, and would be, all in vain. Great wealth had followed and remained but the Western World now seemed to be loosing its sense of itself. Of course, like many, Jamie knew it was time for a change but for the good of the country, it would not be happening under his watch. This was a time for playing the long game. Scotland had to make certain that if it were to slap in a sudden transfer request to NATO and the G8 then certain agreements would have to be realigned and certain relationships renegotiated. Scotland, after all, still needed a little help from its friends. The country had to maintain its disproportionate degree of influence on the world stage. He also knew that Scotland and its people were still held in high esteem by the international community. He was proud. His country was still a fine teacher of rationality and common sense. Nevertheless, to achieve his dream, Jamie knew Scotland would have to utilise and manage its relationships and resources to the max: deep water coastlines, a God-given geographical location, a serious amount of useable and re-useable energy and an intelligent population. He smirked. There was no fucking way Scotland was about to bugger off to play alongside the Albion Rovers of the international community any time soon!

'Brad,' challenged Jamie, 'the First Minister is fully aware of the current situation with the Defence Committee in Washington and as much as we wish to maintain and develop our good relationship with the US, there has to be a trade-off. We've agreed in context it would be beneficial to both nations, and to Hutchinson, to keep Faslane open, in order for the US Navy to still benefit from the facilities. However, you mustn't forget that it is still essentially a MoD base for British subs, so when we win the Referendum, having you or the Royal Navy there just won't be accepted by the electorate. And as much as an independent Scotland will probably recommend a shared Island Defence Force with a new United Kingdom, our people will still want to see the change we have promised them. In other words, we will need to phase out Faslane eventually.'

Brad tried not to release his inner delight on hearing the words, "shared Island Defence Force". Nor did he concern himself with the word "eventually". He would be lying back in his beach house in St. Lucia with three nubile natives by the time "eventually" happened. This was what his strategy had been based upon all along. "A shared and united, island defence strategy with Westminster" was how Drew Wilson had phrased it, an alliance that would result in both Scotland and Hutchinson reaping enormous economic benefits. What's more, Washington and his investors would be cuming in their country club chinos.

Not only would NATO and the US Government continue to increase investment and production into the North Atlantic Defence strategy but now Westminster would have to borrow vast amounts of capital from US investors for it to maintain its own part of the strategy. Either that, or contend with the catastrophe of losing thousands upon thousands of jobs in England. Amusingly, they would still be paying for it long after Faslane was gone.

Zimmerman, though, still harboured one vital concern: would the people of Scotland actually be courageous enough to vote for secession? Retracting the grin, which had been slowly appearing on his face, he returned his attention to the negotiation and to Drew Wilson's back-up list of additional inducements. Without letting Jamie Houston read into what he was thinking, he continued with his suffering benefactor routine.

'What else do you want, Jamie? This deal we are talking about is worth billions to Scotland.'

'As well as to the US Government and Hutchinson, don't forget.'

'Yes, Jamie,' sighed Zimmerman, 'and to us across the water as well. Remember, if our subs continue to use Faslane incognito, I'm sure my guys on Capitol Hill will be only too willing to offer some added incentives.'

'Go on, the country is listening.'

'We could up our input into other industries and ensure a little more capital investment comes Scotland's way: Alternative Energy, Pharmaceuticals, Biotechnology.'

'That's very noble of you, Brad, but let me assure you that we will not accept investment that comes in the form of manufacturing jobs. We already had those in the eighties and nineties and things didn't turn out as expected or promised. It is jobs of substance we need. Scotland already provides services the world requires, and which only Scotland can supply, but we want more. Furthermore, if there was to be investment that does offer something more substantial and ethically acceptable, then we could be talking about a deal.'

'You're not asking for much?' ventured the frustrated

Zimmerman.

'I'm only just beginning, Brad. Nevertheless, I more than understand that you guys are thinking of the long term. So, as compromise on Scotland's part, can I suggest we close down Faslane in stages …let's say over the next thirty or forty years. What's more, I'm sure the consternation that will cause in the US will be more than met with great delight if we offer tax reductions for alternative American investment.'

'These would have to be pretty generous, Jamie.'

'Don't worry, it shouldn't be an issue, especially when Scotland secedes and brings in a reduced corporate tax rate. And if we bung in some pretty big tax concessions to North American companies working in the North Sea, I'm sure we will have provided more than enough to keep your masters happy.'

Jamie felt the power surging through his soul. Here he sat negotiating Scotland's future with one of the most powerful men in international business and he was kicking arse. Faslane could be closed down while the country benefited from an escalation in investment. Knowing what Jamie did regarding the new oil discoveries, disused oil fields being re-opened, and technology being used to drill much deeper on the continental shelf than ever before, the oil business in Scotland was looking good, very good indeed: certainly good enough for Jamie to negotiate with.

'Well, I'm sure what you are proposing is definitely something we can work with' said Zimmerman. 'And I'm also sure the long term outlook will heartily welcomed by both the Hutchinson Board and the guys on Capitol Hill.'

'Listen Brad, Scotland is a country of new found hope. But all along we have never been short of aspiration. We know we can deliver. Just don't be foolish and don't get greedy. Close down Faslane in stages and everybody wins. You can build a base in Iceland if you want, we don't care. Just as long as your guys remember that they will be more than re-reimbursed if they come along for the ride.'

Zimmerman sat up straight. 'Good. Now we're getting somewhere. Long term it is and as you say, there's much to be gained.'

21

gang aft agley?

Wednesday 18th June

2.25 pm – National Security Department – London

Sir Alexander Lamont had disposed of his arrogance and was pacing the office of Sir James Montague, Head of National Security. Montague had told him to wait there and calm down while Montague, being cautious of Lamont's well-documented bad temper, held an emergency briefing with his non-registered and unsanctioned Internal Security Operations Department.

Lack of control was an unfamiliar feeling for Lamont to contend with. He always, always, had a contingency. Good planning had made him the success he was and why he believed himself to be more than just a major player in London. He also believed, that with the enormous revenues generated by UKES's operations across the world and the contributions UKES made to the economy in employment opportunities and in tax, he was the paymaster general of Britain's economy. His company traded in energy: oil, gas, nuclear and renewables and turned over in excess of three hundred billion pounds. Furthermore, with such a demand on those supplies from not only Britain but from further afield, he really did believe he was one of the most powerful men in the world; counting Kings, Princes, Presidents, Prime Ministers, Sheiks, outlawed world leaders and pillars of industry among his peers. He had influence and power, and in normal circumstances, he usually had control.

Nevertheless, was it all about to go wrong? He looked

out across the Thames. 'This sort of fiasco is just not meant to happen.' Finding himself in this sort of predicament would have rendered lesser lights incapable of rational thought, filling them with panic and fear and indiscipline. Lamont knew he could never let himself fall into that mindset, not yet anyway. It was all about disciplined planning. It was about careful organisation and negotiation and the occasional delve into the dark political art of persuasion, where the most productive strategy included bribery and career-destroying intimidation. By relying on his courageous judgement and his stance in the face of calamity, he had elevated himself above the deluded souls. Men who lost control drowned in their own internal anger whereas he had long since given up on that idea of self-persecution. Lamont had no need to brood. And why should he? He knew he wasn't the most popular of men, far from it, and if others deemed him to be a merciless and hard-nosed bastard, then so be it. It wasn't for him to wallow in the despair of his own failures and feelings of injustice. 'If it suited the weak to blame others,' he reflected, 'then they have lost and I have won.' And winning was what it was all about.

He had been planning this operation for three years but in truth, it had been much longer, possibly from as far back as the seventies, and most definitely from the moment the Devolution Bill was passed. Nevertheless, he still found himself sneering with frustration. Had the men who drafted the Bill not seen this day coming? The fucking useless and short-sighted arseholes. Not only did he know that Scottish Secession was at the top of the political agenda, it was fast becoming a reality.

He had made many covert attempts to stop Devolution but couldn't. He just didn't have the clout then that he did now. If he had, he would have made damn sure the very subject would have been cut off at source. Even a political imbecile could have foreseen what would happen. Two governments within one political state might have worked if that political state had been one nation, but Scotland and England? Bloody hell, had these men not been aware of the history, the bitterness, the agitation? Whichever way the debate unfolded, both countries would hold grievances, with England just nudging it with the bookmakers as being the more pissed-off of the two. He could feel it in the people. He could feel their betrayal. At one point, he had been so angry with himself he drifted into a mis-guided and ill-judged moment of thinking he had been out-smarted by the draftees of the Bill whom he thought might have had Secession as their ultimate goal from the very beginning. 'Hell, they were all Scots, weren't they?' Thankfully, he had read the situation and been wrong. He had planned well.

Having watched the mess unfold for the last few years, he could perceive the Scottish people gaining in confidence, but also sensing their unease as the two main parties continued to control affairs from Westminster while dismissing the Holyrood government as insignificant. Furthermore, he could clearly see what the Labour-controlled government and councils in Scotland had achieved. One only had to drive the streets and witness the dereliction in places like Possilpark and Linwood to appreciate their mis-management. Labour had always managed to blame the Tories for the inequality in Scotland but when nothing was done to improve the lives of those in the Labour heartlands, it was obvious to the Scottish voters that it wasn't just the Tories to blame, it was their own party as well. The party founded by Scots, the party controlled by Scots: The Labour Party.

He had always struggled to communicate effectively with the Labour Party but out of fear of what he might lose, he had gone out of his way to warn them of what was to come. When they didn't listen however, he had withdrawn financial support. He even attempted blackmail and still they wouldn't listen. And now they were burning in hell. Yet, he still needed Labour to bounce back and if they weren't going to help themselves, he decided he'd better speak to others who would. In hatching his plan with men who really did hold the power to influence, he had ended up buying a house for the CEO of the BTC, as well as paying-off senior civil servants to push through agreements ensuring Alain DeWitt could expand his media empire without the threat of reprisals. He had even made certain Sir Peter Milligan would remain as Permanent Secretary for another nine years after Milligan had agreed to persuade the PM to appoint a new Secretary of State for Scotland, the snivelling and dreary sycophant, Dan Geraghty. Furthermore, he didn't forget the much-needed muscle either, which came in the form of a violent intimidator called DCC Michael Hastie, a man to whom he had promised a top job with the National Security Department. 'Yes, I had it all worked out.'

Manipulation and coercion, they were his compulsion. Having drummed up anti-SNP sentiment in Westminster and scared the living crap out of those at the Alba Club, Lamont knew this was not the time for negotiation. Neither was it a time for cultural harmony and it was most certainly not the time for the *Settled Will of the Scottish People* to single-handedly destroy a life's work and his immortal memory. 'No fucking way.' It was time to witness the best of Sir Alexander Lamont. It was time for everyone in this great city to see the man who would save the country. He would be master and he would be king. No ifs and buts. Destroy from within. Offer no quarter!

And then there was Elliot Walker.

Lamont hadn't accounted for the events of the last twenty four hours as he watched with growing frustration as his grand plan unravelled. 'How could this be?' Walker was a polite and unassuming lawyer who lived in Surrey, an entirely insignificant man who had no right becoming involved. Heaven forbid! The bloody fool was destroying his own career. 'Fuck him!' When the appropriate time arose, Walker would be an afterthought. He was dead! What's more, DCC Michael Hastie would be the man to do the business: a man just as evil as he, and just as ambitious. Lamont sneered. He enjoyed Hastie's company for no other reason than he could see much of himself in the policeman. Hastie had no time for losing and no time for whinging. In fact, Lamont had compared Hastie to his pet dog, though more Bull-Terrier than pedigree Cocker. Loyal and determined, he had the character to deliver results.

'The news is not encouraging,' stated an expressionless Montague as he strolled slowly into the office. 'There's still no sighting of Elliot Walker or Dixie Armstrong. However, I have had it confirmed to me that they are both in Edinburgh.'

'Tell me, Montague, are all you spooks so bland and so bloody matter of fact that not even a fucking tornado could alter your demeanour?' stropped Lamont.

'Sir Alex, what good would it do if we got ourselves all worked up? Britain has not exactly obtained all this power by loosing the run of things every time someone disrupts our plans. That's what happened in Gibraltar and look at the mess in which we found ourselves there. No, no, no, that just won't do. We need to remain focussed on our objectives, dear boy. Stand firm in the face of adversity and all that. Don't worry, we'll get them and the recording soon enough. And when we do, young Walker will be wishing he was still working on some pointless and brain-numbing tax legality in that most unsecured of offices you call your HQ.'

'And just how do you propose we do that? If this recording is released into the public domain, I am finished. Don't you get it at all, you incongruous arse of a man?'

'And just how do you suppose they are going to release this recording?' asked the indifferent but self-assured Montague. 'We have the Police, the BTC, TFW, the Government and the organised might of the British Security Services on our side. I'd say their chances are minute, if not impossible. Wouldn't you?'

'You pompous fool, Montague. Who knows how many copies they have? We find one; they produce another. And remember, the Tribune is independent. In fact, I can just see that little shit of an editor now, pinching his pug nose and sniggering in delight at the possibilities provided by printing this.'

'Sir Alex, dear boy, we already have three teams in place ready to intercept any communication to and from our fugitives, as well as my own Tech team monitoring the web and ready to pull the Tribune's own website if need be. Furthermore, we have back-up teams in place near the Tribune's office, as well as its printing plant, just in case things get that far. But they won't. There is no way this story will be published. We can close the Tribune down in the morning and who will ever know the reasons why? It's not as if the BTC, BEAR TV and the news agencies are going to broadcast to the nation on their Breaking

News that the National Security Department has raided an independent and legitimate newspaper and closed down its entire operation! No, relax, dear boy. It's all in hand.'

'I hope you're not bullshitting, Montague. You'd better be right on this one.'

'Of course I am. We at the National Security Department are always correct even when we are so blatantly not.'

'Well, just make sure your boys finish the job. We don't want any leftovers at the table.'

'Don't you worry about my men, Sir Alexander, they'll be fine. If I was you, I'd be more worried about your man Hastie losing control and blowing this entire operation wide open. He's not exactly the most diplomatic of executioners, is he? And lest we forget, it was one of your employees who got us into this bloody mess in the first place. It is you who couldn't control your chief litigator and it is you who wanted Hastie to take the lead on this. I mean, who's to say that your man, an imbalanced and panic-stricken policeman with everything to lose, won't start shooting up the centre of Edinburgh?'

Montague had been worried about Hastie's involvement in Lamont's plan from the beginning. Of course, he had used Hastie's skills on many occasions for his own purpose but Hastie was being a little too ambitious, too smarmy and much too eager in securing that fancied move to London. He was also concerned that Hastie's impatience would mean only one thing when it came to handling an operation as delicate as this; that it would become an emotional exercise. And when it came to protecting Westminster's interests, emotion could be the most dangerous of enemies. NSD operatives had to remain impassive when directly involved with strategy. Satisfying personal requirements only heightened the chance of failure. It made for irrational decision-making and damaging after-effects. And he knew he was correct. Who was to say that Michael Hastie wouldn't go over the top in Edinburgh? The NSD psychologist's report on Hastie had certainly indicated it was possible. Yes, Hastie would get results but you might not like how he got them. Hastie got too involved and he spoke to far too many people about his life's plan.

Montague had cautioned Lamont of Hastie's impetuous character, quickly suggesting that the NSD and Lamont would have to operate with extreme caution. That was why he insisted that all operations relating to the matter would have to include the NSD. Hastie couldn't be allowed to treat this as one of his gung-ho Strathclyde operations, where he was answerable only to himself. There had to be guidelines: constant radio communication with HQ, fake registration plates for the cars, and bogus names for his agents. There was also a support team on site to cover up and clean up any mess that Hastie might leave behind, as well as a collection of pre-prepared statements ready to be released to the Press. Hastie might appear to be leading from the front but there was a rather large back-up plan just in case Hastie lost the run of things. That was the NSD way.

*

2.32 pm – Pan-European Hotel – Edinburgh

'I wish I was as calm as your boss,' grunted DCC Hastie to the two NSD spooks sitting next to him in lobby. 'Seems to think there is absolutely fuck-all to worry about.'

Under the guise of looking for three suspects in the attempted murder of Dixie Armstrong, Hastie had called in a favour from his opposite number in Edinburgh to supply extra men. Police check-points had been erected at all the transporttation terminals and major junctions leaving the city centre with nameless but accurate descriptions on hand of Elliot, Paul and Dixie. With three uniforms standing guard on Lothian Road Fountainbridge, Haymarket, Dean Bridge, Stockbridge, Leith Walk, Waterloo Place, Holyrood, and North Bridge, Hastie had been able to order a complete lock-down of the city. He had also extended the favour by asking the Lothian's DCC to supply even more men to sweep the city centre. He was pushing it but he didn't give a fuck. The ensuing chaos was a minor consequence of his actions but Hastie wasn't thinking about the effect on shoppers, tourists and city centre workers. They could fucking wait. This was a tad more important than a latte in a street-side café or a designer dress from Harvey Nicks!

'So, what's the situation as we stand?'

'Sir, we have all the main arteries blocked off and we're doing a site by site search of all businesses from the West End down to the Playhouse and up to the Royal Mile.'

'Are you telling me that we still have no idea where they could be?' Since his men couldn't even recover the number Rory Hamilton was about to call, Hastie didn't wait for a response. He was struggling to contain his anger but thankful his single-mindedness was keeping him applied to the job at hand. 'Have we had any luck on the position of DCI Riley's phone?'

'No Sir. He hasn't used it since our last trace so the best we have is that he is still in the vicinity. I know it doesn't help but the more people we ask, the closer we'll get. Someone must have spotted them. Hopefully, the Tech teams or the checkpoints will come up with something soon.'

Hastie called on his decreasing supply of patience. 'Right lads, it's not a big city so I'm sure they'll slip up at some point. In the meantime, issue a direct order to all teams that if the Press arrive on the scene and start snooping, the word is we're looking for three dangerous criminals on the run. But whatever happens, keep them out of the fucking way!'

Hastie left the two NSD spooks sitting while he took a stroll through the hotel. After calling the NSD HQ with another update, he closed his eyes and breathed deeply, opening them again to find himself staring at a fine collection of Malts on the gantry of the lounge bar. He was seriously considering getting totally blootered. However, as he ordered just a single measure, his phone rang again. Looking down at the name on the screen, he closed his eyes and shook his head. 'Fuck!'

'Sir, how are things?' asked Hastie of his boss, the Chief Constable of Strathclyde. Time for some improv.

'Hastie, I hope you have a bloody good reason for shutting down Edinburgh in the middle of a summer's day. I've already had the Lothians' CC on the phone demanding to know what the hell is going on. In fact, if this nonsense keeps up I'm going to have the First Minister in my ear as well!'

'Yes, Sir, we have reason to believe the men behind the assassination attempt on Dixie Armstrong are here in Edinburgh. Unfortunately, we believe that Dixie Armstrong is here as well, so we are trying to find them before they find her?'

'You mean to say you don't know where she is?'

'No, Sir.'

'Well, have you tried calling her bloody phone? Even for an aging policeman like myself that would be the logical step.'

'We have, Sir. But her phone is switched off so we have no way of knowing where she is.'

'So how do you know she is in Edinburgh, if at all? Did you know her boss called earlier today asking me personally to add extra security to her parents' house?'

Hastie remained silent, trying to fathom what Dixie was up to and if she really was in Edinburgh at all. 'Sir, it's a long story but DCI Riley received a tip-off on where the Range Rover at Loch Lomond came from. And after making a few enquiries, we found out who was driving it and followed them here.'

'For goodness sake, you are meant to be protecting her, not allowing a group of trained assassins get to her first,' blustered the Chief Constable. 'Anyway, you're not making any sense, Hastie. What enquiries? Who did you speak to? Are you in contact with DCI Riley?'

'Yes Sir. It was Paul who put us on the suspect's trail.'

'And do we know where these suspects are?'

'No, Sir, our men lost them.'

'And where is DCI Riley? Is he with you? In fact, let me speak to him?'

'He's leading the operation as we speak, Sir. I'll have him call you as soon as he becomes available.'

'Okay Hastie, but I need this problem fixed immediately. What's more, you could have handled this operation with a little more organisational nous. In fact, it's not like you at all to cause so much disquiet. I trust you can redeem yourself.'

'Yes Sir. We'll have them in no time.'

'Make sure of it.'

As the line went dead, Hastie sighed, finished his whisky

and ordered another. 'But this time make it a treble.'

Hastie stood alone, his life as close to ruin as it was to a top job with the Security Services. If he could only bring these bastards in. Not only was his protégé Paul Riley conspiring to fuck everything up, that dirty bitch Armstrong was at the centre of it all. He despised her. She was a self-congratulatory whore who knew her flirtatious scheming and sultry looks made him crazy with lust and anger. He, however, was a leader. He was the man who set the agenda. He had brought down gunrunners and smashed three IRA cells. He had driven a wedge between drug-pushing gangsters and picked them off one by one as they declared war on each other. He had even brought the Russians to heel in Glasgow's seedy world of prostitution and people trafficking. 'Christ,' he hissed, 'I've made myself a legend in Scotland and for what? To be brought down by a two-faced Fenian scum-bag and a dirty, little scheming slut? No fucking chance.' He would make them pay. He would make them suffer. He would inflict the pain.

The rapid fire shots of malt whisky were going straight to Hastie's head. And of all the things he had learned during his tenure as a cop, it was that he had to remain engaged. He had to be alert and be in control. In every dangerous situation he ever faced, he had been the one making the calls and preparing for every outcome. It was time for the hard man in Hastie to come out to play. First, though, he had to answer his goddamn phone again.

'Hastie speaking. Make it quick.'

'Sir, we have another problem.'

'Go on.'

'Peter Buchanan is in Edinburgh. His car is stuck in the mayhem on George Street.'

'What the fuck is he doing here? I thought he was meant to be in fucking Argyll.'

'We don't know. Our guys in London were tracking him yesterday but instead of heading over to Argyll, he made a detour to some place called Glamis. We didn't think it was that big a deal until he turned up here in Edinburgh.'

Still holding the phone, Hastie let his arm fall as he tried to deduce why Peter Buchanan had gone to Glamis Castle then returned to Edinburgh without prior security clearance. 'What is that bastard up to?' His frustration, now, was grinding him down and he was close to that stomach churning moment of self-resignation. Taking in a deep breath, he stared up at the ceiling, looking for any sign of hope. As he whispered slowly to himself, he felt it drifting away. 'I'd be as well stopping off at the Royal Infirmary and pleading the proctologist for an anaesthetic-free colostomy.'

'Okay,' continued Hastie, 'get him off the street pronto and in here. I'll have a word with him. He's probably no idea what the hell is going on, so if he asks play along with our story 'til he gets here.' Hastie closed his phone. 'Christ, that's all I need, the Leader of the fucking Opposition working himself into a state of panic in the middle of Scotland's capital.'

Four minutes later, the grand wooden doors of the hotel flew open and in marched an agitated but outwardly composed Peter Buchanan surrounded by two NSD goons, four uniforms, Oliver Graham and Pippa Moss. Hastie was standing in the foyer, nodding to his henchmen to usher the group towards the back of the hotel. The hotel staff and some bewildered guests stood back as Hastie pulled the Hotel Manager to one side. 'Listen Cuff-Links, I'm commandeering a meeting room. Get me one down the back, and get it quick.'

The room was small and windowless, and sparse in décor apart from three small water colour prints. There was a side table on which lay an untidy scatter of notepads and plastic pens, and six small bottles of spring water. The chairs were stacked neatly in the corner and a heavy looking table cloth sat folded on the far end of the undressed and wooden conference table. Buchanan and his team were already there when Hastie walked in.

Ollie Graham, dwarfed by the large frame of the plain clothed policeman, stood tall as he introduced himself. 'Hi. Oliver Graham, chief advisor to Peter Buchanan.'

Hastie ignored the outstretched hand as he imparted a long, penetrating stare into Buchanan's eyes. Without turning, he spoke. 'I don't care if you're the chief cocksucker to the fucking Pope; just get yourself and that little tart out of here now!'

Oliver Graham was stunned. 'How dare you? Have you any idea who this is?'

'No. No idea at all. Why don't you enlighten me, Testicle Face!' growled Hastie.

'This is Dougl…'

'Of course I know who he is, you little shit. And do you know who I am, by any chance?'

'Yes, according to your men, you're DCC Michael…'

'It's all right, Ollie,' interrupted Buchanan. 'I'm sure DCC Hastie is only here to look after our safety.'

As the room emptied, Buchanan nonchalantly lifted two chairs from the stack in the corner. Placing one down by the side of the table, he offered it to the DCC. Hastie ignored the offer, preferring to stand close to the door. Buchanan left it there while he picked up the other, taking it round the room so he could face Hastie across the table. 'Okay, Hastie, what's this all about? I've a schedule to keep to and all this nonsense is preventing me from fulfilling it.'

'Listen sonny, you can drop all the political posturing right now. I don't have time for pleasantries.'

'So I hear.'

'Right, Buchanan, I want answers. Truthful fucking answers. Because believe me, telling lies at this present time will not be in your best interests, whatsoever.' This was Hastie at his bullying best. With the influence his bosses exerted in London, he knew the all-clear would be given to push the Tory Leader to his limit.

'Friends in high places?' scoffed a demeaning Buchanan. 'And who might they be? Maybe my chums know your chums, Mr. Hastie? In fact, maybe we can all get together for a Sunday afternoon picnic and a game of cricket?'

'Listen, Billy Bum-Hole, we all know you're the smart-arsed public school boy with an infinite amount of well-heeled connections, keen on congregating in seedy Chelsea apartments to tickle each other's sphincter with a copy of the FT, but on this

346

occasion I am advising you to cooperate because I'm sure the last thing you need to see is a furious and mental Glasgow copper pissing on your political ambitions as they drift down the Thames.'

Peter Buchanan lightly brushed a fleck of dust from his jacket sleeve. Unaffected by the threat, he confidently smiled back. 'Unfortunately, Mr. Hastie, what you fail to realise is that you are the dispensable one. A …what do you call it …Deputy Chief Constable will always be answerable to someone. One misguided judgment or foolish action on *your* part could see *your* ambitions drifting down the Clyde, which, in case you haven't realised, is a much faster flowing river than the Thames. No, I'm afraid it is you have been ill-advised. In fact, if I was you Mr. Hastie I'd be the one on the lookout.'

'Mr. Buchanan, in case you are unaware, I know about your little conversation with Sir Alexander Lamont. One of your friends I presume? However, in case you and your aristocratic bum pals didn't know, he is also a close friend of yours truly. And at this moment in time I would harbour a pretty good guess that his immediate priorities are more attuned with mine than they are to yours.'

Buchanan paused, unsure of his next move. He knew he had to one day rid himself of the men who controlled his life. For the moment, however, his politician's mind decided that capitulation was the better part of valour. 'Please, Mr. Hastie, let's not get caught up in a "my willie's bigger than your willie" tussle. What do you need to know?'

Hastie sneered with delight. He was in the ascendancy. 'What I want to know is why you thought it a good idea to go to Glamis Castle last night without informing us?'

'That is between me and my advisors. What's more, what I get up to is my business and my business alone.'

'Yes, I agree, but when it comes to the security of this country, it becomes my business. We know you've been holding discussions Brad Zimmerman but why Glamis Castle?'

'DCC Hastie,' said Buchanan abruptly, 'as I said, who and where I decide to meet is entirely my prerogative. However, if you really want to know, Zimmerman had some important information for me, which I needed to run by an old friend of mine.'

'You mean to say that when you are discussing plans for the Trident Programme, you turn to a member of the public for advice. Are you fucking crazy?'

'My old friend is not exactly what you would call a member of the public. In fact, he's a very influential man. Not just in this country but in the United States and Canada as well. Anyway, I thought it would be a good idea to meet with him so he could help me rationalise my thoughts on Sir Alexander Lamont's request to formulate a strategy to combat Secession in Scotland. The meeting at Glamis was part of that strategy.'

'So, enlighten me. Who the fuck is your old friend? More importantly, how much influence does he have?'

'Really, Hastie, you don't think I'd be stupid enough to tell you, do you? As for influence, he has too much for you and me to even fathom.

'As ever, Hastie, you are completely out of the loop when it comes to Scotland. In fact, if you had concentrated a little more of your efforts on what is happening here, instead of kissing the arse of Sir James Montague, you would have realised there are many influential individuals who don't want Scotland to suffer again at the hands of the big industrialists down in London. The same bloody things happened in the seventies with the Government and the McCrone Report, and in the eighties with, bless their spiteful souls, the witch and that scum-sucking parasite Press advisor of hers, Hugo Fellingham. No, Mr Hastie, and my apologies to Sir Alexander who you'll no doubt be on the phone to after I leave, Scotland will not suffer again.'

'Christ, I can't believe what I'm hearing. Since when did you become a fucking nationalist?'

Peter Buchanan had been manipulated, lied to and taken for granted: by Sir General James Urquhart, Drew Wilson and Sir Alexander Lamont. Nevertheless, his priorities weren't going to suddenly change just so Hastie and Lamont could maliciously manipulate democracy to suit their agenda of conceit. He knew it was a risky tactic that could render his political career obsolete but his father's words still resonated. He would have no remorse.

'Not quite a nationalist, I'm afraid. You see, Hastie, I attribute my policies to caring for the people of Great Britain and Northern Ireland whereas people like you and Lamont are self-serving antagonists. I mean, why on earth do you think Andrew Drummond is so popular today? The people in Scotland have woken up and, mark my words, will vote for Secession unless something changes soon. In fact, it may even be too late and God help us if it is. Therefore, if Secession happens, I will have no option but to ensure that future relations between Scotland and England are what I would like to call more cordial, with my main priority being that the Queen remains the Head of both states. That is my agenda. Noble and foolish maybe, but at least I can look at myself and believe that what I am trying to achieve will be the best for everyone, not just the selected few. On the other hand, people like you, DCC Hastie, remain obsessed with your buggered-up belief of colonialism and all the strength it presents to your jack-boot philosophy. You think your almighty power can manipulate any situation, even this one today, which, I suspect, has nothing whatsoever to do with an assassination attempt on Dixie Armstrong. You believe the world will go on: Lamont still filling up the bank accounts of his bedfellows in London and you as a top cop with the NSD. No, I'm afraid you are wildly mistaken. My support is primarily with Scotland on this. She has to receive a better deal. Sure, I still want the United Kingdom to survive, and to change, and that's what my friends and I are going to make sure happens: with, or more probably without, the likes of you.'

Taking a deep breath to prevent him from punching the door, Hastie paused. He had to remain in control. 'So who were you meeting in Edinburgh? Or is that classified as well?'

'Mr. Hastie, all that power and information and still you don't know. I wonder who is the dispensable one now? Maybe my willie is bigger than yours, after all,' mocked Buchanan.

Hastie's disposition couldn't prevent the violence from overcoming his controlled interrogation. Turning quickly to the small table, he picked up a bottle of water and lashed it at Buchanan, who just managed to jerk his head to the side as the missile flew by and smashed on the wall behind. As Buchanan glared at the broken glass on the floor, he caught a glimpse of Hastie in the corner of his eye. The policeman was already on the table and launching himself across the room and landing with a kick to Buchanan's head. Stunned, Buchanan fell from his chair as he desperately tried to protect his face from the power of Hastie aggression. A right arm caught him first on the back of the head before a knee pummelled his exposed groin. 'You fucking bastard,' screamed Hastie. Not in the mood for taking it easy, Hastie stood up and kicked Buchanan hard in the stomach. 'You two-faced, dirty bastard. I'm going to fucking kill you!'

The door flew open as Hastie continued to land blows on the Tory leader. Moments later, the rabid DCC was dragged from his prey by two uniforms while Ollie Graham and a hysterical Pippa Moss darted to the aid of their boss. Hastie, beginning to reel in his lunatic tendencies, turned his head and wiped the sweat and the saliva across his shoulder. He was still shaking and seething when Buchanan stood up to dust himself down.

'It's all right, officers,' explained a remarkably restrained Buchanan, 'just a little disagreement.'

The two uniforms stared back in surprise as Buchanan fixed his suit and made to leave. 'I'll be seeing you soon, DCC Hastie. Hope things work out but somehow I think you're well and truly buggered. Enjoy the sphincter bashing.'

As Buchanan and his entourage left the room, Hastie shrugged off his men. 'Get the fuck out of my way. We'll deal with this later.'

Hastie could feel his heartbeat through a sweat drenched shirt as he returned to the hotel lobby. He was marching straight for the bar when one of his NSD spooks came rushing over.

'Please fucking tell me some good news,' grunted Hastie.

'Sir, we've traced a transaction on DCI Riley's credit card. It was processed twenty minutes ago at the Kelso Hotel on the North Bridge.'

22

the northern summer sky

Wednesday 18th June

2.45 pm – Queensferry Road – Edinburgh

As the pulsating commotion in the city centre continued to rumble on, Jamie found himself to be enjoying his stroll through the relative tranquility of Edinburgh's west end; its wide avenues, Georgian architecture and attitudes of gentle persuasion appealing to his renewed sense of achievement. Nevertheless, it still wasn't his beloved Stockbridge. Sure, the West End had a community but not one Jamie could attach himself to on a personal level; an over-abundance of embassies, consulates, lawyers and accountancy firms eliminating any attachment its residents might have had to neighbourly affection. With their empty rooms full of nothing but antique fireplaces and dusty portraits, there was never much sign of life behind the massive panels of olden glass. This was the West End at it was meant to be, embracing the peaceful refinement of Edinburgh's power.

Jamie, however, knew his joy of securing an agreement with the Hutchinson Group could ultimately be a short-lived accomplishment. Not because it was the right thing to do, as he believed it was, but rather he now had to persuade his boss it was the appropriate course of action to take. Andrew Drummond was not in the business of losing votes so whenever Trident was on the agenda there had always been the accepted expectation it would evoke the ethical determination of both the anti-war and anti-US campaigners. Jamie cursed, and that was just one side of the moral and economical divide, the other side including those whose jobs would be at risk if the submarine base were ever to close down. Furthermore, such was clandestine nature of the capricious blend of politics and business, Jamie maintained a perpetual and irritating apprehension concerning the possible actions of those whose international strategic development plans included the Faslane base staying put, and having just encountered Brad Zimmerman, he wondered as to just how far they were prepared to go. Fortunately, he would seek refuge in his knowledge that any deal agreed upon would not go through until after the Referendum.

The warm afternoon sun reflected off the cars and vans and buses as Jamie approached the corner of Melville Street and Queensferry Road. The traffic may have been busy but business in the bars and bistros was slowing as po-faced professionals straightened their ties and made their way back to the office after a light bowl of fresh pasta and a glass of wine.

Deciding he would take the short-cut to Charlotte Square by way of the close at the end of Randolph Place, Jamie crossed the log-jammed street. Glancing to his left, he was surprised to see a police road-block down at Dean Bridge. He shrugged his shoulders; traffic and police were a council issue. What's more, his phone was ringing.

Two minutes later, after Jamie had taken the call, he was inside Bute House snapping impatiently at the First Minister's staff. 'Where the hell is the Mr. Drummond? I need to speak to him, now.' No response. 'Where is he, people?' Not bothering to knock, he took a brief look inside the First Minister's study. No sign. He checked the library and drawing rooms overlooking Charlotte Square. Still no sign. 'Listen folks. I'm not screwing around here. Somebody has to know where he is.'

'He had to go out to the RCB Headquarters,' offered a young intern. 'Some meeting about an over-exposure to the US Sub-Prime Market. Said he should be back in an hour.'

Jamie didn't have time to be pissed-off about not being at that meeting, he had other imminent and more life-threatening issues to be concerned with. He would just have to take the responsibility on himself, hoping and knowing his boss, the First Minister of Scotland, would understand.

*

2.46 pm – Kelso Hotel

Kirsten opened the bedroom door with more than a little trepidation. She had been couped up in there for less than a day but circumstance made it feel like much longer. The room she already despised, a small protective cell in the middle of a city where one is meant to relax, not stiffen with fear at the thought of losing your husband, even if he was a silly bastard.

They decided to leave in pairs by the hotel's two exits. Dixie would go with Kirsten under the assertion that Hastie would not be searching for two females while Paul would chaperon Elliot for no other reason than Elliot would be exposed as little more than pathetically inadequate in the art of evading the NSD and their surreptitious ensnaring tactics. Charlie, yet to be implicated and forever the loner, would go on his own; logic dictating that if something were to happen to the others, not only would he be close by, he would still have a copy of the file.

As he prepared to leave, Elliot, ready at last to become a soldier of destiny, eagerly slung his laptop case over his shoulder. Dixie and Paul smiled; Elliot's lack of experience in the world of authentic death an uplifting tonic for their very real sense of impending danger. Checking her memory stick and Blackberry were secure inside her jacket, Dixie led the way as they split into pairs, each taking a different route to the lobby three floors below.

Kirsten, as the least wanted fugitive, was to do a recce of the immediate vicinity outside the main door. She was to check for police squads on the prowl. Walking cautiously outside, she stood on the small set of steps leading down to the pavement and surveyed the outlook across North Bridge and Princes Street. All clear. As she turned and looked up towards the Royal Mile, she let out a light gasp: one road-block, three policemen, fifty yards

353

up the street, at the junction. Quickly returning back inside, she gave a single nod to Dixie who then pulled out her phone, inserted the battery, switched it on and in seconds speaking quietly to whoever was on the other end of the line.

Dixie was standing just inside the door with Charlie while Elliot and Paul waited in a blind corridor on the other side of the hotel's atrium. Dixie and Kirsten would leave by the main door on North Bridge, Paul and Elliot by Carubber's Close on the Royal Mile, and Charlie out the main door a few seconds after Dixie and Kirsten.

Dixie nodded once to Charlie before grabbing Kirsten's hand. 'Ready?'

Kirsten didn't respond, instead turning to Elliot, and with an increasing heart beat, mouthing the words, 'I love you'.

Elliot's response was not as audacious as before. He saw both love and fear in her eyes. 'I love you, always,' was his silent, smiling reply.

Turning back, a defiant Kirsten spoke. 'Ready.'

Paul and Elliot waited a teasing and stressful thirty seconds before receiving the word to go from Dixie. Running down the narrow corridor, they barged through a side door and out onto the Royal Mile, catching the three uniforms at the road-block unawares. The plods didn't have a hope of stopping any of the gang. Charlie and the two girls had already disappeared beneath the bridge while Paul and Elliot were off and running, down another of the Royal Mile's many closes.

The sweat was continuing to seep through the shirt of DCC Michael Hastie as he waited, impatient and agitated, in the back of an unmarked car on George Street. He sneered with evil intent as he glanced out to the phone box from where his spooks had accosted Rory Hamilton. As businessmen and shoppers hurried by, the radio crackled. It was information from the NSD's HQ in London identifying the exact position of Dixie Armstrong and Paul Riley's phones. They were on the corner of the Royal Mile and North Bridge. Hastie was now less than four minutes and half a mile from finally nailing these bastards.

'Reverse!' he screamed at the driver, 'Fucking reverse!' The rubber burned as the car wheeled round, smashing through two cars coming up from behind. As the car accelerated eastwards towards St. Andrews Square, Hastie opened up the radio channel being used by the Edinburgh Police. 'Suspects leaving the Kelso Hotel. Move in and apprehend.' He then roared at the driver to take a right into St. Andrews Square, again deciding to drive against the direction of the traffic. Cars and buses screeched to a halt as Hastie and his spook car weaved its way towards its pray. Passing the Prudential and Tiles Café Bar on the right, the flashing blue light and the siren rebounded of the ancient walls of the square. At the original HQ of RCB, the car swerved right again and down towards Princes Street. One minute to capture. Hastie once more grabbed for the radio but first he changed the frequency. This time he wanted to speak to his own men. 'Suspects are leaving the Kelso Hotel on North Bridge. Arrests not required. Shoot to kill if necessary. And retrieve all copies of the file!' Turning to one of his spooks, Hastie ordered him to alert all cabs in the city with a description of his fugitives and to place a barring signal on all of their phones. 'There's no way these traitorous cunts are calling for help now.'

When they first heard the raging police sirens, Kirsten and Dixie were already at the foot the old stone staircase beneath the Saltire Hotel. Charlie was about fifty metres behind, ready to warn Dixie of any oncoming police and spooks. On Market Street, the two women were soon running hard beneath the stone skyscrapers of Edinburgh's Old Town. As Dixie glanced back towards the bridge, she heard the sirens of what she correctly thought was Hastie's car rushing up towards the hotel. They were struggling to breathe as Waverly Station emitted pungent fumes from its expended fuels. But on they ran, barging through a crowd of tourists leaving The Dungeons who were giggling at their own fabricated fear, and oblivious to the genuine petrification of Hastie's prey shunting its way through their throng.

Looking ahead with caution, and checking that Charlie was still close by, Dixie and Kirsten ran across the end of

Waverly Bridge and up the steeper end of Market Street, only to see the flashing lights of a police car skidding down Hanover Street, crossing Princes Street, and heading up the Mound. Charlie shouted from behind. They were to take the steps to the side of the National Gallery. Holding each other's hand, they launched themselves down, keeping a close eye on their electric and animated small feet dancing on the stone staircase. The normally affable Big Issue sellers grunted as tourists huddled against the iron fence to let the wild women pass. Up above, Charlie kept watch until they made it down, as the police car screamed past the National Kirk of Scotland and away from the girls. Charlie shook his head as he glared at the building in which Maggie stood on the pulpit. He swore as only the son of a Yorkshire miner could before returning his watchful gaze to the chaos developing down below. He could now see both the North Bridge and Princes Street. Yes, he would wait there until the girls reached Princes Street. And then he would go searching for Rory.

Stepping smartly out of the car at the corner of the Royal Mile and North Bridge, Hastie stood for a second to consider his options. Two glaikit and befuddled officers had seen two women dash from the hotel but since it was at the same time as two men ran out from Carubber's Close, they had decided to pursue the men. Unfortunately for Hastie, the out of shape policemen had given up on the chase when Paul and Elliot disappeared down Anchor Close. They had radioed ahead but that didn't please the furious Hastie. 'You Edinburgh pricks wouldn't recognise a real crime if it crashed into your staff room, pulled out a sawn-off shotgun and blew your fucking heads off.'

Hastie called around his NSD team and demanded an update. 'Two women have just run down by the National Gallery and across Princes Street, one fitting the description of Dixie Armstrong,' came the instant response, quickly followed by another communication telling Hastie that two men had been spotted coming out of Advocate's Close on the Royal Mile.

Hastie' next move didn't take long. He had a suspicion of

where their final destination was. 'Okay,' he ordered, 'that has to be Elliot Walker and DCI Paul Riley up by the castle. I want two men posted at the junction of Lothian Road and the King's Stable Road, and two at the north end of the Grassmarket. I'll head back down to Princes Street and pick up the women.'

Paul and Elliot had easily out-paced the three hefty policemen on North Bridge. After that, they had run down Anchor Close and onto Cockburn Street before doubling back up the hill through Advocate's Close. Edinburgh's Royal Mile was riddled with small closes once used as everyday thoroughfares amidst the appalling living conditions of the sixteenth and seventeenth centuries. At the time of the plague, there had been hundreds buried alive under the city. Jesus, thought Paul, will there ever be an easy way out for the decent folk!

Elliot was also struggling but having given his laptop to Paul, was feeling a bit lighter as they emerged back on the Royal Mile opposite the new statue of Adam Smith. Paul didn't have time to think of all the men who fought for a new Scotland as they ran past the Cathedral of St. Giles, and even less for the philosophical rants of David Hume when they paused for breath at his statue. 'Where to now?' he heaved, seeing what he thought to be two unmarked cars approaching on the King George IV Bridge.

'Up this way…towards the castle,' gasped Paul, dragging Elliot across the street in front of Deacon Brodie's pub and onto the cobbled street of the Lawnmarket. They were sucking diesel.

The Royal Mile was hoaching with tourists, dandering in the middle of the street and strolling from shop to shop. They were a fucking pain in the arse. However, as much as they hampered his progress, Paul also knew they would hinder the chasing pack.

Glancing up at the Castle Esplanade, Paul thought they could take a breather beneath the grandstands being constructed for the Tattoo. *Nah, too fucking risky and too many soldiers!*

Just short of the Castle, they took a left down Johnston Terrace then another sharp left down some well-worn steps leading to the Grassmarket. The dark walls of the old steep staircase hung over them. It was all downhill from here. They had to make it.

Charlie had arrived on Princes Street to see Kirsten and Dixie disappear into a department store across the street to his left. He was also just in time to see three unmarked police cars come racing along from his right. 'Hastie,' he reasoned out loud. 'Fuck it, no time to pop in and see the Titians.'

Most of the traffic pulled into the side of the magnificent street as the whaling spook cars drove ever closer. Charlie knew what he was doing when he stepped casually out. Standing alone in the middle of the street, he stopped, his eyes glaring into the oncoming cars. The NSD spook in the first car, seeing Charlie at the last minute, wrenched at the wheel to avoid him, his car skidding left before crashing into the pillars of the National Gallery. Passers-by screamed as steam and fire erupted from the mangled engine.

Charlie didn't have time to glance over at the carnage. There was no way out. There was no time left for Rory. The following NSD car ploughed straight into him, sending him fifteen feet in the air and forty feet along the street.

'What the fuck?' shouted Hastie from the third car. 'I don't believe it. That was that photographer cunt who works for Dixie Armstrong. What a fucking idiot.'

'What shall we do, Sir?' asked the driver, slowing down to take in the mess.

'What do you think we'll do, you stupid bastard? Have one of our men fleece the body then leave him to die. It's the least the dirty fucker deserves. Anyway, it's the fucking women we're after. Armstrong was seen going into that shop over there to the right. I want two teams on Rose Street, now. They can watch the back and we'll take care of the front.'

Hastie was the starving hunter obsessed with the capture of his despised animals. His tribulations had taken him to the precipice of insanity. 'If they get away,' he muttered, 'I'll be finished, I'll be dead. Just another nobody.' However, retracting himself from his eternal and self-denying depression, he quickly reclaimed his vanity. 'But DCC Michael Hastie is more than that, I'm a fucking legend!'

'Just move it, Kirsten. We've got to get out of here,' said Dixie firmly as she and Kirsten stumbled through the department store and onto Rose Street. Their bodies were warm and damp, their muscles lactic.

As Dixie made to go left along the narrow street, she glanced behind to see two NSD spooks running towards her. She grabbed on to an exhausted and stumbling Kirsten, holding her up as they darted west along the narrow and busy thoroughfare. Weaving between shoppers for a further thirty yards, Dixie took another quick left turn into another Princes Street department store, pulling the petrified Kirsten behind her. She looked into Kirsten eyes and saw tears streaming down a grimacing face. Running through the store and on to an escalator, they leaped and fell as they jinked between the lazy shoppers standing on the moving staircase. Dixie took a fleeting glance towards the ground floor below and swore aloud as she saw the two spooks running into the store. Standing there for a second or two, the spooks cast their eyes above the throng, searching for the two women. One carried on through to Princes Street while the other began to barge his way through the shuffling shoppers.

Dixie eyes flicked from side to side as she hauled Kirsten up to the second floor. Kirsten staggered and lunged forward for more than just help; she was reaching for salvation. However, Dixie knew it wasn't salvation they craved but survival, and to get the fuck out of the store as quickly as possible. Bumping their way between the floor units of expensive clothing and mirrored pillars, to the indignant harrumphs of middle-aged women and obedient husbands, they quietly made their way through a fire exit, down the stairs and back onto Rose Street.

Paul and Elliot came crashing down into the old world of the Grassmarket, holding each other back to avoid tumbling and scraping their faces on the pub-infested street. As Paul did a recce, Elliot stood stunned and alone while a group of afternoon drinkers mocked their calamity. Elliot didn't know which way to turn, his mind gone and his legs wobbling from exhaustion. Paul's mind, however, was keen, and as he bent over and heaved for air, he caught sight of the two suited spooks glaring down at him from the corner of Victoria Street. Unholstering guns from inside their jackets, they jogged towards the shattered renegades. Elliot and Paul crawled quickly to their feet, sprinting hard to their right and barging through the drinkers. This time there was no piss-taking. As the two spooks quickly closed in, Paul moved ahead, screaming at Elliot to run and not look back. On his own, Paul might have stood a chance of shaking off his pursuers but with Elliot by his side, he knew their chance of liberty was expiring fast. Reaching the bottom of the Grassmarket, Elliot and Paul took the quiet King's Stable Road to the right. Up above, Edinburgh Castle and its Union flag hung over them with sneering intimidation as Elliot's childhood nightmare of tripping over his feet while being chased by indescribable fiends became a reality. Paul held him by the arm as their legs struggled in vain to move faster than their brains.

The first shot flew over their heads and ricocheted off the massive cliff face to their right. The second did not; catching Paul in his hamstring and causing him stumble. This time it was Elliot's turn to be the life-support. They staggered on, Elliot leading the way and holding Paul up as he skipped and hopped with increasing pain. Quick glances behind didn't help as the spooks moved ever closer, and neither did the sight of a further two silhouetted spooks standing against the Caledonian Hotel at the junction with Lothian Road.

'Jesus,' pleaded Paul, knowing their plight was almost insurmountable. There was only one option left. Taking a sharp right opposite the multi-story car park on Castle Terrace, Paul crumpled out of sight by the gate at the back entrance to Princes Street Gardens.

As Paul fell, he held Elliot back. Elliot tried to keep going but the force of Paul's weight brought him to a back-wrenching halt. Elliot stumbled, dragging himself back a few feet before sitting up on his knees. Paul was leaning back against the open gate, legs outstretched. Elliot took a quick glance at Paul's leg and then into his eyes. His look of despair angered Paul.

'Elliot,' gasped Paul. He was searching for air, the blood seeping through his jeans and pouring across his shoes. Elliot's face told Paul all he needed to know. Here was his friend with no iniquity to bear against any decent and virtuous soul, ready to save another's life at the expense of his own. Paul couldn't let that happen. 'Elliot, you have to get the fuck out of here now. Follow this path alongside St. John's Church and it'll take you out onto Princes Street.'

Elliot didn't want to leave one of his oldest friends to the murderous exploits of these anonymous spooks. This time he wouldn't stand by and do nothing.

Paul saw the determination in Elliot's eyes but knew one of them had to get to Bute House. 'Don't you worry about me, pal. These numpties will fall before I do. They're only NSD spooks, for fuck's sake.'

Elliot let a smile pass his lips, trying to ease the tension. 'I know. These guys aren't brave enough to go at it mano-a-mano. I think they'll need an entire fucking regiment just to give themselves an even chance. I mean, you're from Glasgow, are you not!'

Paul grimaced, ignoring the well-intended histrionics. He pulled out his gun and released the safety. Elliot looked down at the steel pistol and heaved. Paul, having no time for Elliot's shock, was now peeking round the gate, both left and right, at the four spooks closing in. Each pair of spooks had positioned themselves on either side of the road, hugging the walls, about one hundred and twenty feet away. Paul fired a shot at one closing in from the Lothian Road end before quickly taking cover again. He turned back to Elliot who was still staring at the gun. 'What? You didn't think I'd turn up with a legal document for them to sign, did you?' He pushed Elliot away with his other hand. 'Go Elliot. Now! I'll be fine!'

Elliot stared down at Paul hunkered up behind the gate.

He didn't want to believe it but he knew Paul wouldn't be fine. Elliot was wearing a look of pity, of sadness and of gratitude. 'But Paul, I...'

'No Elliot, fuck off now and take this damn laptop. I'll see you in our old local for a pint.' Paul smiled despondently, telling Elliot that this was it. 'Eight o'clock, Sheep Shagger. And don't be late.'

Elliot stared into the eyes of his friend for the last time, only for Paul to repel the sentimentality by turning again to take a line of sight on the spooks. Elliot dared not turn as he started running but as he heard the shots ring out, a part of him died inside. He disappeared amongst the gravestones of the church as Paul Riley, his lifelong friend and protector, slumped to the ground as a British Government bullet entered his skull.

Hastie's car flew down Princes Street before turning right across the tram-line construction and drifting at high speed towards Charlotte Square. Cars smashed into the back of each other and tourists ran for cover as Hastie's car pulled up at the end of Rose Street, just outside the Floors Hotel. The affairs of State were almost back in the order Detective Chief Constable Hastie had come to expect. He was in control once more, the dread, which had overcome him only thirty minutes before, replaced by his usual haughty demeanour. He slowly stepped out of the car as the tourists on Rose Street stood back for the VVIP. He radioed his henchmen closing in on Dixie and Kirsten, and waited.

Dixie and Kirsten were bobbing between the hoards on Rose Street and only one block from Charlotte Square when the enormous frame of Hastie appeared in the centre of the old and narrow street. Dixie glanced up, throwing out her left arm to hold Kirsten back. 'Kirsten,' said Dixie, nodding towards Hastie.

Kirsten's petrified eyes locked on Hastie. She could feel her heart tighten as she caught the smirk on his face: his eyes offering no hope, no sympathy, no negotiation and no chance. As he swaggered towards them, Dixie and Kirsten made to turn but on seeing the three spooks walking side by side, coming in the other direction, their panic turned into outright terror.

Dixie grabbed Kirsten and pulled her into a nearby bar. Barging through the crowd and knocking over tables and stools, they stumbled towards the rear, hoping to find another exit. Seconds later, as Kirsten and Dixie tried frantically to open the fire exit to the side of the toilets, they could hear the composed boom of Hastie ordering two goons to stand guard at the door and for the bar staff and their bemused customers not to move. The bar fell into a semi-conscious state as Hastie and two more of his men walked quietly in the direction of Dixie and Kirsten.

Kirsten was using her insignificant weight in an attempt to force the door open but her exhaustion and an un-serviced fire-door made it impossible. Meanwhile, Dixie had her phone open, trying to find a number. As Kirsten pushed and kicked, and Dixie frantically struggled to make a call, they felt Hastie's dangerous shadow now hanging over them. As they raised their frightened eyes, Hastie spoke in a slow deliberate drawl. 'It's no use, ladies. Your phones don't have a signal and I've two men on the other side of the door. Why don't you just rest a minute and give me the copy of the file.'

Kirsten began to whimper as Dixie spat on the floor. Her mind was darting from one useless escape plan to another. They were trapped and they were finished.

'Why don't you go and fuck yourself you nasty piece of shit,' growled Dixie. 'It won't matter what you do to us, your dirty little conspiracy will be public knowledge by tomorrow.' Slurping back the saliva dripping from the side of her mouth, she continued. 'You know I'm not the only one with a copy. There are others. And far too many for you to find them all. Eventually you will be brought down.'

'You mean the copies that Paul and Elliot had on them,' lied Hastie. He was enjoying seeing Dixie suffer. 'Too late I'm afraid, you dirty little whore; we already have their wee memory sticks. Unfortunately for you two, your brave and very stupid boyfriends didn't have the sense to give themselves up so we had to make other arrangements.'

'What the fuck do you mean?' screamed Kirsten. 'Where

is my husband?'

'Let's just say, for ease of explanation, that you won't be sitting down for Christmas dinner with either of them this year, or any other year for that matter. And in case you're thinking of inviting a replacement or two to pull the crackers and munch on the turkey, that photographer of yours won't be able to attend, either. I'm afraid he picked a fight with a car a few minutes ago.'

Dixie's eyes were full of hate, full of anger and full of revenge. She lunged for Hastie who shook his head at Dixie's feeble attempts to lash out. He held her arms as she screamed in veracious revulsion before pushing her violently back against the door, sending both Dixie and Kirsten flying outside and into a stack of empty beer barrels.

The alarm rung out loud as Hastie pulled out his gun and began to screw on the silencer. Kirsten was on her knees, grabbing onto his legs and pleading for mercy. He shrugged her off and sneered. 'You stupid fucking bitch, Dixie. What were you thinking? I mean, how the fuck did you think you could take on me, and the Establishment? You really were an arrogant little slut.'

Hastie, full of derision, carefully switched the safety off before holding the gun above their heads. Dixie slowly bowed. She thought about Paul and Charlie and as she grabbed Kirsten's hand, she thought of her kids back in Glasgow. She thought of their future without her and hoped they would one day come to understand what had happened to their mother. Tears began to stream down her face as Kirsten began to mumble Elliot's name. Dixie looked up, staring defiantly at Hastie. 'You're a disgrace; a disgrace to your profession and a disgrace to Scotland. I hope you rot in hell.'

Hastie pinched his lips tightly, ensuring Dixie's words meant nothing to him. The two women were dispensable now. Kirsten was still holding Dixie's hand as Hastie lowered the gun towards Kirsten's head and pulled the trigger. Dixie convulsed as she felt Kirsten go limp but she would be defiant until the end.

'Just do it. Just fucking do it!'

Jamie Houston wasn't overly concerned that the First Minister hadn't given his clearance for the group to use his Residence as a safe house. The situation was, after all, pretty damn important to the country.

Charlotte Square was quiet, the traffic chaos having blocked most routes in and out. Jamie also noticed the policeman standing guard outside the door had disappeared as well. A few minutes later, as he paced nervously and impatiently back and forth in the entrance hall of Bute House, Jamie saw a bedraggled figure staggering alongside the park fence of Charlotte Square. The man was gripping on tight to a briefcase of some sort.

Jamie had been anxious since Dixie Armstrong had called him. He had wanted to send a private car but there hadn't been enough time. His only hope now was that Dixie and her friends would make it to Bute House before it was too late. However, things weren't looking good. There was still no sign of anyone, apart from this guy reeling and swaying around the park. It had to be Elliot Walker or DCI Paul Riley.

Elliot had stumbled through the graveyard and through the Church grounds before crossing the end of Princes Street, onto Hope Street, then into Charlotte Square, unaware that his beloved Kirsten was with him no more; her life ended in a back street alley of Scotland's capital just one hundred yards to his right. Lurching awkwardly on, he almost broke down when he saw the door to Bute House.

A smile came over Jamie's face as he jogged out of the First Minister's Residence, bouncing down the steps towards the frightened figure on the corner of the street to his right. He started into a run but as he did so, a car with tinted windows drew up alongside the exhausted man.

Elliot turned to his left and stared into the car before his eyes returned a terrified glare on Jamie. He tried to run faster but his legs were dead weight. The car crawled alongside him for a few feet before a window opened and a single flash exploded from the back seat. Elliot wobbled. His hands, still gripping the laptop by his side, were of no use to him as his legs buckled and he fell to his knees.

Jamie stared over in disbelief.

Elliot touched his heart and felt the blood seeping gently through his fingers. He lifted his arms and gaped open-mouthed at his deep red hand. Gurgling for his last breath, he looked over to Jamie. Elliot pleaded for help but couldn't hear his own voice. All his strength was gone. As his eyes stared into the bright, summer Scottish sky, he thought of Kirsten and his family and smiled for the last time as his mind drifted off to the expanse and isolation and beauty of his beloved Highlands. He desperately wanted to feel the clean northern air wrap itself around him, to smell the wild mountain pine and to breathe in his homeland. The land he loved and the land he would see no more.

Jamie stood alone, transfixed with both fear and shock, watching in hopeless desperation as two men wearing grey suits and sunglasses stepped out of the car. Looking across to Jamie, one of the men pulled out a hand gun to warn him off. Jamie now knew it was a helpless situation. No special investigation would unearth what was happening here today. No protest and public enquiry would expose the destruction of the British Security Services. It just wasn't the British way.

As the spook with the gun picked up the blood-stained laptop from the pavement, the other bent over and placed two fingers to Elliot's neck. Feeling no pulse, he nodded to a relieved DCC Michael Hastie sitting out of sight in the back of the car. Working quickly, he searched Elliot's pockets and found what Hastie had been yearning for: the final copy of the recording of the Alba Club meeting.

Moments later, as they dragged Elliot's body into the car, one of the spooks turned to Jamie and smiled. Jamie didn't react. He more than understood the inference in the smile. As the man quickly returned to the purring car while it reversed and quietly disappeared into the Edinburgh traffic, Jamie gazed around the glistening walls of Charlotte Square. He thought of what was lost and what could be lost.

23

for a' that

Thursday 17th July 2008

10.22am – West End - Glasgow

Johnnie Di Marco returned to Scotland from the film shoot in South America with an empty feeling of tragic despair. He had walked into his stuffy Glasgow townhouse forty eight hours after hearing about his friends' deaths and three weeks after they had disappeared. Kicking a pile of mail underneath the mahogany table by the door and dropping his bag at the foot of the stairs, he walked into his lounge and collapsed in his favourite old leather chair. He hung his head in his hands and breathed deeply.

He had been having a wonderful time enjoying the wild landscape of Patagonia, working hard through the many chilly mornings but enjoying some great evening meals and parties with the ever-hospitable locals. Nevertheless, when he called home to rub Dixie's nose in the tales of his globe trekking antics, he found himself sitting in a Bariloche bar weeping and shaking, and very much alone.

He had lost his three best friends in what the media had described as three separate and unconnected incidents. Dixie's body had been found in her mangled BMW in the ditch of a back road just outside Glasgow, the result of a late evening, drink-driving accident. Paul had died in a shoot-out with a drugs gang on a housing scheme in Glasgow's East End while Elliot and his

367

beautiful wife Kirsten had fallen to their deaths while climbing the treacherous Inaccessible Pinnacle on the Isle of Skye.

The following day he had gone to visit the graves of Paul and Dixie, sitting for several hours at their fresh gravesides and reminiscing about their days of wild happiness at university and of the quiet weekends of reflection they enjoyed at his cottage. He cried again but this time he was inconsolable. His whaling echoed between the gravestones as his trembling hands reached into the warm summer air. The following weekend, he drove up to Arisaig to offer his condolences to Elliot's mum and dad, and to visit the graves of Elliot and Kirsten. They were lying side by side, overlooking the white sands of Camusdarach and the clear blue waters of the mighty Atlantic. Elliot's yearning had come to an end. He had come home at last.

A few days later, after a lonely and hard-core bout of heavy drinking, Johnnie prepared to face the world again. He would miss his dear friends, he would miss their piss-taking and he would miss their eyes smiling back at him. But life, thought Johnnie, was full of unsuspecting kicks in the balls. Everyone had a tragic story to tell but most of the time they just picked themselves up and got on with the business of life. Johnnie was just another poor bastard who would have to face up to moving on. But he would never forget them. They were his family.

Johnnie took an early morning cold shower and shaved his now stubbly face. He had scripts to read, agents to call and parents to visit. It would be hard and it would be painful but he was not to going to languish in a perpetual pout.

He walked down the stairs and picked up the mail lying by the door. Carrying it through to the kitchen, he poured himself a fine Italian roast. Enjoying the flavour of his coffee while sitting at his breakfast bar, he quickly sifted through the pile, pulling out the junk mail and depositing it in a pedal bin at his feet. He put the bills to one side before first opening anything he thought could be a film script. He then took his paper knife and sliced open the hand-written mail. He smiled as he read welcome home cards from other friends. Glaring out to the street, he thought of Dixie and Paul, and how they would never again walk through his door. He also thought of Elliot and smiled, knowing he was where he always wanted to be. Yes, he would remember all their smiles.

As his attention returned to the last of the mail, he noticed a solitary white envelope lying unopened on the bar. Indifferent as to what he might find inside, he opened it. Hoping it wasn't another love letter from an obsessed stalker, he picked at the Sellotape for a few seconds before ripping into it with his teeth. As he pulled out a few sheets of packing paper, a small silver memory stick fell on the breakfast bar. His curiosity taking over, Johnnie lightly picked it up before unfolding the remainder of the paper to search for a note. There it was. Handwritten. He stared at memory stick and down again at the note. He froze.

Johnnie, I haven't really got time to explain but if anything should happen to me, Dixie or Paul, I trust you will know what to do. Can't wait to visit the cottage again.

Elliot.

Johnnie hadn't heard from Elliot in a few months so to receive the note was a little surprising. And knowing what the three of them were capable of, he was sure it was some kind of practical joke at his expense. This time however, there would be no laughter. With the memory stick in his hand, he strolled through to his office.

Taking a seat at his desk, Johnnie was melancholic as he opened the file. He was thinking of the possibilities of what the little silver stick might conceal.

The file took a few minutes to open. After forty minutes of intense listening, Johnnie sat in silence. He listened to it again, struggling to hold back the tears. His right leg was shaking and twitching uncontrollably. Feeding his hands through his hair, he raised his eyes to the ceiling. For a moment he was still. As his eyes returned to the PC, his hands and arms scattered the paperwork from his desk. He was angry. He was so fucking angry. He wrung his hands between his legs and shuddered. He breathed deeply, slowly shaking his head. He cleared his eyes and picked up the phone.

He called the news office of the Tribune and asked to speak with Rory Hamilton. On discovering that Rory had not been seen or heard since the "failed terrorist plot" in Edinburgh the previous month, he decided to copy the file down to the C drive and upload it onto his private website. He also sent it to the four email addresses he used. When he was done, he unplugged the memory stick, grabbed his car keys and set off for St. Vincent Street.

Johnnie looked around as he locked his car. Carefully placing the memory stick in his wallet, he walked towards the office of the Glasgow Tribune. He was tense but determined. He marched through the main doors and up to the receptionist.

'Good morning, Sir.' She recognised him but remained professional. 'How can I help?'

'I need to speak with the Editor please. I think I have something which might be of interest to him.'

'And may I ask you what it is concerning?'

'Yes, you can. Tell him I have news of Jacob's son.'

Thanks for taking the time to read
A Yearning for Jacob's Son

Much has changed in the world since I finished writing the bulk of this novel in the early autumn of 2008. However, throughout the publication process, you may or may not be surprised to discover the following has happened or will be happening:

-The BBC has been hard at work. Some of its major productions, like *Question Time*, are in line to relocate to Glasgow. The BBC has also made a concerted effort to broadcast big budget and brilliantly made Scottish programmes like the *History of Scotland*, *New Town* and *Monty Hall's Great Escape*.

-The MoD, with support from the government, is planning to move its entire nuclear powered submarine fleet to Faslane within the next ten years. However, some commentators suggest it may be sooner than that. (I wonder whatever for!)

-Politicians, themselves, have not been timid in showering Scotland with their Machiavellian opinions and policies. Recently David Cameron said; *"If we win the next election at Westminster, we would govern with a maturity and a respect for the Scottish people. I would be a Prime Minister who would work constructively with any administration at Holyrood for the good of Scotland, and I would be in regular contact with the First Minister no matter what party he or she came from."*

-Gordon Brown, although he has not met with Scotland's First Minister since April 2008, has once again entered into the debate by stating that, *"economic nationalism and de-globalisation can cause problems for emerging nations."*

-Coincidently, Brown did <u>not</u> add the words 'without oil' to the end of his statement and neither did he make any reference to the civic nationalism espoused by certain ancient nations and for the desire of such nations to trade with the world.

Fortunately, there are still commentators and power brokers in London and south-east England to remind us -regardless of how much they manipulate the truth- what certain people and organisations really think about Scotland, its people and its resources.

RR: Feb 2009

www.rossrobertson.co.uk

And then there were these-

"*We English, who are a marvelous people, are really very generous to Scotland.*"

Margaret Thatcher
(Geocities.com; ©G Rosie-ref: The Times - Feb 12, 1990)

"*The Scots are subsidised to the damned hilt. The first thing is to stop the Scots grumbling. Emasculate them. That would concentrate their minds. The Scots are getting too much.*"

Bernard Ingham
(Alba.org.uk; ©G Rosie-ref: Sunday Times - Apr 29, 1990)

"*If you tell a big enough lie and keep repeating it, people will eventually come to believe it. The lie can be maintained only for such time as the State can shield the people from the political, economic and/or military consequences of the lie. It thus becomes vitally important for the State to use all of its powers to repress dissent, for the truth is the mortal enemy of the lie, and thus by extension, the truth is the greatest enemy of the State.*"

Josef Goebbels

Lightning Source UK Ltd.
Milton Keynes UK
08 September 2009

143489UK00002B/174/P